RANDOM HOUSE
**LARGE
PRINT**

FIRST
LIE
WINS

FIRST
LIE
WINS

Ashley Elston

RANDOM HOUSE
LARGE PRINT

Copyright © 2024 by Ashley Elston

All rights reserved. Published in the United States of America by Random House Large Print in association with Viking, an imprint of Penguin Random House LLC.

Simultaneously published in Great Britain by Headline, an imprint of Hachette UK Ltd., London, in 2024

First United States edition published by Pamela Dorman Books, 2024

Cover design: Ervin Serrano
Cover images: woman by Goldmund Lukic/Stocksy; house by Raymond Forbes/Stocksy

The Library of Congress has established a Cataloging-in-Publication record for this title.

ISBN: 978-0-593-79257-5

www.penguinrandomhouse.com/large-print-format-books

FIRST LARGE PRINT EDITION

Printed in the United States of America

3rd Printing

For Miller, Ross, and Archer

FIRST
LIE
WINS

CHAPTER 1

t starts with the little things: an extra toothbrush in the glass holder next to the sink, a few articles of clothing in the smallest drawer, phone chargers on both sides of the bed. Then the little things turn to slightly bigger things: razors and mouthwash and birth control pills all fighting for space in the medicine cabinet, the question changing from "Are you coming over?" to "What should we cook for dinner?"

And as much as I've been dreading it, this next step was inevitable.

It may be the first time I'm meeting the people gathered around the table, people who Ryan has known since childhood, but it hasn't escaped anyone's attention that I'm already fully embedded in his life. It's the small touches a woman brings to a man's home, like the matching throw pillows on the couch or the faint whiff of jasmine from the diffuser on the bookshelf, that every other woman notices the second she walks through the front door.

A voice floats across the candlelit table, dodges the centerpiece that I was assured was "delicate yet confident," and hovers in the air in front of me. "Evie, that's an unusual name."

I turn to Beth, debating whether to answer her question that's not really a question.

"It's short for Evelyn. I was named after my grandmother."

The women sneak glances at one another, silently communicating across the table. Every answer I give is weighed and cataloged for a later discussion.

"Oh, I love that!" Allison squeals. "I was named after my grandmother too. Where did you say you were from again?"

I didn't say, and they know this. Like birds of prey, they will pick, pick, pick all night until they get the answers they want.

"A small town in Alabama," I answer.

Before they can ask which small town in Alabama, Ryan changes the subject. "Allison, I saw your grandmother last week at the grocery store. How's she holding up?"

He's bought me a few precious moments of relief while Allison relays how her grandmother is faring following the death of her grandfather. But it won't be long until I'm the focus once again.

I don't have to know these people to know everything about them. They are the ones who started kindergarten together, their circle remaining small until high school graduation. They fled town in groups of twos and threes to attend a handful of colleges all within driving distance of here. They all joined sororities and fraternities with other groups of twos and threes with similar backgrounds, only to gravitate back to this small Louisiana town, the circle closing once again. Greek letters have been traded out for Junior League memberships and dinner parties and golf on Saturday afternoon, as long as it doesn't interfere with SEC football.

I don't fault them for the way they are; I envy them. I envy the ease they feel in these situations, for knowing exactly what to expect and what is expected of them. I envy the gracefulness that comes with knowing that everyone in this town has seen them at their worst and still accepts them.

"How did you two meet?" Sara asks, the attention once again back on me.

It's an innocent enough question, but one that unnerves me all the same.

The smile on Ryan's face tells me he knows how I feel about being asked this and he'll step in again to answer for me, but I shake him off.

Wiping my mouth gently with one of the white cloth napkins I bought specifically for this occasion, I say, "He helped change my flat tire."

Ryan would have given them more than they deserve, and that's why I stopped him. I don't mention it was at the truck stop on the outskirts of town where I worked in the small restaurant bar making sure no drink went empty. And I don't mention that while they are familiar with lots of acronyms from MBA to MRS, the only one I'm acquainted with is GED.

These people, his friends, wouldn't mean to, but they would hold such basic things against me. They might not even be aware they were doing it.

I told Ryan I was afraid of how they would judge me once they found out my background was so different from theirs. He assured me he didn't care what they thought, but he does. The fact that he caved and invited them all here and spent the week helping me get the menu **just right** tells me more than the whispers in the dark that he likes how different I am, different from the girls he grew up with.

Allison turns to Ryan, and says, "Well, aren't you handy to have around."

I watch Ryan. I've whittled down our entire meeting to one sentence, and so far, he's let me get away with it.

As he watches me, a small smile plays on his face that lets me know this is my show—for now—and he's happy to go along.

Allison's husband, Cole, adds, "I wouldn't be surprised if he flattened your tire just so he could be there to help you fix it."

Laughs around the table and probably an elbow to the ribs from his wife given how Cole is holding his side. Ryan shakes his head, still watching me.

I smile and laugh, not too loud and not too long, to show that I, too, am amused at the thought that Ryan would go to such extremes to meet me.

Amused that **any person** would have watched another long enough to know that he always filled up at that truck stop for gas on Thursday evenings after spending the day in his East Texas office. That someone knew he favored the pumps on the west side of the building, and that his eyes almost always lingered a little too long on any female who crossed his path, especially those dressed in short skirts. And that same someone would pick up on little things, like the LSU baseball cap in the back seat or the frat tee showing through his white dress shirt or the country club sticker in the bottom left corner of his windshield, to ensure when they did meet there would be things to talk about. That someone would hold a nail **just so** in a valve while the air whistled away.

I mean, it's amusing to believe one person would go to those lengths just to meet another.

———◆———

"I totally nailed it," I say, as I dip the last dinner plate into the sink full of soapy water. Ryan moves in behind me, his arms skimming my hips until they are wrapped around my waist. His chin settles on my shoulder, and his lips press against that spot on my neck in a way he knows I adore.

"They loved you," he whispers.

They don't love me. At most, I satisfied the first wave of curiosity. And I imagine before the first car left the driveway, every woman was in the passenger seat swiping between the group text message picking apart every aspect of the night and the search bar on every social media site trying to track down exactly who I am and what small town in Alabama I came from.

"Ray just sent me a text. Sara wants your number so she can invite you to lunch next week."

That was faster than I anticipated. I guess the second wave of curiosity is barreling toward me, fueled by the discovery that all searches turned up just the bare minimum of information, and they are hungry for more.

"I sent it to him. Hope that's okay," he says.

I twist around until I'm facing him, my hands crawling up his chest until they're framing his face. "Of course. They're your friends. And I hope they'll be my friends too."

So now there will be a lunch where the questions will be more direct, because Ryan won't be there to make sure they aren't.

Standing on my tiptoes, I pull him closer, until my mouth is mere inches from his. We both love this part, the anticipation, when breaths mingle and my brown eyes stare into his blue ones. We're close but not close enough. His hands slip under the hem on my shirt, his fingers digging into the soft skin at my waist while mine slide up the back of his neck, my fingers curling into his dark hair. Ryan's hair is longer than it was when we first met, when I first started watching him. I told him I liked it like this. That I liked having something to hold on to, so he stopped cutting it. I could tell his friends were surprised when they saw him, because from my own social media research, his hair has never touched his collar. And then they looked to me, and I could see their questions. **Why has Ryan changed? And is it because of this girl?**

He drags his hands lower, gripping my thighs under my short skirt and pulling me up so my legs can wrap around him.

"Will you stay?" he whispers, even though we're the only two people in the house. He asks me this question every night.

"Yes," I whisper back. My answer is always the same.

Ryan's mouth hovers over mine but still maintains a sliver of space between us. I lose focus on his face. Even though he's killing me, I wait for him to close the distance between us.

"I don't want to ask anymore. I want to know you'll be here every night because it's your home too. Will you do that? Make this your home?"

I dig my fingers deeper into his hair and lock my legs tighter around him. "I thought you'd never ask."

I feel his smile against my lips, and he's kissing me then carrying me through the kitchen, down the hall to the bedroom.

Our bedroom.

ver since Ryan asked me to move in with him five days ago and I said yes, he's been impatient for it to happen. I woke up the morning after the dinner party to him on the phone with a moving company, scheduling their services for later that day, thanks to a last-minute cancellation.

I convinced him to wait, even if it was just for a week, to make sure this was really what he wanted and not just something he said after an evening of expensive wine and perfectly cooked beef tenderloin. Plus, I mentioned he was getting a little ahead of himself by calling the movers when I haven't packed anything yet.

"If you didn't really want to move in with me, you'd tell me, right?" Ryan is standing in front of the bathroom mirror, knotting a dark blue and gray striped tie, and trying to act like he's asked me some insignificant thing. He's pouting. Something I've seen before when he doesn't get his way.

I hop up on the counter and scoot down the white marble surface until I'm sitting right in front of him. He looks over my shoulder as if he can still watch his progress in the mirror behind me. He's being a little bit of a baby this morning.

I've memorized his face, but I still study it every chance I get, looking for any small piece I may have missed. He's attractive in a classic way. His dark hair is thick and tends to curl at the edges when it gets too long, as it is now. His blue eyes are striking, and even though he just shaved I know by the time I see him tonight his jaw will be shadowed and I'll get goose bumps when it grazes my neck.

Brushing his hands away, I finish tying the tie for him. "Of course I want to move in here. Where's this coming from?"

Ryan looks down at the tie, straightening it even though it's already straight but needing something to do. He hasn't touched me this morning and barely looked at me. Yep, total baby.

Since he hasn't answered me, I add, "Have **you** changed your mind about me being here? I know you think I've been avoiding packing, but I've set aside the entire day today to get it done, and Goodwill is coming by to pick up everything I don't need anymore. But I can call them and cancel . . ."

His eyes and hands are finally on me. "Yes, I still want you here. I didn't know that's what you were planning to do today. But you've picked the one day I can't help you. I'm swamped today."

Today is Thursday, and he'll be fifty miles away from here at his East Texas office for the day. Just like he is every Thursday.

"I know, the timing sucks. But today was the only day I could get off work and the only afternoon Goodwill could send a truck over. I don't have much, so even by myself, it shouldn't take long."

His hands squeeze my sides while he leans forward to kiss me on the lips. His pout long gone, I hook my feet around the back of his legs and pull him close.

"Maybe I can call in sick. I am the boss, after all, and it's high time I abused my position of power," he says with a laugh.

I giggle between kisses. "Save your sick day for something better than packing. And really, there won't be that much to pack since I'm giving almost everything away." I glance through the door to the bedroom. "My stuff isn't as nice as yours, so there's no reason to keep it."

His hands go to my face. "I told you, anything you want to bring here, we'll make room for it. You don't have to get rid of your stuff."

Biting my bottom lip, I say, "I promise you, you don't want my ugly secondhand couch in your living room."

"How would I know if I didn't want your ugly secondhand couch in my living room? You've never let me see it." I try to sidestep this landmine of a conversation by looking away, but his finger pulls my chin back so we're eye to eye. "You don't have to be embarrassed."

"Yes, I do," I say, matching his stare. Then I lean

in and kiss him quickly to avoid another pout. "You'll see it on Saturday when we meet the movers there. I scheduled them yesterday. And Sunday will be spent finding space for my stuff here. Save your sick day for Monday. By Monday, we'll both be exhausted and I'm sure we'll need a pajama day. Pajamas optional."

He leans his forehead against mine, his smile infectious. "It's a date." With a last quick kiss, he pushes away from me and strolls out of the bathroom.

Twenty minutes after Ryan's Tahoe pulls out of the driveway, I'm doing the same in my ten-year-old 4Runner. Lake Forbing is a medium-size town in north Louisiana that is known for its fertile farmlands and deep pockets of natural gas. There is a lot of money in this area, but it's the quiet kind. It takes fifteen minutes to get to Lake View Apartments from Ryan's house, and from what I can tell it's nowhere near the lake this town was named after.

I pull into the empty spot designated for apartment 203, right next to the idling Goodwill truck.

"You're early, Pat," I say to the driver once we're both out of our vehicles.

He nods. "Our first run didn't take as long as I thought it would. Which unit is it?"

Pat follows me up the stairs while his helper opens the back of the large box truck. Stopping in front of the door, I pull a key out of my bag. "This is me."

He nods again and heads back downstairs. It takes me a couple of tries to get the bolt to unlatch; lack of use has made it stubborn. Just as I'm turning the knob, I hear the **thump, thump** of the metal dolly bouncing up the stairs.

I hold the door open as Pat and his helper struggle to get the dolly through the narrow frame.

"Where do you want them?" he asks.

Glancing around the empty apartment, I say, "Just put them in the middle of the room."

I eye the first stack of boxes, each filled with the items I've spent the last four days picking out. Things Pat has been storing for me in that box truck until I was ready for him to bring them here. Things that I will move to Ryan's house on Saturday. Things I will say I've owned for years rather than days.

It takes two trips to get all the boxes upstairs. I pull five twenties out of my back pocket and hand them to Pat. This is not a service Goodwill offers, but for a slip of cash, he was more than happy to help.

The guys are almost out the door when I ask, "Oh, did you bring the extra boxes?"

Pat shrugs and looks back to his helper, who says, "Yeah, they're in the back of the truck. Want them up here?"

If either of them thinks this is strange, they don't let on. "No. You can leave them on the sidewalk in front of my car."

I follow them back outside. As they unload the stack of flat cardboard, I walk to the back of my car, where I retrieve a small black bag from the cargo area. I thank them again as they climb back into the truck. There are only a few things left to take care of.

The layout of the apartment is simple. Front door opens to a small living room with a kitchen against the back wall. A narrow hallway leads to a bathroom and bedroom. Beige carpet meets beige linoleum meets beige walls.

In the kitchen area, I unzip the black bag and remove four menus from nearby restaurants and three pictures I printed from the kiosk at CVS of Ryan and me, plus seven magnets to hold each item in place on the refrigerator. Next, I grab the assortment of condiments and pour half of each one down the sink drain before lining them in the door of the refrigerator. Moving to the bathroom, black bag in tow, I pull out the shampoo and conditioner then pour half of each down the drain like I did with the condiments, before putting the bottles on the edge of the tub. Unwrapping a bar of Lever 2000 soap, I set it on top of the drain in the sink and turn the water on, rotating it every few minutes until the logo is gone and the edges are dulled, then drop it into the small built-in space on the shower wall. Toothpaste is last. Starting from the bottom, I squeeze a portion out but leave a glob or two on the rim of the sink, just like I do at Ryan's house, even though I know he'll fuss about it. Leaving the cap off, I drop the tube on the counter near the faucet.

Last stop is the bedroom. I pull out an assortment of wire and plastic hangers, the last items in the bag, and space them out on the empty metal rod. Back in the small living room, I scatter the neat pile of boxes around until the floor is littered with them. I pick two boxes, one filled with books and one filled with an assortment of old perfume bottles, and pull them open. The box with books is easy to unpack so it's only a minute or so before I have several small piles next to the box as if I haven't gotten around to packing them yet.

The perfume bottles take a little more time. I move the box to the small kitchen counter and unwrap the four on top, setting them down on the Formica surface. The light from the window hits them just right, and the thin, colorful glass acts like a prism, shooting rays of blue, purple, pink, and green around the dingy room.

Of all the shopping I did this week, the perfume bottles were the hardest and, surprisingly, the most fun to find. It's a fluke, really, that I even needed to search for them, but after running across a Facebook post Ryan was tagged in, I knew this was just the sort of item I needed to "collect." He had gotten his mother one for her birthday last year. It was an Art Deco piece, a ball of etched glass wrapped in silver and adorned with small, mirrored squares, and looked exactly like the type of gift Jay Gatsby would have given Daisy. It was beautiful, and from the smile on her face, she loved it.

And if I was the type of girl who collected things, this would definitely be it.

I survey the room a final time. Everything looks exactly as I want it to. That I'm all packed except for the few lingering things I didn't get to, a few random possessions left to put away.

"Knock, knock," a voice says from the doorway, and I spin around. It's the woman who works in the office of this complex, the woman I rented this apartment from on Monday afternoon.

She steps into the room and looks around at the mess on the floor. "I was worried when I hadn't seen anyone here since Monday."

I slide my hands into my front pockets and lean back against the wall next to the kitchen counter, crossing one ankle in front of the other. My movements are slow but calculated. It worries me she's here, checking on me, and that she'll feel the same need to do so on Saturday, when Ryan is here moving me out. I picked a place where neighbors don't bother to get to know one another, and the rent includes utilities since units can be leased by the week. And one week was all I needed.

It must have piqued her interest when I rented one of the few unfurnished units. Usually if someone goes to the trouble of moving furniture in, they plan on staying longer than seven days, but I didn't want Ryan to think my life was so transient that I didn't even have my own couch so the furnished unit wasn't an option. And here we are on day four and there's nothing to show for my stay except eight boxes, strategically placed around the room.

Her hand runs along the top of the nearest box and she's eyeing the perfume bottles on the counter. I know her type. Her makeup is heavy, her clothes tight, and once upon a time she would have been considered pretty, but the years have not been kind to her. Her eyes soak in everything happening around her. This is the sort of place that is rented for illicit purposes, and she rules over all of it, constantly on the lookout for any situation she can use to her advantage. And now she has crossed the parking lot and walked right into my apartment because she knows I've got something going on but can't figure out how to use it against me.

"Just want to make sure you're getting settled in," she says.

"I am," I answer, then glance at the name tag pinned to her low-cut blouse. "Shawna, your concern is unnecessary. And unwelcome."

Her back stiffens. My brusque tone is in opposition to my relaxed stance. She walked in here thinking she owned this situation, understood it on some level, but I've thrown her.

"Should I still presume this unit will be empty and your key returned by five p.m. on Sunday?" she asks.

"As I presume there will be no more unexpected visits," I answer, tilting my head toward the door and giving her a small smile.

She clucks her tongue against the roof of her mouth, then turns to leave. It takes everything in me not to throw the bolt closed behind her. But I'm almost finished here, and there's still more to be done before Ryan crosses the Louisiana state line at five thirty this afternoon.

CHAPTER 3

Ryan's grandfather passed away three years ago, only a year after his wife, and left Ryan his home along with every piece of furniture, every dish in the cabinet, every picture on the wall. Oh, and a hefty sum of cash too.

From the way Ryan tells it, one day he dropped by to check on his grandfather, only to find he had died peacefully in his sleep, and then a week later Ryan was moving in. The only possessions he brought with him were his clothes, toiletries, and a new mattress for the bedroom. Ryan probably would have made room for an ugly secondhand couch . . . if I had one.

His street is lined with large oak trees, their branches shading every inch of sidewalk. The neighbors are all older, more established, and love to tell me how they've watched "that sweet boy" grow up since he was a baby. This is the kind of house you live in when you've finally made it. When you've had a couple of kids and the pressing fear of not being able to pay your bills lessens and no longer has the ability to suffocate you.

But it's too big for Ryan. It's two stories with a wide front porch and big backyard, white with dark green shutters, manicured flower beds, and a brick path that leads to the front door. It would take several minutes to walk through if you needed to check every room—big enough that someone could come in the carport door and you wouldn't hear it from the main bedroom.

I back my car into the driveway to shorten the distance I'll have to carry the boxes. It's not until I pop the rear hatch that I notice Ryan's neighbors to the left, Ben and Maggie Rogers, are watching me from their front porch. Right on schedule. Their morning walk coincides with our departure for work, and their evening cocktails on the porch are already in progress when we arrive back here at the end of the day. But that's the general vibe of this street since most everyone is retired or close to it.

Mrs. Rogers tracks me as I lift the first box from the back of my 4Runner. This clear indicator that I've become more than just an overnight guest will be passed along to the rest of the street when she makes her rounds during their walk tomorrow morning. The Rogerses take Neighborhood Watch to the next level.

They are silent spectators as I unload box after box. Ryan is pulling into the driveway just as I grab the last one. He jogs over the second he's out of his car to relieve me of it.

"Here, let me get that," he says.

I reach up on tiptoes and kiss him, the box keeping us from touching anywhere but our lips.

Before we head inside, he greets the Rogerses. "Evening!"

Mrs. Rogers stands up and walks to the edge of the porch, putting her as close as she can get without falling into her azalea bushes. "Y'all look busy over there!" she hollers back.

With his arms full, he can only nod toward me. "Evie's moving in." His big grin sends a little flutter through me, and I can't help the equally big grin that spreads across my face.

Mrs. Rogers throws a **told you so** look at her husband as her suspicions are confirmed. "Oh. Well, I guess you young people skip over a few important steps these days." She adds a stifled laugh to soften the jab.

Ryan is undeterred. "Our steps may be in a different order but we'll hit them all."

The breathy gasp escapes my lips before I can stop it, and I force myself not to read too much into this banter tossed between them.

Mr. Rogers joins his wife on the edge of the porch. "Well, we need to welcome Evie to the neighborhood properly, then! Join us for afternoon cocktails soon." If Mr. Rogers is bothered by the latest development, he hides it well.

"We'd love to. Maybe next week?" Ryan answers for us.

Mr. Rogers's smile is genuine when he says, "I just got a new whiskey smoker I've been itching to use."

Ryan laughs. "It's been a while since I've had one of your Old Fashioneds. I'm looking forward to it." Then he knocks his shoulder lightly against mine to get me moving toward the house.

Finally, we're inside, and Ryan sets the box down with the others in the wide back hall.

"I went ahead and brought my clothes and shoes over. How was your day?"

He shrugs. "It was long. I would rather have spent it packing with you."

Ryan is always tight lipped about what he does on Thursdays. And while he joked this morning about skipping work today, we both know he never would.

What he does on Thursdays is important.

He surveys the boxes. The empty ones the guys left on the sidewalk for me this morning are now filled with the only items I truly own and will keep here. He pulls at a lock of hair that's fallen out of my messy bun, twirling it around his finger. "Did you get a lot done at your apartment?"

I give him a big smile. "I did! I'm ready for that moving truck on Saturday, but truthfully, we could probably manage with just our two cars. I ended up giving every piece of furniture away. There's only eight or ten boxes left," I say, kicking the box nearest me.

Confusion and a little sadness cross his face. "Evie." He says my name softly. "You gave it all away?"

My thumb runs across his forehead, erasing the creases there. "You live in a home where every single piece of furniture holds meaning for you. A memory. You grew up around these things so they're a part of you. It wasn't the same with my stuff. They were pieces of necessity. Somewhere to sit so I wasn't on the floor and nothing more than that. It was easy to give them away."

The furniture I'm talking about might not have been given away today, but the feelings are true nonetheless.

Ryan slips his phone out of his front pocket and makes a call. I watch him, wondering what he's up to.

"Hi, this is Ryan Sumner. Evie Porter scheduled your services for Saturday but I need to cancel."

With his free hand, he pulls me close, tucking me against his side. He listens to whatever they are saying, then thanks them before disconnecting the call.

"Let's go get the rest. Right now. I'll do all the work since I'm sure you're beat. Give me five minutes to change."

I open my mouth to protest but he seals his lips over mine, my words slipping away. He kisses me long enough that we both consider changing our immediate plans, but then he pulls away and darts out of the room.

"Five minutes!" he yells as he disappears deep inside the house.

I lean back against the wall, checking my watch. It's six thirty. The office at Lake View Apartments is locked up tight and the woman working that desk is gone for the night.

Ryan follows me back to the apartment in his Tahoe. I'm glad I'm not in the car with him when he realizes where we're going, but at least the idea that I was embarrassed about where I live rings true.

He parks next to me and is out of his car in a shot. Before I get my door open, he's at the side of my car. "You should have told me this is where you lived." He's scoping out the parking lot as if he's trying to locate the danger he knows exists here.

Latching on to his belt loops, I pull him closer. "This is exactly why I didn't tell you." I move my right hand into his left one and he grips it tightly as I pull him toward the stairwell. He notices every busted light on the way up.

The lock gives a bit easier this time, and the second the door swings open Ryan has us inside and the door shut behind us. He paces the apartment with his hands on his hips. I hate to admit I like his growling prowl of the room, and the protective instinct vibrating through him is as foreign as it is welcome.

I drop down by the stack of books and start putting them in the empty box I left close by. "Forgot I had a few things left to pack."

Ryan moves to the counter and picks up the closest perfume bottle. Holding it up, he inspects it from top to bottom, then does the same to the other three lined up next to it. "Do you collect these?"

I beam at him. "I do!" And then start to tell him I collect them because they reminded me of my grandmother, but the lie dies on the tip of my tongue. Instead, I say, "I saw a picture of one and I didn't realize how gorgeous . . . and how different they could be. It stuck with me. Started collecting them after that. The purple one is my favorite." It's always best to keep the lie as close to the truth and say as little as possible, but this feels more than that. I don't want to lie to him if I don't have to.

There is no mention that his mother collects perfume bottles as well, or the fact that I have something in common with her, and I won't analyze how it makes me feel that he doesn't let me know this is something we share. Ryan sets the bottle back down and begins opening drawers in the kitchen and then staring at the fridge. He plucks off one of the pictures of us and studies it. It's a selfie we took not long after we met. It was cold outside and we're both bundled up in front of the small fire pit in his backyard. I had brought over ingredients to make s'mores and we had bits of marshmallow and chocolate on our faces. In the picture, I am sitting in his lap and we are smiling big, cheek to cheek.

"That was a good night," he says.

"It was," I answer. It was the first night I spent at his house. The first time I slept in his bed. He's still staring at the picture, and I can't help but wonder what's going through his mind while he thinks back on that night.

Finally, he pulls down all the pics and menus and stacks them on the counter before opening the fridge. "Still have a few things in here," he calls.

"Oh, shoot! Thought I cleaned it all out. Can you just throw it in the trash?"

I hear him gathering the containers, then opening the cabinet under the sink where the trash can hides. He dumps them on top of some take-out boxes and other items I found in one of the outdoor trash containers. Ryan pulls the can out and says, "Anything else need to go in here before I take it to the dumpster?"

I frown while I think about it. "Yeah, there may be a few things in the bathroom that need to go."

He follows me down the hall into the bathroom. I pluck the worn-down soap out of the shower and toss it inside the can. Then I pick up the shampoo and conditioner, testing the weight as if I'm trying to decide if there is enough worth keeping, then toss them in too.

Ryan is digging around in the drawers and cabinets, checking each space. He's more thorough than I thought he would be.

Once we're back out in the main room, he peeks inside a few of the boxes I'd filled earlier in the day.

But then it's more than a peek. It's almost as if he's searching for something.

After he's riffled through three boxes I ask, "Are you looking for something?"

His head comes up and his eyes catch mine. A small smile forces his dimples to appear. "Just trying to learn everything there is to know about you."

The words are ones that any girl would love to hear, but they feel weighted. Heavy. And I wonder if he is choosing his words as carefully as I choose mine.

CHAPTER 4

There are lots of reasons why I haven't stopped by here in the last week—the shopping, the packing, the moving—but I've waited as long as I can. It's fifteen minutes until the official closing time, and even though I can log in and enter after hours, I don't want a record of that.

Just like every third woman I pass, I'm dressed in black leggings, a tee, and running shoes. My long black hair is pulled into a low bun that sits underneath the back strap of my baseball cap. I angle my head down and to the left to make sure the camera in the corner of the room doesn't capture a clear image of me. There are several people in line waiting for the next clerk to help them, including a woman who is struggling with a stack of small boxes, juggling them from one side to the other, before finally spilling them all on the floor. The two people in front of her bend down to help her reclaim her packages while attempting to maintain possession of their own. I skirt around the chaos and move to the back of the store, where the mailboxes line the wall.

Bottom left-hand corner. Box 1428.

These boxes use a code rather than a key, so I use the middle knuckle of my pointer finger to punch in the six-digit code. The door unlatches but doesn't open all the way. Still using the knuckles of my right hand, I swing the door open.

I pull out the small envelope that is tucked in the waistband of my leggings, hesitating a second or two before sliding it into the empty space.

I slam the door shut and reenter the code to lock it back, leaving the store as quickly as I entered it.

CHAPTER 5

'm late for lunch with the girls. Sara and I texted back and forth over the course of the last few days trying to find a day that worked for everyone, and while adding me to their group message would have saved a lot of time, it will take more than one dinner party for that invitation.

They wanted to meet in a small tearoom in the back of a gift shop that sells everything from hand crafted jewelry to smocked baby clothes to high-end skin-care products. They would know every person at every table as well as every shopper they passed on the way to the dining area.

While I might be willing to be interrogated by the women Ryan considers friends, I'm not open-ing myself up to anyone else. Not yet. Not until I'm sure I know more about them than they will ever know about me.

So instead, we're meeting at a small restaurant not far from where I work. It only took a week or so after meeting Ryan for him to push me toward a new job, one that wouldn't make him hesitate when his friends asked him where I worked. I'm the assistant to the event coordinator at a small gallery downtown. The job is easy, and since the head guy, Mr. Walker, is one of Ryan's clients, we skipped the part where I had to turn in three references and list past job experiences.

Beth, Allison, and Sara are already seated along with another woman who was not at the dinner party, but whom I recognize from pictures as being part of their tight group.

I watch them through the window from the sidewalk as I approach. It's more like a diner, and most everyone else is either in business suits or the polyester uniform all courthouse employees are forced to wear. The women are uncomfortable, and from their glances around the small space, I know they're trying to figure out exactly how they ended up in a place where the stench from the fryer will soak into their hair, their clothes, and their skin, and cling to them for the rest of the day. A place where they won't linger once the meal is done.

Sara stands when she sees me, motioning for me to join them. All four women use the time it takes me to walk across the room to survey my appearance. Their eyes glance between the deep slit up the side of my bright-blue maxi skirt, to the paper-thin white tee that does little to hide my baby-blue bra, to the stacks and stacks of bracelets that jingle when I walk. It took me a while to decide what look I wanted to give them—someone who wants to fit in or someone willing to stand out.

Today I'm hard to miss.

"Hey, Evie, it's so good to see you again," she says before sitting back down. Gesturing to the other women at the table, she adds, "You remember Beth and Allison."

"Of course," I answer, nodding to both women.

"This is Rachel Murray. Rachel, this is Evie Porter."

Rachel holds her hand up in a small wave from across the table. "Hi, it's nice to meet you, Evie. I've heard so much about you."

I'm sure she has. "It's so nice to meet you too."

It's a little awkward that the reason we've never met was because she wasn't invited to Ryan's for dinner, but that was his call. He tossed her name around but ultimately decided to exclude her because, as he put it, sometimes she can get on his "ever last fucking nerve." Plus, she's single and that threw off the numbers at the table.

Just as I'm stashing my purse on the floor by my chair, I feel the vibration of an incoming text. A quick glance tells me it's from Ryan:

Have fun at lunch but don't take any shit from them. Call me when you're done.

I bite my lip to hide my smile.

"Thanks for meeting me here. I don't have a very long lunch break," I say while picking up the laminated menu that's wedged in between the sugar caddy and a bottle of ketchup.

Sara snags one of the menus and says, "No problem. We never get downtown so this is fun."

It probably took everything in the other three not
to roll their eyes. This is not their scene. Not at all.

"Okay, so drinks at our house before the Derby
party on Saturday," Beth says.

I've been staring at that invitation on Ryan's
fridge for two weeks. Even though we're nowhere
near Kentucky, we've been invited to a Derby
watch party promising mint juleps and Hot
Browns at a horse farm right outside of town. The
invitation stated that hats, **the bigger the better,**
were encouraged.

The group tries to warm up to me by including me in their small talk, but it's clear that I don't
know the people, places, or events they are referring to, so instead of participating, I watch them.
Watch how they interact with one another, their
mannerisms, the words they choose. They think
this lunch is so they can learn about me, but I'll
come away with much more than they will by the
time we're done.

After our order is placed—waters and salads for
everyone—all four women lean forward and I brace
myself for what's coming.

Not surprisingly, Rachel is up first. "Okay, so
since I missed dinner the other night, catch me up!
Tell me all about you."

I lean back in my chair, wanting as much distance

as I can from them, and say, "There's really not that much to tell."

They expect me to keep going, throw in a few details at least, but they're going to have to work harder than that.

Sara fidgets with her glass, her napkin, her phone. "She's from Alabama," she says, looking at Rachel, answering for me. Sara is the girl who just wants everyone to get along. She probably had pale pink roses at her wedding and purposefully chose the same china pattern as her mother-in-law.

"What part of Alabama?" Beth asks.

"Outside of Tuscaloosa," I answer.

"Did you go to Bama?" Allison asks at the same time Rachel decides to be more direct. "What's the name of the town you're from?"

I look at Allison, deciding to go for the less aggressive question. "I went there for a bit."

Weary glances around the table show me how frustrated they are.

There's an old saying: **The first lie wins.** It's not referring to the little white kind that tumble out with no thought; it refers to the big one. The one that changes the game. The one that is deliberate. The lie that sets the stage for everything that comes after it. And once the lie is told, it's what most people believe to be true. The first lie has to be the strongest. The most important. The one that has to be told.

"I'm from Brookwood, which is really just a sub-urb of Tuscaloosa. I went to Bama for a couple of years but didn't graduate. My parents and I were in a bad accident a few years ago. I was the only survivor. When I was released from the hospital, I realized I needed a change, so I've been moving around ever since then."

Their expressions change instantly. This should end the questions, because they'll look like assholes if they keep prying.

"I'm so sorry to hear about your parents," Sara says, and it's obvious she means it.

I nod and chew on my bottom lip, my gaze not meeting anyone at the table, my body language tell-ing them I'm one step away from losing it if I'm forced to continue talking about it.

Rachel gives me a small smile, like she under-stands my sadness, while the other three squirm in their seats, clearly uncomfortable. They were ex-pecting to find out some gossip, maybe something that could help them dig deeper and possibly un-earth dirt that could be used against me later, if needed. But now they realize they might be stuck with me, because how do you run off the poor little orphan girl?

It's quiet at the table for a moment, then Rachel presses on, no matter how awkward it makes things.

"How did you end up in Lake Forbing?"

I'm starting to see how she could get on your ever last fucking nerve. This is the question I'm most careful about answering. This town isn't big, and it's not a place you'd randomly pick to settle in if you didn't already have family or friends here.

"Came across an online listing for a job. Applied for it and got it so I moved. The job fell through, but I was already here so I made it work."

"Where was the job?" Rachel asks.

"At the hospital," I answer.

"Oh," Rachel says. "Which department?"

Yeah, definitely getting on my last nerve. The other women are nudging one another, each one wanting one of the others to stop this train wreck.

"The billing department," I answer.

Sara, obviously done with our back-and-forth, chimes in, "I can't imagine how hard things have been for you. But I am happy that you found Ryan and that Ryan found you."

The food is delivered, and I'm granted a reprieve when everyone starts eating. Rachel keeps throwing looks my way, trying to figure me out. Good luck.

After several minutes, she spears a tomato on the end of her fork, then points it at me. "It's surprising to see Ryan get serious so quickly. Beth says you've already moved into his place. You've known him what, two months?"

I'm done playing nice.

"Rachel—" Allison whispers.

I hold my hand up, letting Allison know I'm okay. "I get it, I really do. You've known Ryan forever and then here I appear, out of nowhere." A smile stretches across my face. "He's lucky to have you. To have friends who care so much about him." Looking directly at Rachel I say, "So ask me what you really want to know. Am I after him for his money? I mean, that's the real concern, right? That I'm using him?"

Sara stutters out, "No, no, no . . ."

But Rachel says, "I'm worried he's thinking with his dick and not his brain."

Allison drops her head in her hands, clearly embarrassed, while Beth rolls her eyes and says, "Rachel, that's enough." At this point, they are probably glad they don't know anyone else in this restaurant.

Truth be told, while Rachel annoys me, I admire her the most.

I lean forward, pushing my plate away so I can rest my arms on the table. They automatically lean forward too.

"You have no reason to trust me. No reason to believe my intentions are good. But trust your friend. While I may not be comfortable telling you everything you want to know, I've told him. That's the best I can give you today."

There's not much else that can be said at this point. If I'm reading them right, Beth, Sara, and Allison will all go back to their significant others with stories of how humiliated they were by Rachel's behavior rather than any concern over my intentions toward Ryan. And since Rachel didn't make the dinner cut, I'm not too concerned about her sway over Ryan. But most important, no one is questioning who I am or where I came from.

The first lie wins.

We finish our meal quickly, with little conversation, and it's almost a race to see who can leave the fastest. I stand on the sidewalk and watch them scatter to different parking lots, each of them walking with purpose.

The friends always require the most work. I pull my phone out and Google "Evie Porter" and "Brookwood, Alabama," just like I know they will the second they get to the privacy of their own vehicles. The first page is full of vague articles that mention the accident, an accident actual residents of Brookwood might have trouble remembering but would never admit to—because what type of person forgets when two members of their community die? The articles are dated several years ago but didn't truly exist until a couple of months ago. Articles that were created to give me credibility and a reason why I don't like to talk about my past.

Shutting off my phone, I drop it in my bag, then walk the two blocks back to work.

CHAPTER 6

Ryan leans against the open door of the small workroom in the basement of the gallery. Lunch ended less than two hours ago, so I'm impressed with how fast word got to him.

"I heard lunch was awesome," he says with a grin I recognize but a look in his eyes I don't. He's dressed casually today, wearing jeans that he's probably had since college and an untucked button-down that I know is soft to the touch. It's a good look on him, making him seem carefree and younger than he is.

I didn't ask why there was no suit, no tie, no perfectly styled hair this morning while we were getting dressed, and he didn't offer.

"So much awesome," I answer back, matching his smile.

I've got seventy-five place cards scattered on the table in front of me, all needing to be color coded to match the lunch choice selected by the attendees of tomorrow's luncheon. He drops down in the chair next to me, his foot sliding against mine while he picks up two of the closest place cards.

"These two need to be as far apart from each other as you can get them."

I glance at the names written there. I was already informed that it may be a problem for them to be at the same table but decided to do it anyway. I mean, any luncheon where the topic is "Introduction to Art Collecting 101" could stand a little extra excitement.

"Duly noted," I answer.

He drops the cards back on the table and says, "I'm surprised you didn't call after."

I swivel in my chair so I'm facing him. "It wasn't anything I couldn't handle."

"But you shouldn't have to handle that." His hand reaches for mine, then he's pulling me into his lap. I glance at the open door, hoping no one catches us like this. I've only had this job a couple of weeks, and everyone knows I only got it as a favor to Ryan and nothing more.

"This isn't helping my credibility here," I say, even as I snuggle in closer to him.

Ryan wraps an arm around me, anchoring me to him. His finger traces the top edge of my thin tee. "This is killing me right now, just so you know."

I lean into his hand, and he glances at the empty hallway to make sure we're still alone down here, but before he gets any ideas of being naughty at work, I say, "I know you're too busy to come running down here to check on me." I link my fingers with his to stop his exploration. "Which one called you?"

My money's on Sara.

"Sara. She's worried you hate them now." He lets out a quiet laugh, then his expression changes. Gets serious. "Want to talk about it?" he asks.

I shake my head. "No. I'm not worried about what they think." I twist around so I can look at him. "But I am worried about what you think."

Ryan runs a hand through my hair, wrapping the ends around his fist. Holding my face inches from his. "I think you're wonderful."

"Well, I think you're pretty wonderful too." And for the first time, these words aren't spoken only to further my cause. For the first time, I mean what I'm saying.

In moments like this I wish things were different. That this was real life and that my biggest concern was the petty drama between me and his childhood friends. When I wish I was the girl who got a flat tire and he was the guy who just happened to be there to help me. That there was a real future ahead of us.

There's so much he doesn't know. So much I can't tell him. And so much I never will.

Ryan takes in the mess on the table next to us. "I guess there's no way for you to cut out early."

"No. I have to finish these for tomorrow and then make sure all the tables have linens before I leave." I pry myself off his lap and scoot back into my chair.

He leans forward, as if he won't allow too much space between us. "Come work for me. Then we can take off early as often as we wanted."

Ryan has offered this before, but it's the first time it sounds like he really means it.

I get busy stacking the place cards into groups. "Working together would be too big a distraction. For both of us," I say with a quiet laugh, my eyes deliberately on the task in front of me.

His foot tangles with mine. "You're right. I'd never get anything done. I'd follow you around all day, neglecting everything else," he says.

The muffled sound of his phone vibrating has him checking his watch to see who's calling. Ryan groans as he stands up from his chair and digs his device out of his back pocket. "Give me a second," he says as he steps into the hall to answer the call.

It's quiet enough down here that I don't have to try too hard to listen in on his end of the conversation.

"Confirmation?" he asks. A moment later, he says, "One day should be plenty. Send estimated cost and set up arrival for eleven a.m. this Thursday."

Thursday.

"Anything else come up?" he asks. His shoulders stiffen while he listens to whoever is on the other line. I'm prepared for the glance Ryan gives me over his shoulder and all he sees is my attention firmly on the seating chart in front of me. Then he takes one step farther away from me. The pitch of his voice drops lower. I can't make out the words, but he's clearly unhappy and letting it be known. He's all but growling into the phone. This is not a side of him I have seen before.

"Find it," he says loudly, before ending the call.

And now I want to know what he lost.

"All good?" I ask as he pockets his phone and makes his way back to me.

He shakes it off and even gives me that grin that shows his dimple. "Yeah, just a little problem at work." He drops back down in the chair next to me.

I swivel my chair to face his. "I guess if I worked for you, I could help sort through those problems." The work problem he's dealing with is not one I'd be aware of if I took the job he was offering me.

He's tense but still manages to lean closer, sliding his hand into mine. "But you turned me down, so I guess I'm on my own."

We're both dancing around things we can't say.

These feelings for him are leading me down a path I cannot take, so this little reminder of all he's hiding from me and all I'm hiding from him is welcome.

"When do you think you'll be done here?" he whispers, before kissing me gently on the lips.

I pull back just enough to answer him. "Maybe an hour? What time are you off the clock?"

"About the same." Ryan gives me one last kiss then gets up. He's almost to the door when he adds, "You know you can tell me anything, right?"

I nod and fidget in my seat. "I know."

He stares at me for a few seconds, long enough

that an irrational part of me thinks he can see past this glossy outer layer I've created. Then he adds, "Even when my friends act like assholes."

Smiling, I say, "Even then. Don't worry, I don't scare easy. I'll see you at home soon."

Another glance at his phone, then his eyes are back on me. "I like the sound of that."

I watch until he disappears down the hall and around the corner.

———◆———

The place cards are done. Mrs. Roberts and Mrs. Sullivan will be staring at each other across table 1 while I'm sure everyone else will be staring at them. All of my other to-do items have been checked off, but before I clock out for the day, there's a call I need to make.

She answers on the second ring.

"Hey, Rachel," I say. "It's Evie. Do you have a minute?"

Silence. And then, "Sure, what do you need?"

I lean back in my chair and glance down the hall to make sure no one is around. "We got off on the wrong foot and I hate it." I let that hang a few seconds then add, "I'd love it if we could try again."

She's quiet, and then I hear a soft laugh. "I have

to admit, after all the calls I've gotten about our lunch today, this is one I wasn't expecting."

Ryan must have called her, but she wasn't surprised he did. And now I'm curious what he said to her.

"I'm as much to blame with how things went down," I say. "It's really hard for me to talk about my past."

"No, I shouldn't have pushed so hard. It was very **insensitive.**" She says "insensitive" as if that was the main criticism lodged against her in her earlier conversations.

"Truce?" I ask.

"Sure, truce," she answers, her words clipped.

I let out a relieved sigh that I make sure she can hear. "Great! Well, I guess we'll see you Saturday at the Derby party."

"Can't wait," Rachel says, then ends the call.

I smile when I drop the phone in my bag.

Rachel is probably leaning back in her chair, our conversation replaying in her head while staring out the window of her small office, three doors down from the coveted corner one I'm sure she eyed the first day she walked the halls of the most prestigious law firm in town—the office reserved for partners. It's the same firm where on breaks from law school she interned during the week and screwed a junior partner on the weekends. The same law firm that handles anything Ryan needs.

She's picking apart my story, looking for the

truth behind my words. And from my research, she's good at what she does. Something isn't sitting right with her, and she's trying to decide if digging into my background is worth the possibility of losing Ryan's friendship.

Rachel is one I'll need to watch a little closer.

CHAPTER 7

T his is ridiculous," I say, looking in the minuscule mirror attached to the visor so I can make a last-minute adjustment to the swathe of frothy pink fabric residing on the brim of my hat. "I **look** ridiculous."

Ryan turns the SUV onto a long gravel road, passing an open ornate gate with the words HIDDEN HILLS FARM in metal letters stretched out across the top. He spares me a quick glance. "Yours won't even be the biggest hat there."

"Are you sure? Because I totally think they're setting me up." I agreed to go shopping with Sara and Beth for the Derby party and they assured me this hat was exactly what I needed. "And it's not fair I have to tote this thing around on my head all day while you're in khakis and a button-down."

"You look great. As always," he says, then pulls my hand away from the hat and brings it to his lips, where he places soft kisses against each finger.

Moving in with Ryan has upped his romance game: simple touches, sweet words and gestures, going out of his way to make sure I'm happy. When he's not at work, we're together. I can tell from his one-sided conversations with his friends that they are not pleased that I am monopolizing his time. A good girlfriend would insist he see his friends, make sure he didn't lose touch with the people he's closest to—but I am not a good girlfriend.

"Will your friends be mad we bailed on the pre-party?" I ask as we get closer to our destination.

We skipped drinks at Beth and Paul's not because I couldn't stand the idea of being around Rachel but because Ryan couldn't. He's still not over the way she acted at lunch, although at this point it's been blown up to a bigger deal than it really was. She pressed me for information, not punched me in the face, but in small towns among small groups of friends, there is little difference between those two things. Ryan can hold a grudge.

"I'm sure I'll hear something about it, but it's all good."

We've probably beat his friends here, so it will be interesting whom he gravitates to, since he's rarely at a function like this without his core group. When we pull up to the valet stand I'm at least pleased to see that he was right: my hat is not the biggest or the most obnoxious, although that only means we all look like idiots.

Our first stop is the bar.

"Welcome to Hidden Hills Farms," a woman behind the rough wood counter says. "Can I get your names before I get your cocktail?"

While I think this request is unusual, Ryan doesn't hesitate. "Ryan and Evie."

The bartender nods and drops down behind the bar. I take a minute to look at the woman in line behind us, and I'm sure the plastic horse attached to her hat is the same one I got for Christmas when I was a kid—one of Barbie's horses, complete with pink saddle and bow in its mane. The bartender pops back up and starts making us a mint julep. I'm not sure if we have any other choice of beverage since she never asked us what we wanted, but as I eye the healthy pour of Woodford, I'm not going to complain. When she's done, she hands us each a silver cup. Ryan's is engraved with an **R** and mine has an **E.**

Ryan and I walk away from the bar while I'm still studying the cup. "This is pretty over the top," I say. "I mean, if I said my name was Quinn would she have pulled out a cup with a **Q** on it?"

"When I RSVP'd, I told them both our names. I have a whole collection of these at home. This one is number six."

"Ridiculous," I mutter while he laughs.

We surf the crowd and Ryan speaks to almost every person we pass, introducing me to them as his girlfriend while his arm anchors me to his side.

"Well, hey, you two!"

Ryan and I turn around to find his neighbor, Mrs. Rogers, heading our way. I get a pat on the arm from her, while Ryan is graced with a full-frontal hug. I'm amazed at her ability to pull him in so close and not upset the precarious balance of the hat perched on her head.

"Isn't this so fun!"

"So fun," I answer back.

Before long, she wanders off to deliver more hugs, and Ryan gets into a deep conversation with a local judge about an upcoming election, so I take a moment to look around. This place is beautiful. The winding driveway was long enough that you can't see the main road or hear any traffic from the house, making it feel like this party is hidden from the rest of the world—just as its name suggests. The red wooden barn sits on top of a hill and the pasture slopes down in all directions around it like a sea of green lined with white fences. There is a large movie theater–size screen attached to the side of the barn, while smaller screens are scattered in between white linen tables that will show the race. Servers roam the crowd bearing silver trays of mini Hot Browns, individual portions of cheese grits, and delicate tea sandwiches.

The judge ambles off and Ryan jerks in surprise when a couple moves in close.

"Ryan!" the man says while flinging his arm around Ryan's neck and pulling him in tight. The two hug it out while I study the woman with him. She's tall, close to my height, with long light-brown hair. She's slender but muscular, and I can't help but notice how physically similar we are.

When Ryan breaks away, his friend holds out his hand in my direction.

"So you're the girl who's brought Ryan to his knees," the man says with a wide grin.

Ryan turns to me and says, "Evie, this is an old friend of mine, James Bernard. James, this is my girlfriend, Evie Porter."

I place my hand in his and he shakes it enthusiastically. James is tall and thin, with the look of someone who struggles with substances. It's in the hollow places in his cheeks and the smudge of dark under his eyes. The tremor in his hands and the clothes that are a tad too big. Nice dress clothes he probably dug out from the back of some closet just for today. His companion looks to be in better shape, and not just her clothes but her general well-being. Her dress is a cream sleeveless shift that hits midthigh, the shoes are Italian and expensive, and the jewelry is simple but classy. They are a mismatched pair.

"I'm not sure I've brought him to his knees quite yet but I'm working on it," I tease.

James turns to Ryan. "Man, I'm so happy for you."

Ryan and I share a look. It's not like we're engaged, so this hearty congratulations seems a bit much. "Thanks," Ryan says as he wraps his arm around me. We both look at the woman standing next to him and Ryan nods in her direction. "Introduce us to your friend."

James turns around quickly, obviously embarrassed he forgot who was standing next to him. "Ryan, Evie, this is Lucca Marino."

Her name runs through me like a shock of electricity.

"Lucca," I say quietly, rolling it around on my tongue. "That's an unusual name." I realize I sound just like Beth on the night of the dinner party.

She smiles and rolls her eyes. "I know. I'm named after the town in Italy where my grandparents were from. Two **c**'s. No one ever spells it right."

My eyes go to the silver cup in her hand; the script **L** is visible in the spaces between her fingers.

James and Ryan start talking about who they bet on in the upcoming race, but I'm still stuck on the woman.

"Are you from here?" I ask. My mouth is suddenly dry. I take a quick sip of my drink but no more than that.

"No. I'm from a small town in North Carolina, just above Greensboro. It's tiny, I'm sure you've never heard of it."

"Eden," I blurt out before I can help myself.

She flinches slightly. "Uh, yeah . . . Eden. How did you—"

"Just a lucky guess. I knew a girl in college who was from that area." I've got to pull it together. Dragging in a deep breath, I hold it a moment before letting it out in a soft rush of air. Twice more until I feel my heart rate start to slow.

"Do you still have family there?" I ask once I feel centered.

"No," she says with a frown. "It was just Mom and me, but she passed away when I was in high school. Breast cancer."

I had already noticed how similar we looked, but now my eyes devour her. I take stock of every inch of her so I can compare it to every inch of me. Both of us have hair that reaches to our mid-back and has a slight wave to it, but hers is lighter than mine. The color mine would normally be if I hadn't dyed it when I moved here. Eye color: same. Complexion: same.

She notices my inspection and does one of her own. I feel her stare, as it starts at my feet and runs straight up to the big ridiculous hat. Is she surprised by how much we resemble each other? "Have you been to Eden?" she asks.

"I have. The friend I mentioned brought a group of us to some festival. I think it was called something like . . . Springfest? Is that right?"

A test. A test I need her to fail.

A smile breaks out across her face, her eyebrows lifting. "Y'all came to the Fall Riverfest. It's always in September around my birthday. I love that festival!"

No. No, no, no.

I nod to her then turn to Ryan. He's in deep conversation with James, but I interrupt him anyway.

"Hey, I'm going to find the ladies' room. Be back in a moment."

Before he has a chance to say anything or offer to help me find the way, I'm gone. Walking fast in my tight black dress and four-inch heels, I almost drop the metal cup with the letter **E** that is slick with condensation. I nearly fall onto a woman as I close in on the ridiculously nice portable bathroom station that was brought in for this event.

"Oh, are you okay?" she asks, her hand on my arm as she steadies me.

I nod, unable to speak. She shares a look of concern with her husband after I gently shake her off, then they both watch me as I move away.

It takes everything in me to hold it together until I'm in the privacy of one of the bathroom stalls, because I am freaking the fuck out.

As soon as I'm inside and the lock is engaged, I slump against the door. I let out a silent scream and squeeze my eyes shut.

This is not good. This is not good. This is not good.

She is not from Eden, North Carolina—**I am.**

Her mother didn't die from breast cancer—**Mine did.**

Her name is not Lucca Marino—**Mine is.**

Lucca Marino—Ten Years Ago

inch the window open slowly. This afternoon when I tried it, it squeaked around the halfway mark, so I'm trying to stop it just before that point. When there's just enough space to slip inside, I go for it.

The adrenaline rush never gets old.

Dropping my backpack on the floor of the guest room, I quickly shuck the black leggings and carefully pull off the hoodie, making sure the wig cap stays in place and I don't smudge my makeup. Opening the bag, I pull out the sequined black cocktail dress and slip it on. It fits like a glove and is short enough that I'm likely to expose myself if I bend over, so it's perfect for what's happening here tonight.

The long, auburn wig is next. I flip it on, taking a few minutes to adjust it. I've practiced this enough in the dark to know when I get it right. Sky-high heels and a small, black clutch finish the look.

I shove my stuff under the bed then quietly leave the room.

The party is in full swing, and it's a short walk from the guest room to the center of the house. There's a band set up outside and most of the food is spread out buffet style in the dining room, in addition to the passed trays of oysters Rockefeller and mini lobster rolls that I saw being prepped in the kitchen when I was here earlier. My stomach rumbles, but I don't snatch one off the tray when it passes me. I can eat later.

A woman stumbles into me and I have to catch her before she takes us both down.

"Oh, sweetie, I'm so sorry!" she slurs, clutching my arm for support. It's Mrs. Whittington. The second Mrs. Whittington and current wife of Mr. Whittington, not to be confused with the first Mrs. Whittington, who loves to bitch about the second one any chance she gets.

"It's okay," I answer.

She eyes me up and down. "Love this dress! Where did you get it?"

"Oh, a little boutique I ran across while we were vacationing in Virginia Beach," I answer, my accent completely gone. That took more practice than putting on the wig in the dark.

I wait for recognition to cross her face, but in these clothes, with this hair, and the contoured makeup and smoky eyes, there is no part of me that is recognizable. It doesn't hurt that no one expects the poor little girl who works in the back room of the local flower shop to rub elbows with high society as they throw massive parties to celebrate the engagement of a couple whose marriage won't last two years. Honestly, these two will be lucky to make it down the aisle.

Once Mrs. Whittington is steady on her feet—or as steady as she can be in her current condition—I move past her. I would have had trouble coming in through the front door since the parents of the bride and groom are greeting everyone who arrives, but no one will question me now that I'm inside the party.

I pick my way through the open floor plan to a hallway on the other side of the massive den. I don't usually have to make an appearance, but the way this house is laid out left me no other options. The band is literally set up in front of the owner's bedroom windows outside, so through the inside door I must go.

I linger near the opening of the hall that will lead me to the Albrittons' master suite. With my phone in my hand, I'm the image of someone who is look-ing for a quiet corner to make a call. My eyes are everywhere but the phone as I gauge the level of in-terest the other guests have in me. My other hand is in my clutch, my fingers wrapped around a device hidden inside. I take a deep breath then push the small button.

A loud crashing sound makes everyone turn in the direction of the kitchen, and I slip down the hall unnoticed into the bedroom. Someone may search for the source of that crash, but they won't find anything out of place.

The room is dark, but it takes no time to get to the bathroom. I slip on the pair of black gloves from my clutch, then open the drawer in the built-in dressing table, searching for the heart-shaped box I know is tucked inside. I find it. Then I pick through the box's offerings and pull out the sapphire ring, a pair of emerald earrings, and a necklace with a decent-size amethyst surrounded by some channel-set diamonds. I wish the diamond earrings and pendant Mrs. Albritton wore into the store last week were here, but I'm sure she's wearing them right now.

I drop the treasures in my bag, followed by the gloves, then retrace my steps. This is a moment when the fear of being caught threatens to choke me, but I push past it and turn the corner into the main room like I'm exactly where I'm supposed to be.

Thankfully, no one is paying me any attention. I take my time heading back to the guest room, even stopping long enough to snag one of those lobster rolls. It is as yummy as I hoped it would be.

I'm pulling off the dress as I reach for the back-pack hidden under the bed, then shuck the heels. Within seconds, I'm in my leggings and hoodie and I'm slipping out the window.

———◆———

"Mama, I'm back!" I yell as I step inside our trailer. My Southern drawl snaps into place the second I cross the threshold.

"Hey, honey! Who won the game?" Mama asks from her bedroom. My light-brown hair is free of the wig cap and my face is scrubbed clean of makeup. The black hoodie has been replaced with one depicting my high school's name and mascot.

Carrying a brown paper bag, I close the short distance from the main living area to Mama's room. I drop it on the TV tray on the side of her bed before crawling in next to her.

"We lost. But it was close," I say.

Mama digs in the bag and a smile breaks out across her face. "Oh, sweetie, you shouldn't have."

Cinnamon wafts through the room, and my heart nearly bursts seeing this small moment of happiness over something as simple as a late-night treat. "You need to eat more, Mama. You're getting too skinny."

Mama unwraps the bakery paper and the big fat cinnamon roll looks as decadent as it smells. "My favorite," she whispers.

"I know," I whisper back.

While she takes small bites, I pick up one of the square pieces of paper from the stack on the bedside table and start folding it in the way she's taught me. Mama watches me while she eats, not correcting me when I make a wrong fold, instead letting me find my mistake on my own.

After several minutes, the small white origami swan takes shape in my hand.

"Oh, that's a pretty one," she says, plucking it out of the palm of my hand and adding it to the collection on the built-in shelf in her headboard. There are lots of different paper animals in all colors and sizes standing like sentries guarding over her. Mama has always been good with her hands; but no matter how many times she shows me, the swan is the only one I've mastered.

She's about half done with the cinnamon roll when she's wrapping it back up and putting it on the table next to the bed. "I'll finish the rest tomorrow," she says, even though we both know she won't. It's amazing she ate as much as she did.

"What are your plans the rest of the weekend?" she asks as she snuggles back down in the bed.

"I'm working at the flower shop. Big wedding tomorrow night."

She turns her head toward me, her frail hand reaching out to my face. "You work too much. It's your senior year, you should be out with your friends, having fun."

I shake my head and swallow down the huge lump in my throat. "I can do both," I lie. And we both let me get away with it.

"Have you heard back from any of the colleges you applied for yet?" Mama asks.

I shake my head. "Not yet, but should be any day now." I can't tell her I never applied because we couldn't spare the application fee, and as much as I don't want to admit it, she probably won't be here to see I'm still stuck in this small town come fall.

"I know they're all gonna want you. You'll have your pick."

I nod along but don't say anything. But then she's leaning closer and clutching my hand.

"One day soon you'll be all grown." She lets out a laugh and adds, "What am I saying, you're already there. Taking care of me and everything else. I want so much for you, Lucca. A home and a family of your own one day. I want you to have that house we've always dreamed of. Maybe you can build it in that fancy new neighborhood near the lake."

"And I'll have a room just for you," I add, playing along with the fantasy. "We'll paint it green since it's your favorite and you can get one of those beds that has a canopy on top. We can plant a garden in the backyard."

She reaches up and pushes a stray clump of hair out of my face, then tucks it behind my ear. "We'll grow tomatoes and cucumbers."

"And carrots."

Her eyelids get heavy. I know she's only seconds from slipping back into sleep, even though she's probably slept all day. "Of course, carrots. They're your favorite. And I'll make you a carrot cake."

She falls asleep and I lean over to kiss her cheek,

trying not to panic over how cool her skin feels. I add another blanket to the mountain she's already burrowed under before scooting out of the bed.

I head straight for the tiny room at the front of our trailer that is nothing more than a large closet, but it's like stepping into another world when I pass through the door. Before cancer ravaged her body, Mama spent every day in this room behind her sewing machine and craft table. Mothers came from all over North Carolina to have her make pageant dresses, prom dresses, and even the occasional wedding dress for their daughters. When I was little, I'd sit at Mama's feet and watch these plain girls walk in and then somehow be transformed once she got her hands on them. It was in that moment that I learned you can become someone else with the right hair, the right dress, and the right accessories.

Bolts of fabric and rolls of ribbon are stacked against one wall, while the particle-board shelving behind the sewing machine holds jars stuffed full of feathers and rhinestones and any other trimming you could imagine.

When Mama first got sick, I took over her orders. I'd been helping her in this room for as long as I can remember, so it wasn't a big leap. But pageant dresses and custom-made costume jewelry didn't bring in enough money to get Mama the treatments she needed or pay for all the medication she was on. So I had to get creative.

The job opening at the flower shop in nearby

Greensboro was just the answer. Women love coming in the shop decked out in their best jewelry. They love talking about the parties they are hosting and the impressive guest list of those invited. And of course, they need us to deliver the arrangements and make sure everything is just right.

With so much pre-party commotion, it's easy to slip in a forgotten room and unlatch a window. The key is not to take something when I'm there delivering flowers. That brings too much suspicion on the small group who were there early in the day. It's better to let the missus get dressed for the party. Let her pick through her jewelry to decide what will look best. Make sure she remembers what was left in that little jewelry box before the party kicks off.

And then, when the house is bursting with guests and valet and waitstaff and bartenders, the forgotten flower shop girl has a chance to slip back in and grab the pieces that didn't get chosen for the night. The police will inevitably ask when the last time Mrs. Albritton saw these three pieces was, and she will say it was just before the party started, therefore taking the flower delivery people out of the running of possible suspects.

I also learned that it would be best to keep that version of me separate from the real version. Lucca Marino is a seventeen-year-old high school senior who sews dresses and makes costume jewelry to help her mother pay the bills. The girl at the flower store has different hair, different makeup, and answers to a different name.

It takes some time to pry the stones from their settings before I can drop the gold into a small melting pot. Next week I'll drive in the opposite direction, crossing into Virginia, to get rid of the stones and gold. No one ever recognizes their stones once they're free of their settings.

It's a lot of risk for a couple hundred bucks, but we need every penny we can get. I've learned you've got to target the exact right woman. She's well off enough that she hires a professional florist to decorate for her party and has a few nice pieces of jewelry that she feels comfortable enough to shove into a bathroom drawer but not so well off that there's a safe to crack or a security system to disarm.

I work carefully. Looking at each piece through an LED magnifying lamp, it's slow work prying each prong off without damaging the stone. Mama would have had this done in minutes. Well, not really. She'd beat my ass if she knew what I was using her tools for. I had to decide a long time ago that what she doesn't know can't hurt her.

I finish up just before midnight. I still have a paper to write, and Mama needs another dose of her meds before I can crawl into bed. Putting the tools away and cutting off the light, I'm already thinking about the wedding tomorrow night.

CHAPTER 8

Present Day

t takes ten minutes to get myself under control. Panicking was a dumb move, and one I hope I don't end up regretting.

I should not have walked away from her.

I should have discovered whether her knowledge was just of Eden and the general events of my life or whether she knew deeper things, the things only a handful of people could have told her.

I should have pushed her more, found the hole in her story and smashed it open.

I should have seen this coming.

It's been a long time since I've been blindsided.

Ryan is scanning the crowd for a sign of me when I leave the bathroom. He's still in the same place I left him, probably thinking that it would make it easier for me to find him if he stayed put.

But James and the woman with him are long gone.

Ryan pulls me close the second I reach him, his arm sliding around my waist. "Are you okay?" he asks. "You look pale."

The woman's appearance here is concerning, but

I don't know exactly how just yet. It's easy to jump to conclusions and assume this has something to do with my last job, but it's a mistake not to consider any and all other options as well. I've made a lot of enemies over the last ten years, but people you trust can turn on you just as easily.

I remind myself—I only deal in facts.

Nodding, I clear my throat. "Yes, all good. That drink went straight to my head."

He seems relieved that my predicament has an easy remedy and pulls me to the buffet table and loads a plate of food for me. Ryan finds two open spots at a white-linen-covered table and sets the plate between us. "If you don't feel better after eating some of this, we can leave."

But there's no way I'm leaving until I have another crack at that woman. I pick through the offerings on the plate, nibbling on a finger sandwich while Ryan signals to a passing waiter for a bottle of water.

Deep breaths. I need to get back on my game.

"It looks like it's been a long time since you've seen your friend James," I say.

"Yeah, God, probably two years. We were close as kids. He didn't move back after college." He frowns. "Things have been tough for him. Said he's in town because his dad fell and broke his leg. Sounds like he'll be here for a while, helping his mom take care of him."

"Maybe we can have them over for dinner while he's here. Give you two a chance to catch up."

He shrugs. "Yeah, maybe."

I want to ask about the girl. What he knows about her. **If** he knows anything about her. If there was anything he learned after I ran off to the bathroom. But that's so unlike me. This **me** I've created doesn't pry. Doesn't ask unnecessary questions. Doesn't push for information about his friends or their companions. I need the moments that include James and his date to be buried in the blur of the day and not become the chunk of time that separates itself and becomes its own memory.

Because that's all it would take. It's been said that if you want a slice of time to stick out, to be crystal clear in your mind, one small difference in an otherwise normal routine is all it takes. Like if you're the type who has trouble remembering whether you locked your front door before leaving for vacation, you should separate it from all the other perfunctory times you've locked your front door. Something as simple as turning around in a circle just before you slip the key in the lock would do it. A simple movement and forever that memory will be burned into your mind. It becomes clear enough to play over and over again. You see the door, the key turning, the doorknob wobbling when you tested the lock, and there's no guessing whether or not you did it because you know you did.

I don't need Ryan analyzing this moment later, wondering why I had such an interest in his old friend and the woman from North Carolina. Why

I actively wanted to hunt them down so that we could spend more time with them. I don't need these questions to be the turn before locking the door.

There are a lot of people here, but not so many that we shouldn't bump into them again before it's over. For now, I'll bide my time and run through every scenario that might make this make sense.

"That hat looks fabulous on you!" Sara squeals as she approaches the table.

I tilt my head from side to side, the hat bobbling along with me. "Yours too!" I say back enthusiastically.

The rest of Ryan's friend group arrive shortly after her, and from the glassy looks to the pink cheeks, I'd say **drinks before** was a success.

Ryan stands up from the table, greeting his closest friends with a handshake and a firm grip on the shoulder. If they have any issues with us bailing on the pre-party, they don't show it. The guys form a tight circle a few feet away while Sara drops down in Ryan's vacated chair. Beth and Allison pull up ones from a nearby table, but Rachel remains standing a few feet away.

Allison scoots to the edge of her chair then beckons Rachel over. "Here, put a cheek down and we'll share this one."

Maybe Rachel was hesitant because there wasn't an open chair, but I think she was torn because she'd rather hang with the boys.

Once everyone is settled, Beth leans in and says, "I would be so pissed if I showed up wearing the same hat as three other women here." She must be talking about the one with the peacock feathers shooting out of the top and falling like a curtain down the back until they almost touch the ground. I've seen three of those already.

Sara takes a sip from her silver cup. "That's why you have to shop at Martha's. She keeps track of every hat sold and doesn't duplicate. And never offers the same hats the next year in case someone decides to pull from the archives." Then she nods toward Allison. "Or have the florist make you one."

Allison's hat is more like a blanket of red roses, fresh ones it seems, just like the blanket of roses that will cover the winning horse.

I can't help the snort of laughter that slips past my lips. These hats are serious business. Judging by the roll of her eyes and the shake of her head, Rachel seems to be the only one who agrees this party is ridiculous.

They continue to break down everyone here, and I realize I can use this to my advantage. If James Bernard was an old friend of Ryan's, then he was an old friend of theirs too.

I just need an opening.

"Oh!" Allison squeaks. "Can you believe Jeana Kilburn had the nerve to show her face here?"

"Where is she?" Beth asks.

Allison points to a short, round, blond woman nearby who is wearing way too much jewelry. She's hammered. I noticed her earlier when she was walking from the buffet line to a table and almost wobbled right off those high heels of hers.

"I swear, I'll never understand men," Sara says. "If they're going to cheat, why do it with someone as tragic as Jeana?"

Once they've just finished speculating who Jeana's next victim will be, I say, "Ryan ran into an old friend he hasn't seen in years . . . James Bernard. He seemed excited to see him."

All four women whip their heads in my direction.

"He's here?" Beth asks, her mouth hanging slightly open as if she's in awe of my news.

I nod and survey the rest of them and find they all are exhibiting varying degrees of shock and confusion. Except Rachel. This is not news to Rachel.

"He's here with a woman." I don't say her name. I can't bring myself to say her name. My name.

Allison, Beth, and Sara all turn around and scan the crowd, hoping for a glimpse of them, but Rachel looks at me.

Beth swings back around and says, "I can't believe he'd show up here. He must need money."

I take a slow drink from my cup like I've got all the time in the world before lowering it, then ask, "Why do you say that?" My calm and controlled outer shell that is usually locked down tight quivers and threatens to crumble in a million pieces.

"He's trouble," Allison adds. "Nearly bankrupted

his parents with his gambling. They bailed him out more times than they should have. No one knows where he's even been the last few years."

"How did he look? Bad?" Beth asks. "I bet he looked bad. And honestly I'm shocked he found a date. She must be a train wreck too."

I don't mention that his date was far from a train wreck.

"I'm surprised he had the nerve to talk to Ryan," Sara says.

As casually as I can, I ask, "Why?"

Allison answers for her instead. "Ryan tried to help him out a year ago. Gave him a job, set him up with a place to live, everything. James screwed him over so bad. Stole some money from him or something. Ryan was super pissed."

"Yeah, but we all know if anyone is going to forgive him, it's Ryan. Wonder who the girl is?" Sara rattles the ice around in her empty cup. A few more of those and Ray will be carrying her out of here.

I'm even more worried now. James's return isn't welcome, and his appearance here, with her, concerns me. I need to consider the possibility that the woman with my name and my background is using James to get close to me.

Rachel is quiet. Enough so that I'm sure she could answer every question they have.

———◆———

One for the Honey, the longshot, won the race more than an hour ago and Ryan has been on cloud nine since he won a nice chunk of change on him.

We've circled the crowd several times, but we haven't run across James and the woman again. And from the girls' talk, they haven't seen him either. My mentioning him and his companion whetted their appetite and they were greedy for a look at them both.

Ryan leans in close and whispers in my ear, "You know, the best way to spend these winnings would be to head straight for the airport and not stop until we're on a beach in Mexico somewhere."

I turn to face him, wrapping Ryan's tie around my right hand and pulling him close. "I like the sound of that." The words come out in a purr as I step closer so we're touching from top to bottom. Evie Porter has a lot of things, but a passport isn't one of them. Ryan has refilled his silver monogrammed cup several times, and I don't think there is any danger these plans would become a reality—plus, he would never leave without making arrangements at work first. It's fun to play along, though. More importantly, a girlfriend like me wouldn't hesitate to escape to the beach.

"I've been dreaming about you in that pink bikini you unpacked last week." His head dips until his lips are pressed against the side of my neck. We're very close to causing a scene, because this is not the type of party where PDA goes unnoticed.

This is the first time I've seen him drink this much. He's a happy drunk. Handsy. His feelings for me stretch across his beautiful face like an open book, and everyone here gets a peek. "We don't have to be on the beach for me to show you that pink bikini." A quick glance around our immediate area tells me we're already the subject of several whispered conversations. We linger like this a few more minutes, because my goal today was to solidify myself as Ryan's girlfriend, and all anyone will talk about was how he was all over me.

But now that it seems like James and the woman are gone, I'm ready to leave too. The sooner I can get out of here, the sooner I can figure out what is going on.

"You get the valet to pull your car around and I'll drive us home," I say, loosening my grip on his tie and stepping back from him.

Ryan leans in for a kiss and I don't resist him. It's slow and sweet, the kind of kiss that makes you want more.

And wanting more is dangerous.

I give myself thirty seconds to live in the world where this is real. Where my boyfriend is declaring his affection for me in front of all these people and there's nothing to stop this relationship from continuing indefinitely. Where there is no question about who I really am or what my motives are.

But too soon, time is up. "Everyone is staring at us," I whisper against his lips.

Ryan keeps his eyes on me. "Good." Then he pulls me toward the valet stand while digging in his pocket with his free hand for some tip money and the ticket to claim his car. His friends are scattered around the party, and neither of us make any effort to say good-bye.

I throw my heels and hat in the back seat as soon as I'm behind the wheel, then scoot the seat up. Ryan reclines his seat back, just enough that he's still upright but barely. His eyes close as he begins to hum along with the song playing on the radio.

I like seeing him like this. On a normal day, he can be wound up pretty tight and a bit grumpy if there's a problem at work, but now, he's relaxed. Loose. There's that part of me I hate, when my next thoughts wander to what I can find out from him while his guard is down. How many secrets can I pry out of those loose lips?

His hand reaches across the space separating us, his fingers tangling with mine.

"Lucca," he says, and that single word punctures my lungs, making it hard to drag in a breath. My hand on the steering wheel grips tight, and it's the only thing that stops this car from flying off the road and landing in the ditch.

Before my brain can come up with any words, he says, "That girl with James." His eyes are still closed so he doesn't witness my silent hysteria. "She said something weird after you went to the bathroom."

Fuck.

Fuck, fuck, fuck.

Deep breath in through my nose. Slow and steady out of my mouth. Two more times.

"What did she say?" I ask in what I hope is a bored voice.

"Just before they walked away, she said James was hoping to reconnect with me but said it so he wouldn't hear her. Said she'd love to get to know you too."

That bitch.

"Huh," I say. "Why is that weird?"

"The last time I saw him, things were . . . strained. I've learned to be cautious where James is concerned," he says with a grumble. "She seems nice enough, though. Too good for him."

I'm fuming. Still open to all options as to why she's here, but there's no way this is some sort of crazy coincidence.

Ryan turns on his side, his cheek resting on the seat, his eyes on me. "I'm not bailing him out again. Nope. I'm done. He's her problem now."

I drag our joined hands into my lap, squeezing gently. He smiles a loopy smile and I'm hoping this entire conversation is fuzzy tomorrow. "Hmm . . . you like that bikini, huh?" I untangle my fingers from his but keep his hand on my thigh.

He perks up, his eyes sweeping from my face down my body. I slide his hand under the hem of my dress, dragging his fingers against the lace top of my thigh highs. His eyes get big, surprised to find what I'm hiding underneath, but he wastes no time latching on to the straps holding them up.

Not many women wear stockings anymore, and I agree they were invented by the devil, but I've yet to find a man who could resist the garters, and you never know when you'll need a guaranteed distraction.

And what I need more than anything right now is to ensure that when Ryan thinks back to this car ride home, the memory that crystallizes clearer than all the others will not include Lucca Marino.

CHAPTER 9

Present Day

hate coming here during off hours but after yesterday this visit couldn't wait. The UPS store is closed to the public on Sunday mornings, so I enter my code on the keypad to gain entrance, then make my way to the back as quickly as possible.

As much as I try to predict what everyone will do, the one thing that is completely unpredictable is what I will find in the mailbox.

Every job is different, and the only way my boss can control the job—and me—is by keeping me in the dark as long as possible. I'm fed just enough to move forward but not so much that I can get ahead or change the game.

And of course, I'm never told who the client is because, you know . . . control.

The first piece of information I get is the location. I learn everything there is to know about the town where I'll be sent.

The name of the mark comes next.

I'm one of those lucky people who read something once and it's forever filed away in one of those deep corners of my brain. Because of that, it's easy to recall the typed piece of paper that introduced me to Ryan.

Subject: Ryan Sumner

Ryan is a 30-year-old single white male who resides at 378 Birch Dr., Lake Forbing, Louisiana. At 22, he graduated from LSU with a degree in business and a minor in finance then passed the Series 7 exam six months post-graduation and currently works as a financial planner.

Early life: Ryan has one sister, Natalie, who is three years older. Father, Scott Sumner, was involved in a vehicular accident and died from his injuries when Ryan was ten years old. Ryan's mother, Meredith Sumner (now Meredith Donaldson), remarried within the year. Ryan moved in with his paternal grandparents, Ingrid and William Sumner, when he was twelve due to his inability to get along with his new stepfather. Ingrid passed away six years ago from a short battle with cancer. William passed away a year later from a brain aneurysm that burst while he was at home in his bed. Ryan was the one to find him. Grandparents left house and furnishings to Ryan and monetary assets were split between Ryan and Natalie.

Ryan currently resides in the grandparents' house. That house was a sanctuary for him so tread lightly there. If Ryan feels secure bringing you into his home, you're set.

Ryan's dating history suggests he is heterosexual. His longest relationship was with a woman named Courtney Banning during his sophomore and junior year at LSU. The relationship terminated when Courtney left to spend her senior year studying abroad in Italy. When Ryan moved back to Lake Forbing, he rekindled his relationship with high school sweetheart Amelia Rodriguez, but it only lasted five months. Since then, Ryan has dated in a casual manner, mostly when he needs a plus-one for social or work events. Some female companionship results from chance meetings in a bar or nightclub but those are one-time events that do not repeat. **DO NOT RECOMMEND INITIATING CONTACT IN THAT ENVIRONMENT.** Ryan is part of an extremely close-knit friend group and will go out of his way to help them. Friends find him highly trustworthy and dependable. Damsel in Distress seems the best approach.

I ate, slept, and breathed everything Ryan in the weeks before we met. Watched the highlights from his high school football games, stalked his family's social media accounts, and watched hours and hours of daily comings and goings both in person and from video surveillance. And Damsel in Distress was absolutely the right approach.

After the location, I'm given the identity I will use for the job. A name. A backstory. All carefully crafted with the supporting documentation I will need to sell it. I had studied the pictures of Courtney and Amelia that were included in the report. Both have long dark hair, so for this job, Evie Porter would have the same style and shade—but that's where the similarities would end. Because while Ryan may have a certain type he's attracted to, neither of those relationships lasted. Evie would dress to stand out, to be remembered. Her style would be a little bit bohemian, a little bit hippie. Minimal makeup but lots of necklaces and bracelets. Just the thing a preppy golden boy needs to shake things up.

The last piece of the puzzle I get is the job.

Sometimes the jobs are short, lasting a few days to a week. A quick in and out. Other times, it's much longer. A couple of months or more.

I was told I might be in this identity for a while. Ryan's work in East Texas plays a critical role in this job, and getting the information I need would not be easy.

Because my boss isn't happy with how my last job ended, I'm on **very** thin ice. Six months ago, I was sent to retrieve some extremely sensitive information that was being used as blackmail against one of my boss's longtime clients. And when that client is Victor Connolly, head of one of the largest crime families in the Northeast, failure is not an option. But I failed to retrieve it.

Perfection is crucial on this one. Second chances in this line of work are extremely rare. I knew my boss would be testing me on this job. He had to determine whether I was still one of his best assets or whether I had become his biggest liability. I expected this job to be challenging, but I never expected **her.**

Lucca.

Her arrival changes everything, which is why I'm checking the mailbox on a Sunday.

Luckily, it's raining, so I keep the black raincoat cinched tight with the hood up. Droplets slide off and litter the floor with every step, until I'm standing in front of box 1428.

A deep breath and then I key in the number. Swing the door open.

I stare at the empty space while water soaks the carpet in front of me.

Pushing the door closed, I reenter the code to lock it. Once I'm back in my car, I think about how I should proceed.

I was taught it was reckless not to consider every single possibility when on a job, but my gut is telling me that woman was sent here by the same people who sent me. And as Mama used to say, **Better the devil you know.**

There is a number I can call to relay this latest development, but I've been told over and over that using it should be a last resort. It's one step before needing to be pulled out of a job, or if your cover has been blown. It's admitting defeat, or worse— that you got caught.

My boss failed to mention the protocol when faced with an impostor using your true identity, though.

I am in uncharted territory.

Lucca Marino—Eight Years Ago

The bidding for the trip to Mexico is up to twelve thousand dollars. I know they all say "It's for a good cause!" but you've got to be high to pay over ten thousand dollars for a trip that's worth two grand at best.

I'm just glad everyone here has the credit limit to be so generous.

I hold my empty tray just above my shoulder and wander through the ballroom. It's another Saturday night in Raleigh and yet another fundraiser where hundreds of items are being auctioned off. Tonight these tux- and ballgown-clad people are here to support the local opera guild.

A man in his fifties appears in front of me, and he stares at my chest a lot longer than necessary if he's just trying to read the name on my name tag.

"Susan, any chance I can get a Macallan on ice?" he asks.

"Sure thing, Mr. Fuller. What's your member number?"

He's not surprised that I knew his name, and

he rattles off the five digits, even though I already know it.

I take two more orders before I get to the bar, then spend the next ten minutes hunting each member down to deliver their drink. Some patrons I recognize as regulars. They are here for some function or another every weekend. But quite a few are new to me.

I've had this gig for a few months, and it's been more financially beneficial than I thought it would be. Earlier today, after everything was set up and ready to go for tonight, I added a scanner to one of the credit card machines. When the guests pay for the overpriced items they bought, I'll get a copy of every credit card name, number, and expiration date.

The scanner was expensive, and I'm hoping after tonight I'll be able to afford an additional one.

The trick is to hold on to that data for a bit. It won't do me any good if the club is alerted by a bunch of members that their credit card was stolen tonight and then they look closer into who was here. As Mama used to say: **The pig gets fat but the hog gets slaughtered.** No, I'll use those credit cards here and there in small increments a few weeks from now. Not enough to raise a flag or question the transaction right away. With so many numbers at my disposal, those insignificant amounts add up pretty quick.

"The all-inclusive trip for four to Cabo is sold

to Mrs. Rollins for thirteen thousand five hundred dollars!" the MC announces over the mic, then slams the gavel down on the podium. Cheers erupt through the crowd.

Yeah, not going to feel bad about this one.

The band cranks up as soon as the last auction item is sold. The line to check out wraps along the back wall of the ballroom and the waitstaff jump into action so that any member stuck waiting in line doesn't want for anything. I even hold a few places while they excuse themselves to go to the restroom.

As the evening starts to wind down, I stick close to the organizers' table so I can retrieve the scanner.

"Can I be of service?" I ask the woman in charge as her team starts breaking down their area.

"Yes! We could use all the help we can get!" she says, a little overexcited. She reaches over and squeezes my arm in what is probably meant to be a **Thank god you're here** way, but I get a ping in my gut that makes me straighten my spine and survey the scene with a critical eye. Something feels off. I start loading the leftover programs into boxes, then stack them on the cart they will use to transport everything to the parking lot while I keep an eye on everyone else. It seems the same as any other weekend, and I swallow my apprehension. Waiting until they are distracted, I move to the credit card machine and pick it up quickly, popping the scanner out in one swift move.

"What's in your hand?" a voice behind me asks.

A cold chill settles over me. Spinning around, I hold both hands out, the machine in one and the small scanner piece in the other. "I'm so sorry. You can take it out of my pay. I didn't realize how fragile it was when I picked it up."

I offer both pieces to my manager, then look him in the eye. I can tell he's a little thrown for a second or two, but then seems to pull himself back together.

"You can cut the wide-eyed innocent look. We know what you've done. Stealing from our members and their guests." Mr. Sullivan yanks the pieces out of my hands and thrusts them toward the pair of uniformed officers who have appeared at his side. But neither officer takes the device. The one closest to him offers a big plastic bag for Mr. Sullivan to drop the evidence into instead.

My forehead is creased in confusion. My lower jaw hangs open just enough.

There are a few members still loitering around the room, and my interaction with the cops has caught their attention, which causes them to move closer. My mind is racing. I'm thinking about my laptop and modem hiding under the dessert table just a few feet away from where we're standing. The cleaning crew is only minutes away from pulling the tablecloth off and exposing it.

I hold both my hands up, palms out toward Mr. Sullivan. "Wait. You think I have been stealing from people? With that black plastic thing?" My voice is soft and breaks on a few words, as if I'm too choked up to get them out whole. I turn toward the officers, reading their name badges quickly. "Officer Ford, I was only trying to help clean up!" Tears gather in my eyes until a big fat one spills over. I just need a moment to grab my stuff and get out of here. I can't let them take me in. I'm employed under a fake name and social security number that won't hold up under any type of scrutiny. I need to disappear.

Mr. Sullivan turns to Officer Williams, since Officer Ford seems like he's willing to believe me. "I want her out of here. Now."

Williams nods but pulls a small notebook from his back pocket. "Of course, but I'm going to have to get a little information before we go." He points to a chair beside the table and indicates that I should take a seat. I consider running for about three seconds, but without my laptop I won't get far.

I settle in and scan the room, taking in every face still present, while Williams speaks with the organizers and Ford stands next to him.

"Can you tell me how you determined there was a problem with one of the machines?" Williams asks the woman who squeezed my arm earlier.

"Of course," she says, beaming. "We ran a card earlier in the evening and when we pulled it out, we noticed that black piece came out with the card. After looking at the other machines, we discovered it was an addition made only to this machine, and that made us question what it was. We brought it to the attention of Mr. Sullivan, and we determined it was one of those scanner things. We didn't use that machine again."

He's writing everything down. "Can you tell me which one of you was working the machine in question?"

A short blond woman nearby raises her hand. "It was me," she says, then throws me an apologetic look, like she feels bad she played a part in my getting busted.

Williams takes her name and asks question after question.

Mr. Sullivan finally interrupts Williams's questioning. "You should know all of this. The police sent you here so you could wait and watch to see if the perpetrator would try to retrieve that device." It's been about thirty minutes since he first caught me and the members still present are circling closer; it's clear he wants me gone from this room before they butt in. "We want to press charges and I'd like her removed from the property immediately."

"Excuse me, someone left their stuff under the table." One of the guys on the cleanup crew is standing not far away, holding a rolled-up tablecloth in one hand and pointing to the floor with the other.

My equipment has been discovered. The laptop is password protected so they won't be able to get in, but if they take it from me, I lose everything.

The woman in charge walks closer to look at it, then turns toward the cops. "It's not ours."

Ford moves toward the table, and using napkins so he doesn't touch it directly, he picks up both the computer and modem. He looks at me and asks, "I'm guessing this is yours?"

I ignore him. He puts both into a box one of the organizers provided. They take my backpack, retrieved from the breakroom, too.

"Get her out of here," Mr. Sullivan says, his voice full of disgust.

Williams pulls me up from the chair then turns me to face the room. "Give me your hands."

He cuffs me while reading me my rights. My head hangs as Williams ushers me out and Ford follows behind us carrying all my gear. I'm so mad at myself. Mad for getting caught. Mad for not listening when my gut was trying to tell me something felt off.

We're out in the parking lot next to the cop car, and Ford puts the box down on the ground so he can dig out his keys. As soon as the car is unlocked, Williams opens the back door and motions me forward.

"I guess you have to take me in," I say, not really a question.

At least he looks less than enthusiastic when he replies, "Yeah, I do. But if this is your first offense, there's a good chance they'll be easy on you."

Ford moves to put the box of my stuff in the

trunk just as an older man in slacks and a cheap brown jacket approaches us.

"Williams," he calls out, and the officer turns in his direction just before he can stuff me inside the car.

"Detective Sanders," Officer Williams says in a surprised voice. "Did they call you in for this?"

The detective looks me over then turns his attention to Williams. "Yeah, some bigwig in there is worried about his credit card information blah, blah, blah and called the captain. Told me to hustle on down here and handle it so we don't hear shit later."

His arms are stretched out and he clearly wants Ford to hand him the box with my laptop, modem, and backpack, which he does with little resistance.

Officer Williams nods at me. "Want me to take her in or is she with you?"

"With me," he says. "Uncuff her. I'll secure her with my set."

Within seconds I'm free, only to be handed over to the new guy.

He towers over me. "Can you walk with me to my car without causing a problem or do I need to put the cuffs back on you right now?"

"I'll cooperate," I say.

The officers get back in the patrol car and drive away just as we approach his unmarked vehicle. He puts the box in his back seat then turns to me, a small phone in one hand and my backpack in the other. "Call the number in that phone and do what he says, and you'll get your stuff back."

When I don't take either immediately, he shakes the phone around in the air in front of me. "I wouldn't pass this offer up. You won't be getting another one."

I snatch both and stare at him. "You're letting me go?"

He moves to the driver's door without a word. I stand frozen in place until his taillights fade away in the darkness.

Noise from the front door of the club spurs me into action; the crowd is dissipating now that the excitement is over. I run for my car and pull my keys from my bag. The phone is on the passenger seat, but I don't touch it until I'm pulling up at the garage apartment I've been living in.

Racing inside, I throw my backpack on the small kitchen table then take the phone to my bed. There is one contact listed: Mr. Smith.

I press the contact name and hit send. "I was told to call this number," I say as soon as it connects.

"We've been watching you." The mechanical voice catches me off guard and I almost drop the phone. He's using one of those voice changer devices. "First in Greensboro, now in Raleigh. Sorry to hear about your mother's passing."

I go cold inside. There's no way anyone should be able to connect the girl in this apartment to the one from the trailer park in Eden. I've made sure of that.

Or so I thought I had.

"Why?"

"You were able to take something you shouldn't have had access to. It took us some time and resources to find out it was you. I'm hard to impress but somehow you did just that."

Oh shit.

Even though I am freaking out inside, I take a few breaths to calm myself. It didn't take long for me to graduate from the simple pieces of jewelry to paintings, silver, antiques . . . anything I could get my hands on as long as it was small enough for me to carry on my own. And when you dig deep enough on the internet, you can find a willing buyer for anything.

"Do you need it back?" I ask.

"We've already retrieved the item."

This is even worse somehow.

"You've found yourself in a bit of trouble, though. Bad piece of luck your equipment gave you up like that. I might not have been able to get you out of trouble if you had made it to the station."

I lie back on my bed and stare at the ceiling. This feels surreal, and I don't know how to process it. No one has watched out for me since before Mama got sick, but I didn't think my guardian angel would sound like a machine. "I guess I should thank you. How'd you do it?"

"Called in a favor," he says. "I have your laptop, which I'm assuming you'd very much like back. I've

got a job for you, and if you'll hear me out, I'll return your property."

"Even if I pass on the job?" I ask.

"You won't pass. You've been digging for change
in the couch. I'm offering you more money than
you've ever seen and the support behind you not to
get caught as you did this evening."

I don't respond because we both know I'll
be there.

"I'll text you the address. Be there Monday morning at nine a.m."

And then the line goes dead.

———◆———

I'd like to say I wasn't curious about the job and had
every intention of turning it down no matter what
it was, but that would be a lie.

When Monday rolls around, I'm waiting down
the block just out of sight before the sun comes
up. The address brought me to a bail bonds place,
and by eight a.m., there's a steady stream of traffic
in and out, which I guess would be normal for an
establishment like this after the weekend.

I don't like walking into the unknown, and I'm
hoping I'll see someone who looks familiar before
I'm expected. The voice on the phone gave me nothing to go by. I'm not sure an accent would make

it past the voice changer, but something tells me that if he ever had one, he did what I did—spent years wiping away any trace of who I was or where I came from. It wasn't long after I took that first job at the flower shop that I realized my twangy accent created a greater divide between me and the women who came into the store than our bank accounts ever would. The way you walk, the way you talk, the way you move your body screams more about you than anything else ever could.

Mr. Smith and I must have crossed paths in the past if I was able to take something from him. Faces, names, places, events, numbers lock into my memory the moment I hear or see them. But as the clock inches closer to nine, I resign myself to going in blind since the only people on the street are strangers.

The squatty brown brick building sits in the middle of the block with similarly depressing buildings on either side of it. I pull open the door under a blue sign that says AAA INVESTIGATIONS AND BAIL BONDS. And in smaller letters underneath: CHECK CASHING AND PAYDAY LOANS.

A rush of heat mixed with the smell of sweat washes over me once I step inside. The receptionist points me toward the waiting area after I give her my name, then she picks up the phone to announce my arrival to whoever is on the other end. Mismatched chairs sit against walls covered in those posters that combine wildlife photography and inspirational quotes, as if a bald eagle knows the first thing about leadership. I drop down in an empty seat between two mostly dead plants. The only other people left waiting are a couple quietly arguing in the corner and an old man to my right who is hunched over in his chair, snoring loudly.

Several minutes later, the receptionist calls my name and points down the hall behind her desk. "Last door on the right" is all she says.

I pass three closed doors in the narrow hallway before stopping in front of the one she indicated. I take a second or two to center myself, then knock on the door.

"Come in!" a muffled voice yells.

I push the door open and am surprised by the man sitting behind the desk. In my head, I pictured the stereotypical sleazeball: short balding man, leering grin, cigarette burning in an ashtray nearby. But this man looks the exact opposite of that. He's blond. And gorgeous. He stands when I enter, reaching across the desk to shake my hand, pumping it enthusiastically. His light-blue button-down matches his eyes perfectly, and the effect is so dazzling that I know his closet is full of shirts in the same color.

"Lucca! Good to see you. I'm Matt Rowen."

There's no way to know if this is the same person I spoke with last night, but I'm betting it's not.

I nod. "Mr. Rowen."

He throws me a brilliant smile and says, "Call me Matt. Please, have a seat."

Perching on the edge of the chair, I spy my laptop sitting on the corner of the desk.

He notices me eyeing it. "Go ahead. It's yours just for showing."

I pull it off the desk and rest it on my lap, fighting the urge to clutch it to my chest.

Matt flips a pen and catches it, over and over, while he studies me. "I have to say, we've been impressed at the places you've gotten in and out of."

"Who's we? How many creepy guys are in your little gang?" I ask.

He gives me a smirk as if he thinks I'm cute. His phone chimes and he slides it off his desk. Matt's thumbs move across the screen at an amazing speed, his attention firmly on his phone.

"Is that Mr. Smith?"

He ignores me completely.

That's fine. I can wait him out.

Matt finally looks up from his phone and says, "We have a job for you. A chance to make some decent money."

"Doing what?" I ask.

Matt rests his elbows on the arm of his chair and kicks his feet up on his desk, the phone forgotten for a moment. "You'd be doing what you're good at. We'll drop you in a situation and you'll get us what we need. Without anyone being the wiser. You won't believe the difference it will make with us behind you. I'll give you the details as soon as you tell me you're in."

My mind splits, showing two different paths; this is definitely a crossroads moment. Taking the job Matt offers moves me deeper into this world but comes with the support that would make the feel of those cuffs biting into my wrists a distant memory. The other path requires me to go straight. To get out before I'm in any real trouble. Because as Saturday night proved, it will only be a matter of time before something else goes wrong.

Mama always said to be successful in life you need to do three things: learn everything you can, try your hardest, and be the best at what you do.

Saturday night taught me I have a lot to learn.

Just thinking about Mama makes my chest hurt. But I shove it down. She's gone and there's nothing for me in that old life. One day I will go back to being Lucca Marino, small-town girl from Eden, North Carolina, who lives in that fantasy house with that fantasy garden, but today is not that day. Today, I learn how to make the money I need to make that dream a reality.

"Okay, I'm in. What's the job?"

CHAPTER 10

Present Day

t's been three days since the Derby party and the mailbox is still empty. I'm also no closer to finding out that woman's real name or where she's from. And until I know her real name, she is nothing more than **that woman** to me.

But just because I haven't run across her in town doesn't mean she's been in hiding. Everywhere I turn, the name "Lucca Marino" falls from someone's lips as they recount their interaction with her.

I got added to the group text after the Derby party so I could see in real time that Sara bumped into her at that same tearoom that was suggested for our first lunch, and Beth ran into her while getting her nails done. And despite how badly Allison spoke about James at the Derby party, she and Cole went out to dinner with them last night. She gave everyone a full recap this morning.

There was even a picture of James and her at the Derby party in the "People and Places" section of the tiny local newspaper; her hat was looking even more dainty and refined in print than it did in real life.

While I've taken my time insinuating myself into this community, she has come in like a hurricane.

The level of sheer audacity on her part wasn't apparent until I stumbled over James's mom's Facebook post gushing over that woman and the homemade soup she made for James's dad. There were 128 (and counting) comments about how lucky the Bernards were to have her. Since James's mom tagged her in the post, it took only one click to be on her page.

Her account hasn't been active long. The earliest activity was an uploaded profile pic with the caption: **Ugh old account got hacked so let's be friends here!** about a week after I arrived in Lake Forbing.

It was the second post that confirmed it was **not** a harmless coincidence that she showed up in this town, with my name and details matching my own history.

When I was in sixth grade, my class took a field trip to a local farm, where we spent the day playing farmer and doing chores like milking cows and feeding chickens. Somehow, that woman found the group picture we took at the end of the day and posted it as a Throwback Thursday with the caption: **Look what I found while going through some old boxes! Such a fun day! Tag yourself if I missed you.**

In the picture, I sat crossed-legged in the front

row, second from the left, in my jeans and favorite red sweatshirt Mama had trimmed with navy gingham ribbon around the collar, cuffs, and bottom hem.

Several people I went to school with—classmates I haven't thought about in years—tagged themselves in the post. It was a virtual reunion in the comments section, as most of them reached out to tell her they're happy to reconnect, fully believing she is me.

I had gone back to that profile pic and studied it until my eyes were blurry. Her head is turned, that long hair covering most of her face, and she's laughing. It's a great candid shot. The last time those old friends had seen me I was a teenager with baby fat still clinging to my cheeks. It's easy to see why they believe she's exactly who she says she is.

If this were any other job, I would have grabbed my few belongings and gotten the hell out of town the second she was introduced to me, but the ramifications of abandoning this job override that instinct. I can't run. Not yet. Not after the last job.

It has taken everything in me to maintain the level of carefree, happy girlfriend that came second nature before the Derby party, in order to keep Ryan from suspecting anything is off.

A glance at the kitchen clock has me moving. I rinse my coffee cup in the sink before grabbing my bag and heading to the garage.

After a lot of thought, it's time to make the call

I've been putting off, but only from the privacy of my own car. While there is still a slim possibility that someone other than my boss sent the impostor here, it is very unlikely. If my boss were to find out about this woman from any source other than me, there would no doubt be serious consequences. Calling this in is what's expected of me, and right now, I need to be 100 percent predictable.

With my car still hidden away in Ryan's garage, I open the glove box and pull out the prepaid phone, removing it from the package. It will be used one time and then destroyed.

Once it's powered on, I dial the number I memorized at the beginning of this job. The call connects and the robotic voice asks, "Is there a problem?" With all the voice recognition software available, the true sound of Mr. Smith's voice is a secret that's guarded as meticulously as his real name.

"Significant development that makes this call necessary. Made contact with a woman claiming to be me. Used my original name, stated she was from my hometown, used details from my past as hers. Please advise."

The pause is uncomfortably long.

"Yet you waited three days to report this development."

Shit.

"Wanted to be one hundred percent sure it was not a coincidence before—"

He interrupts me before I finish. "I felt you

needed a reminder that you are replaceable. Treat her arrival as motivation to successfully complete this job as opposed to the utter failure of your last one. Once this job is finished to my satisfaction, you will return to being the only Lucca Marino from Eden, North Carolina, in my employ." He pauses for a moment and then adds, "I know how important that is to you."

If the information I was supposed to have turned over to him on my last job hadn't been extremely sensitive, I don't think Mr. Smith would feel the need to threaten me like this. I might not know exactly how badly that woman with my name and my background being here can hurt me, but that doesn't mean she can't hurt me. Mr. Smith doesn't do anything without good reason.

In this line of work, being replaced doesn't mean you're let go without a letter of recommendation. Even if I don't know Mr. Smith's real name, I know enough that I don't get to just walk away.

My free hand grips the steering wheel and I swallow down the urge to scream. When I'm sure my voice is controlled, I say, "I don't particularly like having a threat hanging over me, especially after all the jobs I **have** successfully completed."

"All those previous successes are what made the last failure so difficult to accept. But it also gave you a second chance. You need to remember that while you're sitting on the back deck eating Chinese takeout."

Chinese takeout.

What I picked up for dinner last night.

"I would like nothing more than to finish this job to your satisfaction. When can I expect my next set of instructions?"

"No firm date but within the next two weeks. And to be clear, this is a **reminder,** not a threat. If I were issuing a threat, there would be no confusion."

The line goes dead.

I didn't learn everything I wanted in that call, but I learned enough. I have confirmation Smith sent that woman here, and at least I now have a general time frame for my next set of instructions.

But the most important thing I discovered is that even though his trust in me has weakened, I haven't lost it completely.

Even though I feel like a sitting duck, I must finish what I started.

It's time to go off script.

I start the car and pull out of the driveway, heading to work. Once I'm on one of the busier streets, I swerve, jerking the wheel hard, and my left front tire hits the concrete curb. There's a loud screeching sound, then I hear the tire pop. The car limps into the tire repair shop at the end of the block. One of the techs motions for me to pull into one of the open bays then moves closer to inspect my tire.

"You're lucky we were close by. You couldn't have driven on it this way for long," he says when I exit the vehicle.

"So lucky," I agree. I grab my purse and head inside the shop.

The guy behind the counter greets me when I step up to the counter. "How can we help you today?"

I roll my eyes and say, "Hit a curb down the street and busted my tire." I point to my car through the glass window that looks out onto the shop area.

He asks for my name and information as he fills out the order ticket. "It'll be a couple of hours before it's ready. Got a few folks ahead of you."

"No problem," I say, moving toward the waiting area.

Digging my phone out of my purse, I call Ryan. He answers on the second ring.

"Hey, what's up?" he asks.

"Hey," I reply, frustration lacing my words. "I'm at the tire shop on Jackson. Wasn't paying attention and hit the curb and popped the tire. Luckily, I was close enough to get here before it got too bad."

"You and tires do not get along," he says with a laugh.

"No, we do not," I agree.

He chuckles then asks, "Need a ride? I can call Cole to come pick you up and drop you at home or work." Thursdays are usually the only days Ryan is out of town, but he took a meeting with some potential clients in the town just south of here so he's out of pocket for the day.

"No, I'm going to wait it out. They said it shouldn't take too long. I'll call work. I don't think they'll mind if I'm late since I stayed behind and worked that event last week."

"Okay, let me know when it's fixed."

"I will. I'll see you tonight." I end the call then text my boss, letting him know what happened and that I'll be late. I move closer to the counter and tell the man who helped me moments before, "Text me when it's ready and I'll be back for it."

He nods. "Yes, ma'am."

I exit the store and walk three businesses down to the car rental agency. The girl at the counter is young and way too perky for this early in the morning.

"Can I help you?" she asks much louder than necessary.

"Yes, I have a reservation for a car. Annie Michaels."

She taps away on her computer and then beams at me. "Yes! We're all ready for you!"

I sign the paperwork then grab the keys to a black four-door sedan that's parked out front. Within ten minutes, I'm on the road.

Ryan has gotten into the habit of dropping by my work, so I needed to capitalize on his impromptu out-of-town meeting. But I also needed to account for my time away for my boss. And since everyone in this town knows one another, my stories have to match.

As I pull onto the interstate and head west, I block out everything else and focus on what's ahead. I spent weeks surveilling Ryan's business in East Texas when I first got here. When I finally got my first set of instructions, I realized how important that business was for this job. The search of his Glenview office offered some information but not what I needed to finish here. But that woman's arrival in town had got me antsy and feeling like I needed to go back and make sure I didn't miss anything, so I put the plan in place to head over there when Ryan told me he would be gone for the day.

After that call with Mr. Smith, this job has taken on a sense of urgency I haven't felt before. He wanted to show me I could be replaced. But he also showed me that in the time between the last job and this one, he went to great lengths to groom someone to be me. It's clear there's something big I'm missing, and it's vital that I start over at the beginning and look at everything with fresh eyes.

The game has changed.

CHAPTER 11

Present Day

In Lake Forbing, Ryan runs a local branch of a national brokerage firm. It's located in one of those new office parks where the row of identical buildings looks like cottages. Most of his clients are little old ladies who need help investing their oil and gas royalty checks. He is the local golden boy whom they trust completely. I could probably match his client list to the guest book from his grandfather's funeral, name by name.

In Glenview, Texas, Ryan runs a trucking and transportation business that's located in a warehouse in an industrial area on the outskirts of town. The only signage on the entire property is a rectangular white metal sign with the words GLENVIEW TRUCKING stenciled in black letters. The phone number sends you straight to a voice-mail system, and there is no website or social media attached to this company. He never talks about Glenview Trucking, and I believe very few people, if any, know it exists.

Just as I cross the border into Texas, which is the halfway point between Lake Forbing and Glenview,

I mentally retrieve that typed page of information I was given about Ryan and the business located here.

Glenview Trucking was established in 1985 by Ryan's grandfather, William Sumner. William's son, Scott, joined the business after he returned home from college in 1989. At inception, the business was a legitimate enterprise that served the East Texas and North Louisiana area.

It still operates in its original capacity but in the late 90s, the business model expanded to include brokerage services for stolen goods. It is believed that currently two out of every three trucks that arrive are transporting items bound for the black market. While the illegal side of the business is vastly more profitable, Glenview Trucking is an invaluable front that must be maintained.

Ryan took over operations after his grandmother, Ingrid Sumner, was diagnosed with cancer and his grandfather became her full-time caregiver but limited his on-site involvement to one day a week—Thursdays. Ryan has done an impressive job of keeping the company in Texas separate from his life in Lake Forbing, LA, just as his grandfather and father had done before him.

*Opinion based on research but have no hard evidence to support—Ryan seems to make every effort to maintain the business his grandfather started, and his father worked at until his death in 2004, in Glenview. I believe this business is immensely important to him and he will protect it at all costs.

My last job was unusual in the sense that I knew immediately I was sent to retrieve sensitive information that was being used as blackmail against Victor Connolly, but normally there is a lag between when I get the name of the mark and when I get my first set of instructions. I use that time to dig deep into every aspect of the mark's life so I'm prepared when the time comes to get to work. While I'm waiting to see what the job is, I try to predict what the client hired us to do, even though I never know who the client is.

So that's what I did when I got the name: Ryan Sumner.

At first glance, the financial services business, and its long client list of old ladies with their oil and gas royalty checks, seemed to be the obvious answer. But the more I learned about that part of Ryan's life, the less it seemed likely. There wasn't anyone on his client list who caught my eye as the reason I'm here.

There's always the chance the mark is just a means to get close to one of their friends, but it didn't take long to rule that out as a possibility either. Ryan's friends may be the type to cheat on their golf game, their spouse, or their taxes, but that's the extent of their bad behavior.

But when I looked into the trucking business in Glenview, I knew that's why I had been sent here. It's impressive what Ryan has been able to do in the last six years. He took what was a two-bit operation and turned it into a lucrative enterprise with a reputation of white-glove service that has clients across the country. While there is still the occasional truckload of stolen Xbox and PlayStation consoles that roll through his place, he's transitioned the business to moving more upscale merchandise and to the procurement of specialty items by request. He has become the concierge of the black market.

Basically, Ryan is a thief, just like me.

My first set of instructions verified my suspicions when I learned his trucking business had become profitable enough that it was targeted for a hostile takeover—not the first time I've had an assignment like this.

And while helping the client facilitate the takeover of Ryan's business may have been what brought me here, **my** objective has shifted now that Mr. Smith has brought an impostor on the scene. The needs of the unknown client are now irrelevant to me. I'm going back over everything to discover why Mr. Smith chose **Ryan Sumner** and **this** job to test me.

Just before I arrive at my destination, I stop at an old gas station and pull to the back of the parking lot so I can change. The rental car may be a little out of place in this industrial area, but the disguise is on point. I've traded the pencil skirt and loose blouse for a worn pair of baggy Levi's, a button-down khaki shirt, and a safety vest. My hair is tucked underneath a short wig and baseball cap, while the custom-made silicon facial prosthetics turn my features more masculine. I could pass for a man on his way to work.

I park in the lot for the building next door to Glenview Trucking, then walk toward the chain-link fence that separates this property from Ryan's. This is only the second time I've been here, but I've watched countless videos of Ryan while he was working here. The intel I get before making contact is always thorough so I watched as the coat, slacks, and dress shoes he left the house in were quickly replaced with worn jeans, a T-shirt, and scuffed-up boots.

In the videos, he exits the building from the office door located in the corner of the warehouse and walks to the driver's side of each and every truck that pulls up to the building. The driver rolls down his window and there seems to be an exchange of pleasantries before Ryan retrieves a remote from his pocket to open the bay door.

The structure is large enough that an 18-wheeler can pull into any one of the three oversize roll-up doors that run down the front side of the corrugated metal building, fit completely inside so it can be unloaded in private, and then exit through doors along the back wall. My plan is to enter the enormous building the same way I did the first time I came here.

There's not as much action today. From the reports, the illegal shipments only come on Thursdays, when Ryan is here to inspect them himself. From the increase in volume over the last couple of years, he's going to need to add a second day soon to keep up with demand. The legitimate operation brings in far less traffic. Ryan has done a good job keeping both sides of this business separate, and that includes the employees. There's a skeleton crew here today, and none of these workers are ever present on Thursdays. I should be able to slip in without anyone noticing, since their guard will be substantially lower than that of the guys who are here with Ryan.

I wait on the other side of the fence, near where Ryan's employees park, until a truck pulls up, then

I quickly make a small opening using a wire cutter from my belt. When a man leaves the small office to greet the driver, I slip through and walk the short distance to the back side of the building, just like any other employee would. I pick the lock quickly then quietly open the metal door.

There's only one guy inside, but he's in the back right corner stacking boxes. He seems focused on his task, so I edge my way through the warehouse, toward the office that sits in the front left corner of the building. I peek through the small window set in the door to make sure the room is empty and then slip inside right as one of the bay doors begins to open to allow the truck through.

The office is a complete mess. Stacks of papers cover each of the three desks, along with empty coffee cups and a couple of pizza boxes. Thumbing through the filing cabinets seems like a better use of my time than picking through the trash.

I've turned information on this business over to Mr. Smith twice now. The first time was the general sort that described the day-to-day activity and key personnel, which I was able to get from some of his files here. While that information was helpful, it wasn't what I needed to complete this job. That wasn't surprising given that there are several employees who use this space while running the legitimate side of Glenview Trucking on the days Ryan isn't there. He wouldn't be so careless with sensitive information.

The second delivery included crucial data that make the takeover possible—all the financials, including where the money is and who the clients are. Lists of where he gets the stolen goods and merchandise as well as contacts in local law enforcement and border patrol who turn a blind eye. That treasure trove of information was retrieved from Ryan's laptop. The same laptop he keeps with him at all times. I spent weeks patiently waiting for the right moment to access it.

I had found everything Mr. Smith needed to take what Ryan has spent years building and I was surprised by the pang of regret that hit me when I thought about how huge his loss would be. It was the first time I felt bad for doing my job.

The first time I wanted to give a mark a fighting chance to keep what was theirs.

I've also tried not to analyze why I was feeling this way, especially since I knew how important this job was for my own survival.

So even though I'm back to look through files I've already searched, there's no real expectation I'll find anything helpful. I just want at least one more look in case something new jumps out at me, given that my main focus has now shifted.

The idling engine of the truck inside the warehouse is loud enough that I don't hear the approaching voices on the other side of the door until they are seconds from opening it. The small bathroom is the only spot where I can hide. I scramble into the shower stall, pulling the opaque white curtain closed just as the office door opens and two men enter.

I crouch down, lean against the shower wall, and put my head as close as I dare to the curtain.

From the small gap between the shower curtain and shower wall, there is a sliver of view into the office from the open doorway. The office chair closest to me is occupied, but I can only see the side of the chair and part of the man's shoulder.

"Go ahead and call him in here."

His voice is like a punch in the gut. It's Ryan. Ryan is here. Not meeting clients back in Louisiana but sitting about six feet from me.

A door opens then shuts, and we're left alone. I lean away from the curtain in case he heads in here to use the bathroom.

This is sloppy of me, and I'm never this sloppy, despite Mr. Smith's feelings about my last performance. But if he could see me right now, I wouldn't blame him if he questioned my ability to successfully complete this job.

The sound of paper shuffling is the only thing that lets me know he's still at that desk, since I've lost the visual.

A few minutes later, I hear the door open again, and two different sets of boots shuffle across the concrete floor.

"Hey, man, what are you doing here today?" a

man's voice says. The inflection is high, like he's surprised, but there's a nervous quiver to it that gives him away. He's scared.

There is no answer, so the man keeps talking as if his words are less dangerous than the silence filling the room. "I know I'm only supposed to work on Thursdays, but I needed a few extra hours this week. My ex is on my ass about money again. Wants to send the kids to some damn summer camp up in Arkansas. I'm like shit, they don't have to go all the way to the damn Ozark Mountains to play tag and whatever other bullshit they do up there."

Silence.

"I'm sorry, Ryan. I know I'm not supposed to be here today." His voice breaks when he says Ryan's name, and this has me more curious than anything else. Ryan has yet to say a word, and this man is terrified. All I've ever seen is sweet Ryan. Romantic Ryan. Fun Ryan.

Scary Ryan is intriguing.

"Come on, Freddie. Did you really think it was possible to make a side deal and have my trucks come through when I'm not here?"

His voice is now a bit deeper.

"No. It was dumb. Stupid. Really fucking stupid," Freddie answers. The third person in the room hasn't spoken yet.

There's a squeaking sound as if maybe Ryan is leaning back in his chair and the springs need to be oiled. I can almost picture him. He'd have his hands laced behind his head. Maybe his feet are propped up on the desk. He would look calm, almost casual, but the voice lets you know he's anything but.

"Seth, grab those wire cutters off Benny's desk," Ryan says in a deceptively calm voice.

There's a rustling sound and then Seth says, "Got 'em."

And then there's an edge to Ryan's voice that I've never heard before. "You're going to tell me who else is involved or Seth is going to enjoy using those wire cutters on your fingers." The chair squeaks again and Ryan adds, "What do you think, Seth, one finger for every minute we have to wait?"

"Sounds about right to me, Boss. These are pretty dull, though, so it may take me more than a minute to get one off."

Seth barely finishes before Freddie is talking. He's throwing around names and plans and dates at such a rapid rate that I hope Seth has forgotten about the wire cutters and picked up a pen and paper instead.

"You're not telling me everything," Ryan says. "You and those other idiots are too stupid to pull this off on your own. Tell me who else is involved."

The guy's voice cracks when he says, "That's it, I swear!"

I hear the chair roll briefly, and now I'm imagining him leaning forward, his elbows on the desk and his hands clasped together in front of him. I hear what sounds like a stack of papers hit the floor. "You think I don't know when someone has gone through my shit!"

Oh, hell. This poor guy may take the fall for something I've done.

"Seth, take his phone, then get him nice and comfortable in the warehouse. Get the other guys up here. I'll let Robert know they're ready for him."

"Wait! Wait! There's no reason to call Robert!" the guy shouts. He sounds even more terrified.

From the information I found, the "Robert" he is referring to is probably Robert Davidson, one of his biggest customers. And from my research, Freddie and his cohorts should be terrified he's getting involved.

Ryan waits an uncomfortably long time before he finally answers. "You think the load you were trying to lift today was going to just appear out of thin air? You think Robert wouldn't find out his goods never made it to their destination?" His voice grows louder with each sentence, the edge sharpening on every word. "You and those fucking idiot friends of yours jeopardized my entire operation for a few grand. You didn't even know the value of the merchandise in the truck. You think you're so smart to line up a buyer in advance, but you're so fucking stupid because you made a deal with one of my own guys. I knew what you were trying to do thirty fucking seconds after you made contact with him."

"Shit, Ryan, I'm sorry. I didn't mean to do it. The other guys talked me into it."

"Stop talking before you really piss me off." Ryan's voice is loud enough that I flinch. "You're not my problem anymore. You picked the wrong truck, my friend. Robert wants a few words with you and your buddies. Seth, get him the fuck out of my office."

The silence is almost jarring after the last several minutes. I've never heard Ryan talk to anyone so brutally before. It's hard to reconcile the man I've come to know with the man in the next room.

He works at the desk awhile longer while I hunker down in the stall. Seth is back before long, and it sounds like he settles into one of the other chairs. I hear bits and pieces of their conversation, but it's just normal chitchat between two guys who have known each other a long time. They talk about the Texas Rangers' chances of making the playoffs, and Ryan ribs him about some girl Seth has been hooking up with. There's a long discussion about craft beer that has me wanting to beat my head against the wall if I could do it without giving away my hiding spot.

While I wait for the opportunity to make my getaway, this new Ryan takes shape in my mind. You have to be ruthless in business, even more so when you're working on the wrong side of the law. I knew Ryan couldn't have achieved such success without getting his hands a little dirty. But if I hadn't heard it with my own ears, I would never have believed he was capable of threatening to have someone's fingers cut off one by one. His methods may be a bit barbaric, but they also seemed to be effective, since Freddie gave his buddies up within seconds. I'm glad to have seen this side of him. I need to know what I'm dealing with when it comes to Ryan.

Finally, Ryan and Seth leave the office, and I wait another few minutes before slowly pulling the curtain open. I spot them through the window, immersed in conversation with a trucker who has pulled up, so I sneak out the way I came in, retracing my steps until I'm back to my rental car in the adjacent parking lot.

I check my phone and see I have a message from the tire shop letting me know my car is ready, and another that Ryan left fifteen minutes ago telling me that he's almost done with his meeting and should be on the road soon. While I watch him, I text him back to say I'll pick up dinner on my way home from work. Less than a minute later he's pulling his phone from his back pocket. He steps away from the guys he's talking to, turning his back on them, which means he's now facing me. I didn't see him earlier, so I'm surprised at how tired he looks. And a little haggard. His thumbs move over the screen and a few seconds later my phone buzzes in my hand.

Ryan: Today sucked. Can't wait to see you

I try to ignore what those two sentences make me feel by reminding myself that Ryan will come home tonight, dressed in the suit he left home in this morning, and **lie** about why his day sucked. Then I'll show him the ticket from the tire shop and bitch that they overcharged me.

Even though I expect his lies, does he expect mine?

CHAPTER 12

Present Day

take my cup of tea and drop down on the steps that lead to the backyard. It's one of those days when the sky is so big and so blue that you can't resist being outside. Ryan flips a lawn mower that looks older than him upside down as if he's going to perform surgery on it.

"What's the prognosis?" I ask as he studies it.

He looks up, and there's a huge streak of grease down the side of his face. "I'm calling it." He checks his watch. "Time of death: ten forty-five a.m."

I giggle and he spreads a rag over the machine as if he were covering a dead body. "I guess I'm headed to Home Depot."

"Want company?" I ask.

And then there's that smile. "Always," he answers. "Give me a few minutes to clean up."

He heads inside and I sit back and stare at the sky. It's been a few days since I spied on him at the warehouse and the mailbox is still empty. There was another sighting of James and that woman last night. According to social media, they were at a local craft brewery listening to a popular local band. They have hit every hot spot in town.

The hummingbird feeder that hangs from a tree limb next to the deck draws my attention, and I watch the birds flap their little wings as they dart in and out to get a drink. Every morning, Ryan refills that feeder just like his grandmother probably did.

Mama would have loved it here.

We spent many nights dreaming up the fantasy house we'd one day build. I used to think she just hated the trailer. Or was embarrassed by it. It wasn't until I was older that I realized Mama wanted more for us than just a bigger roof over our heads. She wanted a different way of life. One where you didn't worry about having enough grocery money. One where she wouldn't worry about what would happen to me once she was gone.

"Ready?" Ryan asks from the patio door.

"Yep." I glance once more at the birds, then hop to my feet, following him back inside to the kitchen door that will lead us to the garage.

As we slowly wander down the aisles of Home Depot, Ryan studies each mower, then checks reviews on his phone before narrowing it down.

"I'm going to look at the plants," I say after he has stared at the same three mowers for twenty minutes.

"Grab a buggy. We need something for the front porch." He tears his gaze away from the machines in front of him and looks at me. "Maybe some ferns?"

"The ones that hang?" I ask.

He shrugs, then nods, letting me know it's my decision because in his mind, it's my house too. We are the epitome of a domestic couple. All we're missing is a couple of Starbucks and some hand-holding.

The garden section is an oasis in a sea of tools, lumber, and electrical supplies. I take my time, passing trays of geraniums and petunias and pansies, and think about what I would add to the flower beds in the front yard if it was truly mine to do with as I wished. As if I would be here to see them in full bloom. Distracted by the prettiest pink hydrangeas I've ever seen, my cart clips the side of one coming from the opposite direction.

"Oh, sorry!" And then I nearly freeze when I see it's James and the woman pretending to be me.

"Oh, hey!" she says. "I think we met at that Derby party!"

I hope the smile that spreads across my face hides the internal eye roll at her words. Nodding to them both, I say, "Yes, of course."

Could she not know who I really am? That she was sent here as some threat to replace me? Because she's good. Really good. There's not a flick of recognition nor a long look that sizes me up as her obvious opponent. There is a chance she's still in the "waiting for information" stage of her job, but does she not find the unmistakable resemblance between us as jarring as I do? Even though my hair is darker, it's uncanny.

"Dad usually freshens up the beds for Mom, but he's out of commission right now, so we thought we'd do it for him since it's such a pretty day," James says, nodding to the plants in his cart.

"Aw, what a good son," I say, my back teeth grinding.

"James, hey man!" I hear Ryan say from behind me. He jogs up and the two of them shake hands, then Ryan nods a greeting at the woman. "Lucca." He looks at her then back at me before once again looking at her.

He sees the similarities too.

Ryan clears his throat then turns back to me and says, "I picked one and they're bringing it to the checkout in here. Thought I'd come help with the plants."

James laughs. "Damn, when did we get so old that a beautiful spring day meant yard work? We should be on the lake, icing down some beer."

"Yeah, no kidding," Ryan says, but I know if given the option, we'd still leave here and spend the day in the yard, saving the lake and beer for after the work is done.

"Another time," James says. The small talk lasts a few more minutes while she and I just watch each other. They start to move away, but I put a hand on James's arm, stopping them. "I was just thinking—do you two have plans for tonight?" I glance quickly at Ryan and then back to them. She's been dancing just out of my reach for too long. "We'd love it if you came over for dinner."

She beams at the invitation.

"We'd love that," James answers for them. "What can we bring?"

"Nothing! We've got it." I look at the woman. "Can't wait!"

Alias: Izzy Williams—Eight Years Ago

This is the first job where my fake name and background has the backup to support it. I even googled my new name, Isabelle Williams, Izzy for short, and found that I was listed as a member of the cross-country team who competed at state for a local high school a few years ago. Somehow the picture that accompanied the article included a grainy group photo, and I could swear I was the third girl on the right, complete with short blond hair, like the wig I'm wearing right now.

It makes me wonder how many people Mr. Smith has working for him. Not just people being sent on jobs like me but those working behind the scenes, altering images that show up on internet searches and creating identities from thin air.

The only other person I've dealt with is Matt, but it feels like whatever this organization is, it's much bigger than just him and Mr. Smith.

There was a lot to do to get ready for this job. I was given instructions on how to pull my natural hair up and secure it under the wig so that there was no chance any of my strands would be left uncovered. I was also told to apply a thick layer of liquid bandage to the tip of each finger so no matter what I touch while I'm here, I wouldn't leave a fingerprint behind. I'm to reapply it every couple of hours. I rub my fingers together, still trying to get used to the lack of feeling there. I added the contoured makeup and colored contacts on my own. Mama taught me how a few strokes of powder can change the shape and look of your entire face— although I know she would only have wanted me to use those tricks to enhance my face, not to make it unrecognizable.

It's the first day of my first job for Mr. Smith, and I have to admit, I'm a little nervous. As far as Greg and Jenny Kingston know, I'm the new nanny for their son, Miles. But in truth, Greg has something in this house that my boss wants, and I'm here to get it for him.

There were a lot of instructions of how to handle items, as well. The second I retrieve the item I'm sent for, I am to drop it at a predesignated spot as soon as possible. It's harder to get caught if you aren't in possession of what you stole when they catch you.

Walking up to the front porch, I smooth down my shirt and shorts before ringing the doorbell.

Greg opens the door immediately, as if he has been waiting for me to arrive. He's wearing a gray suit with a darker gray tie, and his hair looks like it hasn't changed since he was a young boy. Short and combed to the side, not a strand out of place.

"Isabelle Williams?" he asks, then looks me up and down. I'm dressed exactly as instructed. Khaki shorts that hit two inches above the knee and a pink polo shirt. I look like I'm ready for a round of golf.

My hand reaches out for his and we shake. "Yes, sir. Mr. Kingston. You can call me Izzy."

He nods and gestures for me to come inside. He checks his watch for the second time since he's opened the door, then yells toward the wraparound stairs that curve up the foyer wall. "Jenny! She's here!"

Both of our gazes are trained on the upper landing as we wait for Jenny to show herself.

She doesn't.

Greg booms her name out again and again we wait.

He's irritated. And slightly embarrassed. "Excuse me one moment," he mutters, and then he's gone. Taking the steps two at a time, he is out of sight within seconds.

"Are you the new babysitter?"

I spin around to find Miles behind me. He's in the middle of a doorway that leads to the dining room, then eventually the kitchen, according to the blueprints I studied.

Moving toward him slowly, I stop when I'm a few feet away and squat down until I'm on his level. "I am. My name is Izzy. What's yours?" I ask, even though I already know his name and just about everything about him. Matt gave me a packet that covered every detail about this family when I agreed to work for Mr. Smith. Miles is five years old, an only child, and I'm the fourth nanny that he's had already this year.

His thumb pops back into his mouth as soon as he tells me his name, even though he looks a little too old for that.

I point to his shirt. "Iron Man is my favorite."

He pulls his shirt away from his body to look down at it as if he needs a reminder of what he's wearing. It's a shirt with all the Marvel characters in their fighting stance poses.

"I like the Hulk. He smashes things," he says, then adds the growl and fists his hands.

I'm about to ask another question, but there's movement on the stairs that draws our attention.

Greg has located Jenny and is now pulling her down the stairs. She almost stumbles once they clear the last step, as if she's unaware there are no more in front of her.

"Izzy, this is my wife, Mrs. Kingston." His grip on her arm seems to be the only thing keeping her standing.

Jenny looks at me and smiles, but it doesn't reach her eyes.

Another thing I know—Jenny likes her Xanax in the morning, her Chardonnay in the afternoon, and a vodka or three in the evening.

I reach out my hand and she clasps it with both of hers. "Izzy, it's so nice to meet you!"

She holds on to me longer than is comfortable, and thankfully Miles moves closer, causing her attention to switch to him.

"There you are, sweetheart! Did you get your breakfast?"

Miles nods but doesn't say anything else.

"Right, okay, I've got to get to the office," Greg says, then turns to me. "You are in charge of Miles. His schedule is written out and taped to the fridge; my number is on the bottom. He can give you a tour of the house and show you where everything is. I'll be home by six."

He ruffles Miles's hair and spins toward the door. There is no good-bye to Jenny or even a look in her direction.

The three of us stand awkwardly in the foyer for a few seconds until Jenny leans down and kisses Miles on the cheek, gives me a great big smile, and drifts back up the stairs.

"Want me to show you around?" Miles asks.

"Yes, give me the grand tour," I say as I follow him through the door he came through earlier.

◆

Mama used to say I would recognize the life I was meant to have. I look around this house and think about what it would feel like if this identity were real and I **was** Izzy Williams, college student and nanny to Miles Kingston.

One thing is for sure, this is definitely not the life for me.

Five days down and I still haven't found what I'm looking for.

What I **have** found is that Miles runs this house. He knows when the housekeeper arrives, he knows where the petty cash is kept so she can pick up the week's groceries, and he knows when Jenny moves from pills to pours. When the wine flows, so do the tears, and we make ourselves scarce.

While she's melancholy when it comes to Miles, Jenny is almost vicious when it comes to me. She's all smiles when Greg is around, but the second he leaves, her claws come out. She doesn't want me in her house. Doesn't want me spending time with her son. But she's too drunk and high to change either of those things.

Miles and I play with Legos. We build forts. We sing songs. And I search and search and search.

Not going to lie. This job gets harder each day. Because as soon as I retrieve what I was sent here for, I'm gone. And who will take care of Miles?

But it's dangerous to think like that. So every day, I add a brick to the wall inside of me that will, I hope, seal myself off from this blond-haired, blue-eyed child who is way too old for his age.

On day eight, I'm able to get inside Jenny's bedroom.
   Finally.
   I don't have access to this part of the house often
since this is where Jenny spends most of her time.
Whenever she ventures out of her room, Miles
sticks to me like glue. Right now, Miles is napping
and Jenny is soaking in the bath, a thin door separating her from me.
   Does she stay in there for hours? Is it a quick
rinse and out? Who knows. But I can't afford to
lose this opportunity just because I don't know
what to expect.
   I wander the room, giving everything a critical
eye. I'm looking for a flash drive, one exactly like
the flash drive in my pocket that I'll leave in its
place. There are tons of places something that small
could be hidden. I have looked in every drawer,
nook, and cranny in Greg's office without luck. I'd
dig through his sock drawer if that's where he hid
his valuables.
   I'm beginning to think that just because the blueprints don't show a built-in safe, they might have
added one after they bought this house, so now I'm
on the hunt for that because I don't want to fail on
my first job.
   Several pieces of Jenny's jewelry are scattered
carelessly across the top of a delicate antique desk.

These pieces are exquisite, and I'm mentally removing the stones from the settings while calculating
the price each would fetch.

But that's not why I'm here, so I force myself to
walk away from them.

I open drawers and rummage through every part
of the room. It's big enough that there's a sitting area
tucked in a corner near the door that leads to the
bathroom. Inching into that space, I stay perfectly
quiet while I listen to Jenny sing off-key in the tub.

The framed family portrait of the Kingstons
hanging on the wall depicts a perfect little trio that
doesn't reflect what life is really like in this house.
I'm sure Jenny shared this picture on social media
to make everyone believe things are as rosy as that
image suggests. I tug on the corner of the frame,
just like I've done to every other piece of wall art in
the house, and stop myself from celebrating when it
swings open, revealing a small safe set into the wall.
I pull on the handle but it's firmly locked in place.

Staring at the ten-number keypad, I start to
sweat. There are a lot of things I can do, but crack-
ing safes is not one of them. I pull out the phone
that Matt gave me for emergencies only.

This is an emergency.

Luckily, he answers on the first ring.

"What's wrong?"

"Nothing," I whisper. "I found a safe. It's got a
keypad and I don't have a lot of time. What do
I do?"

"Take a pic and send it to me."

I do as he asks and then wait for him to get it.

"It's simple. Doesn't look like it's hooked up to a system. Try a four-digit number and see what it does."

I punch in 2580 because I read once that is the most common passcode since it is the only four-digit vertical combo.

"One beep and the little light flashed red once."

Matt is quiet on the other line for a few seconds then says, "Try the kid's birthday."

I read all the important dates from the packet they gave me before I started and have no problem retrieving the exact number from memory. I press in 1017. October 17.

"One beep and two red lights."

"Shit," Matt spits out from the other line. "I bet this is a 'three times wrong, you're locked out for good' system. It probably resets after a certain amount of time. Maybe twenty-four hours. Stay put and try again tomorrow."

And the line goes dead.

I deflate. I need out of this house. Splashing from the bathroom makes me freeze, then I hear Jenny singing that same stupid song she's been singing for two days. The water turns back on, probably because she's been in there so long it's gotten chilly.

I stare at the keypad as my mind scrolls through the important dates and numbers from the Kingston file. Then I think about Greg. I can tell he loves Miles even though he's not a hands-on kind of dad. He'll text through the day asking how he's doing and seems generally interested in talking to Miles when he gets home every night. The code isn't his birthday, though.

Jenny lets out a loud laugh. I can only imagine what's going on in there while she bathes alone.

Why hasn't Greg booted her out of this house by now? He's obviously got enough money to hire all the help he needs. He only talks to Jenny when he has to, although there are times I find him watching her with a sad expression. An expression that shows there's still love there, even though he hates what she's turned into. Could the code be her birthday? Their anniversary? Greg tries to hide it, but he sleeps in the guest room every night, and there is only one picture beside the bed. It's of Greg and Jenny. They are young and all smiles, their faces squished together, cheek to cheek. Behind them, the sky is full of fireworks. There's a good chance this picture was taken on their first date, at the Fourth of July picnic at the country club.

I stare at the keypad, hold my breath, and type in 0704. There are a few seconds where nothing happens and then the light blinks green and I hear the lock slide open.

My breath lets loose and I almost scream for joy. I did it!

I pull the door open and the only thing inside is

the red flash drive with the blue cap, just like the corrupted fake in my pocket I will leave behind in its place. It will also make whatever computer he inserts the replacement into useless. While Greg will freak out and wonder what went wrong, he should be oblivious a swap was made.

As I'm making the switch, Jenny laughs again but it's closer than before. She's out of the bathroom and staring at me.

"I've been watching you snoop around my house for the last week." Her words are slurred and her eyes are half closed. A puddle forms on the hardwood floor from the water dripping off her naked body, visible through her open robe.

This is bad. Very bad. She has caught me red-handed.

"It's not what you think," I say.

She sways and lets out a shrill laugh. "Of course it is. It's exactly what I think it is." Jenny lurches at me, her hands out as if she's either going to grab me or strike me, but her foot gets tangled up in the sash hanging from her robe and she's going down before I can catch her. Her head hits the floor with a loud crack and a thin river of blood runs from under her blond hair. She's out cold.

"Oh shit," I whisper, dropping down beside her. My fingers press against her neck to check for a pulse.

I call Matt again.

"I've got it," I say as soon as he answers. "But the

wife caught me. She's drunk, tripped and fell. Her head is bleeding."

"Is she dead?" he asks in a quiet voice.

"No. But she needs help. Should I call 911?"

"So she can tell the cops she caught you stealing from them?" Matt spits out. "Get the fuck out of there and bring the drive."

"What about Miles?" While there is no love lost between Jenny and me, that little boy deserves better.

"Get out of there now! You can't be caught there like this. Kingston doesn't have shit to go on if you're gone." Matt screams so loud it echoes in the room. "Get your ass out of that house."

And then the line goes dead.

I'm scared to touch her again. Can I leave her like this? Can I leave Miles? But if I stay, I could go to jail. She'll tell them I was robbing them. They may even blame me for her fall. She'll say I pushed her.

I pull the other phone from my pocket, the one Greg calls to check on Miles. The one that is only powered on once I step inside the Kingstons' house.

"Hello," Greg answers.

"There's a problem. I came upstairs to tell Mrs. Kingston I have a family emergency and that I need to leave immediately but she's unconscious on the floor. She must have fallen. Miles is asleep on the couch in the playroom. You need to come home. I have my own family emergency so I can't stay."

"Wait—"

But I've already ended the call. I drop the fake drive in the safe then close it before swinging the picture back in place. Miles is the only reason I'm risking myself like this.

Greg can call 911. He can come home and deal with this. I have to trust the fake name, the steps I've taken to hide my identity. I race down the stairs and peek in on Miles one last time. His little face is lost in sleep, and the origami swan I taught him to make, just like Mama taught me, is clutched in his tiny hand. He'll be fine. His dad will be here soon. He's not my problem.

I dart out of the back door, and creep along the side of the house until I'm on the street and jumping into the car Matt gave me to use for this job. As I'm exiting the gated neighborhood, an ambulance squeals past me followed by a cop car.

I keep my head down and drive the speed limit. Will they pull footage at the guard's gate? Have a pic of me in this car? How soon before the cops start looking for me?

It takes ten minutes to get to AAA Bail Bonds. I was told to never come back here, but this is obviously not a normal situation.

Matt is pacing the street, waiting for me.

My door is ripped open before I come to a complete stop. "What the fuck took you so long?" He pulls me out of the car and into the building. We don't stop until we get to his office.

"I got here as soon as I could," I say as I hand him

the drive and then place the phone I used for my calls with Greg on the desk. I don't mention my call to him—the call I deleted from the log just before I powered it off, in case he checks.

I wonder if Miles woke up and found her before his dad got there.

No. I can't think about him.

Matt has the drive in his palm, and he's tapping away on his phone. He reads whatever's there then flinches when his phone rings.

"Yes." He looks at me, his eyes boring into mine, then passes me the phone.

I hesitate for just a second then take it from him.

"Hello," I whisper.

"Give me the events of this afternoon. Do not leave anything out." Mr. Smith's disguised voice hides the anger his real voice would carry.

I tell him everything, including how I figured out the code to the safe. Everything except the call to Greg.

"You're feeling guilty over leaving Jenny Kingston bleeding on the floor."

It's not a question but I answer. "Yes."

"It was only a matter of time before that was going to happen. If not today, then tomorrow, or the next. She's been working in that direction for a long while."

I'm quiet. While that may be true, I can't help but think it wouldn't have happened today if I hadn't been in her room, rummaging through their safe. She would have come out of the bathroom and sunk into her bed, just like she did every other day I was there. So if she is **successful** today, then that's on me.

"Yes, I know," I answer him.

"You got the job done, but you were reckless. Taking a chance with the safe. Letting that drunk sneak up on you. You're better than that."

And he's right. I am better than that. I should have noticed that she stopped singing. I should have heard her clumsy footsteps cross the bathroom floor. I should have heard the turn of the knob on the door.

"What would you have done if she hadn't fallen on her own?" he asks me.

"I don't know," I answer quickly. And that's the truth. What lengths would I have taken to ensure I got away? I guess I'll never know.

"I'll answer that for you. You do whatever you have to do to save yourself and the job. Because never forget this is a job. You are not a part of that family. That is not your life. Not your world. You're a ghost who drifted through it for a little bit of time. Those people don't give a shit about you, so don't give a shit about them."

I'm quiet as he continues to unload on me. His words are like a knife to the chest.

"I watched you for a long while. You got as far as you did on your own because you are resourceful and can think on your feet. You also have that natural intuition that can't be learned. Those are gifts. Gifts you almost squandered today. I understand you felt the need to call Matt for help when you found the safe, but **calling in is a last resort.** Asking for help becomes a crutch. I need people who can problem solve without outside assistance, because aid isn't always available. That woman slipped up on you because you were more worried about rushing the job and leaning on Matt for help. You should have taken a step back. Done research on the safe. Determined how to get in without the code. Not break your identity by making a fucking phone call while his goddamn wife was soaking in the tub in the next room."

The obscenities seem more vulgar coming from the mechanical voice. It's not the pep talk I expected, but surprisingly it was the pep talk I needed. And he's absolutely right. I was rushing the job. I didn't want to spend another day getting more attached to Miles.

Going forward I have to do better. I **will** be better. This was a tough lesson to learn.

It's crushing for him to lay the truth out like that. Even though I will remember Miles and this job for the rest of my life, he will no doubt forget about me. But Mr. Smith is wrong. I'm not just a ghost who passed through the Kingstons' life.

I am a ghost passing through my own life.

The only one who cares about me is me. The only one who is going to make sure I survive is me.

I am on my own.

He finally says, "Money will be transferred to your account for the completion of this job. Instructions for your next job will arrive within the week. Take a few days to pack your things, since your next job will require relocating. I can't risk you running into the Kingstons."

"Yes, sir."

"The ambulance has already taken Mrs. Kingston from the residence and the police are questioning Mr. Kingston as we speak. Next time I ask you to tell me every detail, don't leave a single fucking thing out."

I take a deep breath and hold it in until there's a slight burn in my chest and my head feels a little fuzzy. Letting the air out in a quiet whoosh, I whisper, "I'll be better. No mistakes." Silently, I add, **And I will never get attached on the job again.**

"No mistakes," he repeats.

CHAPTER 13

Present Day

This dinner party will be very different from the one we had a few weeks ago. I'm setting the table on the back patio rather than the one in the dining room since the weather is nice and the mosquitoes haven't gotten bad yet. Ryan is icing down the beer and wine we bought earlier, placing it in the decorative galvanized tub with **Sumner** etched across the front. Sara gave him the tub on his last birthday; if there is one thing I've learned over the years, it's that Southerners believe the best gift is a personalized gift.

James and that woman arrive just as Ryan is firing up the grill.

We both greet them as they make their way up the short set of stairs to the deck. Ryan takes one of the twelve-packs James is lugging while she hands me a foil-covered platter and says, "I know you said don't bring anything, but James's mom and I made way too many brownies this afternoon."

I pull the edge of the foil back to peek. "Oh yum, these smell divine." I'm already visualizing the Facebook post Mrs. Bernard has probably already uploaded.

"How's your dad's leg?" Ryan asks James as they shake hands.

"Getting better," James answers. "Or at least getting better at not complaining about it."

The woman lets out a laugh while nudging James with her elbow. "Stop. He's a far better patient than his son would be." She turns to me. "There's a never-ending poker game now that he's stuck at home. He's running out of friends who are willing to lose money to him." Her hand falls gently on Ryan's arm. "I know he'd love for you to stop by for a visit. Maybe lose a hand or two to keep his spirits up?"

She's got both men hanging on her every word within minutes of arriving.

"It's not hard for Ryan to lose at cards!" James says.

I laugh just enough that it sounds genuine, then gesture for everyone to take a seat at the table while Ryan adds the beer James brought to the tub.

"I'll just be a second," I say, then step inside to grab the appetizers I made earlier. Once I sit back down, I take a deep breath and soak everything in. It's a gorgeous night, with weather Louisiana is seldom blessed with—warm and breezy with no humidity. It's a shame to waste such a perfect evening on work.

The conversation is easy, with the guys doing

most of the talking. She seems to approach this sort of thing the same way I do: listen and learn.

"We're hogging the conversation," Ryan says with a laugh after a bit, then turns to the woman sitting next to James. "I'd love to learn more about the newest addition to Lake Forbing."

"Yes, we didn't get much of a chance to talk at the Derby Party . . . Lucca." It's hard to say her name out loud. My name. It felt as bitter on my tongue as I thought it would.

She shrugs and sends James a warm smile. "Not much to tell. James and I met a few months ago. We both were working in Baton Rouge. I'm an insurance adjuster and was there following up on a group of claims from the tornado that tore through last fall."

"Yeah, that was a bad one," Ryan says. "I have a couple of clients there. Lots of homes were destroyed."

"It was tragic." She reaches over and slips her hand into James's. "Makes you really appreciate everything you have."

It takes everything in me to keep my sweet smile and engaged expression locked into place.

"So, you just move from disaster to disaster?" I ask.

She cringes. "Pretty much. It gets hard sometimes. But there are breaks in between, like right now. There's nowhere I need to be so I can handle the paperwork from anywhere." Another loving glance at James and another squeeze of his hand, but he's too busy downing the rest of his beer with his free hand to notice.

She's good. The backstory is solid. Delivery is flawless. Facial movements match her emotions. I'm impressed.

James, on the other hand, needs some coaching, although I'm pretty sure he's just a pawn. She's polished while he looks to be hanging on by a thread. I can't imagine any circumstance where this is actually a genuine relationship.

I've been in her spot before. Forcing something just for the sake of a job. The fact that she keeps looking at him like he's hung the moon makes me respect her more than I want to.

She turns toward me and says, "James said you haven't lived here long, Evie. What brought you to Lake Forbing?"

"Oh, I've been bouncing around for a while. My parents died in a car wreck a few years ago and I needed a change of scenery." I bite down on my bottom lip and cast a glance at Ryan—my vulnerability making a quick appearance before I shove it back down. He scoots closer to me, resting his hand on my thigh. "Ended up here and fell in love with this place. I'm a sucker for a cute small town," I say with a nervous laugh. "And for a cute guy who's handy with minor car repairs."

Ryan chuckles beside me. "Anything more than a tire change and I'll need to call in reinforcements."

She leans forward, grin stretching across her face. "Speaking of cute small towns, who is your college friend from Eden, Evie? I'm sure I know her or her family. It would be hard not to in a town that size."

This bitch.

I match her smile. "Regina West. She's got a younger sister, Matilda, and an older brother, Nathan, you may have known. We stayed at her house while we visited but I couldn't tell you the street or neighborhood."

Let's see how good she is and just how thorough the packet she was given on me was. Regina West was a girl I went to school with, but her family moved away in seventh grade. We were best friends growing up, and I would love to find out how much of my past Mr. Smith knows. Nathan moved back to Eden about five years ago after he finished med school and opened a walk-in clinic there. There aren't many family doctors in that area, so he is very well known and respected in the community.

Her brow creases as if she's struggling with how to answer me. "That name does sound familiar . . ." She trails off, leaving the rest of her sentence unfinished.

Nope. I'm docking points. She obviously didn't do any of her own research and relied only on what Mr. Smith gave her. And she would have been briefed on Nathan if my early friendship with Regina had been discovered, because we were inseparable before she moved. I'm guessing Mr. Smith didn't uncover anything on me earlier than high school.

"Is Eden still where you call home?" Ryan asks. "I would think your company wouldn't send you so far away for work."

"I live in Raleigh now. Eden is a great place but it's just really small, you know?" She shrugs then looks at me as if I'll agree with her. "My company is short-staffed, so we're all stretched a little thin. I'm sent where I'm needed."

"Both of you girls have moved around a lot," James says with a loud laugh. "Evie, I'm guessing if you moved in with Ryan, you plan to stay awhile. No more bouncing around? Or is this just a temporary stop?"

"James, you're putting her on the spot." Ryan's voice has a hint of the bite I heard a few days ago in his office in Glenview.

She squeezes his hand hard enough that James squeaks out an "Ow!" And then under his voice he says to her quietly, "Thought you wanted to know if she's staying."

Yeah, there's no way he works for Mr. Smith too. He's not even remotely good at this, and she needs to do a better job of keeping her pawn in line.

"It's a fair question," I say, ignoring his last comment. "I wouldn't have accepted Ryan's invitation to move in if I had plans to move on." Ryan's thumb brushes softly across my leg, so I know he's pleased with my answer.

"Once she sees the plans I'm working on for

the vegetable garden and greenhouse, she won't be going anywhere. It will be a two-person operation, so she can't abandon me."

My attention snaps to him. "You're putting in a garden?"

He shakes his head slowly and his smile widens. "No." A short pause and then he says, "**We're** putting in a garden. You said you always wanted one."

The blush that blooms across my face is genuine, and I wish I didn't have to share this moment with the two other people at the table.

She leans forward, breaking the spell between Ryan and me, and asks, "Can you point me to the closest powder room, Evie?"

But Ryan is already standing up. "I'll show you. I'm heading in to grab the steaks. Need to get them on the grill now or we'll be having them for breakfast."

She follows him inside, and I know she'll take this moment to snoop through our stuff. It's exactly what I would do, but more importantly, **it's what I want her to do.** I've left a little something for her to find that I know she'll report back to Mr. Smith. It's a dangerous play, but I need him to put all his cards on the table. I'm sick of surprises.

The interesting thing about this situation is that I really can't tell if she knows I'm here on a job, just like her. Or is she working me like she would any unsuspecting mark? Did her set of instructions tell her the mention of Eden, North Carolina, would set me on edge?

"James, how do you like yours cooked?" Ryan calls out as he steps back onto the deck holding a platter of marinated steaks and wearing an apron that says **You don't have to kiss me but you could get me a beer.**

"Medium rare," he answers, then moves to the grill.

I sip on my wine while I give that woman a few more minutes to rummage around in my things, then I get up from the table. "Looks like you forgot the veggies. I'll go grab them."

Ryan gives me a nod, then turns back to James.

I enter the kitchen, expecting to see her, but the room is empty. I glance at my watch. She's taking too long.

Quietly, I move toward the stairs. As soon as I make it to the top, she's exiting the upstairs hall bathroom.

"I was afraid you got lost," I say.

She lets out a shriek and jumps slightly back, her hand grabbing at her chest. "Oh, I didn't see you there!" Then her expression shifts into this endearing little grin. "I got caught up admiring those cute family pictures on the stairwell wall on my way up! Ryan was an adorable little boy!"

I look back at the images in question and have to agree. He was a cutie. And bonus points to her for the save. It's a good excuse.

She moves toward the stairs and waits, as if she will follow me, but I step to the side. "I'll meet you down there. Just need to grab something from my room."

She hesitates just a second then smiles as she passes me. Once she's out of sight, I go to our room at the end of the hall. There's only one thing here she could find and I hope she did.

I move to the dressing table and open the drawer. Two pens and a pencil were arranged in a very specific way on top of a stack of papers and she would have needed to brush them to the side in order to read what was written there, and it's obvious she did exactly that. I shut the drawer and go downstairs.

I head back outside with the vegetables, handing the tray to Ryan, then I light the candles I've scattered around the area now that the sun has fully set.

"Everything should be ready soon," Ryan says.

Nodding, I say, "Perfect. I'll get the rest from the kitchen."

It's not long before Ryan places a steak on each plate along with a helping of grilled veggies while I put garlic bread and a big salad in the center of the table.

"Everything looks delicious," she says. "Y'all have outdone yourself."

I cut a small piece of steak and bring it to my mouth, chewing it slowly. "We love to entertain," I say, glancing at Ryan. He gives me that smirk, since we're both thinking of the two weeks it took him to convince me to host our last dinner party.

"How much longer are y'all in town?" Ryan asks.

She looks at James as if she doesn't know the answer.

"Maybe another couple of weeks," he says. "As soon as Dad can get around a little better on his own, I'll feel better about leaving."

"It's good you could take off this much time from work," Ryan says, then takes a swig of beer. This is something he mentioned earlier this afternoon: his worry about why James was really back in town. If James had gotten his life together and was holding down a job like he said, it begged the question: how had he managed to get this much time off?

"The beauty of working from a laptop," he says with a laugh. "Can work anywhere."

"What is it that you do, James?" I ask.

He looks at the woman as if she's the only one who knows the answer. She looks back at him with an expression that can only be described as hopeful that he doesn't completely screw up this answer.

Finally, he turns back to us. "Lucca actually got me a job at her company. I'm working for her."

He could have sold it better if he didn't sound so glum. Instead of us thinking they are equals at work, he sounds like a charity case.

Ryan was not thrilled I had invited them to dinner. He banged around in the garage for a good hour then spent the rest of the afternoon hiding some of the obvious—and easily movable—valuables in the house, including my jewelry and any prescription meds he had in the medicine cabinet. The girls had mentioned James stole from Ryan the last time he was in town, but Ryan never admitted that to me. And you can't tell if there's beef between them by the way they are acting around each other now.

Preparing for this evening was the most strained things have been between us.

Regardless of what Ryan's fears and James's motives are, I'm only concerned with her.

The rest of the dinner is consumed by small talk. Ryan matches James beer for beer until they're both pretty tipsy. She and I clear the plates while James and Ryan throw an old football around in the mostly dark backyard, both of them missing more than they are catching.

She follows me inside and we work through the dirty dishes and put away the leftovers. Mr. Smith told me why she's here, but she's too good an asset to waste as a reminder. And now that she riffled through my stuff, I know she's got an active role; she's not just one who observes. I decide to go on the offensive.

"Have you gotten your next set of instructions or are you still checking your mailbox every day?" My tone is conversational, and from the way the plate slips through her fingers into the sink, I know I've caught her off guard.

But she recovers quickly. Confusion plays across her face when she says, "Instructions?"

"I don't expect you to answer. But I do expect you to pass along that I'm here to do my job and I don't appreciate any interference." Her body language tells me she's genuinely surprised by my words, so I'm guessing she didn't know we share a boss. I lean a little closer. "We have more in common than you know."

The disbelief on her face is still there, but it's more controlled now. "I'm sorry, I really don't know what you're talking about."

"The Sheetz on North Van Buren in Eden—what's the name of the side street?"

Her mouth opens slightly but no words come out.

"It's East Stadium Drive. Same road that takes you to the high school. A road anyone in Eden would know without thinking about it," I say. "Did you already send him a picture of what you found upstairs or will you do it when you get back to the Bernards'?"

She flinches at the tone in my voice. "I don't know—"

I lean in closer. "Can we get to the part where you just answer my question?"

It's a tense minute and then she says, "I already sent him a picture of it."

There would be no way for her to know that what she found was useless, only that it didn't belong in my dresser drawer and looked suspicious. That's all it would take for her to pass it back to Mr. Smith.

And I couldn't resist the opportunity to let him know how I feel about her presence here. He knows I would never keep anything sensitive in this house. So I created a spreadsheet entitled Opera Guild Association Fundraiser with a list of fake names and credit card numbers to symbolize the one I would have gotten from that auction at the country club if I hadn't gotten busted that night. It was enough to catch her attention, and Mr. Smith will know I set her up to find it. I don't appreciate him sending someone into my space.

She starts to move away then hesitates a second. "How did you know?"

"I was expecting you to search through my things and I left it for you to find. But if I wasn't expecting it, I wouldn't have known." I'm not sure why I felt compelled to give her that little bit of praise, since we're not on the same side.

"I better check on James," she says.

Just as we're almost to the door to the deck, I say, "One last warning. It's not a big step from being on the job to becoming the job." There's more I want to say, but I've already said too much, and Mr. Smith won't like that I've spoken to her so candidly.

She pushes the door open and says in that sugary sweet voice, "James, honey, are you ready?"

"Yeah, babe. Ready when you are," he calls back.

Ryan and I walk them out, and I notice that things are not only strained between the two of us but also between Ryan and James.

The good-byes are terse compared to the pleasantness we'd shared during dinner. She gets behind the wheel, since James could barely make it to the car on his own two feet, and we make eye contact as she starts the car.

Ryan and I watch as they back out of the driveway. "Something happen with James?" I ask.

Ryan tenses next to me. "Same ol' shit."

As soon as their headlights disappear around the corner, we walk hand in hand into the house.

CHAPTER 14

Present Day

'm up earlier than usual for a Sunday morning. The events of last night generated an endless parade of questions, ensuring I didn't sleep well. I slide out of bed, trying not to wake Ryan, and slip downstairs to the kitchen. I need to use the next couple of hours contemplating what to do while I wait for Mr. Smith's next move.

I start the coffee machine before flipping on the small television in the breakfast nook. An old black-and-white movie hums along in the background while I stare at the steady drip of dark liquid.

The rumble thundering down the stairs has me spinning in that direction. Ryan skids into the kitchen, his phone clutched to his ear. He snaps his fingers at me then points to the TV. Covering the mouthpiece with his hand, he says, "Put it on three."

He looks panicked.

"I'll call you back," he says, then ends the call.

I change the channel and the local newscaster fills the screen. She's on the side of the road, the warm glow of the rising sun behind her highlighting the bridge that crosses the lake.

"The accident happened shortly after eleven last night. Authorities say the car was going at a high rate of speed when it swerved off the road, breaking through the guardrail at the foot of the bridge, and crashing into the lake. When asked if the driver was impaired, police said they wouldn't have that answer until the toxicology results came back."

The camera pans the scene and a wave of nausea rolls through me. The same car that backed out of our driveway last night is currently being pulled out of the water by a huge tow truck. And then the picture from the Derby party of James and the woman fills the screen.

"James Bernard and his companion, Lucca Marino, were visiting from Baton Rouge. Both were pronounced dead at the scene, and the Bernard family was notified shortly after," the newswoman says.

Holy shit.

Then they cut back to the anchor desk. "Chrissy, this must be awful for Mr. Bernard's family."

And then Chrissy is on a split screen. "Yes, Ed. Mr. Bernard's father is currently at home recovering from a fall, and his son, James, had come to help his mother with his care. They are asking for privacy during this very difficult time. We've made some calls to our affiliate station in Lucca Marino's hometown of Eden, North Carolina, and we'll be sharing what we learn about her on this evening's broadcast."

Ryan stares at the small screen with his hand over his mouth. His expression is blank, as if he is still processing what he's seeing.

When the news moves to the next story, I shut the TV off. Ryan drops down in the closest chair, his head in his hands. I go to him, my fingers brushing through his long strands.

"I can't believe this. We left things in a bad way last night, and now this. He's been a fuckup his whole life. Getting into shit, stealing from me . . . but I thought maybe he was better. And then when we were playing around with that football last night, he asked me for money. I was drunk and I lost it. Told him I was done with him for good."

I don't say anything, just continue to stroke his hair while I consider how this could have happened and what it means.

"We need to go see his parents," he says as he looks up at me. "Was she drunk? Should we have stopped her from driving?"

I shake my head, and it takes a moment for me to find my voice. "No. She had two glasses throughout the night. She was fine to drive." I refuse to let him blame himself for any of this.

This seems to give him some relief but it's short lived. He hops up from the chair like he was sitting on a spring. "I need to see his parents. His mom is going to be heartbroken. His dad too. Fuck, the cops are going to want to talk to us." He squeezes his eyes closed. "We were the last ones to see them alive. They'll have questions for us."

He's rambling, and I've got to center him. And hopefully talk him out of calling the cops. The absolute last thing I need is for the cops to know anything about me.

"One thing at a time. Let's get dressed and go visit James's parents. See if they need any help making the arrangements. We'll worry about the rest of it later."

He nods as he walks in a tight circle in the middle of the kitchen.

"Yeah, let's do that." Then he stops. "What about Lucca? Should we call her parents? Are you still in contact with your high school friend who has family there? Maybe she knows them."

Deep breath in. Hold it. Slowly release.

"Let's start with James's parents. They may have already called her family."

He nods again then sprints toward the stairs. "I can be ready in ten minutes."

I drop down in the chair Ryan vacated.

Run.

Mentally, I'm hauling ass out of this town without looking back.

Breathe.

I need to think this through. I need to think

about this as if I were Mr. Smith. Would he be willing to exert the time and energy it would take to groom her for this job and use the connections he'd need to insert her here only to kill her off just a short time after she arrived?

The only way that scenario seems likely is if she completed the task she was sent to perform and her usefulness had run its course. I don't see how that would have been possible.

I came into this job knowing it was a test—not the first test he's given me in the eight years I've worked for him—so I expected there was more going on here than I was originally told. The only thing that's certain is that woman's appearance here was linked to my boss's displeasure over my performance on my last job, and now she's dead.

For now, I will accompany Ryan to James's parents' home, where we will provide comfort by telling them how happy James was in his last hours of life. I will learn everything I can about the woman who was sent here to impersonate me. I will hold Ryan's hand while he grieves the loss of his friend. Regardless of the harsh words, I know Ryan would rather James had not died in that car wreck last night. Death has a way of letting those hard feelings go.

But most importantly, I will finish what I started.

Two cop cars are parked in front of James's parents' house when we pull up. I knew this was a possibility, although I was hoping they had already come and gone.

Ryan parks on their street two houses down, the closest spot he can find.

The Bernards live in an older neighborhood on the other side of the lake from Ryan, where the houses were built in the mideighties, in various shades of brown brick with low-slung roofs and narrow driveways.

There is a steady stream of people walking toward the front door, just as we are.

"Why are there so many people here right now? This seems like the kind of crowd that shows up to the funeral home," I whisper to Ryan as he maneuvers us through the crowd to the side of the house. I knew he and James grew up together and he spent a lot of time here as a kid so I'm not surprised he's bypassing the front door.

"These are probably mostly neighbors and members of their church. It will be twice this at the funeral home visitation. A lot of these women keep a casserole in the freezer for just this occasion." He looks back at me from over his shoulder and rolls his eyes, adding, "Plus, they're here for the gossip."

Ryan lets us in through the side door and we move down the narrow back hall toward the main living area. There are people wall to wall, and the low ceilings intensify the claustrophobic feel. A group of little old ladies wearing very official-looking name tags and matching smock aprons—probably the Bible brigade from the Bernards' church, if I'm guessing right—scurry around offering water or coffee to those visiting as well as making sure the room stays tidy.

"They aren't in here," Ryan mumbles, then pulls me back into the hall and through another open doorway that leads to a small office.

Rose Bernard's thin, frail body is wedged into the corner of an oversize chair, while Wayne Bernard is stuffed into a wingback chair next to her with his bum leg propped up on a small ottoman. One uniformed officer sits on a stool in front of them while two other officers stand behind him.

The cops' attention pivots to us the second we fill the doorway.

Ryan and I both take a step back. "I'm sorry, we didn't mean to interrupt . . ."

Mrs. Bernard lets out an anguished cry when she sees Ryan. "Don't leave," she cries. "How did this happen, Ryan? Was he okay at your house last night? Did something happen?"

Ryan moves into the room and crouches down next to her, his hands covering hers. "Nothing happened. He was great! They both were. I wouldn't have let them leave if I didn't think they were okay."

The officers share a look with each other when they realize the deceased were at our house before the crash. We've gone from random visitors to possible witnesses to their state of mind before the accident.

Mrs. Bernard leans forward just enough that Ryan can embrace her. Mr. Bernard swallows thickly as he reaches over to clutch his wife's hand in support.

I shouldn't have come. I should have let Ryan handle this alone. Assured him this was a private matter, not a place for a stranger like me, but I was so desperate for any shred of information about the woman that I ignored the risk of what I could face here.

Now I realize how big my mistake is. The officer who was sitting on the stool now has his sights set on us. And because it seems like the only thing stopping Mrs. Bernard from completely falling apart is Ryan's arms around her, the officer approaches me first.

"Hello," he says, as he turns the pages in his notebook. "I'm Deputy Bullock. I'm gathering as much information as I can. Do you mind if I ask you a few questions?"

I'm stuck. I can't say I don't know anything because obviously they were with us last night. And as much as I would like to answer those questions on my terms, now will have to do.

"Of course," I say, then nod toward Ryan. "We rushed right over as soon as we heard what happened. James and Lucca were at our house last night."

With his pen poised over the clean sheet of paper, he asks, "And your name is . . . ?"

I hesitate only a second before I answer, "Evie Porter." I've now officially lied to the police.

"Is Evie your full name or is it short for something else?"

"Evelyn."

"Okay, Miss Porter, how did you know Mr. Bernard and Miss Marino?"

Ryan disengages himself from Mrs. Bernard, promising her he will return shortly, then comes to stand next to me. His right arm slips around my waist and I'm not sure if he's trying to show a united front or if he needs any comfort I can give him.

"Hi, I'm Ryan Sumner. James was an old friend of mine. Evie and I had him and Lucca over for dinner last night."

Deputy Bullock scribbles away and doesn't look up when he asks the next question. "Was Miss Marino drinking last night?"

Ryan looks at me before answering, the pause causing the deputy's pen to stop and his eyes to move from the notepad to us.

"She had one glass of wine when they first arrived around six and then one more glass with dinner. James had a considerable amount more to drink, which is why she was driving," I answer.

Deputy Bullock waits a beat then goes back to his notes. "Would you say she seemed in control of her faculties when she left your home?"

"Yes," Ryan answers.

"Is it possible she had more to drink than you

witnessed? Maybe she snuck another glass or two that you weren't aware of?"

"I guess it's possible but I think that's unlikely. She was around us the entire evening except for when she went to the bathroom."

Drunk driving is the most obvious reason for an accident like this. The question of her alcohol consumption will eventually be answered when the autopsy comes back, but I know she couldn't have had more than two glasses.

"Did Mr. Bernard put up a fight about not being able to drive home?" he asks.

Mrs. Bernard clutches her chest at his question. Ryan, realizing how upset she is, motions for us to move into the hallway.

"No. Not at all. He willingly and gladly got into the passenger seat," Ryan finally says when we've cleared the room.

The deputy nods. He's writing more than what we're saying, but the way the pad is angled I can't see his notes.

"How were things between Mr. Bernard and Miss Marino last night? Any arguing? Fighting?"

"No, not at all," I answer.

"Anything happen that could have caused Miss Marino to be distracted? Upset?" The officer looks at Ryan, shrugging as he adds, "Any talk of old girlfriends? I know how reminiscing with old friends can be. Did she have to sit and listen to

Mr. Bernard's glory days and maybe didn't like what she was hearing?"

"No, it wasn't anything like that," Ryan says, his words tinged with anger. "Neither of us would have wanted Lucca or Evie to be uncomfortable."

The officer holds a hand up. "Okay, I get it, but I have to ask. Just trying to figure out what was going on inside of her head while she was behind the wheel last night."

I know what was going through her head. I not only outed her, I all but threatened that Mr. Smith would turn on her as quickly as he turned on me. And Ryan had just told James he was done with him after he asked Ryan for money. Neither of them was in a good place.

"What time did they leave your home?" he asks.

"A little before eleven," I say.

We answer every question, laying out the evening, starting with the dinner invitation made yesterday morning in Home Depot all the way through our day, until we saw their taillights disappear down our quiet street. Deputy Bullock only looks up when Ryan stumbles over an answer, but mostly his haziness on the details comes from the fact that he matched James drink for drink, and I'm sure the evening is a bit blurry for him.

"When was the last time you'd been in contact with Mr. Bernard before he came back to town?"

Ryan stares off into the distance, seemingly lost

in thought. He finally answers. "Maybe a year ago. He needed money. I sent it to him." He keeps his answer to the bare minimum, and he doesn't mention James's most recent request for financial help.

The deputy looks at me. "And when was the last time you've interacted with Mr. Bernard before his return home?"

I shake my head. "I just met him for the first time a week ago."

Ryan adds before I can stop him, "Evie moved here from Brookwood, Alabama, a few months ago. She didn't know James."

Oh fuck. I watch as he scribbles down that last helpful tidbit from Ryan, hoping the background put in place for Evelyn Porter holds up.

Finally, the deputy pockets his notebook and pen. "We'll be in contact if we have any further questions."

I nod, but Ryan stops him before he walks away. "Have you notified Lucca's family yet?" His arm, which is still anchored around my waist, pulls me closer. "I thought they may want to talk with us since we were the last ones to see her."

"We've called the local police in Eden and are waiting for them to get back to us. They are trying to track down any relatives of hers now."

There are no relatives of Lucca Marino in Eden, North Carolina, but he will find that out soon enough.

"Well, if they have any questions or just want to talk, will you please forward my number to them?" Ryan asks.

Deputy Bullock nods. "Of course."

We help the Bernards back into the main living room after the police depart. Even though there is a line of people wanting to offer their condolences, Mrs. Bernard latches on to Ryan again. He sits down beside her on the couch while she speaks to each person who steps forward. It seems we're stuck here for the foreseeable future. I opt to help out in the kitchen, where most of the church ladies have migrated. No one gossips more than God-fearing, casserole-toting women, so I settle near the coffee pot, offering to refill any mug that comes my way, and hope to hear something interesting until I see an opening to snoop the room James and the woman were staying in.

There are three women in the kitchen with me. Francie seems to be the cook of the group and has taken the wild assortment of food that was brought in and divided it into portions that will go in the fridge for the Bernards to eat later. The other half is being put out buffet style on the dining-room table for visitors to enjoy. Toni is what Mama called a "latherer." She does a good job of looking busy without actually getting anything done. And Jane is the list master. There's a list of people to call. A list of things to buy. A list of dishes that have been dropped off. A list of people who have dropped by. And a list of people who will write notes to thank anyone who brought a dish or dropped by.

Death requires a lot of organization.

Francie disappears into the small laundry room off the kitchen for a few minutes then reappears with a large basket of folded clothes. "I'm going to run these to James's room," she says.

It's clear the weight of the basket is more than she can manage, so I grab this opportunity.

"Please, let me help. I can handle this if you point me in the right direction," I say, my hands already on the basket.

Francie seems relieved. "Honey, that's sweet of you. These were James's and Lucca's things. I didn't want Rose to have to fool with them just yet. His room is the second door on the right," she says, pointing to a hall off the kitchen.

I bolt out of the kitchen and down the hall. It's startling to see this room as they left it last night, thinking they would be back. After dropping the basket of clothes on the unmade bed, I spend time going through the papers on the small desk, but there's nothing of any significance there.

Two open suitcases sit side by side on the floor next to the bed, with clothes spilling out. Toiletries and makeup litter the bathroom countertop. I dig through the woman's bag first, only finding clothes and shoes. I'm surprised they never unpacked, making use of the empty closet and chest, given how long they've been here. I run my fingers around the inside edge of her suitcase, stopping when I pass over a rough, raised area. I dig into the lining and find the Velcro closure then see the familiar brown color of a 4x6 manila envelope as soon as I pry it open.

The same type of manila envelope my instructions come in.

I pull it out and open it, my heart pounding when I see the single sheet of paper still inside.

Subject: Evie Porter
Since initial contact has been
    made, prepare to engage subject
    again. If the opportunity to enter
    subject's residence presents itself,
    use it to search her belongings.
    Concentrate on her personal
    space and possessions. Report
    anything that she deemed
    important enough to hide,
    regardless of what it is. When in
    doubt, document it and send it to
    me. Proceed with extreme
    caution when dealing with her
    things and leave no trace behind.

I study the outside of the envelope and see the address of a shipping store and the mailbox number 2870. He's desperate if he sent her to look through my stuff. He knows I wouldn't ever keep anything of value at Ryan's.

Tucking the instructions back into the envelope, I fold it then stuff it in the back pocket of my jeans.

"Everything okay in here?" Francie asks from the open doorway, startling me.

I glance at her over my shoulder while grabbing a stack of clothes I had removed from the bag. "I thought I'd save Mrs. Bernard the trouble of re-packing Lucca's clothes since I'm sure she'll need to send her stuff back to her family. I didn't want her to have to do it."

That gets me a big smile. "Oh, wonderful. I'll help you finish up in here. I'm hiding from Jane. She'll make me wash the dishes."

Francie and I spend the next thirty minutes get-ting all their belongings back into the two suitcases. I continue to search for the previous instructions and detailed description of me as the subject that she would have received, but I don't find anything else.

I head out to the main room to look for Ryan. I need to get out of here and go talk to the one per-son who can help me decide what to do next.

Alias: Mia Bianchi—Six Years Ago

There are lots of people trying to be the brightest and best help to Andrew Marshall. Smoke blowing and ass kissing are the two main qualities every employee and volunteer possesses. I decide to take the opposite route. It's risky for sure, but I don't care how inflated your ego is, blunt honesty has more value than blind worship, and if Andrew's smart enough to get this far, he knows it.

I'm currently embedded in Andrew Marshall's political campaign as he makes his bid for governor of Tennessee. When I got my first set of instructions for this job, which listed my new identity as Mia Bianchi and the address of my new apartment in Knoxville, Tennessee, there was a handwritten note on the bottom of the page that said: You're moving to the big leagues so don't fuck this up.

Even though I've been working for Mr. Smith for a little over two years, I have never met him in person or talked to him on the phone since the

Kingston job, so I'm guessing that added footnote was from Matt.

Everything goes through Matt.

The second set of instructions came a week after I settled in Knoxville. It listed Andrew Marshall as the mark and informed me that Mia Bianchi would start work on his campaign the next week. My hair, makeup, and clothing were to be flawless. I was to be the brightest person in the room. I was to make myself indispensable. There were seven days to do a deep dive into Andrew Marshall's life and everyone associated with him, including his opponents, so I'd be ready for my first day on the job. Moving up is all I've wanted, so there was no way I wasn't going to be prepared.

I've come a long way from that first job. I was reckless just like Mr. Smith said. It was messy. And luck had been on my side. Jenny was in a medically induced coma for a week. The hit on the head mixed with all the drinking and pills made for a bad combination. When she came to, she had no memory of the entire twenty-four hours before the fall. I was in the clear. Or rather, Izzy Williams was.

I have checked in on Miles a couple of times over the last two years. The Kingstons are divorced now, and it looks like Miles lives with Mr. Kingston and the latest Mrs. Kingston. The last time I stalked the new wife's Facebook page there was a post she shared from an interior design company she'd hired to remove all traces of Jenny. The post showed interior shots of the newly renovated home, including one of Miles's room. When I zoomed in on the bookshelf, I spotted an origami swan sitting on one of the shelves. I'll never know if it's the same one I made with him that day or if he's learned to make them on his own, but seeing that swan displayed as if it holds some importance is proof that I existed there, even if only for a very short amount of time.

Maybe I'm not quite the ghost I thought I was.

The Andrew Marshall job is the first time I've had to settle in, because I was told in the beginning it would be a couple of months before I got any further instructions. It is also the first job that came with a thick packet of cash for expenses, like rent and utilities, and other incidentals needed to become Mia Bianchi. This next rung on the ladder is pretty sweet.

It's taken me three months, but now Andrew Marshall turns to me for my reaction on anything from which tie to wear to whether he should attend a certain event. A nod or quick shake of my head is all it takes to blow someone else's carefully made plans for him.

Andrew Marshall is the only one okay with this.

I don't need eyes in the back of my head to see the target painted there. His staff has dug into my background, trying to find anything that will knock me from my throne, but they've come up empty.

I am Mia Bianchi. Even though I'm only twenty-two, new-hire paperwork shows I'm twenty-seven.

The right clothes and makeup are key. I'm a graduate of Clemson University—**Go Tigers!**—and I excelled in my public policy classes and killed it on the debate team. I can't even begin to understand how someone was able to add my image into a pic of a debate against UNC a few years ago. But there it was. Just grainy enough that if you were looking for me you'd find me, but not so clear as to draw questions from the students who were actually present.

After two years of working with Matt, I know he isn't capable of what it would take to insert me so fully into this engineered life, and I grow more and more curious about the team behind Mr. Smith. I wonder how many people he has out there doing jobs like this.

But those are ponderings for another day.

The subject up for debate today for Andrew Marshall is the American Bar Association event at some fancy hotel in Hilton Head, South Carolina. It's a weekend conference at which lawyers, including those like Andrew, who no longer practice but still keep their license up to date, will get continuing ed credits in between a morning round of golf and afternoon happy hour. It's as much for rubbing elbows and networking as it is for thirty-minute crash courses, like the latest tech for small firms. And since my third set of instructions finally arrived and made it clear that Andrew most definitely should be there, that's what I'm pushing.

But there is another opportunity for him, one

that is better for his campaign, in Memphis at the same time. And given he's running for governor in Tennessee and not in South Carolina, it's an uphill battle.

Andrew's wife, Marie, is weary of me. I have not given her a single reason to think I want her husband in any way, but women are funny. I don't have to give her a reason for her to still expect it.

The surprising thing about Andrew Marshall is that he's a good man. I have searched through every file and personal record I can get my hands on. And since he doesn't suspect a thing from me, I've had access to all of it. There's not a hint of stealing or skimming money, no back-door deals, no promises he wouldn't admit to publicly, he's as in love with his wife now as the day he met her, and he's good to his employees. Even his pets are rescue dogs.

All my past jobs centered around me getting something Mr. Smith wanted or needed—whether it was computer files or documents or any other piece of physical goods or property. But this job was different from the beginning.

Now I know why I'm here. Andrew Marshall **will be** the next governor of Tennessee and Mr. Smith wants to own him on day one.

Since there was no blackmail to be found, I will have to create it.

His chief of staff has just finished laying out all the very good reasons to pick Memphis over Hilton Head. My very good reasons for picking the convention have already been laid out. The Hilton Head choice is a regional event, not just for South Carolina, and there will be some pretty big hitters attending, since the keynote speaker has just announced he's running for president, so media coverage will be on the national level. The networking and potential for new campaign donors is greater. And with social media transforming the landscape of politics the way it has, to become the governor of Tennessee you need to think bigger than Tennessee.

The room is quiet as everyone present waits for Andrew to either accept or reject the invitation to the Memphis event.

Andrew knows my choice. He looks at me and I've got a few seconds to decide if I'm going to help ruin a perfectly good man.

A quick shake of my head seals his fate.

———◆———

Andrew believed I left for Hilton Head a day ahead of him and the rest of the team to get everything set up so we could make the most out of his time there. But that wasn't the reason I headed east a day early, and Georgia was my destination, not South Carolina. On Friday morning I'm in Savannah, an hour south of Hilton Head, waiting for the first ride of the day on the Hop on-Hop off Old Town Trolley.

When it's time to board, I go straight to the back, taking the aisle seat on the last row on the driver's side, hoping no one asks to squeeze past me for the window seat.

The tour company is efficient enough that we are loaded and on the move within a few minutes. An enthusiastic older man is on the mic, his booming voice so loud that not only the occupants of the bus but everyone on the street we pass gets schooled on all things Savannah.

By the time we finish the first loop, I'm the only passenger left from the group I started with, since the others disembarked at different stops along the route.

On the second stop of my third pass, a tall, thin Black man boards the bus and ambles down the center aisle, stopping in front of me.

He's wearing an Atlanta Braves tee and hat and his eyes are hidden behind dark sunglasses. "Is that seat taken?" he asks, pointing to the window seat I've been guarding.

I pull my legs in tight and gesture for him to help himself.

He scoots in past me, sits down, and sets his backpack in his lap.

"Devon, I presume," I say. "I appreciate all the cloak-and-dagger but I have a lot to do and wasting two hours riding in a circle wasn't in my plans."

He nods toward the speaker set in the ceiling of the trolley, and I notice for the first time the tiny little red light hiding behind the mesh material. "You can tell a lot about a person by the way they act when they are left waiting too long."

I focus my attention back on him. "I guess I passed."

His smirk appears for just a second then it's gone. "With flying colors, Mrs. Smith."

It was probably dumb but I couldn't resist using the same fake name my boss does. I found Devon on the internet a year ago when I was looking for some tech I couldn't get on my own that I needed for a job. This is the first time we're meeting in person, which is why he made me jump through hoops before showing his face.

I appreciate the level of paranoia though.

"What is it you require, Mrs. Smith?"

This is where it gets a little tricky. "I'm not exactly sure yet. I have a job in Hilton Head but won't get full instructions until I get there and therefore won't know my needs. Once I do, I'll need it quick, so I'm asking that you be on hand to offer goods and support as needed."

He looks out of the window and doesn't speak. It's a big ask, which is why I wanted to do it in person rather than our usual channels of online communication.

Since the night I was almost arrested at the country club, I've understood the value of having people in place to ensure someone will protect me if things go wrong. The help Mr. Smith sends will take care of me as long as it doesn't hurt him, though. I need to have someone who's looking out for me, **and only me.** It's time I start building my own team.

Finally, Devon turns back to me. "What if you require something I can't put my hands on at such short notice?"

"Then I'm hoping you can work the problem with me and offer another solution."

He's looking out the window again while the trolley stops to load and unload passengers.

"It sounds like you are expecting a problem," he says.

I nod, even though he's not looking at me. "I am. Call it a gut instinct. The job is being set up by someone who doesn't understand the players as well as I do. I'm trying to get ahead of the moment when I'm presented with my instructions and determine the plan won't work."

"This is not how I normally do things," he says.

"I understand. I will make it worth your time. Also, if you ever need help from me, I will be there."

He gets what I'm asking for—a partnership. We've had a solid working relationship the last year; he knows I pay well and I know he delivers.

"We are in a trial phase, Mrs. Smith. The first hint of a problem and I'm gone."

I nod as I pass him a slip of paper from my bag that includes all pertinent information for the weekend. "I wouldn't expect anything less."

Just as the trolley stops, I ask one last question before I get off. "How did I pass with flying colors?"

"You sat here like you had all the time in the world when I knew that wasn't the case. And that tells me everything I need to know."

———◆———

Andrew Marshall and the rest of the team have arrived in Hilton Head. Once I get Andrew settled in his suite, I check into my much smaller room, four floors below. I've just kicked off my shoes and unzipped my bag when there is a quick knock on the door.

A guy in the hotel's uniform smiles at me when I open the door. I look down at the domed covered plate that's sitting on the pushcart in front of him.

"Wrong room. I didn't order room service," I say, and go to close the door.

The guy pushes the cart toward the door just enough to keep it from closing. "Matt sends this with his compliments." His voice is low and deep.

This stops me cold. I've never met anyone else who works for Matt. Doing a quick scan, this guy looks like he's in his midthirties. His hair is short, streaked with gray around the temples, and he's only a few inches taller than me. The name tag on his uniform says George. His face and body are plain enough to make him easily forgettable. But the way his eyes never leave me ensures I won't.

I pull the door open farther and motion for him to come inside. He parks the cart in the center of the room then leaves without another word. Lifting the domed cover reveals a piece of carrot cake and an envelope similar to what I would typically find in the mailbox.

It's unsettling that they know carrot cake is my favorite.

I take the cake and the envelope to the small table so I can dig in while I see what's in store for the weekend.

But after reading his instructions, I'm sure the chances of this plan working are slim. It's a weak plan. Super weak.

Just as I feared it would be.

Matt had bragged that he would be in charge on this job, which led me to believe Mr. Smith wanted to see what he was capable of. I guess I wasn't the only one moving up. But after dealing with Matt for the last two years, I wasn't confident he was ready to be let loose like this, so I reached out to Devon.

The next time there's a knock on the door, I know what to expect. A bellhop, not the uniformed George, pushes a luggage cart into the room then unloads three large boxes. I tip him and off he goes. I get the monitors set up and hook up the laptop, logging into the site on the paper I received earlier. The screen fills with small blocks, showing every angle of Andrew's room and balcony.

Matt somehow got Andrew's wife, Marie, an invite to a very coveted event in Nashville to guarantee she won't be around when a woman approaches Andrew during the cocktail reception tonight to entice him to take her to his room. And I'll be here making sure it's all captured on camera.

I'm almost offended by how dumb this plan is.

Because what Matt doesn't understand is that, if given the opportunity, Andrew will not cheat on his wife. It doesn't matter **how many** beautiful, scantily clad women throw themselves at him. It doesn't matter that he's got a room to himself. It doesn't matter how many drinks get fed to him. He's not a cheater.

Matt didn't do his homework for this job and it shows.

But I can't come out of this weekend empty-handed. It's clear I'm playing a bigger game now with a lot more at stake. I'm past petty theft.

Relief that I brought Devon on board is the only thing that keeps me from panicking. I make the call, and within half an hour, we have a new plan. A better plan.

While Devon scrambles to get what we need, I pick up my cell phone to call Andrew. He answers on the second ring.

"Hey!" he says. "All settled in?"

Andrew's room is one of the largest suites this

hotel offers. There is a huge sitting area and dining room in addition to the bedroom. And there's a camera covering every inch, allowing me to watch as he paces the room, his phone to his ear.

"Yes. All settled. How about you?"

He drops down in one of the large chairs near the window. "Yes. All good here. Looking forward to a little downtime since I don't really need to be at the conference until tomorrow morning. I think I'll skip the cocktail thing tonight and just see everyone at breakfast. Plenty of time to rub elbows at the conference and the dinner tomorrow night. I'll just get some room service then hopefully a good night's sleep."

And that's Andrew Marshall. Squeaky clean and a tad dull.

"You know I'm supposed to fill every minute you're here with things that will help your campaign," I say, laughing into the phone. "Especially since we pissed everyone off by coming here rather than Memphis."

I see him hang his head low. "Mia, I need one night off."

Guilt bubbles to the surface until I remember the Kingston job. **This is not my world. I'm just a ghost passing through.** It's enough that I'm able to shove those feelings way down deep and press forward. "How about this—I've looked at the list of attendees and there are some big hitters here. Why don't I pick a handful for a private cocktail hour in your suite? Very low-key. Mingle with them for an hour then I'll clear the room and let you have the rest of the night to yourself."

Now his head is lying against the back of the chair, his hand rubbing his face. "One hour."

"Got it! I'll have room service send up a bar setup and some food." I disconnect the call and put the rest of my plan into place.

Every man I invited to Andrew's private cocktail party jumped at the invitation. I was very particular with my list, choosing men from all over the South, since this was a regional conference and not just one for South Carolina. And since all my jobs from the last two years have taken place in the South, I'm up to date on the political climate in each state, including the good and bad on every big name here.

Like Andrew, there are a handful of lawyers attending who also hold a range of elected positions, from local government office to the Senate. But I only invited the bad boys looking to play. The same ones who will quote the Bible along with their great love of family, faith, and God at their next rally.

Might as well make the most of this for him politically while I'm at it.

Andrew works the room with one eye on his watch as he counts down the minutes until this is over. The booze is flowing freely, thanks to the girls I brought in to serve it. I hand Andrew a beer and he nods his thanks. He rarely drinks, but when he does, it's always a Miller Lite. Just one.

He sips his beer then says quietly, "Not sure I would have invited Senator Nelson or Congressman Burke."

I'm not surprised by his comment. Both are self-serving pricks, but then so are all the men I've invited here tonight. "I know, but this is part of playing the game. Like it or not, these are the guys who have the most pull."

I nod to one of the girls and the music becomes a little louder. Ties are being loosened. Hands start to stray.

Andrew senses the change in the party, and he looks at me in confusion. He's also sweating a little. His eyes glazing over.

He leans in close. "Maybe we should call it a night. I'm not feeling good."

I give him a sympathetic look. "You don't look good. Let's get you some air." I lead him to the balcony, then help him onto the lounge chair. By the time his head hits the headrest, he's out. The beer in his hand falls to the floor, the spiked liquid spreading across the tile.

"Sorry, Andrew," I whisper, then head back into the party. It's time for the girls to make their move.

CHAPTER 15

Present Day

As soon as I've finished packing up the woman's things, we're finally able to leave the Bernards' house after promising to come back tomorrow to help plan the memorial service for James. That's a visit I will happily let Ryan make alone, since I'd gathered everything I could on Lucca from there.

Ryan drives while I scroll Instagram, stopping on **Southern Living**'s latest post, which showcases a beautiful front porch complete with a white wooden swing and hanging ferns. It's a gorgeous shot. Clicking the comment button, I type: **What a perfect spot for a get-together with a glass of wine! It's five o'clock somewhere!**

I keep scrolling once my comment loads until I'm all caught up, then stuff my phone in my purse.

As soon as we enter Ryan's house, he launches himself on the couch in the den, landing facedown. When I sit next to him, Ryan raises his head up just enough for me to scoot closer so he can rest it on my lap. His eyes fall closed as I gently run my fingers through his hair. Neither of us feels the need to speak.

As I stare down at him, I think about this latest development, now that the initial shock of their deaths has lessened.

There are only two options to consider.

First, the crash was a terrible accident that took the lives of two people.

Second, killing them was a deliberate move by my boss.

My gut is saying it's the second option, while my brain is trying to come up with the reasons why he would make that move. It didn't look like she was finished with this job. Her training for this identity—my identity—was extensive, and it seems premature to take her out now. And why kill them instead of just pulling them from the job? I can't get past the timing.

What does killing them accomplish? Lucca Marino from Eden, North Carolina, is dead.

I made no secret that I fiercely protected my true identity. In that first year, Matt would start every conversation with small talk when he would call to discuss my next job, and I was dumb enough to believe we were friends. My plans of reclaiming my identity to live as Lucca Marino were the one constant topic. I even told him about the house I would build and the garden I would plant.

But her death does not stop me from reclaiming the Lucca Marino identity. It makes it difficult, but not impossible. Killing her off was an extreme move and not one Devon or I anticipated. Mr. Smith said she was sent as a reminder, but I didn't need a reminder of how dangerous this game is.

Which brings me back to the possibility—and hope—that it really was an accident.

And then there's Ryan.

What does it mean for this job if it wasn't an accident?

His grip on me loosens and he lets out a soft snore. Today took a toll on him.

Slowly, I unlatch Ryan from my waist and slide out from underneath him, replacing my lap with a throw pillow. Between the hangover I know he had this morning and the stress of the day, he doesn't even flinch.

A glance at the clock on the oven tells me it's time to get going. I hope Devon will be waiting for me so we can go over everything that has happened in the last twenty-four hours.

In six years of working together, Devon and I have come a long way. He knows exactly who I am and where I came from, and I have made the extremely short list of those he has trusted with who he really is and the details of his past. In fact, I believe there are only three of us on that list.

Pulling out my phone, I open Instagram. I have zero posts and a handful of followers who are mostly bots, but I follow Devon's bogus account

plus forty-seven others, 90 percent of them businesses or famous personalities that post every day.
Out of the forty-seven accounts my bogus account
follows, thirty-two of them are also followed by
Devon's. And even though I posted my comment
on **Southern Living**'s latest post letting him know I
needed to meet up with him tonight at five, he will
answer me in a comment on a completely different
account so no one would be able to link our comments as communication between the two of us.

His paranoia knows no bounds.

I can't give him a hard time about that though
because there is no telling how many times his pro-
tocols have saved us in the past and we didn't even
know it.

Scrolling through my feed, I stop when I get to
the New Orleans Saints account and see the comment from skate_Life831043. This comment from
Devon is the only one visible on my feed since we
follow each other and also mutually follow this account, so I'm saved from having to scroll through
hundreds of comments to find his.

His comment reads: **Who Dat! That's my 3rd
favorite player right there!! #RightOnTime**

First thing Devon does when I get the details on
a new job is scope out five places where he's comfortable for us to meet. The third one on the list he
gave me when we got to Lake Forbing is the coffee
shop on Main. His hashtags always either confirm

the meeting time works or give me an alternative. I have thirty minutes to get there since he'll be #RightOnTime.

I pull a sheet of paper off the pad near the fridge and leave Ryan a note that I've gone to pick us up some food, then slip out of the house.

I'm five minutes early, but I see Devon has beat me here.

It took two years for Devon to share the first personal detail about himself. We were going over blueprints for an office building I needed to get inside of after hours, and he recognized a name from a list of people who had offices on the floor I was trying to access. "He's a tech guy. Spoke at MIT when I was there," he had said. I didn't want to pry, but I also wanted to learn as much about him as I could, so I attempted a joke, hoping to get more out of him. "Were you solving his complicated equations on the whiteboard in the hall?" His stare made me think I'd taken the wrong approach, but then he laughed. A real laugh. And that broke the ice between us. The details were still given to me in small pieces but now I have the full picture of who he really is.

Devon is sitting at the counter that runs along the entire back wall. These spots are mostly used by individuals or couples since the seating is not conducive to conversation with anyone other than the person sitting right next to you. He's working one of those complicated kakuro puzzle books he loves and wearing those huge over-the-ear-style headphones, his head and shoulders moving to a beat even though I know there's no music coming through the speakers.

His IQ is off the charts. If he's awake, he's got to keep that brain busy, like with the book in front of him. He started at MIT when he was seventeen, but he said he knew he wouldn't last long there; not that he couldn't handle the workload but more because he was **bored out of his mind.** His words. What sealed it was when he was given an assignment to build a network system for a simulated online advertising company only to discover it was a real business and his teacher was getting his students to do all the work for his side gigs.

The free enterprise system being what it is, he went straight to the client and made a deal to sell it to him directly at a slightly reduced rate, then clued in every other student in the class, who followed suit.

Then he was in business. It didn't take him long to find the most profitable work isn't always legal. His greatest success was retrieving info people didn't even know they needed, then offering it to them for an attractive price. He loves moving around in those dark places. Thrives on getting around systems meant to keep him out. And if you prove to be loyal to him, he will forever be loyal to you.

I order a cappuccino, then make my way toward him. I choose a stool that leaves an empty space between us. He doesn't look in my direction when he says, "I'm tapped into the coroner's office so I'll have a copy of her dental records as soon as they are uploaded. I don't think a match will pop but you never know."

I give him a small nod but don't look at him either. It won't pop. Mr. Smith wouldn't be so sloppy. I hate that we may never know who she really was.

"And we're sure it's really her? That she really died in that wreck?" This is something he would already have verified, but I still have to ask.

He nods and that's all I need to know he's sure that the body in the morgue is hers.

"I found the last set of instructions he gave her," I tell him.

Devon turns a page in his book as he asks, "What did it say?"

I pull it from my back pocket and slip it inside of a discarded magazine, then toss it in the empty space between us. He won't take it until I'm gone. "You can see it for yourself, but he basically told her to make contact, search my room if she can. It's pretty vague. And she did exactly as he asked. I left something for her to find."

"I don't like this. Not at all," he says quietly.

"You don't think it was an accident?"

He shakes his head just enough to let me know he doesn't.

"But why? Do you think she finished her job and we just don't know it?"

"Or she screwed up and he took her out."

"What do you think James's part was in this?"

"Pawn," Devon says without even thinking about it. "Extensive drug and gambling problem. In dire need of funds. Ridiculously easy to manipulate. Wouldn't be surprised if Smith wasn't behind the dad's broken leg to get him here."

Jesus. I hadn't thought of that possibility.

"And do we think Ryan is involved in this more than just an unsuspecting mark?" We had a conversation before I was sent here and knew who the mark was. Also discussed the possibility that this whole job was just a ruse. Once we found out I was assigned to Ryan, Devon dug as deep as he could on him. Mr. Smith's notes he sends on a job don't compare to what Devon gives me. We learned about his business and how successful it has become. It made sense someone would want it. Mr. Smith had used Ryan's transport services a few years ago to move things on a few jobs I was a part of, so it's easy to see how Ryan was on his radar.

Devon's shoulders shuffle back and forth a couple of times as if he's trying to determine how he feels about this subject. "First, we know anything is possible, right?"

"Right."

"So knowing anything is possible, it's still a long shot in my opinion. Regardless of the shady shit

Ryan has going on, he is too rooted in this community, which goes against everything Mr. Smith looks for in the people he recruits to work for him."

I was a nobody without family or connections. There would be no flags raised if I disappeared. No one to seek out justice for me if things go sideways. That is not true for Ryan. He lives in a house where his neighbors have literally watched him grow up from infancy.

"We deal in facts and we don't have any that point in that direction," he says.

We sit in silence for a minute or so, both contemplating this latest development. Finally I say, "I cornered her in the kitchen. Told her I knew who she worked for. Told her she could very easily find herself in my position."

His pencil stops moving for the first time since I sat down. "L, why?"

"L" is the closest he'd ever come to saying Lucca, since it's such an uncommon name and anyone listening would assume my name is Elle. But even with that precaution, Devon hardly ever addresses me directly, so I feel the weight behind it.

"I needed to know if she thought I was a random mark or if she knew I worked for him too. She didn't, by the way. The surprise on her face was real. And it's not like I discovered some big secret, since he already admitted to sending her."

Devon's pencil goes back to work, and he bounces his head to the assumed beat. "Smith's greatest achievement is keeping everyone under him in line by keeping them blind to everything and everyone else in his organization. No one knows who he is, no one knows where they are in the chain." Mr. Smith is the puzzle Devon has been working on for years.

"And the cops are aware of the name Evie Porter of Brookwood, Alabama," I add in a near whisper, as if I'm confessing my sins.

This admission makes his face turn toward me. "Details?"

I fill him in on our visit to the Bernards' house and the conversation with the police while he works diligently on the page in front of him.

When I finish, he says, "I don't like this. I don't like that I can't see where this is going. I think we bail."

This gives me pause. We have found ourselves in a lot of situations where a positive outcome seemed doubtful, but he's never mentioned bailing before.

"And then what? We knew coming in he was pissed I didn't get the blackmail info on Connolly back for him. We also knew he's trying to determine if I actually **was** successful but kept everything for myself. If Mr. Smith wants to take me out, bailing won't stop him, but it severely limits where I can go from here, especially now that Lucca Marino doesn't exist anymore."

"I still don't like it," he says. "You're going to be a sitting duck while you wait for the next set of instructions. And what if they never come?"

"The only choice I have is to continue moving forward." We both sit in silence for a minute or so, lost in our own thoughts. Then I ask, "How's Heather?"

He ducks his head and I think he's going to ignore me, but finally says, "Good. She's good."

"We stay the course, Devon. That's the only answer."

He hesitates just a moment, then says, "Got the details on the next big shipment coming through Glenview Trucking this Thursday. It's in the **People** magazine in front of you."

"Good. I think it will confuse Smith when he sees I'm still working this job, even after that woman's death." Somewhere between the first and second round of delivering the information on Ryan's business to Mr. Smith, I was regretting the part I was playing. Maybe it was the daydreams that Ryan's home could really be mine or the wishing this identity was real, but in a particularly weak moment, I altered a few key data points on the financials and client names before turning them over. It's not enough that Mr. Smith would notice, but just enough to give Ryan a fighting chance at keeping his business.

I plan to make similar modifications to this latest set of information before passing it along.

Devon doesn't know I've done this and I feel bad keeping it from him. He would think I was taking an unnecessary risk. "I'll drop it by the mailbox on my way home."

Devon's head turns just slightly in my direction. "That's not your home, L."

I flinch at his words, then grab the magazine in front of me, shoving it in my bag. I pick up my cup and stand from my stool. "I'll be in touch."

Just as I start to walk away, he whispers, "Please be safe."

CHAPTER 16

Present Day

After I got back from meeting with Devon, Ryan and I spent the evening stuffing ourselves on take-out food, binging Netflix, and trying to forget about how horrible the day was. The calls and texts from Ryan's friends throughout the day became so incessant that he ended up powering off his phone, which is something he rarely does. Neither of us got much sleep, so this Monday morning it seems especially hard to get up and moving.

Even though Ryan is taking the next several days off, he's still got a full day since he offered to help with the planning of James's funeral. While I probably could have taken the day off as well, I don't want to be available to visit the Bernards again, nor do I want to be forced to devise a way to disappear around lunch to meet back up with Devon.

I'm in the kitchen filling up a travel mug of coffee for each of us when Ryan starts down the stairs.

"I'm heading to the Bernards' first with a few of

the guys," he says. "Mrs. Bernard wants us to help her contact his work and let them know what happened. Then we're headed to the funeral home."

"Yeah, I don't envy you today." I hand him his coffee and start packing my bag for the day. "Shoot, I left my phone on the charger upstairs."

By the time I'm heading back down, Ryan is waiting by the door with his bag slung over his shoulder, his coffee mug in one hand and his keys in the other. "I shouldn't be too late tonight."

I grab my stuff from the chair. "Me either. Call me when you're headed home and I'll duck out early," I say, then follow him to the garage.

Just before I reach the door of my 4Runner, Ryan pulls me in close and kisses me gently. "I'm dreading today," he says quietly. "Is it terrible that I don't want to go over there?"

I run a hand down the side of his face, then wrap my arm around his neck, holding him close to me. He buries his face into the side of my neck.

"I'm so sorry," I whisper in his ear. I can feel my phone buzzing in my purse, but I don't let go of Ryan until he's ready.

I'm not sure how long we stand there holding each other, but he finally pulls away, giving me one last kiss before he lets me go and moves to his car.

I'm getting in my car as he climbs into his. As the garage door opens, he nods for me to back out first. I start inching out of the garage since it's a tight squeeze, watching my passenger side mirror to make sure I'm not going to scrape the door of his car.

As soon as I'm clear, I pull out my phone to give it a quick glance since I rarely get notifications of any kind. It's a text from an unknown number and my heart starts racing. I'm sure Ryan is wondering why I've stopped halfway down the driveway.

I open the text.

Unknown number: 911

Shit. That's my warning from Devon to get the hell out of here. I look up to find Ryan is stepping out of his car, his attention drawn to the street behind me.

I check my rearview mirror, afraid of what I will see there.

Three police cars have pulled up behind me, blocking us both in.

It only takes a few seconds to realize there's no getting past them. It also occurs to me that had I not lingered with Ryan in the garage, I would have seen Devon's text as soon as I received it. Those few minutes may have cost me a clean getaway.

Ryan is out of his car and moving to my door, attempting to open it, but the car is locked since I'm still in reverse. I do a quick mental inventory as to what is in this car that could possibly get me in trouble, but know that there's nothing.

He knocks on the window. "Evie, open up." His eyes track the approaching officers.

With slow and deliberate movements, I put the car in park and cut the engine. The second Ryan hears the lock disengage, he opens my door and pulls me out.

His face is wiped free of expression. Even though I didn't see him while he was talking to that rogue employee, I imagine this is what his face looked like then.

Does he think they are here for him because they have discovered his activities in East Texas? I do appreciate the sentiment when he steps between me and the cops, but the text from Devon tells me they are here for me and he can't save me from what's about to happen.

"Don't worry," he whispers. "I'll handle this."

He does think they are here for him.

The same officer, Deputy Bullock, from the Bernards' house is leading the way up the driveway, his eyes probably twinkling behind the mirrored shades.

"Miss Porter," he says as his hands rest on the low-slung gun belt around his waist. "I'm going to need you to come to the station with me to answer a few questions."

Ryan's hands are on his hips, blocking me completely from the police. "What is this about?"

Deputy Bullock looks around Ryan to me. "There is a material witness warrant for you from

Atlanta PD, in connection with the death of Amy Holder."

I see two of the other officers moving in closer, and I don't want this to get any uglier than it has to. The Rogerses, Ryan's next-door neighbors, have returned from their walk and are watching this unfold, as are several other people across the street. A few cars have stopped down the block. This quiet, tree-lined street has never seen such excitement.

I put a hand on Ryan's shoulder, which causes him to turn toward me. I don't speak but I nod, letting him know it's okay for them to take me with them. He stares at me a second or two, trying to read me so he can understand what's happening. The officers are gentle with me as they lead me to the closest patrol car. Thankfully, no one makes a move toward my car, so I'm hopeful it will still be here when I get out.

Amy Holder was the mark for my last job, the one I didn't complete to Mr. Smith's satisfaction. But my alias for **this** job, Evelyn Porter, should have been a clean identity and should not be connected in any way to Amy Holder or her death. The fact that they are bringing me in for questioning about her death lets me know I've been compromised, and this somehow plays into the next step of whatever Mr. Smith has in store for me.

———◆———

It takes more focus than you can imagine to sit absolutely still. I have not tapped my foot or fidgeted in my seat or looked anywhere other than the light-gray wall that is right in front of me. My breathing remains easy, inhaling through my nose and exhaling between my barely parted lips. My eyes blink in an easy rhythm, not too fast, not too slow.

I know they're watching me through the mirrored wall to my left, but I refuse to give them so much as a twitch of my pinkie finger, because I can't forget what Devon said the first time I met him in real life: **You can tell a lot about a person by the way they act when they are left waiting too long.**

There was a big production of bringing me into the interrogation room and sitting me down at this table. Uniformed officers and plainclothes detectives streamed in and out, each wanting to have their part in this. I was offered something to drink, I was asked if I needed to use the restroom. I was asked question after question, all of which I answered with the absolute bare-minimum response. The last question asked was by me. I asked for a lawyer.

I requested Rachel Murray, although I'm sure Ryan has already called her himself.

Sometime later, Rachel arrives and sits down across from me. I'm quiet while she openly studies me. I wasn't sure what to expect from her—delight in my detainment, or fear of sitting across the table from someone who may or may not be involved with a murder, or confusion as to why I requested her—but I don't get any of those. Her face is as blank as mine, and I'm happy with the route I've decided to take.

She's going to make me speak first, which I respect.

"Will you represent me?" I ask. I absolutely refuse to say anything to her that won't be protected by attorney-client privilege.

"Yes," she answers, then pulls a document out of the bag sitting by her feet. "I figured you wouldn't talk to me without this."

It's a standard agreement stating we are moving into a professional relationship in which Rachel is now my attorney of record. I sign at the bottom, then watch as she scratches her name below mine.

"I'm assuming you're good for the bill I will send you?" she asks.

I nod. "Of course."

She stuffs the document back in her bag and then moves to the door. Opening it slightly, she says, "I am the attorney of record for Miss Porter, so cut the mics and video feed to the room."

The door shuts, then she moves to the window to lower a set of blinds.

Now I have to trust this system and hope no one is about to hear what I'm about to tell her. This little bit of privacy has me shifting in my seat, trying to restore blood flow to the areas that need it.

Her left eye squints as she watches me. "Ryan called me the second they pulled out of his driveway with you in the back seat. When you requested me, I was already here. I was surprised, to say the least."

Finally, I ask, "Do you know what they have on me? Why they think I am a material witness?"

"Officer Bullock ran your name and Brookwood, Alabama, after he left the Bernards'. The warrant popped. He made the call and talked to the officer on Amy Holder's case first thing this morning. They have reason to believe you were at the scene when she died and either have knowledge of what happened in the moments before her death or may have assisted or been a factor in her death. They requested you be brought in, so the local guys headed to Ryan's to pick you up."

Evie Porter and Brookwood, Alabama, should not have **any** connection to Amy Holder in **any** way.

"What proof do they have that I was there?"

"I'm told there is a photo of you at the scene. The local police are saying Atlanta PD hasn't shared it with them so they couldn't show it to me. Not sure if that's the truth or not. Regardless, I have requested a copy of it and have been told it is forthcoming."

I nod, taking it all in. "How do they know the person in the image is Evie Porter, specifically?"

Rachel's head tilts to the side. "I'm not sure what you're asking." And I'm sure she's wondering why I'm referring to myself in third person.

"Is there a complete record on Evie Porter? Anything other than her presence where Amy Holder died?" I ask in a frustrated voice. I'm not ready to tell her everything yet, but I need to know everything she does. I'm not at the point where I can reclaim the Lucca Marino identity, and I need to protect it a little longer until I know exactly what's going on. For now, Lucca Marino is dead and gone and I am stuck being Evie Porter.

Rachel leans forward and rests her arms on the table. "Want to tell me what's going on? I can't help you if you keep me in the dark."

"I knew Amy Holder." She shows no surprise in this admission. "But when I knew her, my name wasn't Evie Porter."

Her head cocks to the side. "What was it?"

"Regina Hale."

"Regina Hale," she repeats.

I nod and she stares at me. "Are you Regina Hale?" she asks.

I shake my head no.

"Is Regina Hale a real person you impersonated?" she finally asks.

"No."

"Are you being vague on purpose?" she asks. "Because if it's more important to keep your secrets than confide in me, I'll show myself out."

God, she's a tough bitch, but a tough bitch is what I need.

"Regina Hale was the name I used when I lived outside of Atlanta. My understanding is that Amy's death was ruled an accident."

Rachel leans back in her chair, her arms crossed in front of her as she openly studies me.

"Is your real name Evie Porter?" she asks.

I hesitate long enough that she knows the answer, but she still waits for my response.

"No."

"What's your real name?" she asks.

"Not Evie Porter," I answer. I'm not ready to give her everything. Not yet.

We watch each other, both of us trying to determine who will break first. Finally, Rachel reaches down and pulls some papers out of her briefcase. "This is from my own personal search. I can find out if the police have anything more than this."

Even though I knew she would do her own search on me, I'm not prepared for the first item she lays down in front of me. It's a photocopy of a student ID from the University of Alabama with the name Evelyn Porter and my picture dated seven years ago.

"What is this?" I ask. I recognize the picture. It's from the first job I did. The Kingston job under the name Izzy Williams, but here it is on a school ID for Evelyn Porter.

Rachel doesn't say anything but hands me another piece of paper. It's a photocopy of a driver's license dated six years ago. Again, the picture is of me but the name on the license is Evelyn Porter. This image is one I used for the Andrew Marshall job under the name Mia Bianchi.

Another page lands on the table. Evelyn Porter's passport dated four years ago. Another picture of me that was intended for a job in Florida under the name Wendy Wallace.

Three more pieces of paper. An electricity bill, a speeding ticket, and a statement from a doctor's office. Three more pieces of proof that I'm Evelyn Porter.

I've spent eight years hiding my real identity, while Mr. Smith has spent eight years creating a new active one for me.

Devon and I are so thorough when we research a new town and a new mark, but not doing a deep dive into the name assigned to me was a blind spot.

Rachel waits for some sort of reaction from me. When she realizes she's not going to get one, she leans back in her chair and blows out a loud breath. "You still want to tell me you aren't Evelyn Porter?"

I'm back to being still. Calm. Composed. My brain may be firing in a million different directions, but I refuse to let anyone know that.

"If you're not Evelyn Porter and you refuse to tell me who you really are, how am I supposed to help you?" she asks.

"I need out of here. I need a few days to get this straightened out."

She's already shaking her head. "I can try but don't get your hopes up. They've been looking for you for a while and they don't want to chance you disappearing on them. All they've got is the formal request to interview you as a potential material witness, not a suspect in her death, so there's that, but I don't see them letting you just waltz right out of here today. I can probably have you out in a day or so, but it will be contingent on you going immediately to Atlanta for questioning."

Time is what I need more than anything else right now. I wait a few seconds, weighing my options, then pull her notebook and pen toward me. I scribble a name and push it back. I don't want to say it aloud in case there are still ears listening in. "Call this man. Say your client was on Hilton Head in June 2017. Tell him to get me out of here. Today."

Rachel leans forward, her face a shade paler than it was before. "You want me to call **him** and mention Hilton Head, June 2017, then what . . . ask him to pull some strings to get you released?"

It's not a question, so I don't bother giving her an answer.

She gives me a quick nod then leaves the room. I'm surprised she didn't badger me about the cryptic message, but I'm learning I didn't give Rachel enough credit.

I never wanted to be sitting here, facing what I'm facing, but I was prepared for it nonetheless. It's time to call in my favor.

The door cracks open slowly, but it's too early for Rachel to be back. I relax into my chair, ready to play the game with the detectives. And then Ryan's head peeks through the open space like he's not sure he's in the right room.

When he thought the police were there for him, he was worried about protecting me. Now he looks at me with apprehension.

"Rachel talked the cops into letting me see you for a minute. I think they're all too scared to tell her no. She did say to expect the cameras and mics to be back on, though."

They probably want him in here with me, hoping I'll say something to him they can use against me.

He hesitates just a moment, then he's by my side and pulling me into his arms. I'm surprised by my own flood of emotion. It's a relief to see him. He holds me close, squeezing me tight, as he mumbles quietly, "What the hell, Evie."

I should step away. Break contact with him.

But I can't let him go.

I don't want to let him go. I blame my lowered defenses on the long day . . . the long past several days.

"Are you okay?" he asks.

"Yes," I answer. "Better now that you're here."

He pulls back so he can look at me. "Rachel says she's working on getting you out of here."

"Good. That's good." He looks tired. The past twenty-four hours haven't been kind to him. First, he loses his childhood friend, then his girlfriend is hauled off in a police cruiser.

He laces his fingers in mine. "What's going on, Evie? That cop said you're wanted for questioning as a material witness in a death of some woman in Atlanta. They think you were there when it happened."

"Yeah, that's what I was told too. I was as surprised as you were that they wanted to talk to me. I had no idea there was a warrant out for me," I say, making sure I don't say anything that I wouldn't say in front of the cops, since they're probably listening.

"Does that mean they think something is suspicious about her death? I mean, why else would they need a warrant to talk to you?"

I take a deep breath and blow it out. "I have no idea why they think I know anything."

He's nodding while I talk as if he's weighing the truth of my words.

Before he can say anything else, Rachel opens the door and slips into the room. Her eyes bounce back and forth between us, the judgment there very clear. I'm lying to her friend.

"Evie," she says with heavy emphasis on my name, "I made the call. It seems to have been successful. We'll know for sure soon."

I nod because I knew it would be.

She looks at Ryan. "Can you give us a few minutes? I need to go over some things with Evie."

He looks between the two of us, I'm sure wondering what we could possibly talk about that he can't hear.

When I don't say it's okay for him to stay, he says, "Of course. I'll be just outside."

And then he's gone.

She waves her hand, gesturing at the room. "Mics and cameras are back off."

I nod, waiting for whatever she wants to say that no one else can hear.

"Are you going to tell him who you really are?" she asks.

"I hired you to handle the legal aspects of my life, not the personal ones."

She's not deterred. "He's my friend."

I don't respond, and we stare at each other a few seconds before she says, "I'll be back as soon as the release comes through. If it comes through."

"It will," I say.

She throws me a look as she leaves the room.

I sit back in the chair and clear my mind so I can start planning.

Lucca Marino—Six Years Ago

take my time driving from Hilton Head back to Raleigh, North Carolina, with the last twelve hours heavy on my mind. I shouldn't care what Andrew Marshall thinks about me now, but I do.

I'm off the grid. Matt has called my phone a million times and texted threat after threat, but I am not fazed.

I park in front of AAA Bail Bonds midmorning on Monday, almost forty-eight hours after I left Andrew at that resort in South Carolina, even though I was instructed never to set foot back here.

Matt is not expecting me.

The last time I was here I was terrified. I had just fled the Kingstons' house after leaving a bleeding Jenny Kingston dying on the floor and a sleeping Miles on the couch.

Today is different.

Today I walk into his office like I own it.

There are a few random people scattered around the waiting room and the same girl at the front desk. She gives me a halfhearted smile when I walk toward her, but her expression changes quickly when I bypass her desk and head down the hall.

"Wait! You need to check in first!" she yells, hot on my heels.

I twist open the door to Matt's office, and she stops herself just before colliding with my back.

"Where the fuck have you been!" Matt yells the second he sees me, then he looks at the reception-ist behind me. "Get the fuck back out front!" She makes a U-turn just as I shut his office door.

I sit in the same chair across from his desk that I did two years ago.

He looks like he hasn't slept since Friday. Since the last time we spoke. Since the last time he could see the video feed he had set up. Right before I cut it.

"My girl looked for Andrew all fucking weekend! Even went and knocked on his door! And where did you disappear to? You pulled a fucking Houdini on this job!" His face is red and bits of spit are flying from his mouth.

I take my time answering him. "Your plan was stupid. I improved it."

He grits his teeth and his eyes scan me at a frantic pace. "What does that mean?" he finally asks.

"Get Mr. Smith on the phone," I say. And now he looks like he wants to murder me.

Matt comes around to the front of his desk and stands over me. He leans down, putting his hands on the arms of my chair to box me in. "You answer to me," he says.

"No, I don't. Not anymore." I raise my arm and look at my watch. "You have five minutes or I walk. And you don't want me to walk."

I'm playing a very dangerous game, but I have to go with my gut. It never lets me down.

We stare at each other for a long, tense moment.

Something happened to me when I took over that job and made it my own. And I'm not going back to how it was before.

"Four minutes."

He shoves off my chair so hard that I'm in danger of toppling backward. I kick my feet out to regain my balance. He picks up his phone. Turning his back to me, he talks quietly to Mr. Smith.

A few seconds later, he's spinning around with the phone on speaker.

"Talk," Matt says.

Silence on the other end, but I don't let that stop me. "Andrew Marshall is a bust. He was never going to cheat on his wife. He's too squeaky clean. And if you forced something, the shame of it would have made him drop out of the race completely. It doesn't do you any good to have dirt on someone who isn't powerful. Ten minutes with this guy and you'd have known that."

Matt's eyes bore into me while I let Mr. Smith's silence fill the room.

"But I got you something better. Senator Nelson. He's held his seat in Georgia for eighteen years. He's on all the good committees. He loves God, his wife, his country. He also loves to have his ass spanked while wearing a ball gag. He's all yours. Just tell me where to send the flash drive."

It's clear I'm cutting Matt out by not giving it to him to pass along. What I don't add is Andrew Marshall is mine now. He will be governor soon, and he realizes just how close he came to being owned while also understanding who saved him from that.

I watch Matt and Matt watches the phone. There is a film of sweat popping out on his forehead.

That conversation with Andrew was hard. When he woke up the next morning still on the balcony, he had questions. And I answered them all. Vigilant. That's what he has to be going forward. No blind trust even if that person proves to be trustworthy. That's a hard lesson to learn. He thanked me, then offered to help me in any way he could to leave this life. To live a life filled with honor, not with crime. Because that's who Andrew Marshall is.

I hugged him and thanked him and promptly left him.

I also know if I ever need him—really need him—he will be there for me.

When it doesn't seem like Mr. Smith will be speaking to me today, I continue. "You may not like I changed the job, and the results may not be the ones you were hoping for, but Matt's plan would have failed. And Senator Nelson is better than a failed plan and wasted resources. If you would like to continue to engage my services, I deal directly with you. Not Matt. I'm good at what I do. Better than him. And you know it."

Silence.

Matt is furious. A deep, red flush is creeping up his neck, and his jaw is clenched tight.

Finally, Mr. Smith speaks. "Matt, give Lucca your phone then go wait in the hall. Lucca, once he's gone, shut the door and take me off speaker."

Matt's eyes look like they will bulge right out of his head. He leaves the office, slamming the door behind him.

I pick up the phone and hit the button to make the call private.

"I'm here," I say.

"I was told there was quite an event in Andrew Marshall's suite on Friday night."

I don't hesitate. "Yes. I invited some big hitters up for a cocktail party once I realized what Matt had planned. I knew if I couldn't get the dirt on Andrew, I better get it on someone else equally or more important."

Silence.

And then finally, more questions. "Where was Andrew Marshall during this party? If you have what you say you have, was he a witness to the senator's behavior?"

"I knocked Andrew out and put him on the

lounger on the balcony. Senator Nelson took one of the girls back to his room, and that's where the event between them took place."

Silence again. The wait between his questions and my answers is unnerving, which I'm sure is the point.

"Matt's instructions were delivered to you at four thirty in the afternoon, and you sent out invites for the cocktail gathering in Marshall's room at five forty-five. How were you able to find the tech and personnel to pull this off in such a short amount of time? Or were you already planning to go rogue before you were given your instructions?"

Assuming he was going to just take what I was giving him was naive.

"As you've said before, I am resourceful and think on my feet. This is just another example of that. I did not go into the weekend believing I would have to alter the plan, but it would have been unprofessional not to have been prepared for any eventuality. It was clear when I got the instructions that Matt had taken the lead on this job. It was sloppy and amateurish."

"And I'm to believe you walked away from the weekend with absolutely nothing on Marshall? That you in fact have not uncovered a single thing in all the time you've been with him that can be used as leverage against him?"

"That is the truth. He's as squeaky as they come."

I can tell he doesn't believe me. After a minute, I check the phone to see if we're still connected.

"While Senator Nelson will be helpful, he wasn't who we sent you after, but I can acknowledge and appreciate salvaging a job," he says. "Moving forward, you'll answer directly to me. We'll see how that works for us. For now. You are quite the surprise. Let's just see if it is a good one or bad one."

I ignore the ominousness of that last part. "My pay will reflect my new position, correct?"

I don't expect the chuckle. "You don't mind pushing me, do you?"

"Would you respect me if I didn't?"

He ignores my question. "Let's see if you're as good as you think you are. There is a situation in Florida you could help with. A sleepy little college town with lots of money. I need you to go there."

"No problem," I say, without hesitation. Even though I don't know what the job is, I know this is my one shot to prove I deserve leveling up.

"Go to the Holiday Inn Express near the airport. Check in under your current alias and wait for further instructions."

And then the line does go dead.

"I'm finished talking to him," I yell at the closed door, and Matt is pushing it open seconds later, jerking his phone from my hand.

"You're going to regret this," he says.

I shrug, then take the tiny paper swan out of my pocket, dropping it on the corner of his desk.

"What the fuck is that?"

"Something to remember me by," I say as I head to the door.

At the same moment I'm walking out of this building, there are small white boxes being delivered to multiple locations. In each box is an origami swan similar to what I just gave Matt. When the swan is pulled open, there's a picture showing the recipient in a very compromising position, with the words "Hilton Head 2017" written underneath it in red Sharpie. And that's it.

I just made my team a little bit bigger, even if the members aren't there by choice. A favor was called in that night I was almost arrested in Raleigh, and that was all it took to get me out of trouble.

There will be a time when I need these men and they will come running. I now have a handful of well-respected, God-fearing politicians in my back pocket. A senator, a couple of congressmen, several mayors and state legislators. And poor Judge McIntyre from Louisiana, who tagged along to the cocktail party with a friend.

CHAPTER 17

Present Day

J udge McIntyre came through like a champ. Just like I knew he would. I'm riding with Ryan back to the house as Rachel follows behind us in her car. She agreed to be held accountable for my actions, so it looks like I'm stuck with her.

In order to walk out of there today, I had to agree to meet with the detectives in Atlanta on Friday morning to answer questions on the circumstances surrounding the death of Amy Holder. If I refused to agree to do that, I would be held at the Lake Forbing Police Department until the escort sent by the Atlanta Police Department arrived and dragged me back there. If I'm not there for that meeting on Friday morning, there will be another warrant issued for my arrest for failure to show.

Yesterday, Mr. Smith's plan was unclear, but that is not the case anymore. While I thought I could always go back to being Lucca Marino, after today it will be next to impossible to lose the Evie Porter identity. As a condition of being released, I was photographed and fingerprinted, so now not only am I in **the system** for the first time ever, I'm in the system as Evelyn Porter.

I was so careful to keep Lucca Marino clean and off the grid—a blank slate that I could shape when I was ready—that I've got nothing to prove I'm actually her. But Evie Porter has a full background and history, including pictures, the freshly uploaded fingerprints, and the material witness warrant for questioning in the death of Amy Holder.

Eight years ago, Mr. Smith saved me from potential arrest, and now he's set me up for one.

Today is Monday and already half gone so I have only three full days to handle this.

It's quiet in the car.

Of all the questions twisting and turning in my head right now, the one that plagues me the most is: **Why would Mr. Smith up the stakes on** this **job?** I may be stuck in this town and in this identity for now, but my work here is done. Was this ever a real job or just a ruse to keep me in one place?

"You can ask me anything," I finally say when the silence becomes too much.

"How did she die?" he asks. "The woman they want to question you about."

"She died in a fire."

He cringes slightly, eyes still firmly on the road. "How did you know her?"

"Through work," I answer. Which is true. She was my last job.

We're a few minutes from his house and he hasn't asked me anything else, so I push him. "You're not going to ask me if I was there? If I know anything about what happened to her? If I played a part in it?"

"No. And it's not because I don't want the answers." He turns and looks at me a second or so before his focus is back on the road. "It's because you're not ready to tell me the truth and I'd rather you not lie to me."

"You're not scared you're shacking up with a criminal?" I ask, no hint of amusement in my voice. "Not afraid I'll set fire to that big beautiful house of yours?"

Push, push, push.

His humorless laugh fills the interior of the car. "My entire street witnessed my girlfriend being taken away by the cops. I've spent the whole day at the police station doing whatever I could to secure her release. And now she's picking a fight with me as I drive us home because I refuse to play games with her." He glances my way again. "Am I happy this is happening? No. Am I here supporting you through it? Yes. Am I scared of you? No. I'm patient enough to wait until you're ready to talk to me about this. But I'm not having hypothetical conversations with you about it."

His words hit me in a way I didn't expect.

Ryan reaches over and slides his hand into mine, softening the vibe in the car. "We'll go to Atlanta and tell them you don't know anything, answer their questions, and then we can get back to normal." He says it so decisively that I almost believe that is an option for me.

I have no idea what normal would even look like.

We pull into the garage, but Ryan keeps the engine running. "I need to stop by my office to pick up a few things since I wasn't able to get by there earlier," he says, staring through the front windshield.

I get out of the car before I say something I will regret. That little speech was making me want to tell him all the things I shouldn't and now he's running from me. I'm almost in the house when I hear Rachel shut her car door, her heels clicking on the concrete behind me.

"Evie, we need to go over some things," she says as she follows me in the back door.

I nod but don't turn back to face her. "I need a shower first. And a little time. Give me an hour." I'm heading up the stairs before she has a chance to say anything else.

I stop cold in front of our closed bedroom door. We never shut this door when the room is empty. I think back to this morning when we were getting ready for the day, each of us moving at a snail's pace, groggy from the weekend. I went down first, then Ryan joined me not long after, but then I ran back up here to get my phone from where it was charging beside the bed.

The door was open when I left the room.

I twist the knob slowly, then give it a push.

The bed is made, which is another thing we rarely do and certainly wouldn't have done it this morning given the state we were in. I scan the room, then suck in a breath when I see what's waiting for me on the nightstand on my side of the bed.

An origami swan.

It's set back against the lamp and small enough not to raise the interest of anyone but me.

I stare at it longer than I should, giving it power it doesn't deserve.

Finally, I reach for it and pull it open. There's another piece of paper inside the body of the swan. There are two pictures printed on one side. This is what the cops in Atlanta have on me, compliments of Mr. Smith, I'm sure. And he delivered it to me in the same way I let Judge McIntyre know what I have on him.

In the top image, I am standing outside a hotel in downtown Atlanta and Amy Holder is only a few feet away, her face angry and her hands raised as she flips me her middle finger. In the second image, I'm following Amy inside the hotel. The same hotel where only a few minutes later every cell phone camera on the street out front caught the black plumes of smoke that poured out her balcony window. It is clear there was a problem between us, and it's also clear I went into the hotel after her.

I remember this moment perfectly. Her heated words. The stares from anyone close enough to hear what she was screaming at me. And then later, the sounds of the fire truck sirens blasting through the air, the people screaming, the acrid smell of smoke.

The perfect piece of evidence, placing me at the scene in a confrontational moment with the dead woman. Knowing Mr. Smith, there are other shots from other angles that are just as damning and that can be passed along to the Atlanta PD whenever he's ready. This is just a teaser to whet their appetite.

The back side of the paper lets me know what he wants from me.

It's a picture of me taken on the same day, but the location is different. I'm leaving a bank a few blocks away from the hotel Amy was staying in.

At the bottom of the paper is a phone number. Retrieving my cell from my bag, I call him immediately.

"I didn't expect to hear from you so soon. You managed to get out of there quicker than I gave you credit for," Mr. Smith says when I answer, the robotic pitch a bit higher than usual.

"You've always underestimated me." It takes everything in me to inject a touch of playfulness into my voice.

"You will turn over what you retrieved from Amy Holder in Atlanta or you will discover this isn't going to end pleasantly for you."

I squeeze my eyes shut and take a silent deep breath. "I explained what happened there. I didn't get it. It's gone. Burned up in the fire."

"Then what is in the safe deposit box?"

I look back at the picture of me on the front steps of the bank. "Please tell me you didn't set me up with the cops because of this picture."

"And you are now underestimating me," he sneers. "I have the video surveillance from the security cameras inside the Wells Fargo branch on Peachtree Street. You rented the box before the Fire Department had fully doused the flames engulfing Amy Holder's body. You never keep anything important on you, and this would have been the quickest and closest place to safely stash what you retrieved. The only reason we're even having this conversation is because I don't know the box number, nor do I have the signature card details."

"It's not what you think," I say. "It has nothing to do with Amy or her death."

The mechanical growl due to the voice changer makes me cringe. "Now is not the time to play dumb with me. You will go back to Atlanta, but I want you there on Wednesday. There is a room reserved for you at the Candler Hotel in downtown Atlanta. You will be met in the lobby on Thursday morning at ten a.m. by one of my representatives, and he will accompany you to the bank and inside the vault. He will remove the contents of the safe deposit box himself. If what you say is true, and the contents have nothing to do with the Amy Holder job, then we will put this matter to bed once and for all and continue forward as we have. And you will find the detectives in Atlanta will quickly lose interest in you."

"And I'm supposed to believe you'll call off the dogs if I show you the contents of the safe deposit box? And what about this job? I'm just walking away from it? For someone who hates failure, why is it okay for this job?"

"With the shit you're in with me, that's what you want to know? The only thing that matters is getting back what Amy Holder took. **All of it.**" He's quiet a moment and then adds, "At one time you were my best asset and now look how far you've fallen."

"I'm still your best asset and we both know it."

The loud bark of laughter startles me. "You walked right in and talked to the cops. There's a file with your name on it now. Did you even put up a fight when they asked for your fingerprints? There's video of you from that interrogation room. Your composure must be commended."

His words are like bullets, each one hitting the target.

"How many Judge McIntyres do you have hidden in your pocket?"

I let out a laugh that I hope doesn't sound forced. "Enough that I can keep dodging the curveballs you're throwing at me."

"Unfortunately, Lucca, you made your choice, so now I'm making mine," he growls.

"Don't act like you haven't been setting me up since the beginning. All these years. I've been one of your best, yet you've just been waiting around for the moment to turn on me."

He makes a tsking sound. "Of course I have. Do you think I wouldn't have a contingency plan in place if one of mine gets out of hand? Don't get sentimental now. This is business."

"Did the woman pretending to be me know what was going to happen to her when she took the job? Did you tell her it was a death sentence?"

"That woman was an unfortunate casualty. She had potential. But I'm always prepared to make the hard decisions. The Holder job is more important."

And there it is. Confirmation that their deaths weren't an accident. "Did she even finish the job you sent her on? Or did she let you down in some way?"

"She was sent to unnerve you. And she did. She was sent to make a name for herself as Lucca Marino. And she did. She was sent to dinner that night to make sure **you** were the last person to see **her** alive so the police would have no choice but to question your evening together. I thought I'd have to step in to make sure they became aware of the warrant out for you, but you made that easy on me too. Her snooping through your stuff was to get under your skin because I knew how much you'd hate that. The spreadsheet you left for her to find gave me a little laugh, though. Nicely played."

The urge to scream at him and throw this phone until it breaks into a million pieces rolls through me, but I can't show him how gutted I feel.

"What guarantees do I have that I won't end up like her? She came in here to do a job and what thanks does she get? A nose dive off a bridge."

"I can guarantee you **will** meet the same fate if you fail to deliver what I send you for a second time." His tone softens when he adds, "I know you'll do whatever is necessary to get that fairy-tale ending you've always wanted. Big house and garden you and Mama planned all those years ago while she was wasting away in that single wide. You can still have all that. I can make Evie Porter a distant memory and bring Lucca Marino back from the dead if you give me what I want."

Does he honestly think I would believe that's a possible outcome?

"I don't know how many times I have to tell you—Atlanta was a bust. Whatever you wanted from Amy Holder, she took with her to the grave. That safe deposit box does not hold what you think it does."

He waits a beat, then says, "This number will be disconnected the second this call ends. You know how it works. If you don't meet my associate in the hotel lobby at the designated time, I'll be forced to give the Atlanta PD everything I have. Those pictures are just a preview of the main show. You can still run, but you're not a ghost anymore." He adds one last thing before ending the call. "And the cops won't be the only ones hunting you down."

And then the line goes dead. I don't try to call back, because he doesn't make empty threats.

I take the paper he left me to the bathroom, drop it in the sink, then pull out the lighter I keep for the candles next to the tub. It only takes a few minutes for it to turn to ash. I wash away all traces of it before the smoke sets off any alarms.

Turning the shower on as hot as I can stand, I undress and step under the spray, desperately needing to wash the last several hours away.

There are a lot of questions that need answers.

There are a lot of emotions I'll need to sift through. The anger that the man I've worked for all these years has turned against me in a way I could never imagine. The disappointment that washed over me upon hearing he built an identity for me from the beginning for the sole purpose of tearing me down. The bitterness that filled me when I discovered he was planning for my demise from the very first job. It all hits harder than I thought it would. Harder than I was prepared for.

But the part that's hitting me the hardest is the death of the woman. She came in and did her job. It's my fault she's dead. That James is dead. If I wasn't playing this game with Mr. Smith, she'd still be alive.

I scrub every inch of my body. Shampoo my hair. Wash my face. Anything to feel clean.

Her death sits heavy on my shoulders, it fills my lungs, it clouds my vision.

The bathroom door squeaks open, making me jump, even though I expect Ryan to come in to check on me once he gets back from his office.

Steam has fogged the glass, so I can't make out his details until he opens the door. A line appears in the middle of his forehead as he stares at me. His expression is one I can't read. Just when I think he'll walk away, he quietly undresses and joins me. He takes the washcloth from me before turning me toward the shower wall. One hand lands on my hip, holding me in place, while the other runs the cloth in long, sweeping passes along my back and shoulders.

I turn back around and bury my face in his chest while the water rains down around us. And I cry. Once I start, I can't stop. Big, broken sobs that wreck me.

Ryan whispers in my ear. Nonsense. Sweet words. Promises.

His soft voice finding the chinks in my armor.

Ten minutes to fall apart. Ten minutes to soak in the comfort he offers regardless of whether I deserve it. I will take these ten minutes then pull myself back together.

The water starts to cool so Ryan shuts it off, then somehow grabs my towel without letting me go. I stand still as he dries me off.

"Want to crawl in the bed? Or want to eat first?" he asks as I pull on a pair of leggings and an oversize tee.

"Is Rachel still here?" I ask.

He nods as he towels off. "Yes, she feels personally responsible for you. She plans to stay within arm's reach until we get to Atlanta."

I take in a deep breath. Then one more. "You don't need to go with me to Atlanta."

Ryan shrugs. "Of course I do. But we're not talking about that tonight. We'll make our plans tomorrow."

My mind is already working through different scenarios now that I know what I'm up against. I'll go to Atlanta after I make a few other stops first.

"What's going on in that head of yours?" he asks.

I don't like that he can read me so well. It shows how much I've let my guard down where he's concerned.

"Just thinking about what they'll ask me. And what they'll do if I can't answer their questions."

Ryan pulls me in close. "I'll be there with you the entire time. So will Rachel. We're on your side. If there's one thing you believe, believe that."

I grasp his hands in mine and pull them to my mouth, kissing each knuckle. "I'm hungry. But I need a minute to gather myself."

He smiles and squeezes my hands. "I'll go pick up some food. Come down when you're ready."

Ryan leaves the room and I sink down on our bed.

I've had my pity party, and now it's time to get to work.

CHAPTER 18

Present Day

Mr. Smith wants me in Atlanta by the day after tomorrow and the last thing I need is to have Rachel there with me. I head downstairs to find she has set up a mini office in the dining room. Her laptop sits on one end while file boxes are scattered down the length of the table.

"Where's Ryan?" I ask in place of a greeting.

She doesn't look up as she organizes a set of files next to her computer. "He ran to pick up food."

I watch her long enough to unnerve her. She stops what she's doing and finally gives me her full attention, dropping down in the chair at the end of the table. "We have to be in Atlanta by nine a.m. Friday, so we need to leave here on Thursday," she says. "I've looked at flights and there's a direct one at four thirty that afternoon. We can get a couple of rooms in one of those hotels near the airport. Let's plan to spend today and tomorrow going over everything so we're prepared."

I sit in the chair next to her, pushing the papers

out of my way so I can lean on the table. "I'll meet you in Atlanta by eight thirty on Friday morning, but there are some things I need to do first. Alone."

She's shaking her head before I finish my sentence. "I'm responsible for you. If you don't show, it's my ass. And while I'm sure you can easily—and happily—disappear, I live here. My whole life is here."

"I wouldn't do that to Ryan," I answer quietly.

She rolls her eyes. "He doesn't even know your real name."

Rachel wants to get a rise out of me and she's pretty close to succeeding. "It's not up for discussion. I could ditch you anytime I want and you'd never see it coming. But I'm being nice by telling you I will meet you in Atlanta on Friday. Just tell me where to be."

We're staring at each other, waiting for the other to break. The back door opening alerts us to Ryan's arrival with the food, and I need this settled before he's in the middle of it.

"I know it may not mean much to you, but I give you my word. I will be there. And when I give my word, I don't break it. Ever."

She lets out a rugged breath. "You don't think we need to spend any time going over your case."

I do need to prepare, but it needs to be with Devon, not Rachel. "I do not."

Ryan peeks his head into the dining room. His gaze darts from me to Rachel and back again. "All good in here?" he asks.

"All good," Rachel says.

"Of course," I answer.

"Y'all come eat," he says, and we follow him back into the kitchen.

I pull out plates and utensils while Ryan sets the food out buffet style on the island. "I got a few different things because I didn't know what everyone wanted."

In the song and dance of getting the meal ready to eat, Rachel watches Ryan and me closely. Watches how we move around the room, how we are always conscious of where the other one is. She is weary of me, and I'm sure it's hard for her to witness, knowing what she does.

I'm scooping a huge serving of chicken parm on my plate when I finally remember Ryan was supposed to have gone to the Bernards' house today. "Was Mrs. Bernard upset you weren't there today?"

He takes a long pull from his beer before he answers me. "I called her and told her I had something come up and wouldn't be able to make it."

I take the seat next to him at the kitchen table. "His funeral will be this week, so I think you should definitely be here for that instead of going with me to Atlanta."

"I already told the Bernards I won't be there because I've got an out-of-town emergency."

I'm shaking my head. "You really need to be there. Rachel and I can handle things in Atlanta."

He drops his fork on his plate and the sound echoes through the kitchen. "Pretty sure I can decide where I need to be."

We're giving Rachel a good show, so I decide to table this conversation until we're in the privacy of our bedroom. She already knows I plan to leave this house alone. I look up at her and say, "I assume you're okay missing the funeral as well?"

"Yep," she says, making that **p** really pop. "Last time I talked to James was about two years ago, when he called begging for money. I gave it to him on the condition he would get some help. I even had a spot lined up for him in a rehab facility. He ghosted me as soon as he got the cash. I was one of the few from our group who didn't see him when he got to town a couple of weeks ago."

Ryan grunts. "Yeah, I have about ten stories like that."

The rest of the meal is filled with meaningless chitchat, and soon enough we retreat to our bedroom and Rachel to the spare downstairs.

Standing in the middle of our room, I blow out a long, slow breath. Center myself. "I need to take care of a few things alone," I say to Ryan as he turns down our bed, not noticing that someone made it up for us. His expression sharpens, but I push on. "I'm meeting Rachel in Atlanta. You're welcome to meet me there too."

Ryan watches me as he strips down and climbs

into bed. "I don't want to talk anymore today." He holds the covers back, inviting me to slip in the bed with him.

I should push, but I'm done with talking, too, so I kill the lights and join him.

———◆———

I'm at the kitchen table, my notebook out in front of me, when Rachel wanders in. I pull out the two sheets I was writing on, fold them until they are small enough to fit in the back pocket of my jeans, then put the notebook in my backpack before moving to the coffee pot so I can fill my travel mug.

"Where are the cups?" Rachel asks.

I nod toward the cabinet over the pot. She ambles over to grab one. "Are you leaving this morning?"

Glancing at the clock, I answer, "Within the hour." I scroll through Instagram on my phone and stop when I get to the latest post from Food Network that shows Bobby Flay in front of a grill with his trademark shit-eating grin. I comment: **Beat Bobby Flay is my #1 fav show!! 45 mins to beat him is impossible! #EveryGoodRecipeIsWrittenDown**

Normally, I would give Devon more than forty-five minutes to meet me at the first spot on the predetermined list, but after yesterday, I'm sure he's refreshing his feed every few minutes like I am. And the hashtag won't make sense to anyone but Devon, but I need him to know I have something to give him so he can tell me where to leave it.

Rachel adds a packet of sugar and some creamer to her coffee, then turns to me while she stirs it in. "Does Ryan know?"

"He does," I say as I continue to scroll, refreshing my own feed. It only takes a couple of minutes for him to post a comment on Spotify's latest post: **See you soon by Coldplay is underrated #TwinkiesAreToo**

Guess I'm looking for the Twinkies when I get to the meeting spot.

I close out of the app, then book it upstairs to pack. I throw some clothes in a bag and move to the bathroom to gather my toiletries. When I come back into the bedroom, Ryan has his own bag sitting on the bed, open and half full.

"Do you think I'll need a suit?" he asks.

I dump the stuff in my arms into my bag before moving to the closet for my shoes. "I need to do this alone." I can't look at him.

"I understand you think you need to do this alone, but you're not alone anymore." His gaze catches mine from across the bed. "I'm coming with you."

I match his stare. "But you would miss work on **Thursday** and I know how important the appointments on **Thursday** are for you." I'm pushing right now to see what I can shake loose.

His head tilts to the side, his eyes narrowing. "I'm

willing to tell you my secrets if you're willing to tell me yours." His voice is deep and a bit unsettling. "You go first." There's a glimpse of the guy who ruled that warehouse yard.

I just cross my arms and look at him.

Ryan throws his hands in the air when I don't take him up on his offer. "I'm not asking any questions. I don't scare easily. And I really don't want you doing whatever it is that you think you need to do alone." We continue to stare at one another until he finally adds, "Plus, my skill set may come in handy in a pinch." And there's that smile. The one that makes him utterly charming.

And as much as I thought smiling was impossible right now, I give him one right back. "And what skill set is that?"

He shrugs and continues packing. "Take me along and find out."

I'm torn on what to do about Ryan. Mr. Smith decided **this** was the job to put me in while we played this macabre game, and I need to know why.

Mr. Smith will expect me to go alone. Until this point, I wanted to be 100 percent predictable, and now I need to be the exact opposite. Plus, Ryan's arguing pretty hard to come along even though he'll miss James's funeral and a week of work. Very curious.

Forcing out a deep breath, I make a show of giving in. "I make all the decisions. If I need to slip off to handle something by myself, there is no argument from you. Not a single word."

He nods. "Don't even think about ditching me along the way," he says with a smirk. "I can see it all over your face."

We both know that option is always on the table.

Rachel is pissed Ryan is going with me but she isn't.

I load our bags into the back of my 4Runner, while closer to the house Ryan is squaring off with Rachel in a heated conversation. I shut the back hatch and turn toward the street, committing it to memory. I will miss it more than I want to admit.

Slipping into the driver's seat, I wait for Ryan. When he hears the engine turn over, he looks at me over his shoulder. Rachel reaches for him when he moves toward the car. She knows things about me that he does not, things she can't tell him since I'm protected by client-attorney privilege, and she's frantic to stop him from coming with me.

He's not having it.

Ryan slips into the passenger seat, then rolls down the window as Rachel approaches his side. He wanted us to take his Tahoe, but this is my show, and if I do decide to leave him somewhere along the way, I'm going to need my own car.

Rachel gives me a look I don't particularly like, then focuses on him. "I'm not joking, Ryan. No later than eight thirty on Friday morning in Atlanta. I'm working on the detectives meeting us in a location other than the precinct, so as soon as that is finalized, I'll let you know where."

"You've mentioned all of this a number of times," he answers. His head drops back against the headrest, his gaze fixed on the windshield. Her hands grip the open window as if she's physically trying to stop us from driving away.

I fidget around in my seat, ready to go. I don't do good-byes. At all.

Ryan must feel my unease because he gives me a nod and I put the car in reverse, letting off the brake enough that Rachel has to pull her hands free and take a step back. "I'll call you," he says to her as we start inching backward. "And don't be surprised if you have to pick me up after she's abandoned me somewhere."

She clearly doesn't think his joke is funny.

Once the window is rolled up and we're on the street in front of his house, he asks, "Do you need me to book a hotel in Atlanta? I mean, I assume that's where we're heading."

"I've got it handled," I answer.

I pull out of the neighborhood onto one of the busy streets that runs through town, then turn in to a gas station. "Can you fill us up while I go in for a few snacks for the road?"

He's out of the car before I finish the question.

"Get me a Coke and some chips. BBQ flavor," he says just before I step inside the store.

I walk down the snack aisle, grabbing a couple of different bags of chips and a package of peanut butter M&Ms, and I spot Devon filling up a cup at the fountain machine. I pull the folded-up paper from my back pocket and slide it under the Twinkies. While I'm checking out at the register, he has moved to the snack aisle to retrieve the handwritten letter that will catch him up on what happened yesterday and give the details of the plan I came up with. It's not the best form of communication, but it's old-school enough that I know it can't be hacked. If everything goes the way it should, I will see him in person soon.

When I get back to the car, I slide into the passenger seat.

Ryan looks at me through the open driver's-side window, where he's still pumping gas. "I'm guessing you want me to drive now?"

"Yes, please," I answer before taking a swig of my Diet Dr Pepper.

"You'll have to tell me where we're going if I'm driving," he says once he's back in the car.

"Get on the interstate and head east."

We drive for a while without a word between us. The car is quiet. No music playing. No conversation. Only directions when needed.

The land flattens out as we head into the Mississippi Delta, where there's nothing but row crops for miles and miles. We're off the main interstate now, bumping along the back roads through the small towns that pop up every hour or so. The kind of towns where the speed limit drops from fifty-five to thirty-five with little warning, so the driver isn't prepared for the speed traps that generate the revenue that supports them.

We stop for gas again, and Ryan insists on paying for it. I insist he do it with cash. He pulls out a bulging wallet filled with twenties as if he is more prepared for this trip than I gave him credit for, and I remind myself that he's as shady as I am.

"I'm sorry you'll miss James's funeral," I say once we're back on the road.

He lets out a deep sigh. "Me too." I don't think he's going to say anything else until he adds, "I spent years helping James . . . saving James. I gave him money, clothes, a place to stay. Put him in rehab more than once. I was a crutch for him. He knew I'd be there. He knew I'd save him. So why bother getting your shit together if there's always someone saving you?"

A few minutes pass before I say, "I don't need saving."

His head jerks in my direction. He looks at me while I stare straight ahead, then his attention focuses back on the road. "I know that. There are things you may need, but saving isn't one of them."

This makes me want to ask questions. So many questions. But he made it clear—he'd show me his but I have to show mine first. So instead of questions, I say, "In two miles, you need to take a left."

Alias: Wendy Wallace—Six Years Ago

love this little town. In another life, I would have graduated from high school and headed straight here for college. I would have gone to every sporting event and play and art showing. Breaks between classes would have been spent in the quad, where I'd complain with fellow students on the unfairness of how our professor graded our last exam.

But I'm not living that life.

I was only in that airport hotel in Raleigh for a day before there was a knock on the door. I opened it to find a guy in a UPS uniform standing on the other side. But upon closer inspection, I realized it was the same guy who delivered my last set of instructions from Matt.

"You're George," I said.

He looked confused. "I'm sorry, who?" he asked.

I pointed to the space on my tee where a name tag would be if I had one. "George. It was the name on your uniform at the hotel in Hilton Head." He seemed surprised I would remember that. "But I'm guessing that's not your real name."

He handed me a plain brown package without any address or shipping label and said, "No, it's not." I'm sure he's not supposed to be talking to me, just delivering things.

"Are you going to tell me your real name or do I just keep calling you George?"

He shrugged. "George works, I guess."

"Okay, George it is." He started to step away, but he stopped when I asked, "You coming to Florida with me? Or do you have other deliveries to make?"

Another shrug. "You'll have to wait and see." And then he was gone.

Ripping the package open, I found a Florida driver's license in the name of Wendy Wallace, along with a slip of paper listing the address of a shipping and container store, including the mailbox number, and the name of an apartment complex and unit number. There were also two keys on a keychain, one key much bigger than the other. And lastly, there was a picture of a man in his mid-to-late thirties. On the back of the picture was his name, Mitch Cameron, and "Get to know everything about him" written underneath it.

I found Mitch Cameron immediately. Everyone knows Mitch Cameron, since he's the head football coach for a college in Central Florida. He is loved and hated in equal parts.

Mitch is thirty-seven years old and has been married to Mindy for the last ten years. Mitch and

Mindy. How adorable. Mitch is also the father of two young kids, a boy named Mitch Jr. and a girl named Matilda.

This family is brought to you by the letter **M.**

It only took four days for me to learn everything about Mitch and what his daily life looked like, although I couldn't for the life of me figure out why a college football coach was the mark. I'm never told who the client is, but I'm anxious to find out what's going on with Mitch that necessitated hiring Mr. Smith.

Every day this week, I've ridden my bike to the practice field so I can watch him at work. Today, I've spread a blanket out, surrounded myself with textbooks just like the half dozen other students studying outside on a fall afternoon, the Florida sun turning my skin a gorgeous tan. I've never spent so much time outdoors.

Mitch seems well liked by his players. He's tough on them but he's also encouraging and not afraid to tell them when they've worked hard. Just like every day, when practice ends and Mitch sends the players to the showers, I pack up and head to the package center to check the mailbox. It's been empty every time I've checked so far, but today I'm feeling lucky.

A little shriek of excitement slips out when I see the small envelope inside. Finally! I slide it in the waistband of my shorts and pull my shirt over it, leaving the store as quickly as possible.

I don't open it until I've reached the safety of my apartment.

There is a single piece of paper inside that lists five names with a date and time next to each one.

I only need to google two names before I see a pattern. Every person on this list is a high school senior who lives within a sixty-mile radius of the university and has had an amazing football career so far. And there is speculation about where all of them will end up playing next fall.

At first, this seems ridiculous to me. Why am I here? To monitor some football coach and a handful of eighteen-year-old boys?

I deep-dive into high school and college football. I realize the millions and millions of dollars that universities make on the backs of these players before they go pro. If they're lucky enough to go pro.

It is a big business.

There's also a lot of talk about players getting paid under the table to pick one college over another—stories of bagmen dropping off cash late at night and communicating by burner phone, and even more mind-blowing are the college boosters, aka old people, who spend big money in the hopes that their alma mater might possibly win a championship. They throw cash at programs and expect results. And if they don't get them, the money stops. There's a real question as to who is actually running these programs: the school's athletic director or the wealthy few writing the checks. All you need to do is google "T. Boone Pickens" and "Oklahoma State University" to get the general idea.

There is a big push to change the rules and allow college athletes to profit off their name and likeness. In fact, most people in the industry believe the NCAA will allow student athletes to accept endorsements as early as 2020 or 2021, but for now, it is strictly forbidden. If caught paying players, schools are fined huge sums and could even lose opportunities to go to bowl games at the end of their season, which kills their recruiting efforts. But the worst penalty is to the athlete. They lose their eligibility to play. Anywhere.

The last few jobs, I've used this time in the lull between getting information but still waiting for exact instructions to guess what the client has hired us to do.

Since the prospective players' names were given to me, I'm guessing they play into this somehow. Is Mitch a dirty recruiter? Is the client a rival school who wants Mitch's program in trouble?

I concentrate on the dates and names. I map out where each player lives, I learn their stats, I scour their social media.

Five names. Five dates. The first takes place in one week. I'm going to need some tech and help installing it, so I follow the steps Devon has set up and ask him to come to Florida.

———◆———

I planned to watch Mitch Cameron court these players, but I didn't anticipate I would also catch coaches from other schools visiting them too. These guys are the best of the best from this area and everyone wants them. While the university Mitch coaches for is a good one, there are a couple of bigger and better ones not far from here, so the competition is strong.

It was easier than I thought it would be for us to get in each player's home to set up once Devon arrived with the equipment we needed. All their houses are in poor neighborhoods with little to no security in place. It's hard to ignore how much money is at stake for colleges with a winning season, yet these boys aren't even supposed to get their dinner paid for by anyone associated with the school. It doesn't seem fair.

A week into spying on these guys, there's another note in the mailbox.

All recordings, videos, and images of the subjects from the previous list that document meetings, conversations, or discussions (even discussions between family members) regarding <u>any</u> football program should be turned in. A

courier will arrive at your
apartment every night at 10 pm for
pickup. Do not leave it in
the mailbox.

I knew Mr. Smith would be keeping a close eye on me, but I didn't realize just how close. It also weighs heavy in favor of the client being from a rival school. Mr. Smith doesn't want the conversations just between the players and Mitch, but their conversations with all the coaches. But the coaches aren't the only ones showing up to talk to these guys.

It's quickly obvious who the most valued player is: Tyron Nichols. Tyron lives in one of the poorest Black communities in the same town as the university. His house consists of three small bedrooms and one tiny bathroom, but is home to Tyron, his parents, a grandmother, and five younger siblings. His parents work long hours while the grandmother tends to the kids who aren't in school yet. It's clear his parents have no idea what to do with all the attention Tyron is getting.

But Tyron is smart. Even though he's been offered money, he hasn't taken any of it. Because when it comes down to it, Tyron is the one with the most at stake. If he loses his eligibility, he doesn't play. There's a close to zero chance he'll go to the NFL, where he'd finally get paid what he's worth, if he doesn't have a successful college football career first.

I watch on my small screen when men in starched button-down shirts show up at Tyron's door. I notice how he handles himself with them and then later listen in on the conversations he has with his brother, who is only one year younger, about what's being offered.

By the second week, I'm exhausted. Even though Devon and I are dividing and conquering, it takes us all day to skim through footage from all five locations and separate the relevant parts before George knocks on my door in his UPS uniform.

The only good thing is that George seems to be warming up to me. The first pickup or two, it was all business, but now he lingers in my doorway and chats a bit. I even gave him a few slices of pizza last night for the road since he looked as worn out as we did. Makes me wonder how much area he's covering in a day if he's got to be back here every night.

While we've gotten some dirt on some of the other coaches, Mitch Cameron hasn't stepped out of bounds once in any of his meetings with potential players. He's up front about his desire for them to be a part of his team, he's courteous to the family, complimentary about whatever food or drink is put in front of him. He is the perfect guest.

I'm having flashbacks to my time with Andrew Marshall, and there's a tight twist in my gut about what I might be asked to do.

I'm ready to know what the job is.

After another long day of scrolling through videos, I drop the thumb drive in an envelope and glance at the clock. George should be here any second.

Once Devon saw the last set of instructions, he wouldn't come to this apartment at all since he doesn't like the idea of George being so close by, so I've had to add in a trip to get what he's recorded. Those meeting spots change daily.

Two quick taps on the door lets me know he's here.

"Hey, George," I say, handing him the small package.

His forehead crinkles. "You're not looking so good."

"Always the charmer." I roll my eyes. "You watch surveillance videos all day long and let me see what you look like."

He hands me a manila envelope. "Got something for you tonight. Thought I'd save you a trip to the mailbox since I have to come by here anyway. Just don't rat me out."

My relief is evident. "Finally. And don't worry, your secret is safe with me." I'm ready to tear into it but I notice George is lingering in the hall. "Is there something else?"

He nods once, then says in a near whisper, "Since this is your first job where you're dealing directly with **him,** if it feels like a test, it is."

I stare at him with wide eyes, silently begging for

him to tell me more. But with those cryptic words, he's gone.

I can't rip open the envelope fast enough.

Cameron needs to be removed from his position without negative outcome financially or publicly to him, the university, or the program or any future prospects.
No scandal.

I had a lot of theories of what I'd be asked to do but this didn't make the top ten. And while the desired outcome and parameters are very clear, these instructions still feel very vague.

If it feels like a test, it is.

Well, here we go.

———◆———

It took a few days for me to walk through my options and weigh the potential for success against the risks of breaking one of the rules Mr. Smith laid down.

I can't load some underage porn on Mitch's computer and blackmail him into quitting because, for one, there's no guarantee that won't turn into some scandal, and two, if he quits, he forfeits the rest

of what's left in his contract—six million dollars—
and that would hurt him financially.

Blackmail on his wife leads to the same results
and blackmail on any member of the college opens
them up to scandal and also hurts them financially,
since they'd have to buy out his contract.

I feel like I'm boxed in.

I feel like I'm going to fail his test.

The only thing to do is start back at the beginning. He wouldn't set me up to completely fail, so
I'm missing something. He wants me to prove myself, so there is a way to get this job done—I just
need to find it.

———◆———

The Ford dealership is shiny and new; the main room
is a big open space with lots of glass and chrome.
Salesmen circle the front doors like sharks, but I
push my way through without breaking my stride
or making eye contact with a single one of them.

There's a young blonde at the welcome desk who
eyes me up and down quickly, then pastes a gigan-
tic smile on her face.

"Welcome to Southern Ford! How can I help
you?"

"I need to speak with Phil Robinson."

"I'm not sure he's available . . ."

"Give him this." I drop a white envelope on the counter in front of her. Phil owns five Ford dealerships that are scattered throughout central Florida, but he keeps his main office in this location.

It only takes a moment for the receptionist to return and lead me to him. Phil meets us at the door. His eyes track me from the tips of my shoes to the top of my head. I'm feeding him the details I want him to have, to remember. My clothes are nice but not too nice. My jacket looks like it was fitted especially for me but it's obvious my skirt is off the rack. My jewelry is minimal but tasteful. My hair is pulled back and the makeup heavier than what I normally wear. I'm thirty, easily.

My hand is out as I approach him, and he hesitates a second or two before caving.

"Mr. Robinson, thank you for seeing me," I say as we shake hands.

He motions me inside his office and I do a quick survey of the room. He's a super fan and one of the college's biggest boosters. There are framed jerseys and game balls. Pictures with players and coaches, including Mitch Cameron. Phil sinks into his chair behind his desk while gesturing me to take the one across from him.

"What is the meaning of this?" he asks. He's opened the envelope and pulled out the picture of stacks of cash sitting on the tailgate of a Ford truck with a sticker of his dealership's logo on the back window. There is no room for small talk.

"I'm here about Roger McBain."

Phil's face shows confusion, but there's red creeping up under his starched white collar. "I don't know anyone named Roger McBain."

My forehead crinkles as if I'm really taking him for his word and am somewhat confused, then I pull out more pictures. Pictures that show Phil and Roger together. "Huh, you two look pretty chummy here." Then I put my iPad on the desk so it faces him. I press play on the video that is waiting on the screen. It's a recording of a dinner with Phil, Roger, and a handful of other megadonors. Their discussion comes to life where they detail which high school prospects they want Roger to approach and how much money they will offer to each one. Phil even offers to throw in a couple of cars if necessary. "Anything to keep them from going to Florida State," he says. There is also some bragging about how successful they were last year in scoring some of the best recruits. I end the video right after Phil says, "Giving away that F-250 was worth those twelve touchdowns."

Phil stares at the screen from across the desk, and I can see the color drain from his face.

The one group that was not mentioned on that sheet of paper from Mr. Smith were the boosters. The mark: protected. The school: protected. The program: protected. The prospects: protected.

But not a word about those wealthy, overly invested boosters.

Mr. Smith knew I'd not only see the players talking to the coaches, but I'd also catch men like Roger McBain approaching them on behalf of boosters like Phil Robinson.

"Roger works for you. You tell him the players you want to commit to your alma mater, give him the funds to entice them to do so."

I came with receipts and he knows it. He's quiet, toying with a black ballpoint pen in his hands.

"I have just as many pics of you with the athletic director, the university president, and half the coaching staff so it's not a stretch to assume the school knew what you were doing and even condoned it. Think the NCAA will give them a three or four season bowl ban?" This is my only bluff, because I can't really pull the school into this, but Phil doesn't know that. I just need him scared enough that I can tie the school to his activities. The last thing he wants is to be the guy who brought down the whole program.

He finally speaks. "What is it that you want?"

Even though I knew there was zero chance Phil would let the team suffer for something he did, I am relieved he's crumbling under my threat.

"We want Mitch Cameron gone. You and your little friends will insist he be let go but you'll be nice about it. You're to say you don't agree with Mitch's vision. You'll say it's time for a rebuild. And then you'll buy out his contract. No reason for the school to eat that six million dollars when it's all your fault."

His lips peel up over his teeth like he wants to growl at me. "You are under the impression I have more power than I do."

"Nope. I believe in you, Phil," I say brightly. "I believe you can get it done."

"Why?" he asks. "Why Cameron?"

"Just like you, we want what's best for the school. We're all on the same team, Phil."

He doesn't like my answer and he doesn't ask anything else. I gather my things, taking my time getting everything back in my bag. "I'll expect an official announcement no later than Monday morning."

And then I'm gone.

———◆———

Three days later, I'm back in my apartment, one eye on ESPN and one eye on the continuing footage coming in from the prospects' homes. There haven't been any more notes in the mailbox and no more nightly pickups from George. I'm in the waiting game to see if my gamble paid off. It's not unheard-of for boosters to want a coach gone and to raise the money to buy them out. But that's usually at the end of a losing season when the coach is doing a poor job.

The breaking news on ESPN takes my attention away from the grainy footage of one of the players' houses as I focus on the words flashing across the bottom of the screen.

COACH MITCH CAMERON IS OUT IN FLORIDA

And then the details. The university had terminated their contract with him, and money raised by the boosters will cover his buyout. The reason given was that Coach Cameron and the athletic director had a different vision for the future of the program.

That's it.

Not even a minute later, there is a knock on the door and I almost jump out of my skin. Smoothing my hair back, I take a few deep breaths before I open it. And there's the familiar face in the brown UPS uniform, a package in his outstretched hand.

"Hey, George!" I take the package and say, "Looks like I passed."

"Looks like you did." He smiles and leans against the doorjamb. "How does it feel?"

"Feels pretty good," I answer.

He lingers a few more seconds, then pushes away. "See you soon."

And then he's gone.

I tear open the package the minute the door closes. Inside is a single typed page, a receipt, and a flip phone.

The paper reads:

The balance of your fee has been deposited. Details included. Keep the phone charged and you will be contacted for your next job.

That's it. I check the deposit receipt and read the note again. I eye the figure on the receipt once more. That's a lot of money. And it's mine.

It takes only a few minutes to pack up what I need from the apartment, but I'm not going back to North Carolina. I need to find a spot where I can't be found, a safe place to land between jobs. I've paid attention over the years and know how important it is to save for that inevitable rainy day. Maybe I can tuck away in another small college town like this. One where I can get lost in the sea of students.

I picture it. Visualize myself in a sleepy little town like this. A cute little house on a quiet street. Somewhere safe.

Now I just need to see it done.

There's one thing I need to do before I go. My "new to me" Honda rolls to a stop in front of the small house, and I lock the door before I make the short walk across the tiny yard.

Tyron answers the door a few minutes after I knock.

"Hey, can you step out here for a second?"

He's clearly confused but does what I ask. I walk

back to my car and lean against the trunk while he stands on the curb next to me. This is more privacy than we would get inside his house.

"You don't know me, but I wanted to give you some advice. You have a very bright future ahead of you and you're smart, but you need to be smarter. Assume someone is listening. At all times. Assume someone will rat you out. I know you like to talk to your younger brother about all the offers . . . and extra incentives . . . but you need to stop. Keep your own counsel."

His eyes are big. Like freaking-out big.

"And get what you can. Take it all. Make no promises and sign with the team you want regardless of what any other team offers you. But be smart about that too."

I talk for a few more minutes and he seems to absorb everything I tell him. He asks questions and I answer what I can. I give him tips on where to put the money so it grows. How to keep a low profile. How to never trust technology. Just as I'm about to leave, he asks, "Who are you?"

I give him a smile and say, "Someone who has had to grow up fast, just like you." I'm just about to turn and leave but ask one last thing. "Have you thought about where you want to play?"

He shrugs. "Not sure yet. Probably going wherever Coach Cameron ends up."

I nod. "Yeah, I hear he's looking for a new school now."

"Yeah, he said that was coming but not to worry."

Something about the way he says it makes me straighten. "When did he tell you that?" I've watched every interaction between Tyron and Mitch in that house and I never heard him say that.

"I ran into him about a week ago. He was kind of cryptic and shit but I got what he was saying. He wanted me to know he wanted me even if he wasn't in Florida."

Ran into him.

A week ago.

Mitch Cameron was let go this morning. He shouldn't have known that was coming a week ago.

Very interesting.

CHAPTER 19

Present Day

t's late afternoon when we pull into Oxford, Mississippi.

Oxford is a picturesque little college town that makes anything seem possible. I direct Ryan to a hotel right off the square that is a favorite with the college students. They study in the lobby during the day then take a short elevator ride to the roof for cocktails once the sun sets.

"Of all the places I thought you'd take me, this wasn't one of them," Ryan says as we pull into the parking lot.

This college town is home to Ole Miss, one of his alma mater's rivals.

"Ever been here?" I ask, mainly just to keep him distracted. It was a long, quiet ride, and I don't really want to get into why we're here.

"Yeah, we came once when LSU played here." He throws the car in park and turns to me. "Are we staying here for the night?"

I shake my head. "No. I need you to go up to the

rooftop bar. Eat something. Get a beer. Pay in cash. I'll meet you back at the car in one hour."

I open the car and hop out. He's right behind me.

"We should stick together," he says. There are a group of girls weighed down by backpacks and purses, with Greek letters stretched across their shirts, giving us curious glances.

I wait for them to pass then close the distance between us, putting both my hands on his chest. "We talked about this. The fact that you're here, in this town with me, while I'm dealing with what I am, is huge. I know you think I'm shutting you out, but you are the only person I've let in for years. But I need this hour. Don't make me get it another way."

We stare at each other for a minute longer, then he pulls me closer, kissing me on my forehead. "One hour," he says. "You need the keys?"

If Mr. Smith is tracking my car, which is possible, I want him to know we're in Oxford but I don't want him to have the exact location of where I am right now. Not yet at least.

"No, I'm not going far and would love to stretch my legs."

Ryan moves toward the hotel, and I start walking in the opposite direction. I turn down a quiet little street, not far from the square, and stop in front of a beautiful white house with a wraparound porch. Pink blooms explode from the hydrangea bushes in front of the house, and the hummingbirds flutter around feeders hanging from the limb of the huge oak tree.

Overflowing pots of spring flowers perch on each brick step. There is a small seating area on the left side of the porch and an old-fashioned swing hanging on the right side. I stand in front of the door, looking right then left, then wander to the seating area, where there's a small couch and a rocking chair, both pieces covered in the signature red and blue colors of the university and the words "Hotty Toddy!" printed across the throw pillows. I fluff a few of the pillows, dusting off a thin layer of pollen that settles on every single surface this time of the year, spending a little extra time getting the cushions on the rocker just where I want them.

This is the home of my dreams, the safe haven I always wanted.

Too bad it's not mine.

I shove down the wave of longing and move back to the door. A few minutes after ringing the doorbell, a blond teenager opens it.

"Hey," I say. "Is your dad home?"

"Sure, let me get him," she says, then closes the screen door in my face. I hear her yell for him and then his heavy steps coming from somewhere deep in the house.

The screen door opens slowly and Mitch Cameron asks, "Can I help you?"

I knew it was risky coming to his home, but this time of year and this time of day, there's nowhere else he would be. And nowhere else I wanted to meet with him.

"Can I have a minute of your time? My name is Wendy Wallace and I was the one who helped you get out of your coaching job in Florida," I say.

He steps back as if I've physically assaulted him. A glance over his shoulder tells him we are alone, but he doesn't want his family to see me so he steps out onto the front porch, the door closing behind him.

I never expected to be invited inside.

"I'm sorry, I'm not sure what you're referring to . . ."

I move to the seating area, sit in the middle of a small couch while he watches me, trying to figure out my game. We stare at each other for a tense few seconds, then he eases into the rocking chair next to me. "I'm really at a loss as to why you're here, Miss . . ."

"Call me Wendy. And I'm sure you are."

I let the awkwardness settle over us. I invite it in to be the third member of this conversation. I let it unravel Mitch like nothing else could.

He throws his hands up and his voice goes to a higher pitch than is normal. "Look, I'm not sure why you're here or what you want but I was fired. And I was blindsided by it, so maybe you've got the wrong idea about something."

I lean forward and drop my voice to a whisper. "I'm going to cut through the bullshit and get right to it. You hired my boss to get you out of your contract. You hated the athletic director, and those boosters were a pain in your ass. And after meeting some of them, I can see why. Leaving on your own meant walking away from a shit ton of money, so you hired someone to get you out of it. But you're an honorable enough guy that you didn't want to wreck the program in the process. Which means you've got some sense of decency in there somewhere."

Mitch has leaned back in his rocker, his elbows resting on the arms of the chair. He looks afraid to move.

"Since asking what I need or want makes you think you're admitting to something, I'll save you the trouble. I need some money. I came in and did my job. You walked away with a big paycheck and quickly got a new job offer. A job offer I'm assuming you knew was coming. I think it's only fair you help me out now since I helped you out then."

His jaw ticks and his eyes roam from the top of my head down my body.

"Worried I'm wearing a wire?" I stand up and throw my arms out to the side. "Feel free to frisk me."

He is not amused. But before he says anything else, his phone beeps. Pulling it from his pocket, he looks at the screen a second before tapping against it. A few seconds later, he's finished and shoving the device back in his pocket.

I sit again since it doesn't seem he's going to take me up on my offer to see if I'm wired. We watch each other while he rocks slowly back and forth. It's almost like I can see his mind spinning.

"Who are you really?" he finally asks.

"I'm no one," I answer.

Mitch Cameron is living up to his reputation of a coach with nerves of steel.

"Well, No One, you've made a mistake. I loved my job in Florida and would have stayed until retirement if they would have let me. I was fortunate enough to land on my feet here and now this is home. And I protect my home. It's best that you leave. Now."

I deflate on the couch and his lips tuck in, stopping him from saying anything else. I can see the pity in his eyes when he stares at me.

Getting up from the small couch, I move toward the porch steps. He remains in the rocker.

Just as I'm about to step off the porch, I turn back to him and let my frustration bubble to the surface. All of the anger and the fury of my boss turning on me after eight years. And I let it explode out of me. "You know what? You're an asshole. I did you a huge favor and now I need some help and you know what? You're a fucking dick. Fuck you and fuck all the way off, you fucker."

His face turns red and he stands up so quickly the rocker almost turns over. I'm focused on his chair, but thankfully it rights itself at the last minute. It would not be good if everything fell out of his chair right now.

Mitch spits when he shouts at me. "You have thirty seconds to get off my property or I'm calling the cops! No one comes to my house and talks to me like that, little girl!" He's not worried about drawing attention now.

I need to make sure he's good and pissed, so I throw him the middle finger before stomping down his front walk. That does the trick. He moves away from the rocker and stops on the top step, his hands balled in fists. I'm on the sidewalk in front of his neighbor's house when he finally looks around to see if anyone heard us.

I scream, "Screw you, Mitch!" for good measure then jog down the block.

My temper is back in check by the time I'm a couple of streets away. That was out of control. Reckless. I let myself go in a way I've never done before.

And it felt really good.

I check my watch. Ryan should be back in the parking lot of the hotel waiting for me. I don't spare another glance behind me.

By the time I get to my car, Ryan is sitting in the driver's seat with the car running. I jump into the passenger seat and say, "Go." I'm trying hard to hide the smile that is stretched across my face.

His hand rests on the gear shift, his face turned toward me. His mouth quirks when he says, "That smile says you've been up to no good. Need me to peel outta here like a good getaway driver, or do you want to give me a general direction to go?"

"Leave Oxford and head north toward Tennessee." He's teasing me and I'm sort of falling for it.

"I got you some food," he says, nodding to the back seat.

Reaching behind me, my hand closes on the white plastic to-go bag. Inside is a cheeseburger with everything except onions and an order of sweet potato fries.

"Thank you," I whisper.

We pull away while I grab the burger, taking a huge bite. He's quiet while I eat, and I'm finding it hard to swallow past the lump in my throat. It's the food that got me. And that he knew I liked sweet potato fries more than regular ones. And that I hate onions unless they're cooked. The thoughtfulness of it has been so rare in my world.

I eat quickly then push all the trash back in the bag it came in when I'm done.

"So, just Tennessee?" he asks.

I nod. "Yes."

His jaw flexes and he seems to struggle with holding back what he wants to say. Finally, he just spits it out. "You made a point to mention how important my appointments on Thursday are. I have a business in Glenview, Texas. It's different work than what I do in Lake Forbing. I acquire things in a questionable way then sell those things for a significant markup. It's not something that is public knowledge at home and I plan on keeping it that way."

I'm floored by this admission. "But you're telling me," I say.

He glances at me, studies my face, then turns his attention back to the road. "Figured I'd go first."

Neither of us say anything else. We ride this way for miles, him staring ahead at the road, me watching the blurred scenery from the side window.

"I'll tell you everything. But not right now. I have to get past Friday." It comes out as a whisper, but I know he heard every word. Because after Friday, I will know everything I need to know.

"I can live with that," he says. "But come Friday, we're putting it all on the table."

My phone dings, saving me from having to say anything back to him, and a wave of relief courses through me when I see the notification.

Ryan glances my way and notices the change. "Good news?"

Nodding, I say, "Yes. Just what I needed."

I open my phone and pull up the app that allows me to see an exact replica of what's happening on Mitch's phone right now. And sure enough, he did exactly what I hoped he would do. He reached out to Mr. Smith to complain about me.

It was a risky move visiting Mitch. I didn't think he would invite me inside, but you never know when you're dealing with deep-seated Southern manners. But luckily, he wanted to ensure there was distance between me and his family, and we kept to the porch. And when he sat in the rocker, right on top of the device I planted there just moments before, it was only a matter of him opening the message Devon sent to his phone while I was sitting across from him and we were in.

Given that he is just now getting in touch with my former boss tells me he thought about it for a bit, which speaks for that level head of his. I'm sure he worried about the risk of making contact again, but my showing up on his doorstep was far more threatening, which is why I had to make a scene before leaving. I could see he felt bad for me at first, and that wasn't going to cut it. I needed him pissed. And a little bit scared of me. Enough to take the risk of reaching out.

There are a lot of things we don't know about Mr. Smith. Despite Devon's impressive skills, he has been unable to discover his real name or where he lives. The other thing we have been unable to uncover is how clients contact him and how they communicate. After dealing with Devon all these years, I know it's not something as simple as a fake email address. So this is where Mitch comes in. Of all the jobs I've done, this was the only one where I felt certain who the client was, based on that slip from Tyron Nichols. Mitch Cameron knew he was being fired in Florida a week before I approached that megabooster. And he knew to speak to Tyron away from the listening devices in his house when he told him he'd want him on his team no matter what school he was coaching. Only one way he would have known those things.

Mitch Cameron was the client.

Now he is deep in a message board created to celebrate the love of a seventies band named King Harvest. I'm guessing most of these messages are meant for my boss, while a few just really love the one hit this band had, "Dancing in the Moonlight." The new message window pops up and Mitch starts typing.

Gridiron Boss: I just heard Dancing in the Moonlight for the first time today.

That's it. This must be how they make initial contact with Mr. Smith.

"Decision time," Ryan says. He nods at the upcoming signs. "Straight to Memphis or somewhere else?"

"Not Memphis. Head northeast," I say, and he flicks the turn signal on. "We're going to Nashville."

He glances my way. "Not Atlanta?"

"Not yet."

He nods. "I'm going to pull over for gas since that's a pretty good stretch. Get some more snacks."

At the next exit, Ryan fills up the tank then heads into the store.

I'm glued to my phone, waiting for a reply to come through to Mitch. And while Mr. Smith may be hesitant to answer Mitch's message, I'm hoping the overwhelming curiosity about what Mitch wants, added to the high probability that he is tracking me and knows we were in Oxford, will get the better of him. I need him to react the way I expect or I'm dead in the water.

Now that I know where to look, I open my browser and find the message board so I can snoop around instead of just seeing what Mitch is looking at. Since Devon can also see Mitch's screen, I'm sure he's doing the same. There are a lot of posts that say: **I just heard Dancing in the Moonlight for the first time today.** I always knew I wasn't the only one working for my boss, but by the sheer number of posts, he's got a lot more going on than I originally thought. There are a few usernames that could possibly match up to jobs I've done in the past, but I can only see their initial post. I'm sure the conversations with Mr. Smith are moved to private messages.

It's only another minute or so before I get a notification that Mitch has a response to his message.

Kingharvestmegafan: What can I help you with?

Gridiron Boss: a girl showed up at my house. Said she worked for you. Wendy something. Asked me for money! She was out of control. Told me to fuck myself when I

**told her to leave.
Screamed it loud enough
for the neighbors to hear. I
paid you too much money
for some crackpot to
knock on my door!!**

**Kingharvestmegafan: My apologies for the
unexpected visit. I assure
you, she will be taken care
of and you will not be
bothered again.**

"There you are," I whisper. "Got you."

———◆———

It's late when we get to Nashville. Ryan pulls up in front of a run-down motel on the edge of town; my door is open before he puts it in park.

"Wait here. I'll get us a room," I say, one foot already out of the door.

He cuts the ignition. "Are you sure? I can—"

"I'm sure. Wait here." He's been frustrated with me since we left Oxford because I have dodged every question he has asked.

A few minutes later I'm back in the car and give Ryan the room number. We park right in front of the door since I asked for a unit on the ground floor. While we could afford nicer accommodations, I prefer to be able to make a quick exit if the need arises.

We packed light so it doesn't take long to get settled in.

"I'm hitting the shower," Ryan says. "I'll find us some food after I get out."

As soon as I hear the water turn on, I pull out my phone and scroll Instagram until I find a comment giving me the meeting time for tomorrow. I comment on a different post letting Devon know I received his message.

When the bathroom door opens, Ryan exits in nothing but a towel.

I could look at him all day. His body is exactly my type—fit and trim but not overly muscular. Ryan must see the glint in my eye because instead of moving toward his bag, he crawls across the bed toward me. His mood has greatly improved.

And I give myself this moment. I push away the plans rolling around in my head. Hit pause on my timetable. Relish these few stolen moments where we can be normal.

I pull him close and his weight settles over me. My hands drift up to his hair, still damp from the shower.

"It's been a helluva week," he says, his lips only inches from mine.

"And it's only Tuesday," I answer. Then my expression turns serious. "Regretting coming on this road trip?"

"Not yet," he says with a laugh.

Ryan kisses that spot on my neck that he knows I love, and I feel it down to my toes.

"What if I did it? What if I had something to do with Amy Holder's death?" My whispered words hang in the air between us. This is self-sabotage at its finest.

He stills. Then his head lifts and his eyes meet mine. "That's not a question I need the answer to." Ryan leans closer, his lips landing softly on mine. It's not long before we're skin to skin, and I lose myself in this moment as his hands and mouth roam slowly down my body before working their way back up.

His hands grip me tighter, he holds me closer, as if he's afraid I'll disappear, then he buries his face into that sensitive spot where my neck meets my shoulder. Whispered words flow out of him, broken sentences that shouldn't make sense but do.

I soak up every word as my nails dig into his back. Show him I feel the same way without having to say it.

Alias: Helen White—Four Years Ago

For this job, I'm Helen White and I'm the farthest west I've ever been: Fort Worth, Texas.

I've always wondered why every job I'm given is located in the South, but I guess Mr. Smith must have others who work for him in other parts of the country, so the South must be my territory.

It feels very corporate.

But Texas is new for me. Everything just feels different here. Bigger and louder for sure, but there's something else to it. It's almost culture shock.

On the surface, the Fort Worth job is supposed to be a simple retrieval. Some painting worth millions was stolen years ago and is believed to be hidden inside the sprawling home of oil tycoon Ralph Tate. Whoever hired us for this job has apparently tried to buy it from Ralph for years, but Ralph won't sell, so we're going to steal it from him instead.

But I'm not the only one trying.

Mr. Smith loves his games, and this job is the prime example of how twisted he can be. He told me I'm not the only one he's sending after it, but he didn't say exactly how many of us are throwing their hat in the ring. Because this is a contest, and the one who gets the painting out of the house first gets a bonus. A big one.

I find I want to win badly. Based on my last few jobs, I feel like I'm getting closer and closer to the top of that ladder, but walking away with that painting would confirm I'm the best he has.

After researching the art in question, I was a little disappointed it's not one of the big ones, like that yellow poppy painting by Van Gogh that's still in the wind. The one I'm after is worth about five million and it's not even cute. I was given the details on this job thirty-six hours ago, and the more I dig into it, the more I'm convinced Mr. Smith wants the painting for himself, so he's made a game of getting it.

It wouldn't be the first job where there is no client.

The security system of the Tate house is a nightmare and doesn't make any sense. At all. It looks more like an obstacle course. No matter how long I'm in this business, I'll never understand rich people.

Ol' Ralph believes his system is impossible to breach, but I've got Devon on my team. There is nothing I've requested from him that he has not delivered, and he can say the same about me.

I walk into Buffalo Wild Wings and scan the restaurant for him. He nods when we make eye contact and I make my way through the crowd to the booth where he's waiting.

Sliding in across from him, he passes me a beer. If we were in private, I'd throw my arms around him, pulling him in for a hug since I haven't seen him in a while, but he insists that in public we do nothing to draw attention to ourselves. But I do get a small smile and I return it with a much bigger one.

"Those colors look good on you," I say. He's wearing a Cowboys jersey even though I know he hates them. He wore it because he knew more than half of this restaurant would be wearing apparel celebrating the home team. As I glance around the room, all I see is a field of blue, white, and silver.

"Don't start. The things I do for you." He rolls his eyes and fake gags.

"You love me, I know it." I tip my bottle, tapping it against the neck of his. "Cheers!"

"Yeah, yeah," he mumbles, then takes a swig of his beer. "First time you've been sent to Texas. Not sure I like it."

Devon's weariness for anything new is the one constant in my life. "Maybe my territory is expanding," I say with a laugh. He tilts his head to the side, his expression telling me he's not so sure, but he doesn't say anything else once the waitress approaches the table.

"Hey, hon," she says. "Can I get you something to eat?"

I look at Devon and he says, "I got the burger and fries. It's good. You'll like it."

I nod and say, "Same for me." Once the server has walked away, I pull a manila envelope out of my bag and hand it to him, filling him in on everything I know so far. I sip my beer while he reads what I've given him, relaxing for the first time since I crossed the state line into Texas. I know Devon arrived at least an hour before I did and did a sweep of the place for any bugs or recording devices, even though absolutely no one knows we'd be here.

Our food is delivered and I people watch while Devon carefully reads each page.

A kid stops a few feet away from our table and says, "This phone sucks. I can't get this pic to download." He and his friend examine the device and then walk away. I chuckle and Devon looks up at me.

I point to the small black device on the table. "How big of a dead zone did you make?"

He chuckles as he glances at the kid. "Twenty-five-foot diameter." Then his attention is back on the plans in front of him.

I gaze around the room, noticing everyone is having similar issues with their devices. Devon is causing chaos around us. "Everyone is freaking out."

"I'm saving a lot of people from making bad decisions right now." His eyes go to the rowdy bar not too far away for just a second or two. "They'd thank me later if they could."

Finally, he turns over the last page and looks at me. "I've never seen a security system designed like this."

"Can you hack it?"

Devon cocks his head, giving me a look. A look that says **Don't dare insult me like that.**

"Lay it out for me," I say, with a smile.

He digs through the stack of papers and pulls out a floor plan. "This setup is gorgeous. Super hot. There's no reason for how it's laid out and that makes it exquisite." He points to one section and asks, "The painting is believed to be in this room in the middle of the house, correct?"

"Yeah, it's his trophy room, where he keeps those stuffed exotic animals he killed in Africa. I've found a few pictures from inside that room. There's also one of those commercial cigar humidors and a tequila collection that'll make your mouth water." I pull a piece of paper from the pile. "And this drawing shows the addition made to the room shortly after that painting went missing. Looks like there was a false wall added that retracts. My best guess is that the painting, and whatever else he's obtained illegally, can be hidden behind that wall if he's got people in the room he doesn't trust to see it."

Devon studies the drawing of the addition, then goes back to the main set of blueprints. "You'll need to be at the keypad outside the room where you believe the painting is kept"—then he moves his finger across the page, tracing lines that represent cables and wires—"while I'm here at the backup system to prevent it from kicking in right away. Neither can be accessed remotely. It's devastatingly simple but chaotic. And you will only have maybe five minutes. Five minutes inside a room we haven't seen, so there's no telling what else awaits you there. No other way around it. It's magnificent, really."

He doesn't have a special someone, but if he ever gets one, I hope he feels the same way about them that he does for a well-made security system.

"Why only five minutes once I'm inside? If you disarm it, does it not stay disarmed?"

He shakes his head slowly. "Nope. Mr. Tate has employed a system that records every second of what happens in that room and there's an alarm that goes off if the feed is interrupted for longer than that amount of time. But I can't override or bypass it because that system **is in the room.** Can't be accessed remotely either." He points to two areas and goes into a complicated description of wires that need to be short-circuited and lots of other things that I don't understand.

"The timing has to be perfect. Absolutely perfect. Down to the second. The alarm only rings in the guardhouse, so you won't even know you've tripped it until it's too late."

Devon's eyes continue to roam the plans, while his head shakes slowly back and forth like he can't believe what he's seeing. "As much as I love this, it's not right. I mean, who does this? I don't like this for you. There's something else going on."

"I think it's a game. I was already told I wouldn't be the only one trying to get the painting."

"But why?" he asks. "Is Smith sending multiple people in or are there some other players involved?"

"I think this is all Mr. Smith."

"But why?" Devon asks again. "This doesn't make sense."

I shrug. "It wouldn't be the first time he did something like this. I think he gets bored and decides to play games. Rich people are weird."

Devon's head tilts to the side. "Can you say no to the job?"

This gives me pause. "You really don't think I should do it?"

"I don't know." He's chewing on his bottom lip as he studies the drawings.

I lean forward trying to see it the way he does. "I'm not sure I can say no. I've never turned a job down."

"I need some more time with this. How soon do you want to try for it?"

I shove a few fries in my mouth while I consider my next move. "I need to go to Austin for a few days. Tate is having a huge Fourth of July party at his house this weekend. Might be the best time to hit him if you can get it all figured out by then. Get everything we need while I'm gone." It's a risk putting it off since I don't know who else or even how many other people are trying to get that painting, but it's a risk worth taking, especially if Devon needs more time on his end.

I pause a moment before adding, "You're going to have to find a way to get into the party. This isn't a job where you can pull the van up close by and do your thing from there."

He nods. "I know."

Devon is comfortable in those dark spaces, behind the scenes, but that won't be possible on this job.

I knock my foot against his under the table. "You got this."

He drags a fry through a mountain of ranch dressing. "I guess we'll see."

———◆———

This cover of "Sweet Home Alabama" would be pretty good if the lead singer wasn't off-key and whiny, because the rest of the band is killing it. I bang my head to the beat regardless.

I got to Austin just before they took the stage and I've been front row for the entire show. The lead singer has noticed. He's stared at my chest for the past two songs, so I pull my tight V-neck down a bit more to make it easier for him.

Once they finish the set, he catches my eye then nods toward backstage.

Shoving my way through the crowd, I push past the curtain to find him waiting for me. He pulls me in close and kisses me, hard, completely forgoing any introductions. I give him a little leeway before I pull away.

"Y'all sounded so hot out there," I say, my hands roaming up his chest while his fingers dig into my hair, which has recently been dyed a beautiful shade of cobalt blue.

"I like this color," he says.

"I'm a big fan of Blue Line." I rub up against him. "The biggest."

He nods his head toward the back door of the club. "Want to get out of here?"

His bandmates hear him and yell his name, "Sawyer! You're not fucking bailing before we get this gear loaded!"

He pulls me close, tugging my hand around his waist. I dip my fingers right under the waistband of his jeans, my nails scratching gently into his skin. "Yeah, let's get out of here," I say.

"Gotta go! I owe you one," he yells without ever looking back at them.

"Fuck you, Tate!"

I believe he would have been booted from this band long ago if dear old dad, Ralph Tate, wasn't funding this little endeavor, because he's easily the worst member in talent and usefulness.

"What's your name?" he asks, ignoring everyone behind us.

Helen White is not going to cut it.

I wrinkle my nose and bite my bottom lip. He stares at my mouth like I knew he would. Then I whisper, "Kitty."

He makes a cat noise. It takes everything in me not to roll my eyes.

Sawyer gives me a grin while he grabs my ass with one hand and pushes open the back door with the other. He's going to be a tough one to wrangle. But if there's one thing I know, it's how to handle trust fund babies with big egos.

—◆—

The Tate Fourth of July party is a big shindig complete with pig chases, lasso roping contests, and a thirty-minute fireworks display planned for just after the sun sets. It is one of the hardest invites to get.

Unless you're his son's band groupie.

Sawyer and I, along with twenty of his closest friends, show up an hour late. I've done as much recon on this little group as I can, trying to see if anyone else is using him to get inside the house, but they have been fried since last night, so I think I'm the only plant. It didn't hurt being the girl to show up with the edibles to ensure they stayed that way.

We pull up to the valet stand, the other four cars in our caravan behind us. Sawyer throws his keys at the poor pimple-faced teen manning the station. "Keep it close. We're not staying long."

I sidle up next to him, my hand slipping around his back, and we walk inside the sprawling house. "But you promised me fireworks," I say, my lips pouting.

"I got your fireworks, Kitty Cat," he says, while grabbing his crotch.

While this is the easiest way to get into the party, it is also the grossest.

As soon as we enter the house, I hear someone shout "Sawyer!"

We both turn to find Ralph Tate staring at us from the top of the stairs. I knew I'd be memorable walking in with Sawyer so I played to it. My jean shorts are short enough that I have a little ass hanging out of the back, and the American flag bikini top leaves little to the imagination. My hair is blue in honor of my country on its birthday and my great love for Sawyer's band, Blue Line. Some well-placed temporary tattoos, smoky eyes, and fire engine red lipstick complete the look. I am hiding in plain sight.

Ralph Tate approaches us slowly and I can feel Sawyer tense up next to me. He wants to cause a scene. Wants it to look like he's thumbing his nose at Daddy's money. But I know he'll crumble the second Daddy threatens to take the money away. These boys are so predictable.

"Son, I believe you mentioned a few friends would be joining you." He eyes the group behind us. "This is a bit more than we planned for."

Sawyer spreads his arms out wide. "It's either all of us or none of us."

This fucking tool. I hold my breath, hoping Ralph isn't about to throw us out just to put him in his well-deserved place. Luckily, Mrs. Tate steps in to smooth things over.

"Honey, we always have room for you and your friends!" She's not his mother since she's only about six years older than him, but she likes the show as much as Sawyer does. Ralph disappears outside while the missus points us in the direction of food and booze. I dig my phone out of my back pocket to send Devon a quick text: **Tick tock**

Sawyer gets swept up by a group of girls he's known since childhood, while I slip away to the bar, swaying just enough to make it look like I'm as high as the crowd I showed up with.

"Vodka cranberry," I say.

Devon is behind the bar. I would not recognize him if I didn't know it was him. He's wearing the same uniform as the other servers, but he's got a pretty groovy mustache going on and dreads in place of his normally short hair. When he told me his revised plan, I was surprised he was willing to interact with so many people, but happy he's getting out of his comfort zone. He's stood in the shadows long enough.

Devon hands me a drink that I know will contain zero alcohol, then checks his watch. "No changes. Cameras out at four seventeen."

Since we knew we wouldn't be the only ones attempting this job, he tapped into the security system within hours of leaving Buffalo Wild Wings, and he's been watching the house ever since. He texted me the number four last night, letting me know how many failed attempts to get the painting there have been so far. I don't have the details yet, but since he said "no changes" it seems like no one has tried it the way we have planned.

"How many on deck?" I ask.

"Three but hopefully they're waiting until the show," he answers. I nod and slip away.

We tossed around waiting until the fireworks started to make our move like he believes the other three people here for the painting will be doing, but we knew we might face a crowd if we wait that long. So we're going for it in broad daylight.

I drop down in a chair near the patio door and watch the clock. We have timed this to the second, so as soon as it hits 4:17, I put my drink on the small side table and make my way into the house. Once I've cleared the main area, I walk with purpose to the bathroom located off the back hall. I've memorized the floor plans so there are no wrong turns. I lock the door once I'm inside and pull the bag Devon stowed in the cabinet earlier. There is a black wig and server's uniform, a pair of gloves, a watch, and a big black trash bag. I put everything on over my shorts and bikini top in record time. I shouldn't be caught on any cameras, but Kitty is too memorable if I bump into someone in the hall. Once I'm out of the bathroom, I send Devon a text: **Go**

Making my way through the house, I get to the back hall where a left will take me to Mr. Tate's trophy room.

I turn right.

I keep my head low as I pass through the kitchen, holding the trash bag in front of me like a shield. No one spares me a second glance since it looks like I'm on my way to take the garbage out.

A few more turns and I'm in front of the door to the laundry room.

I send another text: **Ready**

There's a small keypad outside the door, and the light flashes from red to green. I open the door and step inside, put the trash bag on top of the dryer, then pull out a small black device from inside the bag. I hold it up to the cabinet doors next to the washer, entering the series of numbers that Devon has texted me. You cannot tell there is a lock on this cabinet from the outside, but in a few seconds I hear a click and the doors pop open.

Inside the cabinet is a clothes rod full of hunting clothes. Grabbing a fistful at a time, I remove all the clothes from the cabinet, then hold the black box against the panel that was hidden behind them. Devon sends me another set of codes that I plug into the device.

A few seconds later, it pops open, and I'm looking at a very expensive but also very ugly painting.

I take the painting, leaving the replica that was hidden in the trash bag in its place. Luckily, the painting isn't very big. Once the clothes are all back on the rod, Devon helps me work my way out of the system, locking each door in place.

Within minutes, I'm back in the hall outside the laundry room and moving toward the garage. My heart races as one of the men hired to patrol the house turns the corner, nearly bumping right into me. He catches himself by grabbing on to my arm.

"My apologies. Shouldn't have taken that turn so quickly," he says.

I give him the laugh he's looking for. "No worries," I say.

He waves an almost empty water bottle at me then dips his head to the trash bag in my hand.

I open the bag and he chucks it in. "Thanks," he says.

"No problem," I reply, and hope the painting can handle a little bit of water.

Keeping my head down, I walk out the side door to the garage, where the trash bins are located. I strip out of the uniform, leaving me in my shorts and bikini top, and shove the clothes and wig in the garbage bag with the painting, then tie off the bag before dumping it all in the garbage can. Once I'm in the backyard, I text Devon: **I took out the garbage**

He will retrieve the bag before cutting the cameras back on.

Twenty minutes after I set my drink down on that side table, I'm picking it back up. The ice has barely melted. I take a deep drink, then go find Sawyer. He's sitting on the side of the pool and I squeeze between him and a blonde so I can take her spot next to him. She's not happy.

"Where you been, baby?" he slurs.

"Looking for you."

He throws an arm around me, pulling me close, then starts talking to the girl on his other side.

I sip on my drink and take a deep breath. I owe Devon big for this job. The day after we met at Buffalo Wild Wings, he showed up in Austin.

I found him on the children and teens floor of the Central Public Library, where he was teaching three middle school girls how to play chess on the life-size board. For all his rules and procedures, he's a complete softy when it comes to kids. I slid into one of the many chairs in that area and let them finish. As soon as the girls were lining up the over-size pieces for a new game, he picked up the cardboard tube and motioned for me to join him in one of the private study rooms. Next to the black box that would ensure that no one was listening in on our conversation, we bent over those blueprints a second time.

"Are you sure the painting is in that room?" he had asked.

I leaned across the table and tried to see what he saw, but nothing jumped out at me. "That room is more fortified than any other spot in that house. The false wall addition implies he's hiding something there. You said the system is . . . what was the word you used? Exquisite? Everything points to the painting being in that room."

"But you said you think this is a game, right? You won't be the only one there looking for it?"

I nodded and he pointed to a small corner of the house.

"You see this right here?"

I moved in close and squinted like that would help me see what he wanted me to see.

It didn't.

"Give it to me like I'm dumb," I finally said.

His finger tapped on the space labeled **Laundry Room.** "See all the wires running to this room?"

I nodded again.

"This is overkill for a room that houses at most a washer and dryer."

It didn't take me long to catch on. "So you think the trophy room is bait. Send everyone to a room protected with a ridiculous system they can't get past. Once they trip it . . . which they will . . . guards get a silent alarm and go scoop them up. Meanwhile, that painting is hidden next to the deep freeze."

Devon gave me a huge smile. "That's exactly what I'm thinking."

"And you're still good to come in with me? Play a part?" I asked.

He nodded. "Already working on my disguise." There was actually a hint of excitement in his words I would not have expected.

And he was right. By now, Devon has secured the painting and has left the Tate property. I'll hang out as long as Sawyer wants, then ditch him once we leave here.

I dig out the small white paper swan that I'd tucked away in my back pocket this morning and set it in the water. It bobs and weaves its way across the pool.

I take another sip of my drink. It won't be long before the fireworks start.

———◆———

I'm expecting the call but jump anyway when the phone rings. The burner was waiting on my kitchen table the second I got home from the party.

"Yes."

"The blue hair looks better than I thought it would," Mr. Smith says in his mechanical voice.

"It's going to be a bitch to remove."

He laughs quietly. "The package will be picked up shortly and details on the next job will be delivered along with confirmation of your deposit, which includes the bonus."

I open my laptop and log into my account, where I can already see that the money has been deposited. I start the process of moving it, just like always.

"I'll be here."

I think he's about to hang up, then he adds, "I must say, I'm impressed you recovered it."

"How many people did I beat?" I'm doing a little fishing of my own. I don't think he's going to answer so I push just a little. "Was I the underdog?" I want to know how many more rungs of this ladder I need to climb to make it to the top.

He lets out a soft chuckle. "You've always had an ego problem, Lucca."

"I call it confidence, and it's worked well for me so far," I purr into the phone.

The silence stretches but I wait him out. If he wasn't going to tell me, he would have hung up by now.

He finally says, "I'm only going to tell you this now since you were the victor and had the nerve to ask."

When he doesn't say any more for a full minute, I say, "You've worked me up and I'm right on the edge. Don't be a tease now."

That laugh again. "Let's just say I needed to see who of mine would rise to the top under less than ideal circumstances. And who can recognize when the most obvious path is the wrong one. Congratulations."

"Was there even a client? This didn't feel like a real job."

"The job is always real, but you may not always be aware of what the end goal is."

Before I can say anything else, Mr. Smith says, "Answer the door. I'll be in touch soon."

The call ends and I move to the door. Peeking through the peephole I see my guy in his usual UPS outfit holding a small box.

"Right on time," I say as I pull open the door. He hands me the small box, and I give him the painting wrapped in brown paper. "Want to come in for a drink? We can get drunk and spill all our secrets," I say with a wink. "You know you want to, George."

"You know I can't do that no matter how much I want to."

George and I have developed an easy camaraderie over the years. It's hard to make friends in this business since I'm always on the move. Devon is really the only true friend I have, but sometimes we go months without seeing each other. George is the only other constant in my life. Well, other than Mr. Smith, but I'm not sure he'll ever be more than a mechanical voice to me.

"So blue hair, huh?" he asks.

I shake my head around. "You like it?"

"I like the blond hair you had in New Orleans. That may be my favorite."

I laugh. "Well, I may be blond again after I strip this color out."

"Okay, Lucca, got to get this to the big guy. Stay out of trouble."

Leaning into the hall when he starts to walk away, I call out, "I'm going to wear you down one of these days and talk you into staying for a drink!"

He stops a few feet away and turns back around to face me. "If anyone could tempt me into breaking the rules, it would be you." He steps back in closer and adds, "Just remember, the bigger the job, the closer you're watched. Eyes are everywhere."

I watch him walk away while I consider his warning. It's not the first time he's given me one and, I hope, not the last.

CHAPTER 20

Present Day

Ryan follows me to the door of our motel room but doesn't step outside. I turn around, lean in, and kiss him gently.

"I won't be long," I say in a soft voice.

His arms wrap around me, pulling me close. "You sure you're okay? Don't want me to come with you? You may need another getaway driver."

My laugh is loud enough to feel real. "I wish, but this is something I need to handle alone. Plus, I know you need to check in with work. Gotta keep all those old ladies happy."

He peppers me with quick kisses while his hands roam. "Call me if you need me."

One last kiss and I'm walking away.

Ryan watches me from the open doorway until I turn out of the lot. Today is important, and I need to clear my head and remind myself why I'm here. I have some time before my next stop, so I drive around in a random sort of way to center myself.

It also gives me time to identify who's tailing me and screw with them.

Because I know someone is back there. Since the Tate job, someone has always been there.

My mind wanders back to that job as I cruise through a neighborhood. I think back on that complex security system that guarded some stuffed dead animals, a cabinet of cigars, and not much else. That was not as much a job, but more a twisted game where he pit us all against one another.

Devon had watched that house as religiously as Mama had watched Victor Newman in **The Young and the Restless**—never missed a second. He studied who came in and out, he made sure I was aware of every camera so I had the least amount of screen time, and he identified every person who came for the painting.

When the painting was delivered and my fee had been deposited, it was time to move on, but I couldn't stop wondering about the others who showed up and failed. I couldn't shake my curiosity about who they were and whether they wanted more from life than moving from job to job like I did.

Because Devon is Devon, he sent me exactly what I wanted almost before I had to ask for it. He didn't even make me feel weird when I said I wanted more than screenshots of them from the video feed, I wanted names and addresses. Mr. Smith sent six of us into that job, and I wanted to meet them all.

That was the first time I had ever been that close to learning who else worked for him, and I didn't want to waste this opportunity. I knew it was possible that not all of them would want to talk to me, but I was hoping to get to speak to at least a couple of them.

We may have been competitors on the Tate job, but why couldn't we be allies going forward? This was not the first job that I realized the value of having someone on my team who answered only to me. And this time, I would have been one of the failures if it hadn't been for Devon. I convinced him that it wouldn't hurt to reach out to them. We could combine resources. And brainstorm strategies.

We could build a community.

At the end of the search, Devon could only give me one name and address. I drove all the way to Cape San Blas, Florida, between jobs. Walked up to the cutest little pink house, where half a dozen wind chimes hung from the front porch and the doormat had a drawing of the sand and surf, and the words **All we do is beach, beach, beach** printed on it.

That search for the others who attempted the Tate job and the conversation with the one person I did manage to talk to changed everything for me.

For the first time, I wanted to quit this job, this way of life. Flee and start a new life, one with purpose, like Andrew Marshall spoke of that morning in South Carolina. The shiny gloss of this life had worn away, leaving all the scratches and dents behind. But it isn't a job where you turn in your two weeks' notice. Not if I ever wanted to go back to being Lucca Marino and everything else that meant.

So I stayed. I kept taking the jobs he offered like I had an option to refuse them.

When I was sent to Louisiana and given the name Ryan Sumner, I thought I was prepared for the job ahead of me.

In theory, it's easy to believe I could handle whatever he threw at me.

In reality, there was no way to prepare myself for what he did. Mr. Smith struck where it hurt the most.

It's too late to run, so I need to see this through.

I finally arrive at my destination and find a spot to park. After I throw some quarters in the meter, I duck into a CVS to buy a prepaid phone, a single-dose pack of Advil, and a bottle of water. There's a headache building behind my left eye that I need to get in front of. Leaning against the back of my car, I balance the phone against my shoulder once I hit send so I can use both hands to throw back two pills and chase them with water.

Devon answers on the second ring but doesn't say a word in greeting.

"It's me," I say.

"Twenty-One C hotel in one hour. Coffee shop in the lobby."

"Number?"

"Five fifteen." And then he ends the call.

It's a short drive to the hotel, and thankfully I find a parking spot around the corner from the front door. In addition to this being a hotel, 21C is also home to a museum, so the lobby is teeming with people and I'm forced to weave through the crowd, dodging rolling bags and swinging briefcases, until I get to the coffee shop that sits to the right of the main entrance. A huge banner hanging over the hall that leads to the convention rooms catches my attention.

REELECT ANDREW MARSHALL— PROMISES MADE, PROMISES KEPT

I skip the long line for coffee and find a small table where I have a good view of the lobby.

Forty-five minutes later, a smile stretches across my face when I see Governor Andrew Marshall stride through the front door. There are quite a few people with him, two who I recognize from my short time in his employ. Early polls show he'll win his reelection by a landslide, and his name is already being batted around as a potential presidential candidate.

I leave my jacket on the table, so no one takes my place, and walk toward them. He spots me when I'm about ten feet away, and I can see recognition dawn on his face even though I look different than I did six years ago.

He separates from his group and closes the distance between us.

"Mia?" he asks.

"Yes, Governor. It's me."

"How have you been?" he asks. I can tell he wants to reach out in some way, to hug me or shake my hand, but neither seems right under the circumstances, so he ends up shoving his hands in his pockets.

"I'm good. I've been following your career. I couldn't be prouder."

He shrugs. "I had some good advice early on that I believe has helped me tremendously."

I take a deep breath and ask, "Can I speak to you a moment in private?"

One of his aides has materialized next to him. "I'm sorry, but Governor Marshall has a tight schedule. He's due to speak at a luncheon in just a few minutes." She has a hand on his arm and is trying to pull him away, but he stops her.

"Margaret, it's fine. I have a few minutes."

I gesture to the coffee shop and he follows me back to the table I saved. Once we're both sitting, he asks, "Are you in trouble? Is that why you're here?"

I give him a tentative smile. "Maybe a little. I'm okay. For now."

Andrew leans forward, his elbows resting on the table, his voice dropping to an almost whisper. "I owe you and we both know it. What can I do to help?"

Shaking my head, I say, "I'm not ready to call that favor in yet, just needed to make sure it's still on the table and you're still willing to give it."

We stare at each other while he tries to read me,

but I'm giving nothing away. "If it is in my power to help you, I will."

I nod, knowing this is the best I'm going to get from squeaky-clean Andrew Marshall. "That's what I needed to hear. And now enough about me and my problems. How are you?"

He leans back in his chair, his eyes never leaving mine. "I'm good. Balancing the job and the reelection campaign, so it's a busy time. But I have to ask, Mia, are you good? Happy?"

God, if he only knew. "A few rocky spots left to smooth out, but I'm getting close."

This gets me a smile finally, although it's smaller than I wish it was. He glances at his watch, signaling our time is up.

"You need to go," I say, making it easier for him to leave.

Andrew stands up and pulls a card out of his pocket, then hands it to me. I study it while he says, "My private cell. Just let me know what I need to do."

And then he's gone.

I drop back down in my seat and watch him walk away. Holding the card in front of me, I read it over again.

A loud screech pulls my attention from the card, and it lands on the man dragging out the chair Andrew just vacated. It's George, but instead of the UPS uniform, he's dressed in a dark suit.

He drops down in the chair, catching the flicker

of surprise that washes across my face before I hide it away.

"You look good in a suit."

He smiles and says, "You're supposed to be in Atlanta."

"I'm working my way there. Needed to make a couple of stops first," I answer.

"What are you doing?" he asks in a soft voice. His concern for me is apparent. "You're playing with fire. Andrew Marshall won't do anything that gets his hands dirty, we both know that."

My eyes never leave George's face. "I don't know what you're talking about. I was just passing through town and thought it would be nice to catch up with a few old friends."

He frowns. "You can lie to everyone else, but don't lie to me. Not after all this time."

"Then you don't ask me questions you know I can't answer."

George rubs a hand across his mouth then says, "Mr. Smith thinks you need a bit more incentive."

I let out a loud, frustrated breath. "You going to send the detectives another picture of me on a public street?"

"Not me," he says. "I'm just the messenger. The next set of images will make it increasingly hard to get you out of trouble. He's not playing around."

I nod slowly, considering his words. "Any other messages you need to deliver?"

His eyes crinkle at the corners as he really thinks

about what he wants to say. "Just one from me. Head to Atlanta. You can still make it to the bank and get into that safe deposit box by tomorrow afternoon. Give him what he wants. I don't want to do what he'll ask me to do if you don't. Please, Lucca."

This knocks me back a bit. This is the most candid he's ever been with me.

All I say is, "Thanks for the heads-up."

I stay in my seat while he rises from his. "Tell your guy he's getting sloppy. I clocked him coming in through the service entrance in a maintenance uniform."

He always calls Devon "my guy." Devon and George have played their own cat-and-mouse game over the years, trying to figure out who the other one really is, but I don't think either have been successful. At least I know Devon hasn't been.

"Wish we could have gotten that drink," I say.

He laughs. "Get your ass to Atlanta and maybe we can." Just as he's about to walk away, he turns and adds, "Good luck."

I shrug and give him a smile. "Who needs luck?"

His laugh carries with him out of the coffee shop.

I sit frozen in my seat another ten minutes, running through our conversation over and over.

The urge to run floods my system.

But running means I'm looking over my shoulder not only for Mr. Smith but for the police for the rest of my life.

Finally, I get up and head to the elevators. I hit

the button for the eighth floor once I'm inside. I walk down the hall to the door that leads to the stairway. I go up and down by elevator and stairs three more times until I end up on the fifth floor and I'm positive no one is following. Knowing Devon, he's had the cameras monitoring this floor on loop before he walked into the hotel.

I knock on the door to room 515.

Devon opens the door and says, "The look of shock when George sat down was a nice touch."

"He told me in Fort Worth that 'eyes are every-where,' but I never know if it's him or someone else watching, so I **was** a little surprised when he sat down." I sit in the chair next to him. "He said you're losing your touch. Saw you come in through the service entrance."

Devon's upper lip curls back. "Does he think I just coincidentally entered the building the second y'all arrived?" He rolls his eyes and adds, "He only spots me when I want him to."

Devon has a monitor and printer set up on the hotel room desk, and I study the images he has on the screen. Andrew and I are in the frame but we are not the main focus. George is. While I'm chatting with Andrew, he's in the lobby, sitting in a wingback chair, holding up a newspaper but watching me.

"I'm assuming George got audio too. Was he able to hear everything Andrew and I said?"

Devon pushes another couple of buttons and

replays the conversation between Andrew and me. "Yeah, the old man in the Titans cap. Guessing the mic was in his cane since he handed it over to George on the sidewalk outside the hotel after he left the table."

I find him on the screen and sure enough, the cane is leaning against his table, angled toward me.

"I wasn't sure how Andrew would react when he saw me, but it was the best I could have hoped for," I say. It was a risk coming here, but it was clear six years ago that he felt like he owed me one so I was confident that sentiment would resurface. I just needed him to say it out loud, and he didn't let me down. I'm also sure Mr. Smith will interpret it the way I want him to. He won't think Andrew would help me just because he's a nice guy, he'll think Andrew has to because I've got something on him. Mr. Smith always thought I got dirt on Andrew Marshall but kept it for myself. Which is why it's so easy for him to believe I did the same with the info on Victor Connolly. He thinks I retrieved it from Amy Holder and kept it for myself instead of turning it over to him.

Renting the safe deposit box seems to be what threw my loyalty into doubt.

And a guilty verdict means the only thing keeping me from taking a nose dive into the nearest body of water is the contents of a 5 x 7-inch box locked behind a bank vault door.

"Is Connolly just sitting back and waiting or should we be worried about him?" I ask.

A few keystrokes and the screen changes. "So far he's sitting back, but I'm keeping a close eye on him."

I stare at a picture of the man in question. From my own research, I know he's sixty-seven, but he looks older in the images Devon has collected. What little bit of hair he has left is completely white, and years and years of sun exposure have not been kind to his skin. But while he may look like he's some aging old man, there's no doubt he's extremely dangerous.

Connolly's businesses are a mix of legitimate and illegitimate, as you would expect. You have to show how you can afford the fancy cars and private planes and houses scattered around the country. But the substantial income he claims on his tax return is nothing compared to what he brings in through nefarious means.

This is why Mr. Smith is going to such great lengths to make sure Victor Connolly remains a happy client.

And I don't need Mr. Smith making me the sacrificial lamb to Connolly if he starts to become unhappy.

So now Devon and I are on the offensive.

I knew Mr. Smith had more evidence against me, but I didn't want to wait until I was sitting across from those detectives to find out what it was, so I'm forcing him to burn it now. He thinks he's going to scare me by sharing the rest of what he has on me with the police, but I'm glad I'm flushing it out while I can still do something about it. While I still have a chance to run if I need to.

"How soon before you have Mr. Smith identified?" I ask.

The detour to Oxford had three purposes. First, I wanted to look a bit unhinged. Wanted Mr. Smith to feel like I was out of control and worry about where I would go next. It's harder to anticipate a person's next move when they are acting erratically.

Second, we needed to determine how clients get in touch with him. I knew Coach Mitch would only have one person to turn to when I came knocking. **Hello, King Harvest.**

And lastly, we still don't have Mr. Smith's true identity, and we need that more than anything else. By discovering the fan site and Mr. Smith's username, Devon is backing his way through the system, hoping to find something that will lead us to him.

"I'm close," is all he says and I don't push for more.

He pulls out the handwritten pages I left for him under the Twinkies yesterday. "It's not your fault he killed the woman and James."

I nod even though I should have known he'd go to those lengths and I should have said more to her that night before she left. Warned her in some way.

"You still think we should bail?"

He takes in a deep breath then lets it out while his eyes scan my face. "I'd rather bail and regroup than continue down a path that leads to you either being thrown in jail or killed."

I'm shaking my head before he finishes. "Bailing now doesn't save me from either of those options."

The ding from the computer behind him interrupts whatever he was going to say. An alert has him changing the screen to show he's finally gotten into the Atlanta PD system.

"I'll pull up the file on Amy Holder and we can see what they've got." A few images fill the screen, and Devon says, "According to the dates of these entries, these images were uploaded a month before you got to Lake Forbing, so they have to be the ones that supported the material witness warrant."

We both move closer to the screen to get a better look.

"This pic of you dragging Amy from the car is not your finest moment," he says.

"It couldn't be helped."

He continues to click through the images. "You do a really good job of angling yourself away from the camera. Did you know where your shadow was?"

George is rarely the one who follows me around during jobs unless it's a particularly important one like when I was on my own for the first time for the Coach Mitch job. Being my shadow has a lot of down time and I'm sure he's got more important things to do. Most times I can pick out who's watching me, but other times, like that night, I couldn't. It was too dark to see anything farther than three feet away.

Shaking my head, I say, "No. I mean, in most of these situations, I had a good guess of where they would be . . . where I would be if I was the one watching."

"Okay, here we go. New images were just added to her file, so let's see what Smith sent in. You must have really pissed him off. He didn't waste any time."

The note attached to the pics makes it look like it was sent by a detective from another department who stumbled on this critical piece of evidence while investigating another case. And while Devon could probably wipe it from their server right now, Mr. Smith would just resend it later. Best to leave it in play.

With a few keystrokes, we can see the latest piece of evidence against me.

It's a video.

He pushes play and there I am.

CHAPTER 21

Present Day

It's late afternoon when I pull into the motel parking lot. I see Ryan pacing back and forth in front of the open window of our room, phone to his ear. He ends his call then steps outside as soon as I'm parked.

Before I can shut off the engine, Ryan is at the car door.

"I kept trying to call you." I can tell he's agitated I ghosted him all day.

"I texted that I called the motel office earlier and got us another night," I say, then lean in to kiss him before he can respond. We stay tangled up for a few minutes, long enough to soothe any worries that there is a problem between us. "Sorry, that took longer than I thought it would."

There were decisions to be made and plans to put in place once we watched the video. I have to hand it to him, Mr. Smith has all but turned the key in the lock on my jail cell.

Ryan follows me into our room and watches as I pull out a change of clothes from my bag. "I talked to Rachel earlier," he says. "She'll be in Atlanta to-morrow afternoon. She was hoping we would get up early and head that way so you two would have a little time to prepare before the interview on Friday. Looks like it's around a four-to-five-hour drive."

"Okay." I move to my bag and grab a change of clothes. "I'm going to get cleaned up."

"Hungry?" he asks.

"Starved."

"There's a pizza place on the other side of the gas station next door. I'll run over there while you're showering." He steps close, giving me a quick kiss, then leaves the room.

Moving my stuff to the bathroom, I dig through my toiletries bag for some Advil. My headache from this morning is back. I can tell the bottle is empty before I pull it out.

I hesitate a second about whether to call Ryan and ask him to pick up some for me or to just head to the vending machine in the elevator corridor, where I know there is an assortment of single-dose packets like I bought this morning.

My head is pounding, so I opt for the vending machine since the pizza could take a while.

I'm still dressed, so all I need to do is slip into my shoes. I'm almost to my destination when the conversation drifting from the open space where the vending machines are makes me pause. It could be any of the guests staying here, but my gut tells me to be on alert.

I inch closer. Leaning against the brick wall behind me, I slow my breathing and close my eyes. I
invite my other senses to take over, hoping to pin-
point what has me feeling like this. Deep breath in,
deep breath out.

Two voices, both male. One much deeper than
the other.

I relax into the space. Open myself up to the
sounds only a few feet away. Words float my way
and it's easy to pick out the ones that hit home:
Atlanta and **Amy Holder.**

I slide my phone out of my back pocket and
text Ryan.

**Me: Stay at the restaurant until I tell you to
come back. Please don't ask questions**

I press send.

And then hear the familiar chime coming from
the same direction as the vending machines.

What. The. Hell.

The faint rumbling of voices continues as I watch
the small dots jump around as he replies. My ringer
is off so there's no sound once it's delivered.

Ryan: Ok let me know what you want me to do

"Fuck, something's got her spooked." Ryan's
voice fills the space and I freeze. They've moved a
little closer to me.

And then another voice I recognize. "Did she say what's wrong?"

George.

He's talking to George.

"No. I need to get back. I'll let you know when we get to Atlanta."

"And if she doesn't make it on time tomorrow?" George asks.

I take a deep breath. No, no, no. Not this.

"I'll let you know what I want to do. I don't like all that information out there like that."

"I'll wait to hear from you," George says. "And here, picked this up but couldn't get it to you before you left town."

I quietly take a few steps away, then hustle down the side of the building back to our room.

My phone vibrates in my hand, alerting me to an incoming call just as I'm opening the door. Ryan's picture fills the screen.

I don't answer until I'm inside. "Hey."

"Hey, what's happening? Are you okay?"

"Yeah, I'm fine. Freaked myself out." My voice is frazzled but I'm hoping it plays to what I'm telling him, not because of what I've discovered.

"I'm coming back. Hold on, I'll be right there," he says, and ends the call.

I shuck off my shoes and jeans, then move into the bathroom. I cut on the water in the shower before wrapping one of the thin, white towels around me. I give myself a moment to take several deep breaths in and out to slow my racing heart.

Then I hear the door opening.

"Evie!"

I poke my head out of the bathroom. "In here."

He's by my side in seconds. His arms pull me in and close around me like a vise. I force mine to do the same to him. "What happened?" If I didn't know who he had just been talking to, I would be flattered by his concern.

I squeeze my eyes closed and count to five. Another deep breath in, deep breath out.

"It's nothing, I swear. Heard something outside. Ended up being one of the janitors banging around out there."

Opening my eyes, I see our tight embrace reflected in the bathroom mirror behind him. And papers rolled up like a tube shoved in his back pocket. Those must be what George handed him.

I watch the mirror disappear as steam from the shower fills the tiny space. I count the seconds between the drops of water as they leak from the faucet.

Because I have to separate myself from this moment. Need to focus on something other than the desire to react to what I just heard. Need some space between him and me if only in my mind.

Ryan's mouth is next to my ear. "You okay?" His actions are exactly as they should be, and I mentally scroll through each and every moment we've shared, starting with the first one in the parking lot with my flat tire, scrutinizing them with the certainty of his involvement.

I nod, not trusting myself to speak.

He met with George. He talked to George with the same familiarity that I would.

There were so many times when it felt like Ryan was a whisper away from telling me every secret he'd ever had. He even talked openly about his business in Texas in the car. There were many times I teetered on the edge of confessing everything.

But he was playing me, while I was ready to risk everything for him.

The sorrow clouds my vision. My thoughts. Everything inside of me.

His hands slide up my body to my face. He pulls back so he can look at me. His eyes search mine as mine search his.

"It's not like you to get spooked," he whispers. He's right.

Did he study me the way I studied him? Was there a sheet that said **She enjoys sweet potato fries and two sugars in her coffee**?

"I've been fighting a terrible headache all day. Then I heard a loud noise and it got the best of me." I look toward the shower. "I better get in before I run out of hot water."

He runs his hands down my back once more, then steps away. "I gave the cashier an extra twenty to deliver the pizza to us, so it should be here by the time you get out."

I can't lock the door when he closes it behind him because that's not something his girlfriend would do. I step into the hot water, and it's the jolt I need. Like a punch in the face. It clears the haze but does nothing for the grief that has settled in my veins. I am gutted.

I give myself five minutes to mourn the possibility of us. Five minutes to grieve what could have been. Five minutes to destroy the idea that it was possible that I was the kind of girl who could live in a perfect house with a perfect guy on a perfect street.

And I remember this is not my world.

I'm just a ghost who drifted through for a bit of time.

When I'm back in the main room in fresh clothes and wet hair, Ryan is clearing off the small table for us to eat on. I was starving half an hour ago, and now the thought of food makes me want to throw up.

But I sit at the table and choke down a slice. I fill the silence with mindless chitchat. Because that's what his girlfriend would do.

"I'm worried you won't have enough time with Rachel to be prepared for Friday," he says after taking the empty boxes to the dumpster outside.

Those papers aren't in his back pocket anymore and I'm hoping they didn't get thrown away too.

"Rachel and I will have plenty of time. Promise."

I climb in the bed, burrowing deep in the covers. "It's cold in here. Can you turn the air down a bit?"

Ryan moves to the unit under the window to adjust the temperature.

He rummages around the room a few minutes then heads to the bathroom. It's not long before he's crawling into bed next to me. I let him pull me close. He doesn't speak and doesn't push for anything more. We're connected from our head to our feet, and I can feel the steady beat of his heart where it's pressed against my back. There are a few moments where I think he's gearing up to say something, but words never surface.

I replay the conversation between Ryan and George over and over and over.

"You seem distracted. Want to talk about what's on your mind?" The whispered question so close to my ear feels intimate. Like we're really in this together.

"I'm just tired."

He doesn't push for an answer, but instead runs his fingers through my hair just the way he knows I like. It's a while before either of us fall asleep.

CHAPTER 22

Present Day

'm up before the sun.

It took me forever to fall asleep last night, and when I finally did, I was restless. Ryan always sleeps hardest in that last hour before he wakes for the day, so this is the best opportunity to look for the papers he had when he came back from meeting George.

Ryan's grip on me has lessened during the night so it's easy to slip out of the bed without waking him. Crawling across the floor, I make my way to his bags. He's got the duffel with all his clothes, shoes, and toiletries, and a laptop bag for his work stuff. I've been through this bag a number of times, dug through the files on his computer, and checked his internet history, but other than the things I've already found for Mr. Smith, he's careful about what he leaves lying around.

Now I'm realizing it's because he knew I'd be looking. I only found what he wanted me to. So stupid.

But those papers George gave him should be here somewhere unless he read them and then threw them out with the pizza boxes.

The air unit under the window kicks back on and drowns out the sounds of his bag being unzipped. The laptop comes out first since it takes up the most room. There's a yellow legal pad he takes notes on while he talks to clients and a spiral-bound prospectus on some mutual fund I've heard him push on a few of the calls he's taken since we hit the road.

A stack of papers are tucked away in the inside pocket. I go through them, sheet by sheet, most of them relating to the financial services business, and I'm preparing myself for the possibility that they aren't here, until the edges curl up on the last few sheets in the pile as if its muscle memory has kicked in.

These were the ones that were rolled up.

Spreading them back open, it doesn't take me long to recognize what this is.

Alarm bells slam through my head.

This is the last batch of information I left for Mr. Smith. Devon had slipped it to me in that **People** magazine, and I had gone through it to decide what I wanted to turn over. The small handwritten note in blue ink in the bottom corner of the last page, where I tell him I will check the box again the next day, lets me know this is the original, not a copy, since all I had in my purse was a blue ink pen.

This shouldn't be here.

I turn around and take in Ryan's sleeping form and the puzzle in my head starts to rearrange. Even if I consider that Ryan is higher up the ladder than I am, he shouldn't have this. Not the originals like this. Not delivered to him by George. Not when it sounds like George picked them up from the mailbox and brought them directly here, to him.

The idea that Mr. Smith wanted this business for himself seemed like the most likely scenario, but what if it's more than that? There is no danger of me screwing up the hostile takeover of a business he already owns. No reason to keep me on a job that's not a job at all.

My mind races, tripping over theories and speculations and suspicions, while the air conditioner purrs and Ryan sleeps.

The meeting between Ryan and George yesterday confirmed a couple of things. George knows where we are because Ryan told him. And the way they interacted with each other spoke to a closeness that only forms over time.

I have been trying to put a face to Mr. Smith for years. Turning to look at Ryan three feet away, it's hard to believe he could be the boss I've grown to despise.

No. No, that's not right. He's too young. Timeline doesn't match up.

As I shove everything back in the bag the exact way I found it, I mentally scroll through every conversation with Mr. Smith.

The first time I talked to him was eight years ago. Ryan was still at LSU and has no connection to North Carolina.

Mr. Smith handed me off to Matt, who I dealt with solely over the next two years. I didn't speak to Mr. Smith again until after the Andrew Marshall job six years ago.

Six years ago.

Ryan's grandmother fell ill with cancer six years ago. Ryan stepped in to handle the trucking business—both the legal and illegal side—for his grandfather, so he could stay home to care for his wife, and eventually took over the business fully after he died not long after.

Was that all he took over?

No.

No.

Ryan is going to Atlanta with me where I'll talk to a bunch of cops. Would he open himself up like that?

And then I'm back at the Bernards' house in my mind. Seeing that small room where we answered every question asked of us. Where that detective learned Evie Porter was from Brookwood, Alabama. Because Ryan told them. **"Evie moved here from Brookwood, Alabama, a few months ago. She didn't know James."**

No, no, no.

And then Monday morning in the garage. Where Ryan lingered. And I ignored the 911 message from Devon. Because Ryan wasn't ready to let me go. I remember thinking, **Had I not lingered with Ryan in the garage, I would have seen Devon's text as soon as I received it. Those few minutes may have cost me a clean getaway.**

But wait. No. Mr. Smith responded to Mitch on that forum after we left Oxford. Ryan was driving. I think back on the moment I saw the message come across. I was in the passenger seat of my car. Ryan had just filled it up with gas and gone inside for more snacks. He was in the store while I was watching the conversation between Mr. Smith and Mitch.

The memory of the moment between Ryan and George boots up and I watch it again through a different lens. The familiarity is still there, same as I would have with George. But it's Ryan making the decisions. George deferring to him. George delivering the papers to him.

This job was a test. Testing my loyalty.

And shit, Ryan would have known immediately that I'd altered the information on his business before I turned it over. He has direct proof I wasn't doing the job I was sent to do. And I was worried about him losing his business to Mr. Smith.

I knew I would be watched closely.

What better way to watch me than when I'm sharing the same space?

No.

Not going there. Not yet.

While it's easy to jump to conclusions, it's also very dangerous to make assumptions.

I crawl back to my side of the bed and snatch my phone off the nightstand and pull up Instagram.

Scrolling through my feed, I stop on the Skimm's

post recapping the five biggest news stories of the day and comment: **That is breaking news! Too hot for me to handle! #OnTheRoadAgain #PartyOfOne**

It's a good chance Devon won't see this for a couple of hours, but I need him to know I'm out of here and leaving Ryan behind.

Once my comment loads, I grab my purse and keys, abandoning everything else. I had already planned to stop at Goodwill on my way out of town to get what I need going forward, so I'll just have to add a few more items to my shopping list.

The click of the motel door opening echoes through the room, but luckily Ryan doesn't stir. I'm in my car and pulling out of the parking lot within minutes. As soon as I hit the interstate, I dump the phone I've been using as Evie Porter in Lake Forbing, and thanks to the little black box from Devon, if there is a tracer in my car, it's not providing any information. Before, I wanted Mr. Smith to know where I was going, but not anymore.

Once I've been on the road about two hours, I stop to buy a prepaid phone and call Devon.

"Hey," I say, when it connects.

"What happened?" he asks.

I fill him in and we're both silent a few minutes. "You know what I'm thinking," I finally say, not wanting to voice out loud who I think Ryan really is.

"You know I'm thinking it too," he replies. "But no assumptions . . ."

"We only deal in facts," I say before he can. This has been our mantra.

I'm still in the parking lot of the store where I bought this phone, pacing the length of my car again and again. I tell myself it's because I'm stiff, but it's fear that's driving me.

"I'm back in Lake Forbing," Devon says. "I'll take care of my part, you take care of yours." Before I can end the call, he says, "I'm close on the message board. Keep that phone so if I need you I can get you since I'm guessing you don't have access to your Instagram account. The risk is low enough."

I'm not sure what parameters Devon uses to gauge the risk versus reward in these situations, but I trust him enough that I don't question his reasoning.

"Okay." I pause a moment, then add, "If it looks like things are not going to end like we hope tomorrow morning, haul ass. Drop what you're doing and disappear."

"L, you know I'm not abandoning you."

"Between Mr. Smith and the cops, we both know the chances of me walking away from this are slim. And there are other people to consider. Heather, for one, will need you."

"Same goes for you," he says. "It's never too late to bail. Just get up and start moving."

"I'll check in when I'm done today," I say, then end the call. This entire conversation felt so much like a good-bye that I couldn't bring myself to actually say it.

It's midafternoon when I pass the WELCOME TO EDEN sign. It was a long drive with only a stop to buy the burner phone to call Devon, and in Winston-Salem to buy some clothes at Goodwill.

My eyes drink in the town I once called home. Memories flood in so fast that I almost drown in them. The fast-food restaurant where I hung out with friends and the fabric store where Mama and I spent hours poring over new arrivals every week are still there, but those buildings have been ravaged by time and neglect. I turn on the road that runs in front of my high school, and it's almost physically impossible to breathe when I see the worn path through the grass between the side door and the parking lot that I traveled a thousand times.

The last time I was here feels like a lifetime ago.

It also feels like yesterday.

But as familiar as everything is, I am still a stranger here. There's no one I would call up and visit.

One last turn and I'm on my old street. I pull into the trailer park and get out without cutting the engine. I study each one of the single-wide mobile homes crammed into this space, comparing what they used to look like to now and remembering who called each of them home. I save the middle one on the left side for last.

I cringe when I think about how embarrassed

Mama would be for anyone to see it in this condition. Even though it wasn't much to look at when it was ours, she always made sure it was neat and clean and the narrow beds near the steps had flowers planted in them. Now they're full of weeds, and there's a blue tarp covering some damage to the roof and a broken-down truck up on blocks next to the door.

It hurts to remember the girl I once was. The one who called this place home. That girl was happy here. Really happy. Even when Mama got sick, that young, naive girl thought she could take care of her. Thought she could save her from dying.

But that little girl learned a lot in that trailer. She learned that no matter how hard you try, sometimes it's not enough. She learned the only person you could trust, the only person you could truly rely on, was yourself.

A woman peeking out from behind a curtain in the trailer closest to me reminds me I didn't drive all this way for a walk down memory lane.

There is one reason I came back to Eden.

Once I'm in my car, I turn around and hit the main road again, stopping at Sheetz to refuel and do a quick wardrobe change in the bathroom. Then it takes only a few minutes to get to the newer area of town, where the businesses sit in a long row behind plate-glass windows.

I park near Dr. Brown's office at the far end of the strip and make my way to the door.

"Can I help you?" the receptionist asks when I approach the counter.

"Yes, property management sent me over. We're checking the breakers in all the units. There was an electrical problem in the pet store last night, but thankfully someone was there to get it under control before it started a fire. Shouldn't take but a couple of minutes." I was lucky enough to find a uniform shirt and a pair of khakis at Goodwill that I could make work so I look the part.

"Oh!" she says, motioning me to pass through. "Of course, let me know if you need anything."

I give her a big smile then head toward the back of the office. Luckily, all the employees are with patients in the exam rooms so I go unnoticed as I slip inside the mechanical room. I bypass the electrical box, going straight for the main server and inserting the drive from my bag then running through the keystrokes Devon wrote down, guaranteeing the files are uploaded.

I'm out of the room in five minutes. Moving back to the reception area, I nod to the girl at the desk. "You're all good, enjoy your day."

I'm leaving Eden for the last time ten minutes later.

Calling Devon, I say, "It's done," the moment he answers.

"Sending you a screenshot," he says. "The Coach Mitch gamble paid off. We know who Smith is now."

My heart rate skyrockets and I pull over on the side of the road as I wait for the image to load.

And there he is. Even though the screen is tiny, his familiar face is all I can see. I stare at it longer than I should.

Finally, I put the phone back to my ear. "We deal in facts now," I say.

"Yes, we do." He pauses then says, "This doesn't have to change anything, L."

I swallow hard. "I know. Make the calls. I want to get through the cops first. Then I'll worry about the bank. If I can't shake the cops, the rest of it doesn't matter, so they are the priority right now."

"Okay. Remember what I said. It is never too late to bail. Just start walking."

I'm nodding even though he can't see me. "And you're handling things in Lake Forbing?"

"Already done. Got in the house without a problem. I'll tip the police off first thing in the morning," he says. "And the next river you pass, toss that phone in. Don't have it on you when you meet with the cops."

"Will do. I'll grab another one when I get to Atlanta so next time you hear from me should be after I'm done with those detectives. And if I can't call, you'll know . . ."

"Nope, no doomsday talk just yet. I'll wait to hear from you." And then Devon ends the call.

I stare at his image a few more minutes before deleting it.

Alias: Regina Hale—Six Months Ago

t's the first time I've been bored on a job. I'm in Decatur, Georgia, and the only thing I've been given was my new identity, a membership number for the local country club, and the name Amy Holder, along with a set of instructions:

Amy Holder is in possession of some extremely sensitive information regarding Victor Connolly and the Connolly family business. She is threatening to use the information against Victor in exchange for money. I cannot stress to you enough how crucial it is to retrieve this information before she can make good on her threat. You are being trusted with this job and confidentiality is imperative. Neither of us want to get on the bad side of a man like Victor Connolly. You are to watch

Amy Holder and learn everything about her. Do not engage until I tell you to but be ready to act at a moment's notice.

Like clockwork, Amy pushes through the double glass doors of the bar at 5:25 p.m. For the last two weeks, she has stayed home until around five in the evening, then she commutes a measly two miles to this country club, where she'll drown herself in vodka martinis until closing.

Amy is five foot seven with an athletic build and honey-blond hair that hits right below her shoulders. The makeup is light, the jewelry is nonexistent, and she rocks a perpetual resting-bitch face.

By the time she slips onto her favorite stool, a bartender with a name tag that reads Morris, in a pressed button-down shirt with the club's logo, delivers the first of many drinks with a warm smile and a cheerful hello. Devon has definitely gotten more comfortable in playing an active role over the last few years.

"Would you like to see a menu, Miss Holder?" he asks.

"Maybe a little later," she replies.

"Of course, just let me know when you're ready," he replies as he walks away.

This exchange is also a constant: same question, same answer. She won't ask for a menu, and he won't offer one again, but all it takes is a slight nod and her glass will be refilled within seconds.

I've been in and out of this bar for the last eleven days, but it's the third night in a row that I've settled in for the duration, not bothering to hide anymore. She sips her drink and ignores everyone around her. If she has a phone, she has not once taken it out and looked at it. There's not a single person here, myself included, who hasn't glanced at their phone at least once, even if it is just to check the time.

But not Amy.

Amy will sit at the bar and drink anywhere from four to six martinis, then she'll grab her purse and drive the short distance home, some nights swerving back and forth across the yellow line the entire way. She lives in a townhouse that is worth more than it should be because of its location. She'll wake up the next morning and start the whole process again.

And since there is no way to get inside her house without losing sight of her, hanging around this club is my only option.

From my place across the room, I track groups as they come and go just as I've done night after night. The bar area fills with members heading in from rounds of golf and tennis as they either celebrate or commiserate over the day's game. The restaurant caters to the families looking for a dinner out. Both areas are loud and chaotic.

This sitting around and waiting is getting to me.

Usually, I get a little lead time before a job starts, but within twenty-four hours of getting word from Mr. Smith, I was crossing the city limits into

Decatur. Because of the frantic nature of my arrival, I assumed I would be making contact immediately, but I have been instructed to do the exact opposite. And now two weeks have gone by and all I've done is watch her drink her dinner.

That doesn't mean I don't know what's happening here.

The reason I'm in a holding pattern is because someone else is working behind the scenes trying to make a deal with her to return the information on her own. Not that they are playing nice, but because it's the best way to make sure they get back everything she took.

The only thing protecting Amy right now is that she is still in possession of the blackmail material. And regardless of whether she turns it over willingly or I have to take it from her, the second it's out of her hands she'll feel the full wrath of Mr. Smith and the Connolly family.

And just as I was warned after the Tate job, I have no illusions that I am alone here. Amy Holder has become the number-one priority to Mr. Smith, so there will be nothing left to chance.

I move to the bar, choosing a stool three down from hers with a big open space between us, and signal for another glass of wine.

Devon sets it down in front of me and asks, "Would you like to see a menu?"

With a smile, I say, "No, thank you," and he moves off to help a group on the other side of the bar. Even though I'm not sure if I'll need him for this job, I've gotten to where I don't want to do a job without him. We've become an inseparable team.

"You're new here," Amy says.

I take a minute to glance around to see if she's talking to me. When it's clear she is, I answer, "Yes, just moved to town." I turn on my stool to face her, opening myself up to a conversation.

She scans me up and down, then turns back to her martini.

"I know what you're looking for, but you're not going to find it here." She swirls a finger in her drink and then brings her finger to her mouth, sucking the liquid off it. "You won't find it! Tell your people!"

I can't help but shrink back from her outburst.

Amy brings her glass to her lips and takes a deep drink, finishing it off, then waves the empty glass in the air. "You'll never, ever, ever find it!" She's loud enough that several heads turn her way.

She spins around to face me, gives me a big toothy grin, then turns back to the bar. "Gone," she shout-whispers.

I identified the guy who was sent to watch me watch her a few days ago. Older guy who stays in the back corner of the room, dressed like he's just finished a round of golf. I know there's a high probability he's sending Mr. Smith real-time updates on what is going down right now, so I have to tread carefully, since I was told not to engage her. I don't want to be taken off this job.

"I believe you have me mistaken for someone else. I don't know what you're talking about," I say, then turn back to face the bar, taking a sip of the wine in front of me. Mr. Smith will be pissed I'm the reason she's losing it.

Watching her in my peripheral vision, I see her shoulders deflate almost as if she's frustrated with me. I watch her for several seconds, then she beams when another cocktail lands in front of her. "Morris! My hero!" she squeals.

The crowd's interest in her dies down and the volume rises as the conversations around us resume.

I swivel just slightly in her direction so I can watch her a little more easily.

She notices I've turned and she follows suit. "The first time you showed up at the club was Monday before last at six seventeen p.m. You wore a light-blue tennis skirt and white sleeveless top. Hair pulled back. You ordered a vodka cranberry. The next night you got here at five forty-five p.m. wearing a floral shift dress. You had two glasses of Chardonnay." She's pointing the plastic drink stirrer at me while she rattles off the exact arrival time of each visit I've made here, including what I ate, drank, and wore, her volume increasing as she goes. "And every night, your midnight blue Lexus

SUV follows me home." She even recites the license plate number.

I'm glancing around the room, noticing we've attracted an audience again. My shadow in the back corner is openly staring at us. The only other time I have been confronted like this was by another drunk woman, Jenny Kingston. Images of her lying on the floor, blood pooling around her head, flood my memories, along with the question my boss asked me after: **What would you have done if she hadn't fallen on her own?** It's a question that has haunted me for eight years.

I have to try to salvage this situation. "I'm new to town and this seemed like the best place to meet people."

"I get it," she says. "I know they want it back, but we both know I'm dead if I turn it over."

I glance around the bar, looking for any cameras or mics so I can determine just how much Mr. Smith will hear about what went down tonight between us. There's nothing obvious, but I can't rule it out so I keep up the charade.

"I'm not sure what you're talking about, but if you need help, I can—"

"You're not here to help me. No one can help me. But I had no choice. I'd already be dead if I didn't take it." She doesn't give me time to respond but instead says, "Just go away already," before settling back into her cocktail.

I stay at the bar long enough to finish my wine

FIRST LIE WINS 343

and close out my tab, then I slide off the stool and walk out of the bar.

Once I'm in my car, I drive on autopilot to the small apartment that was set up for me. There's no doubt Mr. Smith has already heard about the scene we made in the bar. I don't think what happened tonight would be enough for him to pull me out, but he'll be watching closer than ever now.

———◆———

It's three days before I make my next move. I'm hiding across the street from her house, awaiting her arrival home. The second set of instructions came the morning after Amy confronted me at the country club. I was right. Mr. Smith was not happy with me.

Timetable moved up due to your inability to follow simple directions. Use whatever means necessary to locate and retrieve any digital device including cell phone, computers, tablets, hard drives, etc . . . If it can store digital information, take it from her. I shouldn't need to remind you how sensitive this information is and how you are to handle it.

We've thrown away any semblance of being sub-
tle and the warning there is clear—the information
I recover is for his eyes only or I'll find myself in the
same place Amy Holder has found herself. I'm not
to befriend her, get close to her, draw things out. I
am to take everything from her. Immediately.

Amy's headlights shine across the yard as she
swings into her narrow driveway, the right side
of her car barely missing the trash can. It's a five-
martini minimum night for sure.

The car cuts off but the driver's door doesn't open.

Minutes tick by and she's still not out of the car.
I wait until ten minutes pass before I leave my hiding spot and slowly walk down the driveway to
where she's parked. As soon as I get close enough
to the car, I see her slumped form draped over the
steering wheel.

Opening the driver's-side door, I catch her before
she falls out onto the concrete. I dig through her
purse to find her keys, shoving them in my pocket.
Grabbing Amy underneath her arms, I drag her
from the car and up the driveway. She loses one
shoe and then the other. I almost want to flip off
the camera I know is pointed at me, but I resist
and keep my body turned away from the street as
much as possible. It's slow and steady until we get
to the front door. Blessed silence meets us as I get
the door unlocked and open.

I don't stop moving until I get her to the couch.
Once she's lying down, I go back outside to grab

her shoes and purse, and take a moment to search her vehicle. It's as clean and empty as the day she drove it off the lot.

I start snooping around her house because, at this point, I wouldn't put it past Mr. Smith to have someone peeping through the windows to make sure I do. The house is as immaculate as her car. There is no technology here. There is a landline phone but no cell, computer, or tablet of any kind. And no chargers that would indicate the tech exists but is just not present. There is one television, but the only channels it receives come from the antenna attached to the top. I check all the usual hiding spots, but it is as if nothing past 1980 has ever entered this house.

I even search for notebooks or notes or scratches of paper in case she went the old-school route. Nothing.

I sit in a chair and watch her sleep for a little longer before finally calling it a night and letting myself out of her house.

———◆———

Amy relocated to a hotel in downtown Atlanta the day after I searched her house. That was four days ago. I'm in my car watching her stumble out of a corner bar the way she does when she's had at least four martinis.

I'm getting new instructions almost daily, since Amy's behavior is changing just as rapidly. The latest tells me Mr. Smith has lost all patience.

Amy is out of control. Bring her in immediately. Non-negotiable.

Bring her in immediately. This is new for me. And bring her in where? Do I grab her and wait for someone to approach me? Stuff her in my trunk? Mr. Smith is acting as erratically as she is. He is freaking out, and I have to wonder how much pressure he's getting from Victor Connolly to resolve this matter.

Hopping out of the car, I cross the street, maintaining a reasonable distance behind her.

Amy steps into the street as soon as the crosswalk turns green. Her bright-red coat billows behind her as she knocks into people not getting out of her way fast enough. She nearly trips on the curb when she gets to the other side.

She's making a complete spectacle of herself.

Ignoring the group of sightseers ahead of her, she barrels her way across the sidewalk in front of her hotel.

Amy pauses there, and I veer to the right so I'm off the street but not standing too close to her.

She's planted herself right in the way of foot traffic, and she's jostled by the pedestrians trying to move past her, spinning in a circle until she comes to a stop facing me. Her eyes lock on mine.

The recognition on her face is clear.

She raises her hand, pointing a finger at me. "You. What are **you** doing here? I thought I told you to go away."

I shrink back a few feet, edging toward the corner, but before I can slip away, she moves a little closer and yells, "You can go back and tell that cocksucker Smith to go fuck himself. He's not as clever as he thinks he is. He's been screwing over people for years and I've got all the details! I've got so much shit on him. More than he even knows!" A scowl stretches across her face, and then she flips me the bird before turning around and waltzing into the lobby of the hotel as if she didn't just lose it out on the street.

The shock of what she just said about Mr. Smith washes over my face, then I school my expression into the blank slate I've spent years perfecting, because I know I'm being watched right now. I scan the street, looking for the older guy Mr. Smith has planted here. This will be the first he hears that sensitive information she stole wasn't just from a client. He will, no doubt, be furious to learn this. He barely trusts me to see what she took on Victor Connolly, so there is no way he would have sent me on this job if he thought there was a possibility I would be retrieving information on him. The last thing he would want would be for me to recover something that could be used against him. Something **I** could use against him.

For years, I've been looking for information on him. Anything at all that will clue me in to who he really is. He's right to worry about what I would do if info about him came into my possession.

You do whatever you have to do to save yourself and the job. That piece of advice Mr. Smith gave me early on has stuck with me. It's the advice I let guide me on every job.

This job is far from over.

I follow her inside, sticking with the plan I'd made. It takes a few minutes to get to the door that leads to housekeeping. I find a bag in one of the supply closets that has a hotel maid's uniform stuffed inside. I change quickly, then pull my dark hair up in a tight bun. Digging through the bag, I find the mic and earpiece at the bottom. Once I have the mic clipped to the inside of the collar of my uniform and the earpiece pushed inside my ear, I'm ready to go.

Devon is usually against this type of tech since it's easy to pick up the frequency if you're close by, but there was no way to get around it. "I'm ready."

In the earpiece, I hear Devon say, "Good to start. Be careful." He got inside the building yesterday to hack into their system and is now working it from a van parked at the curb. He'll have one eye on me and the other on the hotel's security feed. The plan is to freeze the camera when an area I need to move through is empty, then he'll unfreeze it after I've passed through. I'll work my way through the hotel in stops and starts, invisible to the cameras above me.

The cleaning carts are pushed off to the side, where they wait for the graveyard shift to restock them, since all the rooms were cleaned hours ago. I grab the closest cart, shoving my black duffel into the space left for dirty linens, and call for an elevator.

"Elevator is empty. I'll wait for the hall to clear before I open the doors."

"Copy," I say.

The doors open and I push the cart inside, pressing the button for the fifth floor. When the elevator doors open, I move the cart out into the hall.

"Hold there," Devon says. "Amy has just gotten off the main elevator and is making her way to her room. We need her on that camera, so I'm not cutting it until she's inside."

I check my watch. "What's taking her so long? She should have already made it in."

My gaze bounces from one end of the hall to the other, praying no one decides to come out of their room right now. I don't want one single person mentioning the presence of a maid with a cart on this floor at this time of day.

"She's at her door. On her fifth try getting the key card in the slot."

"Good grief," I mumble.

"Okay, she's inside. You are good to go."

And I'm off, pushing the cart down the corridor then turning toward Amy's room when I get to the main hall.

Skidding to a stop in front of her door, I rap on the door and yell, "Housekeeping!"

It's less than a minute before Amy opens the door. I don't give her a chance to say anything, I just shove the cart through the door, backing her up with it, then let the door swing shut behind me.

CHAPTER 23

Present Day

I arrive at the Westin hotel in downtown Atlanta right on time. Rachel is waiting for me in the lobby, although I can tell she isn't happy I've cut it so close.

Since I was a no-show for the reservation made for me at the Candler Hotel, and I blew past the deadline set for me at the bank, I had to time my arrival just right.

"I wasn't sure you were going to make it," she says as I approach.

I spot the figure standing a few feet behind her. "I gave you my word I'd be here," I tell her.

"Can I talk to you?" Ryan asks as he moves closer to us.

Rachel says, "He called me and said you ditched him." I don't miss the tone or the raised eyebrow, but I ignore it.

I look at Rachel. "Our appointment starts in a few minutes, right?"

Rachel glances at her watch then motions for me to follow her to the elevator. "Ryan, let us get through this and then we'll figure the rest out, okay?"

She thinks we're having a simple lovers' quarrel. I don't correct her.

Ryan drops down in a chair in the lobby and watches us until the elevator doors close.

When we reach our floor, I push Ryan from my mind and focus on the task ahead of me.

"How'd you pull this off?" I ask Rachel. I'm honestly amazed she was able to move the meeting from the police station to one of the meeting rooms at this hotel. She's good, I have to give her that.

"We were unaware there was a warrant out, and we traveled all this way to answer their questions. We're here in good faith to put an end to this misunderstanding, so a visit to the police station was asking for too much."

I'm glad she's on my side for this but having seen the video I know the police received, they probably went along with her request so they don't spook me and risk me not showing.

"Remember," she says as we march down a hall where the meeting rooms are located. "Do not answer anything unless I give you permission. Do not offer anything extra."

I nod while she studies me. We're stopped outside of a door labeled Room 3.

"I was also going to tell you not to let your feelings show, but you have that down pat."

This actually gets a little smile out of me because God if she only knew.

She pushes open the door and I follow her inside. I was expecting a long table and chairs setup but this is cozier. It's a small room with a couch and two oversize chairs grouped around a coffee table next to a wall of floor-to-ceiling windows with an incredible view of the Atlanta skyline. "The key here is that we're cooperating and have nothing to hide," she says moving toward the center of the room. She registers my surprise at the room and adds, "I liked the optics. How can anything bad happen in such a warm, inviting space?"

There's a fresh pot of coffee and a plate of blueberry muffins in the center of the coffee table.

"You take that chair," Rachel says, pointing to the one on the left of the couch. "And I'll take this one. The detectives can snuggle together on the couch between us."

I settle in while she drops her briefcase on the floor next to the table.

"Not going to lie, I'm feeling underprepared. We haven't had a moment to talk about that day and how we are handling this."

Leaning back in my chair, I cross my legs and say, "I'm going to need you to trust me and follow my lead."

She watches me from across the coffee table and I know she has a ton of questions, but thankfully they remain unspoken. Before there's any time for awkward silence, there's a knock on the door.

"It's your show," Rachel says, then gets up to open the door, stepping aside so a man and a woman can enter the room. I stay in my spot, making them come to me for introductions and handshakes.

"I'm Detective Crofton and this is Detective West," the man says once they are standing in front of me.

From her spot in front of the other chair, Rachel motions to the couch and invites them to have a seat. Detective West glances at the couch, then at Rachel, and finally at me. She's realizing she won't be able to look at us both at the same time.

They hesitate a few seconds but eventually take seats on the couch. It takes another minute or so of them repositioning themselves and trying to get comfortable before they seem ready to begin.

Detective West is a reed-thin white woman dressed in what has probably been her uniform of the last decade: white shirt, black blazer, black pants. A simple gold band on her left ring finger is the only piece of jewelry she's wearing. She's got those lines around her mouth that let me know she loves to pull on a cigarette. Detective Crofton is her exact opposite. He is a tall Black man and was probably a linebacker in his former life given his size. His shirt has a blue paisley pattern and the tight cinch of the belt holding his tan pants up shows he's recently lost some weight around the waist. There's a simple gold chain with a cross hanging around his neck.

FIRST LIE WINS 355

And the peek I got of his socks right before he sat down tells me he has a sense of humor. Cats riding unicorns on a pale pink background.

And then I wonder if this is a true representation of them.

Or are they like me? Hiding behind a mask.

Because I was deliberate when I dressed this morning, striving to show them the image of me I wanted them to see. Plain white tee with jeans. Zero makeup and hair pulled back in a ponytail. I look easily five years younger than I really am.

"Can I offer either of you some coffee? A muffin?" Rachel asks.

Detective Crofton pats his midsection. "Not me. Strict orders to lose twenty pounds and I'm still five from my goal."

Detective West pulls a small notebook out of her bag and flips it open. "Let's get started," she says, ignoring the offer of refreshments while Detective Crofton pulls out a small recorder and presses the red circular button on top. Detective West says in a deep, scratchy voice, "Detectives West and Crofton questioning the material witness, Evelyn Porter, in the death of Amy Holder." She adds the date, location, and time before meeting my gaze.

Rachel holds a hand up. "I would like it on record that Amy Holder's death was ruled an accident. And that we are here cooperating with officials to clear my client, Evelyn Porter, of any part in what happened to Miss Holder."

"Your note is on record," Detective West says. Then she turns to me. "Why were you living under the identity of Regina Hale in Decatur, Georgia, at the time Amy Holder died?" she asks.

Well, we're getting right to it. Forcing Mr. Smith's hand ensured he'd give them everything he could to bring me down. I look at Rachel and she gives me a small shrug, reminding me it is indeed my show.

"I was in a very toxic relationship and moved to put some distance between me and my ex. He didn't want me to leave, and I was afraid he'd come after me. I went to the police, but the only thing they were willing to do was give me a restraining order, and we all know how ineffective those are. So I used a fake name hoping he wouldn't find me."

This gives them pause. Rachel's left eyebrow raises just slightly, as if she's impressed with the answer.

"Where were you living when this happened?" Detective West asks.

"Brookwood, Alabama."

My boss went to great lengths to make me Evelyn Porter, lifelong resident of Brookwood, Alabama, so I'm putting it to work.

"We'll need to call and check out that story with the Brookwood Police Department," Detective Crofton says in a quiet voice.

I nod. "Of course. My ex-boyfriend's name is Justin Burns. His brother is on the force there. His name is Captain Ray Burns."

Detective West scratches the information onto

her notepad. If they did call, they will learn there is a Captain Ray Burns and he does have a brother, Justin, close to my age. Justin has a record too. A couple of DWIs and a disturbing the peace when the neighbors called the cops on him and his girl-friend fighting in the front yard.

If they don't find a record of his altercation with me, they won't assume it didn't happen . . . they'll assume Justin's brother was able to keep that one off his record.

The first lie wins.

I am nothing if not prepared.

Detective West seems to be the one in charge of asking the questions, and even though my an-swers so far seem to have taken a bit of wind out of her sails, she presses on. "How did you know Amy Holder?"

"We were both members of the Oak Creek Country Club," I answer.

She checks off something in her notebook, as if she's going down a list of predetermined questions. "There was no memorial service or funeral for Amy Holder. She was an only child and was not married, nor did she have any children. Are you aware of any family or friends she may have had?"

Rachel sits forward in her chair. "We're not here to answer questions about Miss Holder's life. We were told you had very specific evidence that my client was at the scene. Can we cut right to that, please?"

Detective West shuffles through the papers in her lap. "We're getting to that, Miss Murray," she says to Rachel, then turns back to look at me. "When was the last time you saw Amy Holder?"

Here we go. I learned a long time ago to stick to the truth as closely as possible. "I moved away from Decatur in early September, and I know I saw her before I moved but I can't tell you the date." In fact, you can tell the truth if you word it the right way, using the right intonation. They will take **I can't tell you the date** as I can't remember it because of the tone I used instead of the truth, which is **I can't tell you the date** because it would incriminate me.

"At six twelve p.m. on August twenty-seventh, Amy Holder entered the American hotel. Twenty-seven minutes later, her room was engulfed in flames," she says, her voice flat. "Have you ever been in that hotel?"

"I've eaten in the restaurant located inside the hotel." Which is true.

Detective Crofton pulls out an iPad. He lays it in the middle of the coffee table, and Rachel and I both lean in to see what's on the screen. He pushes the play button while Detective West says, "This is the security feed of Miss Holder entering the hotel prior to her death."

We all watch the grainy video of Amy shoving past a family of four as she crosses the street, then getting bumped by a guy who was looking at his phone instead of watching where he was going, which causes her to spin around. That red coat makes her easy to pick out, especially as she waves her arms around and throws me the bird. From this angle, I am in the background and slightly out of focus.

The video finishes playing and Detective West looks at me. The screen is frozen, and I'm just barely visible in the corner of the frame. "Does this jog your memory, Miss Porter?"

Before I have a chance to say anything, Rachel answers for me. "Are you insinuating that blurry figure in the back is my client? Half of the white women in the state of Georgia have brown hair. That could be any one of them." She leans forward and presses the button to replay the video. "What I see is a woman who is clearly intoxicated. Miss Holder was a known smoker who died in a fire that was the result of smoking in her bed while drunk. If you have something that implies Miss Porter had anything to do with the death of Amy Holder, and for God's sake, an actual picture that looks anything like my client, we'd like to see it."

Okay, damn, Rachel. I'm impressed.

Detective Crofton flicks the screen to the next video. "This was taken by an eyewitness."

Downtown Atlanta is not a particularly busy hot spot during the week, although it can get pretty crowded on the weekends. Devon tracked down every piece of video of that day, from security cameras to videos on social media, that either tagged that location or a nearby business. We only learned of the existence of this video less than forty-eight hours ago, so I'm guessing the "eyewitness" and I share the same boss.

The angle is directly even with Amy's room, taken from the building across the street, so there is a straight, unobstructed view, unlike the real eyewitnesses on the ground, who had to aim their cameras up and only caught a sliver of the room in question once the smoke started to pour out of the balcony window.

The video opens to the camera panning the building until it stops on the open balcony doors of Amy's room. The balcony railing is a solid structure, so you can only see the top half of the room, the bed not quite making the cut.

There's audio, but Devon and I believe it was added later so it wouldn't seem odd that this video just happens to capture me in the moment it does.

Detective Crofton turns up the volume and we hear the guy's voice.

"Hot maid alert! Maybe we'll get turndown service."

And then there I am, dressed in the hotel's housekeeping uniform. I'm deep in the room but in plain sight through the open balcony doors. I'm looking down at where the bed would be if you could see it through the balcony wall. And it's a very clear image of me, unlike the one we just viewed.

I remember that moment clearly. I had just pulled the box of matches from my bag and was about to run one across the striker. It was the moment right before the bed went up in flames. A few seconds pass and the memory comes to life on the small screen, and then I'm obscured from view as thick plumes of black smoke overtake the room.

CHAPTER 24

Present Day

remain calm and don't let any emotion show, which is easy since this is not the first time I've seen this video.

Okay, this is it.

Both of the detectives are looking at me expectantly.

"That's Lucca Marino," I say after a few quiet seconds.

The two detectives look at each other, then back to me.

Detective Crofton asks, "Lucca Marino?"

"Yes, the woman in that video is Lucca Marino."

I spent years and years protecting the identity of Lucca Marino. Making sure I could go back there and be that girl. I've already bought the land to build the dream house Mama and I planned. Already have the landscaping plans for the garden Mama would have loved. But when that name was threatened, I realized it was just that. A name. I spent years protecting the idea of Lucca Marino, but I'm no longer that naive little girl. While it was hard to finally make the decision to let her go, the truth is she's been gone a long time. I don't need to be Lucca Marino to keep the memory of Mama alive. Or to do the things Mama would have wanted me to do.

All eyes are on me, including Rachel.

"Let me get this straight. You're saying that's not you," Detective West says.

My eyebrows raise and my mouth drops open. And then I tilt my head and give them a quizzical look. "The woman in that hotel room is Lucca Marino. I don't know how else I can say it." They could hook me up to a lie detector and I'd pass with flying colors.

Rachel breaks in. "My client is referring to a woman who recently spent time in Lake Forbing, Louisiana. She was in a car accident a week ago and did not survive."

I nod and add, "Lucca lived here when Amy died. She knew Amy."

"Do you know her connection to Amy Holder?" Detective West asks. She has pulled out her laptop and is presumably doing a search on Lucca Marino.

"Again," Rachel says. "We're not here to answer questions about Miss Holder's associates."

I hold a hand up and say, "It's okay, Rachel. I can answer this." I've got to frame this just right. "Amy was mixed up with some bad people. Lucca was a part of that. That's all I can tell you." Again, it's all in the tone.

They hand me a few more pictures, images I

already knew they had, including the one of me dragging Amy from her car to her house.

I look them over and shrug. "The person in all these images is Lucca Marino."

Detective West is engrossed in the information she has pulled up on the screen. Detective Crofton leans in closer and mumbles, "The resemblance is striking."

Guessing they found her picture, I lean to the side and glance at her screen. Yep, it's the one from James's mother's Facebook post about that stupid soup. She's got her hair pulled back, no makeup, jeans, and a plain tee. We could be twins. Mr. Smith may be regretting finding such a perfect match.

By now Detective West should also be pulling up records that Devon created, which will show Lucca Marino rented an apartment in downtown Atlanta in the time frame around Amy's death. For good measure, there will also be a couple of parking tickets for a vehicle registered in that name down the street from where Amy lived, proving she had been in that area.

When Devon and I parted ways in Nashville, I drove to North Carolina, but Devon went back to Louisiana. When these detectives call the Lake Forbing police and ask about Lucca Marino and her time there, they will be told about the file folder full of pics and information on Amy Holder discovered in a forgotten bag in James's room. The bag Devon planted there. He also called the police, as one of the helpful church volunteers, alerting them there was one more personal effect of Lucca Marino to add to the others they'd collected to ensure they had it in their possession.

"Why would Lucca Marino follow you to Louisiana?" Detective West asks.

I shrug. "That's not something I can answer."

I'm not here to solve their crime, I'm only here to ensure they look in the direction I want them to.

My boss worked really hard to find someone who looked just like me so she could assume my identity and make it hers. He splashed her all over social media and made sure she was the talk of the town. He locked it up tight, covering all the bases. And then he killed her off.

Killing her off also made it impossible for them to question her, so there's no one to go against what I'm saying to the detectives today.

Mr. Smith thought he was just making it difficult for me to one day go back to my real identity, but yesterday I put the final nail in the coffin, so to speak. Thanks to the uniform from Goodwill and my last stop in Eden, the woman's dental records now match a set in a dentist's office in Eden, North Carolina, under the name Lucca Marino, making the ID of her body complete.

If I'm losing Lucca Marino forever, it's going to be worth it.

The two detectives are lost to the computer screen while Rachel eyes me from across the table. I stare right back at her.

"Detectives," she finally says, "we've come all this way, and yet there's absolutely nothing connecting my client to the death of Amy Holder. Now unless there's something else . . ."

"We will check into this new information. But to make sure we cover everything we need from you, can you tell us where you were the night of August twenty-seventh?" They're not ready to pull the plug on this yet.

I relax in my chair. Calm. Controlled.

"I looked back at my calendar after I learned from the police in Lake Forbing there was a warrant out for me, so I could see where I was when Amy died. I went to a friend's house that night for dinner. He and his wife just had a baby and they invited me over to see him."

The only lie in my response was the date of the dinner. That dinner took place the week before.

Detective West has her pen poised over her notebook. "Can you give us the name and number of who you dined with that evening?"

"Yes, of course. His name is Tyron Nichols."

Detective Crofton's head pops up. "Tyron Nichols who plays for the Falcons?"

I smile. "Yes, he's an old friend."

Another truth.

Holding up my phone, I say, "I told him I had an appointment with you this morning. He said to call if you need to verify anything with him. Would you like me to get him on the line? I know he'd rather me not give out his private number if it can be helped."

Detective Crofton jumps at the chance to talk to one of the best-known players on the Atlanta Falcons.

I decide to FaceTime him because seeing is believing.

Tyron appears on the screen. He's sitting in his chair in his home office. On the wall behind him are framed prints, articles, and jerseys depicting his time playing football in high school in Central Florida, then later at Ole Miss under Coach Mitch Cameron, and then his rise to the NFL. He's come a long way from that naive eighteen-year-old kid whose biggest dream was a full-ride scholarship to play college football in the hopes of one day being able to give his family a better life.

"Hey, girl," he says in his big booming voice.

"Hey, Tyron. Do you have a sec to talk to these detectives?" I roll my eyes for good measure.

"Sure, put 'em on."

I hand my phone to Detective Crofton, who looks absolutely giddy. "Yes, hello, Mr. Nichols. I'm Detective Crofton with the Atlanta PD. We need to verify Miss Porter's whereabouts the night of August twenty-seventh. She says she was at your home that evening."

I sit back in my chair and find Rachel staring at me again. I give her a small smile.

"Of course," Tyron says. "She was here that night. It was the week of our home game against the Saints. During the season, Tuesday nights are the only nights I'm home for dinner, so that was the best time for her to come over and see our son."

Detective Crofton is satisfied but Detective West is less starstruck and has another question. "What time did Miss Porter arrive and depart from your home that night?"

"I picked her up after I left the practice facility, which would have been around five. She stayed pretty late since we haven't seen each other in a while. Her and my wife got into a bottle of wine sometime around nine or ten, I guess?" He lets out a loud laugh. "And then, of course, they had to break out the karaoke machine. Lord, those two think they can sing."

Locked up tight.

Detective Crofton says, "Thank you. We've got everything we need. We appreciate your cooperation."

"Sure, anytime," Tyron says.

Detective Crofton hands the phone back to me and I look at Tyron on the screen. "Thanks for clearing that up."

He laughs. "No problem. You're coming by for dinner since you're in town, right? You won't believe how big Jayden has gotten."

"Of course! I'll call you when I leave here and we'll make a plan."

I end the call and turn my attention to the detectives.

They are looking at me, then they look at each other, sharing a silent communication.

Detective West closes her notebook. "I think that covers everything we have for today. If we have any further questions for Miss Porter, we'll be in touch."

It only takes a few seconds for them to pack their belongings and leave the meeting room.

Rachel and I are still sitting across from each other.

"You didn't know who Lucca Marino was when she first showed up with James at the Derby party," she says.

I shake my head. "If you remember correctly, I mentioned he showed up with a woman. I didn't comment on whether or not I knew her."

This is why I tell the truth as often as I can.

Rachel gets up from her chair and smooths down her skirt. "Well, this seems like it's all wrapped up in a neat little bow."

I shrug. "I'm just relieved it's over." It's not over. Not for me. While I've dealt with one of the threats against me, it's the other one that poses the greatest danger.

She grabs her briefcase and heads toward the door but doesn't open it. "Yes, me too. I'd hate to think you had anything to do with that woman's death."

Looking right at her, I say, "If there's one thing you can believe to be true, Lucca Marino was the woman in the room with her that day."

We watch each other for a few seconds, then she slips out of the room without another word.

While Rachel gets to walk away from here

without a thought, I'm facing a different situation. My departure won't be as smooth as my arrival.

I pull the new clean phone from my bag and call Devon once I'm out in the hall.

"I'm clear with the police," I say, as soon as it connects.

"Good," he says. "Now let's handle the other problem."

"Ryan was here when I arrived. I need him gone. Can you help with that?"

I can hear the familiar clicking sound that means he's hammering away on his keyboard. "What's he wearing today?"

The image of him forms in my head. "Jeans. Blue Oxford button-down."

"Okay, I'll call the hotel security and report him for suspicious behavior. It won't stick for long but should probably give you enough time to get out of the building. Switch to the Bluetooth earpiece. I want to be on the line with you."

I dig the small flesh-colored ear bud that Devon designed out of my bag and sync it to the phone. I pull my hair out of the ponytail and slide the earpiece inside my right ear. It matches my skin tone and having it hidden behind the curtain of my hair should make it hard to spot.

I shove the phone in my back pocket and head out into the hall. The fact that Devon has insisted I keep this line open when I'm walking into the lion's den hits me hard. He's making himself vulnerable right now for me.

"In case I can't say it later, thank you for everything. Thank you for being my friend."

He clears his throat. "We're not doing that shit right now. Head in the game. Just start walking if you need to. It's never too late to bail."

I push the metal bar at the end of the hall that leads to the stairwell. The concrete room is damp and dark and my voice echoes off the walls. "I'm headed down."

When I get to the lobby level, I push open the door slowly and peek out just in time to see two uniformed hotel security guards approach Ryan. They move closer to him, saying words I can't hear while he glances around the big area. They motion to him to follow them, but he argues, still paying more attention to the elevators than the men in front of him.

They grab him, one on each side, and he momentarily seems to put up a fight before relaxing in their hold. As they escort him away, he throws one last look behind him.

As soon as he's gone, I slip out of the stairwell and whisper, "Moving to the exit."

"I'm tapped into the street cams so I'll see you as soon as you clear the doors."

The closest exit is a door that lets out on the side street. I'm steps away when I hear, "Hey, Lucca."

I spin around and freeze when I see who it is.

"Fancy seeing you here, George."

"Get him on the street," Devon says in my ear. "I don't have eyes on you in there."

"You shouldn't be surprised since you stood me up yesterday," he says.

I nod toward the door to let him know we're taking this outside. He nods back as if he's good with it.

"Gotcha. Start walking north to the intersection," Devon tells me.

Even though I can't see the cameras, I feel some relief that someone else in the world is watching out for me, even if there isn't too much he can do for me right now.

"You're plan B if the detectives strike out, right?" It takes everything in me to keep my voice strong and steady.

George laughs. "I was supposed to be plan A. If you just gave him what he wanted, you wouldn't have had to bother with those cops."

I shrug and look at him as he walks beside me. "Until next time I piss him off. He'd just pull the card out again. I mean, there's no statute of limitations on murder."

"Maybe you should have thought about that before you lit that match," he says quietly.

"Ryan has left the hotel." Devon again.

I take a deep breath and let it out slowly. Then one more. "My regrets are long, and I'll have to live with the things I've done." And then I meet his gaze. "You don't have to do this."

We stop a few feet from the crosswalk and he stares at me, his eyes roaming my face. "I don't want to do this. But I have to get what's in that safe deposit box. We both know that's the only option right now. My hands are tied, Lucca. You haven't left me any other choice."

"And then what?" I whisper.

His hands go to his hips and he steps away from me, his eyes sweeping the streets. He turns back to me. "Maybe I'll be distracted while I check what's in the box. Maybe I won't see that you disappeared."

He wants me to think he'll let me go. And he might right now, but it wouldn't be long before I see him over my shoulder.

The light flashes that we're clear to cross the street and we walk the next two blocks in silence, until we're standing in front of the bank.

"If you were gonna walk, now is the time," Devon says in my ear. "Once you go inside, there's no turning back."

George starts up the steps to the entrance of the bank while I'm frozen.

"You coming?" he asks.

I shake it off and follow him instead. Walking away was never an option.

Alias: Regina Hale—Six Months Ago

The smell of sulfur stings my nose as the match flame comes to life. I hold it steady for a second or so to make sure it's going to stay lit, then throw it on the bed. Flames stretch and grow as it feeds off the synthetic fibers of the comforter and really take hold once it latches on to the bright red coat.

Throwing the last of Amy's belongings into the black duffel bag, I take one last look around the room to make sure I got everything, then toss the bag back into the housekeeping cart. Flames shoot up, and thick black smoke fills the room. That's my cue to go.

I pull the hotel room door open and push the cart into the hall, straight to the service elevator that is waiting. Once I'm back on the ground floor, Devon is there waiting for me. I pull out the bag, then hand off the cart to him. We don't speak when we part ways, him going through the parking garage to exit on the other side of the block while I move through the kitchens to the door that lets out onto a narrow alley on the side of the hotel.

I unlock my car and sink into the driver's seat. My hands shake as I pull out my phone and tap in the number I have for emergencies.

Mr. Smith answers on the first ring.

"What the fuck happened?" He's already heard about the fire.

I let out a shaky breath I'm hoping he can hear. "When I entered her room, she was already in the bed. She was extremely intoxicated and had a lit cigarette dangling from her mouth. I approached her with a syringe of Rohypnol but she became violent the second I was near the bed. The cigarette fell out of her mouth and landed on the bedspread. There was an empty bottle of wine next to her, but the contents must have soaked into the bedding, because the entire bed was engulfed in flames within seconds. I reached for her but she . . . was already on fire. Her clothes . . ." My voice cracks and I shudder out a moan. "It was horrific. And so fast. She was just . . . engulfed in flames." I sound frantic. Scared. My voice is trembling.

He's quiet on the other end. "Was there anything of use in her room?" he finally asks.

"I don't know. I was going to look after I had her subdued but had to leave the moment the fire alarm sounded," I answer quickly. "I wasn't able to recover anything."

"You didn't take anything with you?"

"No. Nothing." I'd stuffed the black bag under my jacket, so there's no reason anyone should have seen me with it.

I wait for a response or another question, but there's only silence. Finally, he says, "I understand she hurled a threat at you on the sidewalk in front of the hotel. One that involved me."

"She was completely intoxicated. Acting crazy," I tell him, but don't deny what she said.

"It would be very convenient for you to come into possession of something that could be used against me and tell me you didn't." There's a chill in his voice I've never heard before.

With a shaky voice, I answer, "I don't know what she had on you. I didn't find anything at her home, in her car, or in that hotel room. If she had it in there with her, it is nothing but ashes at this point."

Silence. Silence that lasts forever.

What feels like an eternity later, he says, "We'll be in touch." Then he ends the call.

I lay my head on the steering wheel and take a deep breath. My heart pounds. My hand fumbles as I attempt to turn the key in the ignition. It takes a few minutes, but I finally get the car into drive, and I'm pulling away as more and more fire trucks arrive.

Two blocks away, I find a parking spot in front of a Wells Fargo bank and head inside.

CHAPTER 25

Present Day

Once we've entered the bank, we move to the desk where I will sign in to get inside the vault.

"Hi, how can I help you?" the woman asks.

I give her a smile I don't feel. "Hi, I need to get into my box."

"Of course! Box number and name?"

"Regina Hale. Box number 3291." I pull out the ID I used in my last identity and the small key I've kept stashed away for months. She opens the ledger to the page for my box and I sign underneath the last—and only—time I've accessed this box. The day it was opened.

"You've got company outside. He just arrived. Standing near the steps," I hear Devon whisper through the earpiece.

I let out a slow, deep breath while George and I follow the bank attendant through the vault and into a private room, where the walls are lined with little brass doors and a large table sits in the middle.

She slides her key into one slot while I slide my key into the other one. We turn it at the same time.

Once the door pops open, she says, "Feel free to put your drawer on the table and take all the time you need." Then she leaves, shutting the door behind her. It's silent except for the clock on the wall. **Tick, tick, tick.** The room feels like it's closing in on me.

George reaches inside the box and pulls the drawer out, the contents still hidden beneath the closed lid. He sets it on the table.

He stares at me. Five seconds. Then ten. We both know there is no going back to the way things were after this. I can see a touch of sadness and maybe even a little regret in his gaze, but I refuse to let any of my emotions show. Finally, he returns his attention to the box in front of him. Slowly, he pulls the lid off.

The only thing inside is a small, white origami swan.

A look of confusion flashes across his face for one second, then two.

The confusion shifts to anger. An anger so consuming that it feels like it sucks the air out of the room. His eyes narrow and his brows snap together. His jaw clenches.

Tick, tick, tick.

"I guess I don't need to call you George anymore," I say, if only to drown out the clock.

He picks up the swan by one of the little wings and twirls it around. Then he takes his time, slowly opening it up, verifying that the paper is blank. There's no question that there is no information on either him or Victor Connolly in this box.

I was prepared for a lot of different reactions, but the unrelenting attention on the empty box wasn't one of them. "I used to think you picked Mr. Smith because you were a big Matrix fan or lacked imagination, but you are literally Mr. Smith. Mr. Christopher Smith. Pretty ingenious, actually. Your name is already one of the most generic names out there." I'm rambling.

A laugh escapes him but there's no humor behind it.

He finally faces me, the unfolded paper still in his hand. One step, then two. Each step he takes toward me, I take a step back.

The paper slips from his hand and floats to the floor.

Another step forward.

Another step I take back.

"When did you figure it out?"

"Figure out that my boss and my delivery guy were the same person? Figure out your real name? Yesterday afternoon," I answer.

He nods to the open safe deposit box. "But this has been waiting for me for much longer."

I nod.

"While I'm impressed you were able to discover what so many others have tried and failed to in the past, you knowing my name doesn't change a single thing." There is an edge to his voice that tells me it's taking everything in him to remain in control. "Where is the information Amy Holder stole from me? You left that hotel just as her room went up in flames, and this was your first stop. Don't lie to me again and say you didn't keep it for yourself." He glances to the hundred or so other boxes lining the walls, and I can see what he's thinking, that I've got more than one box and it could still be close by.

"Oh, I got what Amy took, I just didn't leave it here," I say, gesturing to the other side of the room. "But I knew you would think I did. That was one of the many lessons you taught me: **It's hard to get caught if you aren't in possession of what you stole when they catch you.**"

We're only inches apart now that my back is against the wall. The metal handles of the boxes behind me are digging into my skin. I use the pain to help focus. I may be at his mercy in this room, but there is a crowd on the other side of this door. It won't be easy for him to walk out of here without me, since the woman who let us in is waiting to lock the box back up.

"You failed a job for your own benefit."

"You're assuming I failed. That job was successful, you just didn't understand what the end goal was." I'm throwing his words back in his face, and from the look he is giving me, I know I'd be dead if we were anywhere other than where we are.

He crosses his arms. "It seems we are more alike

than you would want to admit. Instead of completing the job you were hired to do, you took advantage of the situation."

The words hit their mark, but I can't let him get in my head. "I've learned . . . so much from you over the years. But probably the most important thing I learned was—**Do whatever I must to save myself and the job.** Those are words I worked very hard to live up to."

"You've come a long way since that trailer park in North Carolina. I had high hopes for you, but what a disappointment you turned out to be," he sneers at me.

"I was your best asset and we both know it. You know nothing about disappointments."

He's leaning over me, forcing me to tilt my head back to see his face. "How long have you been planning to betray me?"

"Four years," I answer, without bothering to correct him. "Only half as long as you have been planning to betray me."

I can tell he's thinking back, trying to determine what happened four years ago that would make me turn on him.

Finally he says, "The Tate job."

I nod. "The Tate job."

He leans back and spreads his arms out. "Are you going to get to the point of all this? I'm assuming there is a reason for this little stunt."

"Amy told you she had information on Victor

Connolly and the crimes his family has committed, but what she really had was information that shows **you'd** been double-crossing **them** for years. Not a good idea to screw over one of the biggest crime families on the East Coast. She had it all: wire transfers, documents, and communications that show you've been skimming money, selling their secrets, and using information to your benefit instead of theirs. You've made them think you are protecting them when in reality you're their biggest threat. But it was useless to have blackmail on you when I didn't know your real name, Christopher."

All humor has been wiped from his face. "Cut the bullshit. What do you want, Lucca?"

"Absolutely nothing. And it's Miss Porter now. I've expended all the energy that I care to on you. This is just a friendly warning, since we go back so far. You have some old friends waiting for you outside. We really shouldn't keep them waiting any longer." I stare at him two seconds, then three, before I add, "Did you think I wouldn't have a contingency plan in place?"

One eyebrow raises as he stares at me. He's always been good at wielding silence like a weapon, and this moment is no different.

"Today doesn't end the way you think it does," he says, his face just inches from mine. "You better look over your shoulder every chance you get, because I promise you one day I will be there."

"You've already taken the one thing I've cared

about. Lucca Marino is gone, dead and buried. There's nothing left for you to hold over me."

He moves away from me and it takes everything in me not to collapse on the floor. He throws the door open and it slams against the wall.

Just before he leaves the vault, I say, "Don't get sentimental now. It's just business."

He's on his phone the second he hits the bank lobby. The woman who let us in the room approaches me but I wave her off. "We don't need the box any longer. The key is still in it."

"No problem, Mrs. Hale, I just need you to sign the closing documents . . ."

I ignore her and follow him out of the bank and see the exact moment he spots Victor Connolly and several members of the Connolly family waiting on the steps outside. He hesitates a few seconds then ends his call, sliding his phone in his back pocket. He seems to stand a bit taller before walking out to face the man he has stolen millions from. He doesn't look back at me once.

He's ushered into the back of the SUV, while Victor Connolly nods at me before getting into the front passenger seat. We had all the information Amy had collected sent to his hotel room last night with the promise of delivering the man who betrayed him today. I do believe Mr. Smith has probably gotten himself out of a lot of bad spots in the past, but I don't believe he's walking away from this one.

"Damn, L, I wish I would have hooked you up with video, too, because I would have loved to see his face when he opened that box," Devon says in my ear.

"I feel like I'm going to vomit." Now that it's over, the adrenaline that has been fueling me is leaving quickly. "It's hard to reconcile the guy I knew as George with Mr. Smith."

"A total mind fuck. Grab a cab. Your flight leaves in an hour and a half."

◆

Just landed, I text before throwing my phone on the passenger seat.

It's a thirty-minute drive to my destination, and I am exhausted. I'm not sure I can make it the last few miles before falling asleep. Thankfully, the driveway comes into sight before too long. I turn in, then make my way down the winding gravel road.

The front light is on, which I appreciate since it's completely dark outside. I drag myself from the car, hauling myself up the porch steps. Leaning on the bell, I don't let up until the door jerks open.

"That's a little much, don't you think?" Devon says as he pulls the door open.

"It's been the longest three days of my life." I fall onto the couch and kick my shoes off. "I'm sleeping for three days straight."

"There's a bedroom down the hall," he says, but throws a blanket over me, then cuts out the lamp on the side table because he knows I'm not moving.

"I guess everything went well?"

It takes a lot of effort, but I lift my head. She's in simple pajamas and her hair is sticking up in every direction, and the petty part of me is glad I woke her up after the week I've had.

"Looks like I won't be going down for your murder after all."

Amy Holder lets out a laugh as my eyes fall shut and I'm dead to the world.

Lucca Marino—Four Years Ago

The Tate job in Fort Worth, Texas, was the first job where I knew for sure I was not the only person doing jobs for Mr. Smith. Since Devon had been watching the security feed for days before I showed up, he was able to get images of the other people sent there for the same purpose. When I asked Devon to track down everyone who tried to retrieve the painting from the Tate home, he did what he could.

And it's why I'm standing on a sandy street in a small Florida town, staring at the cutest pink beach house. I can't see the ocean from here but I can hear it.

The front path is just a collection of oddly shaped stones in a loose line leading to the porch. If she's anything like me, she already knows I'm out here.

When I'm a few feet from the door, it opens.

"Hi," I say, with a big smile on my face.

"Can I help you?"

"Amy Holder? Can we talk a minute?"

She's on guard, as she should be. Same as I would

be in her place. Your safe haven is one you protect at all costs and rarely suffer strangers showing
up unannounced.

"You can say what you want from there."

I nod and think about the best way to proceed. "I need to talk to you about the Tate job in
Fort Worth."

Raised eyebrows are the only reaction I get
from her.

"We have the same employer," I add.

Her arms cross in front of her chest. "You
should leave."

Damn. I can see it in her eyes. She's about to
take off.

I hold up my hand as if I'm going to stop her
from fleeing. "I would feel the same way you do
right now if someone showed up at my place like
this. We really need to talk, but I'm going to put
the when and where in your hands." Digging in
my bag, I pull out a pen and a receipt from the gas
station where I just filled up, then scribble my info
on the back. Looking right at her so my sincerity is
clear, I say, "My number. And my real name. The
one only a few people have. It's important that we
speak. I'll be in Panama City Beach until I hear
from you."

I walk back to the street, put the paper in her
mailbox, and leave without her saying another
word. I'm taking a huge risk by doing this, but I
don't have another choice.

It's five days before she makes contact.

She gives me only fifteen minutes' notice to meet her at a farmer's market near the beach. It's crowded and loud and exactly the place I would have suggested if I were her.

"The only Lucca Marino matching your age and ethnicity was the one mentioned in an obituary for Angelina Marino of Eden, North Carolina."

I nod. "And that's all anyone will find until I decide otherwise."

We walk through the stalls, dodging little kids, until we get to a small area full of picnic tables. There's an empty one in the back corner, and she sits down on one side while I sit down on the other.

"So, talk."

I jump right in. "I have a friend who helps me on jobs. He piggybacked on the security system prior to me going in on the Tate job. You were there right after me. You lifted the forgery I left behind."

She's quiet for a moment then finally says, "I got my ass chewed out that I handed over a fake and didn't know it."

"That was probably the ugliest painting I've ever seen. I can see why you wouldn't think anyone would re-create it," I say to break the tension.

She laughs. It's quiet and short lived but I'll take it.

Then my smile fades when I think about what I'll have to tell her. "Did you know we weren't the only ones there trying to recover it?"

She nods. "Yeah, I was told it was some sort of bullshit test. Winner got a bonus."

"I think it was more than a test," I say quietly. "My friend was able to identify everyone else, and I went looking for them, just like I did you."

"And?"

I clear my throat. "And it's just us. We're the only ones left."

Amy sits up a little straighter. "What do you mean?"

"Mr. Smith was cleaning house, and this was his way of determining who he was keeping and who he wasn't. And it's not like he can just fire us after the things we've seen and done."

I list the names of the others and causes of death while she stares at me, unblinking.

"I think you were spared since you actually figured out the puzzle by going to the laundry room even though you walked away with the fake."

When I asked Devon to locate everyone he had on video, it was for selfish reasons. This is such a solitary way of life, constantly moving and lying about who you really are. I didn't see the others only as competition. I saw them as potential friends. Others who would understand the challenges of living and working like this. A group where we could be our true selves and possibly even help one another, even if just as sounding boards when tasked with a difficult job. Devon was a bit more hesitant to track down the others, but I won him over. Neither of us were prepared to learn that everyone but Amy was a

victim of some grave accident or sudden fatal illness
shortly after that job.

Amy still hasn't said anything.

"It's only a matter of time before we're on the
wrong side of one of his tests. If it wasn't for my
friend, I wouldn't have known to go to the laundry
room. He literally saved my life."

She looks away from me and stares out into
the crowd.

"I'm not waiting around for him to take me out,"
I say.

Finally, I get a reaction. She frowns as she considers my words and what they mean. "So you're what,
quitting? I tried that . . . there's no quitting." Her
voice cracks, and it's clear there is so much she's
not saying.

"Mr. Smith has got to go," I say.

She's shaking her head. And looking like she's
about to get up. I've spooked her.

All I can do is push forward. "I've been thinking about this for a while. But I can't do it alone.
If you're in, we are going to have to take our time.
Gather everything we can on him. Something to
use against him. As dirty as he is, you know there is
someone he's screwed over. We get the details then
we turn him over to them. Let them take him out."

Amy stares off to the side, her jaw clenched tight.

I keep talking. "And we've got to find out who
he really is. It doesn't do any good to tell someone

he's double-crossed them unless we are also handing over his identity."

She's shaking her head. I've thrown a lot at her and she's not processing it as fast as I'm saying it.

"We'll protect ourselves at all costs," I add. "When it comes time to turn the table on him, we need to control everything down to the last little detail."

She stands up and takes the first step to walk away, and I ask, "Do you have any family that he can use to get to you? Someone you'd do anything to protect?"

She contemplates whether or not she wants to answer me for a long time.

"Yeah, there's someone." It's all she says and I don't push for details.

"Then we'll have to make sure they are protected."

She finally turns to look at me. "What about you?"

"No. I don't have anyone."

I watch her as she debates what she wants to say. "Have you ever told him no on a job? Ever refused to do something he asked you to do?"

I shake my head. "No. I haven't."

She looks off, giving me a frustrated laugh. "You have no idea what he will do if he finds out what you're planning."

I'm a little worried she didn't say what **we're** planning, but she hasn't walked away. Yet.

"He'll try to wreck us but if we get in front of it, it could be like one of those controlled explosions,"

I finally say. "Like when the only way to get rid of a bomb is to detonate it. We'll control as much as we can, so when things explode, like we know they will, the fallout won't be as bad."

She laughs again as if I'm naive. And maybe I am.

"So you're really doing this," Amy says a bit later.

"I don't think **we** have any other option," I answer.

CHAPTER 26

n my line of work, there are the short cons and there are long cons, and I've just finished the longest one of my life. I'm feeling a bit out of sorts now that it's over.

I was only slightly joking when I said I was going to sleep for three days, since I slept for most of two. Devon and Amy tiptoed around me, making sure there was food close by and not peppering me with questions like I know they wanted to.

Because this was a long job for them too.

"You're finally awake," Devon says as he sinks down in the chair next to the couch.

"Barely," I say. "It's like a hangover but without the fun of getting one."

He laughs. "So too early to bust out the champagne?"

"It's never too early for that," Amy calls out as she enters the room, taking the chair next to Devon. "Morning."

"If you say so." Just as I'm thinking about how badly I need coffee, Amy sets a mug down in front of me.

We're quiet for a moment, then Amy says, "Wish

I could have seen his face in the bank vault when he opened the safe deposit box."

Devon laughs. "I said the same thing."

Shrugging, I say, "I wanted a jaw-dropping look of astonishment that I had bested him, but I only got a raised eyebrow."

For the next half hour, I fill them in on all the details of the meeting with the detectives, since Devon wasn't listening in for that.

"God, you're lucky he basically sent your twin or you would have been toast," Amy says. "Even with the alibi from Tyron, it would have been hard to convince them that wasn't you."

I shrug. "We could always have risen you from the dead if prison loomed too close. I'm not actually a murderer."

Amy laughs. "Well, yeah, there's that too."

"It was a good thing Amy was already in that laundry basket before the filming started. I checked that building right before I delivered the body from the morgue, and the room directly across from hers was empty." Devon frowned then added, "I hate when someone gets the jump on me like that."

I push my foot against his. "Don't beat yourself up. You've saved our asses more times than either of us would like to admit. Can't be perfect all the time."

I thought I had asked Devon for everything until I asked him to get me a dead body. A very specific dead body. Newly dead. White. Female. A Jane

Doe who no one would miss. Approximately five foot seven inches with long blondish hair that we dressed in that unmistakable red coat.

For our plan to work, Amy Holder needed to die in a big splashy way.

When we first started preparing for this day, the day we would be free from Mr. Smith, none of us knew just how long it would take to get here.

Although the execution took longer than any of us wanted, the plan itself was fairly simple. While we worked through our own jobs, we would look for proof that he was double-crossing any of his own clients. Something big enough that he would fear for his own well-being if it got out. And most importantly, we had to discover his real identity.

Amy was right, though. We had no idea what he would do when he started questioning our loyalty.

We had to flush out anything he had on us early on so we could adapt our plan accordingly. Amy stumbled on the Connolly double-cross, and that was all we needed. So Amy became the sacrificial lamb. She would be the disgruntled employee who would go rogue on a job. If Mr. Smith was holding something in his back pocket that could bring her to heel, he'd be forced to use what he had on her.

And he didn't disappoint.

It took Amy a long time to tell me about her sister, Heather. They had both been put into the foster-care system when they were young, just after their mom overdosed and no other family showed up to take them in. They were sent to separate families and lost touch. Amy found Heather after she started working for Mr. Smith, using the same resources available to us to do our jobs. We both knew that if Amy had found her, Mr. Smith probably had too.

And that's where he hit her. Mr. Smith had evidence ready to go that would result in Heather's arrest for drug use and distribution, and her young daughter, Sadie, would be placed in the foster system. Amy's and Heather's worst nightmare.

Devon pulled Heather and Sadie, relocating them to a different state under different names, just after Mr. Smith delivered his first threat against them. This was a temporary fix, but a fix all the same.

We controlled that explosion.

It also didn't hurt that Heather and Devon hit it off, and he's been very protective of both of them ever since. No one was going to be able to get near her or her daughter.

"What does this mean for Heather and Sadie?" I ask Amy now. "Will they head back to Tulsa?"

"She likes Phoenix. It wouldn't surprise me if they stayed there. The fresh start has been good for them." Amy grins and turns to Devon. "I heard you may be relocating to Phoenix too."

"Maybe," Devon says with a shrug, but the smile gives him away.

Once Heather and Sadie were out of immediate

danger, Amy relocated to Atlanta, where she would act wild and unstable. Mr. Smith would be left with only one option—send someone to retrieve what Amy had.

Our biggest risk was assuming that I would be given the job. We timed Amy going rogue to coincide with me just finishing a job, so I was available. And truth be told, I was one of the best he had working for him. We had a contingency in place in case he didn't send me, but thankfully the job was mine.

And while Mr. Smith had people there to watch me watch Amy, they didn't look closely enough at the bartender who served Amy her drinks or notice that Devon didn't put any alcohol in them. It didn't strike them as odd that every time Amy screamed at me, making sure to let critical information slip at the precise moment we needed it to, it was always in a very public setting—which guaranteed it would trickle back to him.

Or that Amy chose Atlanta to ride out this storm she created, which was also home to one of my oldest and most famous friends, who would happily supply me with an alibi. Tyron made sure we knew Tuesday nights worked best for him.

Amy played her part perfectly. She was on a dozen security cameras when she left the bar and walked across the street into that hotel. Staggering the whole way. It was no stretch that she would have been careless with her cigarette in that state. I pushed Amy out of that hotel room in the house-keeping cart, then Devon took over as she continued her escape to the parking garage and into the car we had waiting there. She's been hiding in this cabin ever since.

I wanted Mr. Smith suspicious of me, but I wasn't prepared for him having hard evidence that would implicate me in her murder.

That came as a surprise to all of us.

After Atlanta, the first part of our plan was done. We had enough to bury him. Amy's "death" ensured she was safe from any further retribution.

All we needed was his real name.

It was my turn. I needed to push him to use what he had against me. Control my own explosion.

While we knew Heather and Sadie were a weak spot for Amy, we weren't as confident about where he'd hit me. So I had to play along until he showed his hand.

The road trip was my own version of instability. I knew Coach Mitch was my best shot at discovering who Mr. Smith really was, and we could finally play that card now that we had the proof against him.

I needed to poke at Mitch, and I knew meeting with Andrew Marshall would send Mr. Smith over the edge, since he's always believed there was a small chance I had the politician in my back pocket.

It lit the match for the bomb he had ready for me.

Or so he thought.

"Any word on Smith's whereabouts now?" Amy asks, pulling me from my own thoughts.

Devon is tapping away on his laptop. "Nothing confirmed. The Connollys will deal with him their own way, which means I don't believe we'll find any identifiable body parts."

I cringe at his words. It's the least of what he deserves after everything Mr. Smith's done, but Devon knew I would struggle with being the one who hand-delivered him to his fate.

But it had gotten to the point where it was him or us.

"I can say this now that it's over, but there were a few moments when I thought he got the best of me," I say quietly.

Devon lets out a groan. "Yeah, Fake Lucca threw me. I never saw where that was headed."

"Wish we could have pulled her out in time," I say.

Amy leans close and squeezes my arm. "We would have if we'd had any idea that's what he was planning. But she's his last victim."

I nod and try to take some comfort in that. "Did you figure out how deep Ryan is involved?"

Devon looks up from his laptop. I've put off asking this because I wasn't sure I wanted to know the answer. After Devon planted the info on Amy in James's parents' house, he flew to Virginia, where

Mr. Smith lived. While Mr. Smith was following me into that bank, Devon was hacking into his personal computer. Once Devon knew where to look, the floodgates were opened and he was able to discover every facet of his business.

"His only involvement was what we already knew. Smith used his services over the years. As Ryan's business increased, so did Smith's interest in him. I believe he intended to take over Ryan's business, just as he had said to you. From what I've gathered so far—and it will be a while before I've gone through everything—Ryan knew him from those previous transactions but wasn't privy to the scope and breadth of Smith's organization."

Amy sits up in her chair, her eyes darting between Devon and me. "Then why was Smith giving him the info on his own business?"

Devon shrugs. "Not really sure. I'm guessing Smith had his reasons for doing that, but short of asking Ryan, we may never know."

"Well, then I guess we'll never know," I say.

Amy lets out a laugh. "Seriously? You're not going to ask him?"

I can't help the grimace that takes over my face. "I can't ask him!"

"Sure, you can," Devon says, his focus once again back on the laptop.

"What would be the point? The job is finished. And I'm on the straight and narrow from here on out. No more illegal activities for me."

Amy rolls her eyes. "Going straight doesn't mean you have to be finished with him. He's morally gray, you're morally gray. Plus he's superhot and probably great in bed."

"I give her three months before she's calling me and saying, 'Devon, so there's this job . . .'" His high-pitched impression of my voice has me laughing as I roll my eyes.

"I give her one month," Amy says.

I throw a couch pillow at both of them.

We stay in the cabin another three days while Devon digs through the rest of Mr. Smith's files he copied from his computer. But this time away from the real world can't last forever.

"Okay, ladies, I'm out," Devon says, loaded down with his backpack and bag. His car is already packed with his equipment. He's the first one to leave, and Amy and I take turns giving him hugs, but I'm the only one who follows him out to the porch.

"We did it," I say.

His smile stretches across his face. "That we did." He pauses before saying, "When you get over thinking you're done with this life, let me know."

"I **am** done," I say, although it lacks conviction. "And we can get together for fun! It doesn't always have to be work related."

Devon walks to his car, laughing. "Of course we can. I'm ready when you are." He throws his stuff in the back seat before taking off.

Amy is the next to leave. "You'll text me when you get settled, right?" she asks me.

"Yes. And then I'll see you in a couple of weeks." I help her get her bags to the car, then we throw our arms around each other and stay there for a long moment.

Then she, too, is gone.

I stay a little longer at the cabin. There are things to do, plans to make, decisions to consider, but for one blessed week there is quiet.

Alias: Evie Porter—Four Months Ago

t's Thursday and Ryan Sumner is right on time. He pulls up to the gas pump on the farthest side, just like always.

He's a bit casual today, his usual button-down replaced with one of those pullover golf shirts with the logo of the local club. I wonder what made this Thursday different.

I tug my skirt up just a fraction higher and run my hands through my hair, making sure it falls just the way I want it to.

I knew coming in that this was going to be my most dangerous job. Mr. Smith sent me here to break me.

I'm going to play this one by the book. I won't step out of line, won't get ahead of the game. I will let it unfold around me. And wait for Mr. Smith to hit me with everything he's got before I hit back.

"Hello," I say, as I walk up to his car.

He's startled but hides it quickly and easily. "Hey," he replies, a grin spreading across his face. He's cuter in person.

I tilt my head in the direction of my car, which is sitting off to the side, its left rear tire completely flat. "Any chance I can get some help with that? My dad taught me how to change my tire years ago, and in theory, I remember the basics, but it's a little more daunting when you're faced with it in real life."

His smile grows and it lights up his whole face. And it's a very lovely face indeed.

"Of course," he says. "Let me just finish up here and I'll pull around."

I give him a high-wattage smile right back, then return to my car.

He parks beside me and eyes me when he gets out. I'm leaning against the side of the car, showing off in just the right way. Ryan goes to his trunk, retrieving his jack, before kneeling down in front of my flat tire. I crouch down beside him, his eyes lingering on my legs a few seconds like I hoped they would.

I know from my research that he likes to play golf and tennis, though he's not exceptionally good at either one. I know he went to LSU and was social chair for his fraternity. I know he dated a girl through sophomore and junior year but that she broke it off before she left to study abroad.

"You look really familiar," I say, as he loosens the first lug nut off my tire.

He glances at me and says, "I was just thinking the same thing."

"Did you know Callie Rogers? We were friends at LSU."

From his expression, I know he recognizes the name but can't place her. I studied the girls who had been in sororities around the same time he was there, girls who were tagged in posts of his friends' friends but never with him. Their names would be familiar but not familiar enough that he would ever ask them about me.

"Was she friends with Marti Brighton?"

"Yes!"

"I think I met her a time or two when she was with Marti," he says, then gets back to work.

Once the mutual connections have been made, I'm no longer thought of as a stranger and the conversation is easy. Even though Ryan has finished changing the tire, he lingers. We're both leaning against the car now, turned toward each other.

"I should buy you a drink!" I say. "The least I can do for saving me."

He leans in a few inches closer. "I'll let you buy me a drink if I can buy you dinner."

Ryan is smooth.

"I feel like I already know you, but we haven't been officially introduced." I hold my hand out, not far since we're already so close. "I'm Evie Porter."

His hand slides into mine. "Ryan Sumner."

"Well, Ryan," I say. "Drinks and dinner sound like a great idea."

"Follow me?" he asks.

"Right behind you," I answer.

We pull into a small bistro, and he's at the driver's-side door before I can open it. Ryan holds his hand out, helping me from the car.

We step inside the restaurant, where he asks for us to be seated on the patio. It's still chilly outside this time of year even though we're in Louisiana. My short skirt offers no protection, but I'm relieved when I see several heaters scattered around the area. Twinkle lights stretch between the trees that border the patio. It's a dreamy spot for a first date.

We order wine and appetizers, and we talk and talk and talk. He leans toward me and I mirror him.

"Tell me more about you," he says, just as our main course is served.

Thoughts about Mama and that small trailer we called home—that Mama made a home—wash over me, and for the first time, I don't want to tell the first lie. I want to tell him how she taught me to sew and how we made dresses for every stuffed animal I had. How we had tea parties and acted like we were royalty. I wanted to tell him about the map of the world that hung on the wall. We would throw a dart and then learn everything we could about the place it landed on.

But I stick with the script and tell him my parents died in a car wreck and I'm just trying to find my way. I weave more truth than I should into the story. Give him more of myself than I've ever given anyone else.

His hand slides across the table and I steel myself for how good I know it will feel. And it feels good.

Too good.

So I pull away slightly. Not enough to make him feel rejected. Just enough to give myself some distance. I mentally wall up my emotions, brick by brick. Ryan Sumner is a job. One that won't last. He's charmed with Evie Porter, a figment of my imagination.

It's time to remember exactly who she is and why she's here.

It's time to get to work.

Evie Porter—Present Day

Ryan is in the front yard pushing a lawn mower back and forth along his perfectly green grass. The sun is setting and the dying light is throwing a golden glow over the two-story white house, making it shimmer.

He spots me as he makes his second pass and kills the engine immediately. He's wearing old, faded khaki shorts and a light blue tee that is frayed around the edges.

I'm on the sidewalk watching him watch me. Neither of us moves for several minutes.

It's been three months since that morning in the hotel in Atlanta.

He meets me halfway. Grass trimmings coat his legs and shoes, and his hands are streaked with grease.

My eyes scan his face for any little change since I saw him last. "I'm hoping you still want to talk," I say.

Ryan pulls a rag from his back pocket then uses it to clean his hands. After a long moment, he finally looks up at me and nods toward the house. Without waiting to see if I'll follow, he starts making his way around the side of the house to the backyard.

My eyes snag on the three long rows of plants that are bursting with vegetables in the back corner of the yard.

Ryan arranges the two Adirondack chairs so they are facing each other rather than sitting side by side, motioning for me to take one. I choose the one that puts my back to the yard. I can't look at that garden right now.

He grabs two beers from a nearby cooler, passing one of them to me. "I thought it would be better to talk without the prying eyes of the neighborhood watch. Although I should thank you, the little old ladies on this street have given me a wide berth after the spectacle in the driveway, and they've grown weary of throwing their granddaughters at me."

"I'm available any time you need your good name tarnished," I say, then take a sip of my beer.

"It was never as shiny as you once thought it was. We can stop pretending whenever you're ready."

I take a deep breath and blow it out slowly, hoping to calm my nerves. "I'm not sure I know where to start. I've . . . been pretending a long time."

Ryan's head tilts to the side as he studies me. While Devon, Amy, and I can speculate until we're blue in the face, we don't know Ryan's side of this or what he knew about me or Mr. Smith. The only thing we do know is Ryan did business with Mr. Smith in some capacity, but he has been the sole owner of the operation in East Texas since his grandfather died.

I also know there's something unfinished between us, and I had a strong desire to see him again that time has not lessened.

"I should make you go first since you've taken your sweet time to come talk to me." He puts his beer on the little side table, then leans back in his chair, his head resting in the cradle of his joined hands. "You were something I wasn't prepared for. Did I know you were trying to get information on the business in Glenview when I fixed your flat tire? No. Even before I met you, I could tell something was wrong there. Things had been moved around at work and at home. Shit missing. It got worse after I met you, but I didn't link it to you. Not at all." He gives me a lopsided grin and a shrug that tells me he knows he should be embarrassed, but he's not. "An associate I've done business with off and on over the years told me he was hearing rumors that someone had infiltrated my operation and was selling info on my shipments to the highest bidder."

"An associate?" I ask.

He shakes his head. "No more from me until I get a little from you." He takes a deep drink from his bottle then puts it back down on the table.

"You were a job. I was . . . having trouble with my boss and he wasn't happy with me. When I got assigned to you, I wasn't sure if this was a real job. Not in the usual way. My boss . . . he liked to play games. Test me to make sure I was still loyal. Needless to say, I wasn't sure if you were playing me too."

Ryan's eyes narrow as he tries to understand what I'm saying, since I'm not being as clear as I should be. "That sounds . . . fucked up. Your boss seems like an incredible asshole."

My laugh surprises us both. "You have no idea." It's so much harder than I thought it would be to just be honest. "If the associate that warned you someone was selling the details on your shipments was the same guy you were talking to in the motel corridor in Tennessee, then you met my boss."

He leans forward, the laid-back attitude long gone. "I didn't know you heard us talking. Is that why you freaked out and left? And yeah, that was him. But he was **your** boss?" His eyes glaze over as he tries to sort through his confusion. "He told me you were the one stealing files from me."

"Yeah, that sounds about right. Pitting two people against each other is his favorite pastime." Or should I say **was** his favorite pastime. "He thought it provided the best results. One side working against the other, no one trusting anyone. And he conveniently watches from the sidelines."

We're studying each other. Comparing what we once believed against what we're learning about each other right now.

"When did he tell you it was me? And why would you stay with me when you found out I was betraying you?" I ask. Ryan keeping me around made sense when I thought he was Mr. Smith.

"He texted me just before we left the police station. Asked me to meet him. Said he had some information for me. That's where I went when I dropped you here and told you I needed to go by my office." He laughs, but it's hollow. He looks off toward the backyard. "It's easy to see how he played me, looking back. Told me someone approached him, offering a partnership since they knew he'd used my services in the past, and thought he'd like to cut out the middleman. But he made me believe he was on **my side.** Was making sure they didn't succeed. He told me you were using me to get close enough to get my financials, my client records, shipments records. Handed me 'proof.' Said you were meeting with your contact in Atlanta to give them the rest of the stuff you had on me, and they promised to help get you out of this trouble with the police. I agreed to stick close to you. I wanted to know who was behind this. Who sent you to do their dirty work. I was so fucking pissed off. I sat in my car in the driveway and read through everything he gave me."

Ryan finally turns to look back at me, leaning forward in his chair with his elbows resting on his knees. "But then I was more confused than ever," he says, his voice strong but quiet. "Everything he gave me as proof of what you had taken from me was altered. The dates of big shipments were a week later than what I planned. The cargo smaller. The buyers' names changed. It didn't make sense. And it was enough for me to doubt what he was trying to make me believe. And then I went inside. I went looking for you. And I found you in the shower and you were so . . . broken. Crying so hard I thought you'd break in a million pieces. It was the exact same way I felt. I knew there was a big piece I was missing." He gives me a sad smile. "I was going to ride it out and see where we landed."

His stare is so intense I have to look away. Coughing to clear the lump in my throat, I finally say, "He wasn't the only one playing a game. I needed him mad at me. Madder than he already was. I needed to lose his trust completely. But I also didn't want you to lose your business to him. I didn't want it to become another cog in the wheel of his organization. So I changed the details."

Ryan reaches forward, his hands sliding around the legs of my chair, and pulls me a little closer. "Tell me the rest of it."

Taking a deep breath, I tell him about Devon and Amy, without giving away their names. I tell him about Eden, North Carolina, and living in that trailer with Mama until she died. I tell him about Mr. Smith and George and how I didn't know they were the same person until it was almost too late. I told him about the woman who claimed to be me and how her life and James's were cut short just so Mr. Smith could make a statement.

At some point while I was unburdening myself,

Ryan had pulled me into his lap. My head leaning against his chest, his hand brushing through my hair as he listened to all my secrets.

"I'm sorry James got wrapped up in this. If I had known what was in store for them, I would have found a way to pull them both out."

"I know you would have."

We sit in silence long enough that the sun starts to set.

———◆———

I should be ashamed of how easy it was to fall back into the daily routine with Ryan. The only difference this time is we're both honest about how shady we are.

It's Thursday and Ryan is headed to East Texas.

"I'll be home by six," he says as he fills his travel mug with coffee. He's dressed in jeans and a tee since he doesn't have to act like he's headed to his local office.

"And I'll be here." I move in close, wrapping my arms around him.

He buries his face in my neck and peppers me with kisses. "Want me to pick up some steaks on the way home?"

"Hmmm, that sounds good. There's a ton of squash and zucchini we need to eat so we can grill those too. The neighbors run from me now."

Ryan laughs. "That's what happens when half of the backyard is a garden and we have to palm veggies off on everyone." One more kiss and then he mumbles against my lips, "Try to be a good girl while I'm gone."

Laughing, I say, "I'll try but I make no promises."

He leaves and I watch him drive away until he's out of sight.

I top off my coffee and head to the small home office I created for myself out of one of the guest bedrooms. It takes a few minutes to settle in and get everything powered on. Devon created this space, and we take every precaution.

I place the call on the secured line and Amy picks up on the first ring. "Morning," she says, although she still sounds half asleep. She kept her same first name but now goes by the last name of Porter as well. I guess I wasn't the only one looking for a connection with someone else.

"Morning," I say back, as I log on to the King Harvest fans message board. The alert box pops up, showing there are new messages, while the first few bars of the chorus of "Dancing in the Moonlight" plays over my computer speakers.

"Two new messages," I tell her.

I hear Amy yawn and then she says, "Open them up and let's see what they're looking for, Miss Smith."

It's my favorite part of the morning.

ACKNOWLEDGMENTS

Writing this book brought about a lot of changes: I moved from the young adult market into the adult market and started fresh with a new agent and publisher. And the experience has been nothing short of amazing!

First, a huge thank-you to my agent, Sarah Landis. From our very first conversation, your enthusiasm and love for **First Lie Wins** has been unmatched. I gained not only a fierce advocate for this book but also a new friend. I'm so thankful for your guidance and support.

Thanks to everyone at Sterling Lord Literistic, especially Szilvia Molnar and the foreign rights team. I'm thrilled **First Lie Wins** will be published around the world!

To my film agents, Dana Spector and Berni Barta, thank you for believing in this book and finding an incredible team to adapt it. Y'all are the best!

There is something magical that happens when a book finds the perfect home. Pamela Dorman,

Jeramie Orton, Marie Michels, and Sherise Hobbs—y'all are the dream team of editors and I'm so grateful to have your expertise and support! Thank you for all your hard work and dedication to helping shape **First Lie Wins** into what it is today. And thank you to everyone at Viking/Pamela Dorman Books and Headline, including Diandra Alvarado, Matthew Boezi, Jane Cavolina, Chelsea Cohen, Tricia Conley, Tess Espinoza, Cassandra Mueller, Brian Tart, Andrea Schulz, Kate Stark, Rebecca Marsh, Mary Stone, Christine Choi, Molly Fessenden, Jason Ramirez, Lynn Buckley, and Claire Vaccaro. I know there are so many people behind the scenes and I appreciate all of you.

To Megan Miranda and Elle Cosimano, thank you for being the absolute best critique partners and friends a girl could ask for. I can't imagine doing this without you.

I'm so fortunate to have so many people cheering me on. To my husband, Dean, and our sons, Miller, Ross, and Archer, thank you for being my biggest supporters. I love y'all so much and am so thankful for you every day. Thank you, Mom and Joey and the rest of my family, for always being so proud of me. Thank you to my friends who are always there for me. And a special thank-you to Aimee Ballard, Christy Poole, and Pam Dethloff, who made sure my hair, clothes, and background were always perfect for every video I've had to film. It takes a village!

Last but certainly not least—thank you to my readers! Whether this is the first book of mine you've ever read or if you've followed along with me from the beginning, I appreciate each and every one of you!

ABOUT THE AUTHOR

ASHLEY ELSTON worked for many years as a wedding photographer before turning her hand to writing. She lives in Louisiana with her husband and three sons. Elston has written six young adult novels; **First Lie Wins** is her adult debut.